When All the Girls Are Sleeping

YOUNG ADULT BOOKS BY EMILY ARSENAULT

The Leaf Reader
All the Pretty Things
When All the Girls Are Sleeping

when all the girls are sleeping

EMILY ARSENAULT

Delacorte Press

Text copyright © 2021 by Emily Arsenault
Jacket art copyright © 2021 by Leo Nickolls

All rights reserved. Published in the United States by Delacorte Press,
an imprint of Random House Children's Books,
a division of Penguin Random House LLC, New York.

Delacorte Press is a registered trademark and the colophon
is a trademark of Penguin Random House LLC.

Visit us on the Web! GetUnderlined.com

Educators and librarians, for a variety of teaching tools,
visit us at RHTeachersLibrarians.com

Library of Congress Cataloging-in-Publication Data is available upon request.
ISBN 978-0-593-18079-2 (trade) — ISBN 978-0-593-18081-5 (ebook)

The text of this book is set in 11-point Sabon MT Pro.
Interior design by Jen Valero

Printed in the United States of America
10 9 8 7 6 5 4 3 2 1
First Edition

To Lisa

1

Thirteen Nights Left

The window is open now, but I don't feel the winter wind. I don't shiver. I don't chatter. Rather, I feel only a sensation of it blowing through the space that used to be me.

This is what it means to be a ghost. To watch all the other girls live—laugh, talk, sleep, eat, dance, study, scream—while you flicker and fade into the shadows. To wait till night to slip out of nonexistence and into these silent halls in search of your former self.

You won't find her.

But still you look. Night after restless night.

2

February 10, 2018

Dear Members of the Windham-Farnswood
Academy Community:

It is with deepest sadness that I inform you of the loss of one of our students early this morning. Taylor Katherine Blakey, a senior, fell to her death from a Dearborn Hall window between one and two a.m. I and other school faculty have been in close contact with Taylor's family. Please keep them in your thoughts and prayers in the coming days and weeks.

Campus security and health personnel, along with the Heathsburg town police department, will be conducting a thorough investigation of the incident.

Counselors Elizabeth Haden, Brenda Alenski, and Charles Utley will be available to students at Dearborn Hall and the health center, and will be visiting the classes in which Taylor was enrolled. They and other school personnel are working with students and staff who were close to Taylor. Students are also encouraged to call or visit the health center office if they need assistance during this difficult time.

Classes will continue as scheduled today and throughout the remainder of the week, but we urge all students to take the time and assistance they need as we all grieve together.

Sincerely,
Dr. Shawna Ivins
Dean of Students

3

Monday, January 28, 2019

I felt my roommate's gaze on me as I stretched and pulled up my window shade. She was already dressed in a red cardigan over long underwear and a jean skirt.

"Are you okay?" Star asked softly, twisting one of the cardigan's shiny black buttons so hard I thought it would come off in her hand.

"Umm . . . sure," I said, but felt one side of my face twitch at the half-truth of it.

"I woke up at about two a.m. and you were, like, playing with your phone." Star frowned, letting her hand fall from the button.

"Couldn't sleep," I admitted. "Sorry, you should have said something if the glare was keeping you up."

"It wasn't." Star pulled a hairbrush and hair clip from her desk but just stood there holding them, watching me.

I looked out the window so I wouldn't have to figure out what kind of expression should be on my face. Outside, there was a powdered-sugar dust over the dirty crusts of ice and snow along the crisscross of paths in the middle of the campus green. It felt like it was never not going to be January.

"I'm just an insomniac," I said. "And sometimes it's better if I don't fight it."

I'd been on a YouTube tear last night, trying to push back various little guilts and delayed responsibilities—among them, the email from Taylor's brother. He'd sent it over a week ago and I still hadn't replied.

Star buttoned her cardigan over her chest, looked at the effect in the full-length mirror between our beds, and then unbuttoned it again.

"Why do I have these particular boobs?" she asked. I wasn't sure if she was asking me or the universe.

"Why do *I* have *these* particular boobs?" I said, just in case.

"Because those are the right boobs for *you*. I, on the other hand, seem to have gotten someone else's boobs."

"Whose boobs do you think you have?" I asked, stretching.

"They're someone's mom's boobs. They're the wrong size. They're too big, but not in a good way. They're the wrong personality."

Star stuck her elbows out and flapped her arms, slamming the elbows down on the sides of her chest as if to forcibly compress it. Then she sighed and hung her arms resignedly at her sides before bending down to collect a few fallen papers from next to her desk. She had endless photocopies of 19th-century letters strewn across her half of the room. A history nerd, Star lately seemed to be drowning in her senior research project.

"I mean," she said, "are you stressed out?"

"Stressed out?" I paused, trying not to look pointedly at the avalanche of homework on her desk. "I'm not the one disparaging my boobs first thing in the morning."

"I meant the staying up all night."

Star sat on her bed and tilted her long, makeup-less milkmaid face to one side. Sometimes her sincerity embarrassed me. I had to remind myself that that was my problem, not hers.

"Oh, it wasn't *all* night," I said, nearly chirping this reassurance. I'd fallen asleep sometime close to three a.m.

Star wrestled with the sides of her sweater, still clearly distracted by her rogue boobs. I bit my lip to keep from smiling. I opened the door to head down the hallway for the bathroom.

I shuddered. The sensation hit me right away, even before I'd stepped out of our dorm room. It was freezing cold in the hallway. More freezing than usual, even. Dearborn Hall was a drafty 19th-century building with crotchety old radiators. Their unpredictable hissing and banging was probably a big part of why some girls said the building was haunted.

The bathroom was ice-cold, too. But I needed a shower—to wash away some of the grogginess and worry of my relatively sleepless night. At least enough to get me through the first couple of classes.

✦✦✦

When I made my way down the stairs to breakfast, Alex was standing in the second floor of the stairwell, looking small against its majestic arched window.

Sometimes, when you saw her from far away—before you

had a chance to hear her speak and remind you how smart she was—she looked tiny and vulnerable. She was pale, just barely five feet tall, with brown hair that had a little bit of blond-red in it at the end of the summer or when she was standing in sunlight, like right now. Since her arms and legs were like twigs, other girls often whispered that she might be anorexic. She wasn't. I could attest to that, having been her roommate freshman year and then actually friends with her more recently. Alex ate plenty. She was just one of those fast-metabolism girls.

"Hey," I said.

"Hi there." Alex turned from the window and seemed to force a smile.

"How's the flower-bulb thing going?" I asked. I hadn't had a chance to catch up with her in a few days. She was always busy and usually had a few different projects going at once—almost all of them having something to do with science. Most recently, she'd been spending her spare time at the greenhouse, where she was chair of some committee to do a public bulb show. They were charging admission, and the money was going to an organization that protects state wetlands.

"Good," she said. "There are a couple of juniors helping me."

I nodded, feeling a little guilty that I wasn't helping her myself. College applications had been killing me lately, and I hadn't felt up for any new stuff this year. I did cross-country in the fall because we had to do a sport. I did newspaper because I always had. But even that had felt like a ball and chain.

Alex sighed, gazing into the tree branches that were at eye level.

"So tired of the cold," she murmured.

"Yeah," I agreed, a little surprised at her melancholy, and unsure if she was referring to the temperature of the hallway this morning or the midwinter weather generally.

We were both staring out the window now. It was an unusually sunny morning for January. The snow seemed to sparkle. I watched Alex scan the landscape till her head was turned to the right. She was looking at the spot on the brick pathway where Taylor had landed last February. Then her gaze darted quickly back to me. Like she didn't want me to see her looking there.

I didn't blame her for looking. A lot of us probably didn't know how to look at the place on the walkway where Taylor had died. I usually went in the front entrance of the building—rather than the side door, which would basically force me to walk over those bricks. And when I forgot myself sometimes and went in that direction, that night would inevitably come back to me. The yellow tape. The ambulance and the police cars. The horrified expressions of the handful of seniors who had seen her before the residential director had managed to gather everyone in the dining hall to keep them away from the scene. Those expressions came back to each of those girls occasionally until they graduated last June. I was glad they were gone now. But I wondered if the same expressions occasionally came over them still—troubling and mystifying their new college friends.

"Breakfast?" I said weakly.

"Yup," Alex agreed, and we went down the last steps together.

Maylin had already finished her cereal by the time we joined her at one of the round wooden tables. She took out her red lipstick and retouched her mouth while she watched us dig into our bowls of yogurt and granola. She looked impeccable. Maylin was probably the only Windham girl who wore full makeup, wrap dresses, and heels to class. She had to get up an hour before everyone else to pull it off, but she said it made her feel more confident.

"Do you miss Jake?" she asked me, sweeping her long black hair up into a clip, away from her wet lips. "I mean, do you *ever* miss him?"

I held in a sigh. Talking about my ex with Maylin wasn't a new conversation. Jake was my boyfriend last year. We met at the Farnswood half of Windham-Farnswood. The school community as a whole was kind of coed, kind of not. All of the girls' dormitories were on the Windham campus, all of the boys' ones at Farnswood, about two miles away. Freshmen and sophomores had single-sex classes on their own campuses, but upperclass students had coed classes. A shuttle went between the two campuses for this. So most of the Windham boyfriends came from Farnswood, of course. Unless you were resourceful enough to have a boyfriend from back home, or to sneak your way into parties at the nearby state university and snag someone there.

"Actually . . . not that much," I said.

It was mostly true now—even if it hadn't been true a couple of months ago. And it felt like what Maylin *wanted* me to say. Jake left after he graduated and his college is in Maine. Massachusetts to Maine wouldn't have been an unreasonable distance for some to carry on a long-distance relationship. But Jake and I chose not to. The outward ease with which we'd come to this decision seemed to fascinate Maylin, so she and I had had this

9

conversation several times already this year. Her boyfriend, Wes, was Canadian, and he was dead set on going to McGill University in Montreal. Maylin, on the other hand, had mostly applied to warm and sunny places.

"Do you ever text him?" Maylin wanted to know.

"I did on his birthday."

That was back in September, and I'd actually hidden Jake on my social media since. Even though it hadn't been a really bad breakup, I didn't need a play-by-play of who he was hooking up with in college.

"Do you think he has a new girlfriend by now?"

I shrugged. "Stands to reason he would."

I glanced at Alex, who was probably grateful to be left out of this conversation. Alex had a Farnswood boyfriend for about two months last year, but she was mostly mysterious about it. She seemed to have trouble fitting him in with all of her studies and causes. According to Maylin, Alex also mentioned a couple of times that she wished he'd shower more.

"Are you thinking of moving to Canada, Maylin?" Alex asked.

"Canada probably doesn't want me," she said dully. "And I don't know any French."

I gazed at my half-eaten yogurt. My brain wasn't functioning very efficiently this morning. While Alex and Maylin continued to talk about the pros and cons of following a boy to Francophone Canada, I took out my phone and clicked on Taylor's brother's email. It had been more than a week since I'd last read it.

Hi Haley,

I hope you're doing well at Windham-Farnswood and having a not-too-stressful time with college applications, etc. It was a sad Christmas without Taylor, but we all went to Colorado together just to be in a different place than past holidays. I've finally had the stomach, lately, to go through some of Taylor's old things. I managed to get into her phone last weekend. There are lots of pictures of you two together, and I was remembering how fondly she spoke of you. I also found this weird long video, and I wondered if you had any idea what it was? Maybe she'd shown it to you before? Just curious. Write back when you can—I know you're probably busy.

Take care,
Thatcher

All very respectable and polite. This was the older of Taylor's siblings—he'd graduated from college last year. Below his message was a big file—a video. And I had a feeling I knew exactly what it was without even looking at it. I just didn't have the heart to explain it to him.

You see, Thatcher . . . your sister wasn't really all that nice. She filmed some poor self-conscious girl making out with a Farnswood guy at a party. . . . It was a real shit show.

And could someone like Thatcher—smooth and smart and even-keeled, I could tell from our one meeting at Taylor's memorial—understand that kind of thing? And why was he named *Thatcher*? What were the other kids in the family named? I was trying to remember. *Thatcher, Taylor, Tinker, Spy.*

Something like that, probably. People with money were so weird to me sometimes.

"How're you girls?" someone said behind me.

I turned to see our residential director standing there. She slipped into the empty seat next to me. I did my best not to suck in a breath as Anna's glossy brown lipstick formed an overly sincere smile.

"Haley, I haven't talked to you in ages. I didn't even hear how your holidays were."

"Not bad," I said. "My grandmother always has a nice Christmas Eve."

"Well . . . wonderful." Anna touched the back of her hair, near her ear. Maybe she was checking to see if her bobby pin was perfectly secure. She always wore her hair like this—neat bun behind slicked-back brown hair that matched her lipstick startlingly well—like she was drawn by a cartoonist who had only one shade of brown. She was maybe trying to look the part of the housemother from central casting. But she was a little too pretty for the part, in my opinion. A stereotypical housemother would be older than Anna—who was about thirty—and would maybe have a wart somewhere on her face.

Alex looked at her phone and said, "Oh! Haley, are you done eating? Still okay to help me with that thing in the greenhouse?"

I hopped up. "Yeah. Nice chatting, Anna."

"Alrighty," Anna said. "That works. I wanted to touch base with Maylin anyway."

Pulling our backpacks on, Alex and I made our way toward Dearborn's front door.

"Thanks," I murmured.

"No problem," Alex said.

There was, of course, nothing happening at the greenhouse right now, but Anna didn't need to know that. And Alex knew Anna wasn't my favorite person.

Alex and I quietly understood each other most of the time—even though we had a weird history. When we were roommates freshman year, we didn't talk to each other much. Alex was shy, and studied constantly. We didn't hang out with the same people back then. She only started to come out of her shell, and begin showing people how supersmart she was, the next year. By then we weren't roommates anymore. But we sort of reconnected last year through our mutual friendship with Maylin.

Maylin, who was now stuck talking to Anna. Really, it wasn't fair of me to dislike Anna. I'd barely spoken with her. She was new to Windham. Last year's Dearborn residential director, Tricia—who was also the soccer coach—was quietly let go after the Taylor tragedy. She didn't do anything wrong. The school just wanted the appearance of a fresh start, clearly. Anna, a counselor, was brought in as a new and calming presence. Maybe it had something to do with the way I was raised pre-Windham, but I didn't really trust people in the "feelings" professions.

"She means well," Alex added, just because someone had to.

"Yeah," I replied, so she wouldn't feel the need to elaborate. "I wonder what she wants with Maylin, though? Is Maylin in trouble?"

"I wouldn't worry about it," Alex said quickly.

I nodded, chastened. Of course. *None of our business.* Alex's default. Gossip ignites pretty easily at a girls' school, and Alex always refused to fan the flames.

We headed toward the science building, as we did most mornings, although we didn't have the same class. I was in AP Bio. Alex, overachiever that she was, had taken it last year, and was taking both AP Chem and Physics this year.

She asked how bio was going and I said okay, grateful for the small talk. It kept me from turning around and looking at the old brick building from which we'd emerged. It could be pretty on an early fall afternoon. But in the morning in midwinter, it usually looked to me like a movie mental hospital.

♦♦♦

The bio lab had a huge window with a good view of the oak tree near the entrance. While Mr. Cortes talked about stem cells, I stared down at the snow-covered bench beneath the tree. Taylor and I used to spend a lot of time under there my sophomore year.

One time I was especially exhausted because I'd stayed up all night writing a history paper. She had a thermos full of the strong coffee she always used to brew in her room. On that particular morning, I drank most of it. I was chugging the last of it when Taylor said in a low voice, "Look at that squirrel. It's, like, scratching its armpit."

I'd followed her gaze to a spot in the leaves where a squirrel *was,* indeed, scratching its armpit. More slowly and deliberately than one usually associates with squirrel movement—although the Windham squirrels tended to be more casual and less human-cautious than regular squirrels. It seemed to notice us looking, then seemed to scratch more aggressively and deliberately, its little black eyes challenging us somehow. Taylor started to snicker quietly, muffling her laughter as if it might offend the squirrel. I started laughing too, maybe not because the squirrel was funny, but because I was giddy from lack of sleep. And because almost everything Taylor did—at least back then—was sort of contagious.

"It reminds me of when we caught Eric Hale touching himself in the closet at that party last year after midterms," she said. "He was so drunk he didn't even stop."

Those words dashed the giggles out of my mouth. Taylor loved to laugh at simple, silly things. She watched endless "Funny Cat Video" compilations. She liked jokes about farts and foul-mouthed parrots. But she also had an insatiable appetite for gossip—the darker and dirtier the better. So I suddenly felt sorry for Eric Hale. I felt sorry for anyone who Taylor knew too much about.

It was a category that included me, I was certain.

Taylor's gaze had shifted from the squirrel to me. Her eyes looked as dark and primal as those of the animal before us—maybe more. She knew her words scared me. Even though they didn't have, on their surface, anything to do with me.

This was one of the many things about Taylor that none of the memorials said. That she was intensely interested in people's secrets and especially their vulnerabilities. She liked to step into them—to splash around in them like puddles.

"Haley, are you with us?"

"Yes," I said, snapping my attention back to Mr. Cortes, smiling as studiously as I could manage without looking like a smart-ass.

"Remind us what the three general properties of stem cells are?" Mr. Cortes asked.

I glanced around the room. Several kids were looking at me expectantly—among them, my friend Anthony, staring through his weird flap of curly overgrown bangs. Like me, he used to go to off-campus weekend parties with Taylor—often thrown by her day-student friends. And like me, he was a bit of a loner now that that crowd was pretty much gone and graduated. We were closer this year than we'd been in the past. Now that we were both leftovers.

There was a vague concern—or at least sympathy—in his expression that helped me regulate my breath and focus on Mr. Cortes's words. I cleared my throat, glanced down at my notes, and answered the question.

***

"Nice save there," Anthony said when he met me outside the science building. "Cortes is such a sadist. I always like it when he thinks he's going to get a delicious little charge out of humiliating you and then he . . . doesn't get there."

Sadist is one of Anthony's favorite words. He has a strangely dark worldview for a rich kid with happily married parents.

I shrugged. "Let him try. In a few months, it won't matter."

"Are you okay today?" Anthony asked. "I was thinking in class that you don't look so great."

"I didn't really sleep last night," I admitted.

"Oh," Anthony said. "I'm sorry. All-nighter?"

"Not exactly. But it's not a big deal."

"Do you like my stubble?" Anthony asked, running his fingertips over his cheek. "Did you notice it at all?"

I reached out and touched his chin line.

"It's . . . downy," I remarked.

"That might be because I've been exfoliating while I'm growing it."

"Weird," I said, my shoulders relaxing at the silly familiarity of being with Anthony. "Is that a thing?"

"I don't know. It's *my* thing, I guess."

I led him to the humanities hall and pulled the door open for both of us.

"What were you doing up all night?" he asked.

"Not *all*. Just, like, half. I watched YouTube videos on my phone way later than I should have. You know I have a complicated relationship with sleep."

We started to part ways—me for my first-floor classroom, him for the stairs.

"Text me later," he said.

"Yup," I said, went into my class, and slid into my back-row seat. I still had a few minutes before the bell and Ms. Holland-Stone often traipsed in a minute or two late, sucking down a latte from the overpriced café across from campus. I took out my phone and clicked on Thatcher's email again. I sighed, eyeing the attached video file.

Muting my phone, I held it close to my face. I'd click on it really quickly, just to verify: the video of the dim room, Jocelyn and Charlie barely visible as they started to kiss. The whole dark and dirty business. And then I would just go ahead and lie. *Dear Thatcher. Glad to hear you're okay. Yes, I remember this.*

Taylor showed it to me. She accidentally left her camera running at a party, and she thought it was kind of funny. I know she meant to erase it, I guess she never did. . . .

Lies, lies, lies. It's not like I'd never lied before, and this would at least be sort of for a good cause: a grieving brother who didn't need to know how nasty his sister could be sometimes. *But then . . . how could he not know?*

I clicked on the video.

It started with blackness. And then more blackness. Not the dimly lit couple fumbling around on Charlie's unmade bed.

And then a flash of a window, with a little light leaking through its blinds. A moment later there was some jouncing of the phone, and then light, and then a glimpse of Taylor's face.

I felt my stomach drop at the sight of her. I hadn't seen her in almost a year. I had even avoided looking at photographs of her. And this wasn't the video I was expecting at all. I had no idea what it was. But it wasn't the infamous party video.

Ms. Holland-Stone walked into the room, tossed her black coat on her desk chair, and took a long sip of her coffee, closing her eyes for several seconds as if she couldn't bear the sight of us until the caffeine kicked in.

"Ladies and gentlemen," she said once her eyes had fluttered open. "We're only halfway through the French Revolution. The heads are still rolling."

I clicked my phone off, pausing the unknown video, and shoved my phone into my backpack, taking a breath and trying to focus on Ms. Holland-Stone instead of the pulsing in my ears.

4

"Hey, Haley. Are you getting the pasta? I really shouldn't. But it's been a while since I carbo-loaded."

I hadn't seen Maylin sneak up behind me at the lunch bar. I sucked in a breath, wondering how I was going to shake her off. My plan had been to find a quiet corner table and watch the full video. I had a feeling I wouldn't want anyone else to see it but me.

"You should have pasta whenever you want, Maylin."

Maylin grabbed a plate from the salad bar, scooped some chickpeas and spinach onto it, but then frowned at her selections.

"Maybe I will. Look . . . Haley?" Maylin inched her tray toward the pasta bar. "Alex wasn't sure I should tell you why I was talking to Anna this morning. But I told her I *should* tell you because I accidentally told like three other people and you would probably hear anyway."

Maylin clearly had an agenda, and it was not to talk about her diet.

"Uh-huh," I said, scooping myself a generous helping of penne with red sauce.

"I don't know if you noticed how cold it was in the hallway

this morning in Dearborn. I was the first one up. I wanted to be the first one in the big corner shower before the hot water was gone, you know? Like I do? But when I left my room, the hallway was freaking freezing, like worse than usual."

"Yeah, uh, I noticed, too."

"Well, it probably wasn't as bad once you were there, because by then everything was closed up again." Maylin straightened the utensils on her tray, oblivious to the two girls behind her waiting to serve themselves. "But when *I* was on my way to the bathroom, I noticed that the supply closet was open. And the window in there was open, too. Now, Anna thinks Ms. Engels must've left it open to air it out yesterday, or something, and that the door must've come open overnight from the wind, or something, and she's going to make sure it never happens again."

Maylin finally took a breath, plus a small scoop of pasta. Her rushed storytelling was hard for me to follow, especially when it felt like the unfinished video was burning a hole in my pocket.

"Look, um, Maylin?" I said, getting out of the way of a redheaded girl who was trying to reach for the pasta sauce. "I hate to say this, but I've got some calculus I forgot to do that I thought I'd cram while I eat."

"Oh!" Maylin put a dramatic drizzle of olive oil on her pasta, her long, willowy arms looking ridiculously elegant as she did so. "Okay. Sure. We can talk about this later. Where should we sit?"

We. I held back a sigh. I didn't want to hurt Maylin's feelings—but I really wanted to watch the video in private.

"I was . . . um, thinking I would sit by myself? Just this one time, to get the stupid calculus done."

Maylin studied me, pushing her hair behind one ear. "Are you . . . upset?"

"No. Why would I be upset? I'm just afraid of getting a zero for calculus homework."

Maylin hesitated. "Oh. Okay. Good."

I brought my tray to the only empty table in the room—the corner one that didn't have any windows near it. For show, I had to take out my calculus book and tablet. But then I put my phone in my lap and earbuds in, watching the little screen from behind the tablet. Before I hit Play, I glanced up to see where Maylin was. She'd found Alex, and was eating with her along with a couple of other seniors. As Maylin picked up her fork, I saw her eyes wander toward me, then dart away when she saw I was looking. It was only then that what she'd been telling me registered. *The supply closet was open. And the window in there was open, too.*

The "housekeeper's supply room" used to be Room 408, Taylor's old room. The room she'd jumped from. The school had repurposed it into storage for brooms and mops and window cleaner so no one would have to sleep there this year. It was a weird move on the administration's part—there was already a similar supply closet on the first floor—but I supposed they thought the grim optics were better than simply keeping it unoccupied and locked.

Maylin had said "supply room" instead of "Taylor's old room." Maybe because it was easier to say. She'd woken up this morning and found Taylor's old door open, and the window open, too, frigid air flooding the fourth floor.

Just the door open was one thing. Maybe Ms. Engels, the housekeeper, hadn't closed it hard enough. Or forgotten to lock it. Maybe she never locked it, since all it contained was cleaning supplies, presumably. But the window? Why would she open the window? In the freezing January weather? *Taylor's* window?

I pulled my plate of pasta toward me, then slid it away. I clutched my phone in front of me and hit Play.

At first the video was just blackness. But it was accompanied by a couple of deep, trembling breaths, and then Taylor's voice saying, "Say it again. Say it again, bitch."

The voice was low, but it was definitely Taylor's.

She took another breath.

"Say it again," Taylor repeated. "I dare you."

Then there was silence.

A long silence. More darkness. More breathing.

I paused the video, glancing around the lunchroom. Everyone was just going about their business, eating their pastas and chicken-avocado wraps, chatting—which was reassuring. Maylin was talking to someone at her table, laughing, no longer interested in me.

When I hit Play again, there was a gasping noise coming through the earbuds, and then the phone camera seemed to be somersaulting for a second. Then the picture actually showed something. A window. Taylor's window. You could see a little light coming in around the blinds.

There was a thump and then a scratching sound.

The picture lingered on the window for a moment. Then

there was more jolting. And a light came on, revealing Taylor's old room as I remembered it—with the red rug and the concentric circles of the dark tapestry on the wall.

And there was Taylor herself, looking into the camera. She was more wide-eyed than I remembered her ever being. It seemed like there was a little mascara smudged on one of her temples—like she'd not been looking in a mirror when she'd wiped her makeup off.

Stunned, I paused the video. I wondered if Taylor had ever told her brother about the ghost that supposedly haunted the Dearborn dorm. Or if this was some kind of prank video related to that.

Probably it was just that, I told myself, pressing Play again.

"I was all the way across the room. It was coming from the window," Taylor was whispering now in the video.

Was there possibly someone else in the room with her? No one replied. So it seemed Taylor was just talking into her phone.

She looked away from the camera, her brown hair falling over her face as her neck turned.

She got up and staggered over to the window. Her face looked weird from the upward angle. Although the screen was blurred, I could hear the sound of blinds being raised. Taylor steadied the camera phone to focus out the window. You could see the lamppost that lit the walk outside Dearborn.

I clenched my teeth and paused the video.

I didn't like seeing Taylor near that window.

The window she eventually jumped from.

The window that was open this morning.

But I felt compelled to keep going.

Next there was a faint sound on the video, like a sigh or a whisper. It felt like there were words in it, but I couldn't make out what they were.

The screen was jostled again, then blurred again.

I heard a bang and a clatter. And then the camera seemed to be still, taking in a bright light, high ceiling, and cream-colored wall that I recognized as the hallway of Dearborn.

And then for a whole minute the screen showed the empty hall. And then a minute more. There were six more minutes of the video. I skipped ahead. Still the empty hall. In the final seconds, there was the sound of a door groaning open. And Taylor came out of the bathroom, scooped up the phone, and stopped the camera.

I closed my eyes. Above all else—even the scratches and whispers and the creepiness—it stunned me to watch someone in such swift and familiar motion and know she was, nonetheless, gone. And yet there was something about this Taylor that was unfamiliar. She seemed manic and frightened. I was used to Taylor being coolly detached.

I restarted the video and watched the first minute again. I paused it a few seconds after she turned her light on. There was a black and aqua-blue object leaning against the wall near her window. *Her new snowboard.* We weren't friends anymore when she'd bought it, but I'd seen her make a big show of carrying it into Dearborn from her car. When had that been? Two weeks before she died, maybe? Even less?

I'd rolled my eyes at the sight because it was her second snowboard. The old one had been orange and pink. And she hardly ever used it. I'd always secretly thought she had no real interest in snowboarding—just liked for people to think she did. Or liked to waste money on snowboarding stuff. I'd seen a couple of unused bars of snowboard wax lying around her room.

I felt a pang of guilt for having judged her. Because now it seemed a relatively small thing—throwing away some money, getting a little joy out of a spending spree before she died.

I shook my head. There were only a few minutes left until my next class, so I opened up my email to Thatcher's note and started to reply.

Hi Thatcher,

I am not sure what this is. Was there a time/day stamp on it? That would help.

Because her new snowboard is in it, it must be January or early February of last year, right?

All best,
Haley

I hit Send.

I'd waited a week to open the video and now felt bad. Had it bothered him as much as it did me, and he was too polite to say so?

There was some dispute about what happened to Taylor the night she died.

The school administration essentially blamed her death on some "potent marijuana brownies" she'd been enjoying alone in her room. And there's no disputing that the edibles were there, and that they were made with a generous amount of a very potent strain of weed. And the story was consistent with the picture most people had of Taylor by then. She broke a lot of rules. She'd been given a couple of chances after minor offenses—probably because her family gave a lot of money to the school, although no one wanted to admit that directly. She was kind of a loner at that point—she'd hung out with upper-class students most of her time at Dearborn, so she was a little bit at sea her senior year. Kind of like me this year. But she, un-like me, spent weekends visiting college friends.

Those brownies—she'd possibly eaten more than one and then left a half-eaten piece on her desk—let the administration off the hook in a number of ways. There wasn't really a signifi-cant drug culture at Windham-Farnswood per se, except for the occasional outlier like Taylor. But the pot brownie made it so there didn't need to be a particularly thorough discussion of the suicidal possibility of Taylor's jump. If they could reasonably claim she'd had a bad reaction to the brownie, then there wasn't a suicidal tendency that staff or students could've perceived or reported. Never mind that pot isn't LSD, and that people don't usually leap out of windows after doing weed. It *was* a par-ticularly potent edible, cooked up by her other brother's col-lege friend, and that was apparently close enough in the eyes of Windham-Farnswood's conservative administration.

How much of this explanation I believed came and went de-pending on the day, depending even on the time of day, how pes-simistic I'd been feeling, how much sleep I'd gotten, how much light was coming in the window at any particular moment.

And I certainly didn't know how I felt now.

5

October 28, 2017

WINDHAM STUDENT WEEKLY

"Haunted Halls and White Nightgowns: Ghost Story Traditions at Windham-Farnswood Academy"

BY BRITTANY FORD, '20

It's that time of year again. Everyone's planning their costumes for the annual haunted walk through the Upper Pond path, and the culminating party at the assistant dean's house.

But another spooky Windham tradition is, of course, its ghost stories, most often told about the three oldest buildings on campus—Mary Putnam Hall, Cole Auditorium, and Dearborn Hall.

Students report feeling inexplicably cold sometimes in the Mary Putnam student lounge. And there's the occasional flickering stage light in Cole Auditorium. But everyone knows that the vast majority of the ghost stories at Windham involve Dearborn Hall.

Dearborn is the senior dorm and the oldest building on campus. It was built in 1879 as a gift to the school by

Jonathan Dearborn, in honor of his wife, Sarah Dearborn, who had attended Windham in her youth. It was built in the style of the Elizabethan renaissance at his request. The architectural style of the building—with its high, stepped brick gables and mullioned windows—gives it a stereotypical "haunted castle" kind of look, which has probably helped maintain its reputation over the years.

The most frequently told Dearborn story is that of the Winter Girl. The Winter Girl is a ghost who is said to haunt Dearborn—but only ever at the beginning of a new year. Legend has it that she must have died in January or February. As seniors return from holiday break each year, they can only try to prepare themselves for the Winter Girl's late-night visits—sometimes it's her humming or whispering in the halls. Others say she knocks on your door in the wee hours—slowly, three times—a night or two before she intends to haunt you or your room.

For some historical background, I talked to Eugenia Noceno, our school librarian and archivist.

"The story I've most often heard is that a student hanged herself in her room at some point in the late 19th century," she said. "The story usually involves something about her being jilted by a boyfriend—and in the seedier versions, she was pregnant at the time. And now she comes back to haunt the place of her final dark moments—pale and haggard and in a white nightgown, of course. It's never been clear to me which room or even which floor she supposedly occupied. But in any case, there is actually no record of any student ever dying by suicide on campus, in the 19th century or otherwise. There have been about five student deaths on campus in the school's entire history. None of them were suicides, and none of them occurred in Dearborn Hall."

Dearborn residential director Donna Yeager reports that there were no Winter Girl sightings last year or the year before that. The previous year—Ms. Yeager's first as a residential director at Dearborn—was a different story, however.

"First and last time I heard a story about her, she was humming and whispering to a student who decided to break the room curfew to go down to the basement to do laundry by herself at two a.m. That was in '15. No actual sighting. I have to say, I think that particular student was pulling a string of all-nighters and was under a lot of stress—as seniors often are during the storied 'haunting' time of late winter."

According to Ms. Yeager, students sometimes refer to the ghost as "Sarah."

"Not everyone calls her 'the Winter Girl,'" she reports. "I'm not sure why they call her Sarah. Maybe since the plaque on the doorstep mentions Sarah Dearborn, the building's namesake. Maybe that's where that comes from. But Sarah Dearborn died of natural causes in Philadelphia in 1936."

Conflicting ghost stories notwithstanding, most of the current seniors I spoke to say they're not worried about the Winter Girl, aka Sarah.

"I think Dearborn is really cozy," said Heather Mesloff, '18. "I just don't get a haunted feeling from being here. It looks a little spooky from the outside, maybe. But when you're in the building, it's got the usual dorm sounds and smells, like the Imagine Dragons playing and burnt micro-wave popcorn stinking up the kitchenette and lounge. It just doesn't feel ghosty. You'll probably feel the same way when you're a senior."

"I'm not going to worry about the Winter Girl until winter," said Amy Liu, '18. "I think it would be cool to see her, actually. Last semester at Windham, see the ghost. That'd kind of be a nice finale at the end of this whole Windham experience."

It was pretty easy to call up this cheesy old article from the newspaper archive online. I remembered it well since I'd proof-read it for Brittany after she'd written it. I hadn't thought much of it at the time. Sometimes I felt like Windham-Farnswood was obsessed with its own dumb traditions.

Nonetheless, after class I read and reread the article in one of the dusty library carrels in the stacks, nibbling a contraband granola bar out of sight of the librarians. I was hungry now since Taylor's video had wiped away my appetite at lunch.

Of course I'd known about the Winter Girl since I was a firstie. It seemed like girls talked about the Dearborn ghost until they actually lived in Dearborn—when they were mostly too old and jaded and distracted to care about an old ghost story. It was certainly true of me; I'd really not thought that much about the Winter Girl this year. Not yet, anyway. I'd forgotten the detail about how she was supposedly most active in January and February.

I stuck my earbuds in my ears and called up Taylor's video again. Holding my breath, and putting the volume up as high as it would go, I waited for the part where there seemed to be whispering in the room.

Saaaaa, it seemed to say. And then something like *mule*.

Was it Taylor whispering? Playing a prank on someone she'd planned to share this footage with later? Was the whisper maybe saying *Sarah*?

I backed up the video and played that part again.

It didn't sound like Taylor to me, but with whispering it can be hard to say.

And no. It wasn't saying *Sarah*. Because there was an *mmm* sound after the *Saaaaa*.

Saaaaam. Mule.

I listened longer.

Saaaaam. Mule. Washing.

That's what it seemed to be saying. Or rather, *Samuel? Samuel Washing?*

Someone's name. There was some garbled stuff after *Washing*. Maybe *Washington*? Maybe that was the name of the storied lover of the jilted girl in the newspaper story?

Maybe. And maybe I needed to give this Winter Girl thing a little more attention now.

I knew exactly who I'd talk to about it first.

♦♦♦

By nine o'clock, Star was in her octopus pajamas, gazing at the Caroline Bromley papers scattered all over her bed—as usual.

Caroline Bromley was a Windham student in the early 1890s who eventually became a journalist and a relatively influential

31

figure in the women's suffrage movement. Star, a history buff, was doing a senior project on old Caroline—on her life at Windham, and Windham's possible influence on her as a social reformer and a suffragette.

I wonder which room she stayed in when she lived in Dearborn, Star would randomly muse sometimes. Or *I wish I knew who her roommate was.* Or *I wonder if the girls had access to newspapers back then.*

But tonight Star was so engaged in her work that she said nothing—just occasionally flipped between pages and then leaned over and typed something on her laptop, which she had wedged between her hip and the wall. When I heard her yawn, I started to worry she'd want to turn in early. I definitely wasn't ready for the lights to go out.

"I wonder if Caroline Bromley believed in the Winter Girl," I said.

Star looked up, surprised.

"Yeah." She nodded. "I've wondered if it was a thing then, or if that all started later."

"Dearborn was probably a brand-spanking-new building when she stayed in it," I pointed out, just to get Star talking more. "People don't usually tell ghost stories about *new* buildings."

"Maybe they did then, though," Star said, studying me. She was curious where I was going with this. I wasn't sure myself.

"I don't know," I said. "We often think of the 19th century as the source of all our ghosts in old houses. People didn't think of the 19th century that way when they were *in* it."

Star seemed to be considering this. "Of course not," she

said, "but they were definitely into the supernatural. Have you heard of the spiritualist movement?"

"Um . . . I don't think so," I admitted.

"It was the mid-19th-century craze for doing séances, trying to speak to the dead. Anyway. Never mind. I guess it helps to remember, though, that for them this place wasn't a creaky old spooky building." Star glanced up at the crack in the ceiling. "It probably *felt* very different," she said, sighing. "New. Fancy. State-of-the-art."

Star's eyes settled on me for a moment—before they darted back to the ceiling. Maybe she'd heard about what had happened with Taylor's room this morning—since Maylin had mentioned she'd told a few people. Star probably wasn't sure if she should say anything, given that I'd been Taylor's friend.

There were a couple of things I wished I could explain to Star. For one, that she didn't need to tiptoe around me. Something that Anthony, Alex, and Maylin knew—but few others— was that Taylor and I weren't *really* friends when she died. We'd drifted apart a few months earlier.

But I'd never been sure how much I should explain this to people, when they regarded me with such care and sympathy. It would be gross to say out loud.

We weren't really friends anymore when she died.

And it felt terrifying to even think it. Because wasn't the next logical step to wonder, *Would she have died if we were still friends?*

"You want to Twizzle?" Star asked.

I tried to smile. Some nights, Star liked to split a Coke. She'd pour it into mugs and give each of us a Twizzler as a straw. I had a feeling, based on a few things Star told me about her hippie-ish parents, that they didn't let her have much sugar when she was a kid and this was one of her little boarding school rebellions.

"I maybe shouldn't have caffeine," I said. "Since I couldn't really sleep last night."

Star puckered her lips skeptically. "Coke doesn't count as real caffeine. Coffee would be another story."

I shrugged. "Okay, just a few sips."

Star grinned and opened her little fridge. After she pulled out a can, she turned to me.

"Funny you should ask me about Caroline and the ghost," she said.

"Funny how?"

"Well, you know how I've been doing a lot of research in the archives?"

"Yeah?"

The school archives were in a special part of the Windham Library on the top floor, and Star hung out there whenever it was open. Not all private high schools have archives, but because of Windham's unusually long history and status as one of the earliest girls' secondary schools in the country, it had a fairly big special collection of old letters and other documents.

"I found something in November that I thought was kind of cool."

Star put down the Coke can and opened one of her desk drawers.

She pulled out a paper photocopy of a large black-and-

34

white photograph. I recognized the photo as one she used to have on the corkboard behind her desk earlier in the year. It was a photo of about forty girls—Caroline Bromley among them, presumably—assembled in front of our dorm.

Dearborn Hall, 1891 was written lightly below the photo, in elegant slanted handwriting.

"Caroline's in the picture?" I asked.

Star pointed to a girl third from the right in the second row. She was one of the few girls in the photo who wasn't looking directly at the camera. She seemed to be looking beyond it, off to the side. She actually looked slightly confused.

"She's fairly easy to identify in photos because she was so short. But in this one we don't have to because it's labeled."

She handed me another photocopy.

"On the flip side of the paper—someone wrote all the names."

They were written in tiny, almost unreadable script.

"Cool," I said.

"The girl on her right is her friend Abigail Ashton. Abigail was a big letter writer her whole life, and lots of the letters—mostly to her parents and her friend Eleanor at home—ended up here in the Dearborn archives. There are even a couple letters to Caroline when they were adults."

"And on her left?"

I asked because the girl on Caroline Bromley's left had her arm tucked around her, and her head was cocked so it was almost touching Caroline's.

"Yeah, isn't that interesting? That's Leonora Black. All three were friends, at least for a little while. I know because some of

Abigail's student letters mention both Caroline *and* Leonora. I don't know if they stayed friends with Leonora, though. If they did, Leonora didn't keep in touch writing letters like Caroline and Abigail after they'd graduated. At least—that I know of."

Star opened another folder and rifled through it. I waited politely, unsure if I wanted to read a bunch of old letters right now. What I really wanted was someone to talk to about Thatcher's video—about the strange whisper in Taylor's room. But I didn't know Star well enough to trust her with all that. Bringing up the Winter Girl had felt about as close as I could manage.

"Here's two where she mentions both of them," Star said, handing me two photocopies, both of which she'd annotated in pen at the top:

AA: Caroline, LB.

I read the first:

November 10, 1888

Dear Eleanor,

Isn't November so dreary this year?

I am eager for my Thanksgiving visit home. I try not to talk about it in excess, as my dear friends Caroline and Leonora do not have the means to do so themselves. They go home only for the Christmas holiday. Oh, how I wish I could bring them with me!

Since our last letters were in October, I've not

yet told you about the All Hallows celebration here. It was great fun. There was a literary theme of fantastical stories. Caroline, Leonora, Sally, and I all dressed as characters from Alice's Adventures in Wonderland. Can you believe they let me be Alice? Caroline and Sally have fairer hair than me, but they wanted to be the silly Tweedle twins, as they are shorter and look uncannily alike. (And I believe Sally would have been loath, nonetheless, to receive the attention of playing Alice. As a twin, she could shrink behind Caroline.) Leonora, with her stature, was the queen. I spent the night saying "Curiouser and curiouser!" When called upon in class the following day, I wished to keep repeating it.

I am eager for another letter from you.

Your friend,
Abigail

May 1, 1892

Dear Mother,

Happy May Day! Are your daffodils happily blooming?

Graduation is only a month and a half away now. I am poised to be salutatorian. Surely you will tolerate my boasting. You know I would never do so out loud, with the girls and the teachers. But quietly here with you—huzzah! Perhaps you will hide this letter from Father.

I do hope Leonora and Caroline and I remain friends after we leave Windham. In recent weeks, I've felt a division between the two of them that I am at a loss to repair. Neither seems willing to explain. They don't argue, but don't seem as sweet to each other as they once were. Possibly they are both trying to lessen the pain of the final goodbye in June.

I am counting the days until you come for graduation.

Yours affectionately,
Abigail

I looked up. "Are these the only ones?"

"No," Star replied. "She writes about Caroline and Leonora a lot, but these are part of a handful that mention them all together, like a trio."

"Oh. Okay."

"But what really got me thinking about the ghost was this girl here," Star said slowly. She reached for the old dormitory photo and slid her finger over to the image of a tall girl at the end of the back row. Her mouth was turned down in a rather severe way. And her gaze was intense—almost mean. She was standing slightly apart from the rest of the girls. Or maybe it was just that the girl immediately next to her was leaning away from her.

Star tapped the sheet with the tiny scrawled names. "It says her name is Sarah Chase."

"Ohhh," I said. Everyone knew that the Winter Girl's name was *Sarah*.

"I mean, is it just me, or do you get the creeps looking at her?"

"Hmm," I said, studying the tall girl.

She didn't look like a friendly person—I had to give Star that. But that was often true of people in such old photographs.

"I wonder at what point people decided it was okay to smile at a camera?" I said softly.

Star opened the Coke and poured it into two mugs.

"Right after the Second World War, maybe?" Star said. "I feel like I see more people smiling in pictures after that. Maybe people had more to smile about then. And more people had cameras. So it was less of a formal thing where you had to be serious about it."

She used to live here, I thought, eyeing the severe Sarah Chase. *Maybe even in this room.* When the school was smaller, almost all of the girls stayed in one building.

"When did this become the senior dorm?"

"I think that was established sometime in the late '40s or early '50s, when enrollment went up. This couldn't have been the whole group of residents that year, though. Maybe it's just all the girls in one grade, or something."

I tried to shift my gaze away from the girl, but something about her expression kept drawing me back in. I felt like she knew I was looking at her. Like she knew something about me, and disapproved. I thought again of the faint whispering in Taylor's phone footage.

I felt the mug being placed into my hand but wasn't able to close my fingers around it. And in the next second, the mug was on the floor in pieces. Coke sliding across the hardwood and browning the edge of our indigo rug.

"Oh!" Star jumped. "Sorry. I should have made sure you had it."

"No, it's my fault," I said. "I'm out of it."

I started picking up the mug pieces as she wiped up the Coke. Then she poured half of what she had left into a different mug, which she placed carefully on my desk.

"Do we know anything about Sarah Chase?" I asked.

Star shrugged. "She's not really connected to my research about Caroline. She just . . . caught my eye. I haven't looked her up in other documents or whatever."

Star hesitated, glancing warily over at the new mug of Coke she'd given me—as if it was now, in light of our conversation, embarrassing in some way.

"Hey, where's my Twizzler?" I said. "It's not a Twizzle without a Twizzler."

"Right! Uh . . . They're in my drawer."

She fumbled around at her desk, opening a couple of drawers before finding the package of candy. She pulled two out and dropped one in each of our drinks.

We sipped silently for a moment before Star said, "I wonder what kind of treats Caroline and *her* friends had when they lived here."

"A cup of cider with a cinnamon stick, maybe," I said, grateful for the awkward change of subject and suddenly realizing she'd called me her friend.

This was our first year as roommates and not just classmates. I wondered at what point that had happened. Sometime before the holiday break, probably—when we had stayed up late guzzling soda and finishing papers and labs due before we all went home.

Last year Star's old friend and roommate, Jocelyn, had left abruptly around November—after the fiasco with the make-out footage. My junior- and sophomore-year roommate, Maya— with whom I'd gotten along fine, but who wasn't really a close friend—had requested, and gotten, a single for her senior year. I didn't want a single room. Particularly following Taylor's death, I was admittedly reluctant to consider sleeping alone in Dearborn. I'd known Star since we'd been on the same floor freshman year. We'd never been friends, though.

Taylor had always thought Star was kind of dopey. Sometimes she referred to her as Star Crunch or Little Debbie. Although the nickname was fitting, I thought Star was a really pleasant and easygoing person. So last spring I asked if she'd room with me. And I wouldn't ever tell her about the nicknames.

"I'd like to think something a little more scandalous." Star sucked on her Twizzler. "A hot toddy, maybe."

I smiled. My phone vibrated and I glanced down to find an email notification with a message from Thatcher. I swiped quickly to read.

It looks like she took the video on 2/7/18.

"Another Twizzler?" she asked. I hadn't even bitten into my first one, and I was still trying to make sense of the message.

Thatcher didn't clarify that the date was only three days before Taylor had died. He didn't need to.

"Haley?" I heard Star say as I felt my fingers tingle again. I gripped the mug tight, focusing on not dropping this one.

"Uh, sure," I replied, putting my phone down and silently taking the candy.

6

I can hear Star's rhythmic breathing. She's already asleep.

It always feels the same, in a way, lying in the dark and listening to your roommate sleep. Still, over the years, I've gotten used to my different roommates' unconscious quirks.

Star's are long, deep breaths—like a sleeping baby in a cartoon. Maya, before her, would make curious, conversational little sounds in her sleep. "Hmmm? Mmmm?" And freshman year, Alex was a dead-silent sleeper except in the middle of the night, when she would occasionally huff and puff like a diminutive dragon, and a few times seemed to wake up with a quick, defiant yelp.

When you're an insomniac, you learn to live with the sounds of the people who sleep next to you in the dark. Those sounds become the rhythm to which you run the reel of your unwanted thoughts.

Tonight, as on so many nights, mine are about Taylor again. This time—Taylor screaming.

Not the actual sound of her screaming, which I never heard myself. But the question of whether she ever screamed at all that night. The night she died.

The girl who lived on the right side of Taylor's room—what

was her name?—said she heard Taylor screaming in her room before she jumped. The girl who lived on the left side of her— her name was Lily—said there was no screaming. That there was some commotion, and then she heard Taylor's window screech open and then something outside—and that's what woke Lily up. And when she looked out the window and saw Taylor on the ground, she started screaming. So that's probably what the other girl heard.

It's always felt important to me to know which girl was correct. Because who screams right before they deliberately jump out a window?

In the end, everyone decided the truth lay somewhere in between. That both girls were half-right. That Taylor probably didn't scream before she jumped, but on her way down.

But now, after seeing Thatcher's video, I wonder. What else might have been happening in her room that night—that made her scream?

7

Twelve Nights Left

How does a ghost break through silence? How does a ghost convey words? How shall I?

Scream them like the banshee that I am now? Or whisper them like the sweet, soft-spoken girl I once was? Write them in smoke or wind or water?

I have no friends here to teach me how.

I am all alone. I have to figure it out myself— how to push the weight of the words from my world into theirs.

8

Tuesday, January 29

My phone alarm dinged gently.

When I opened my eyes, the first thing I saw was Star sitting at the edge of her bed, arms twisted behind her, braiding her long wet hair down the back of her neck.

"Hey," she said. "The Coke didn't keep you up, did it? You sleep okay?"

"Yeah," I said, yanking open a drawer and picking out a black jersey dress and dark purple leggings. I threw them on, deciding I didn't need a shower.

After I'd pulled on my clunky black boots, I grabbed my book bag, threw open the door, and was relieved that it didn't feel especially cold. A few minutes later, after I'd brushed my teeth, I was tromping toward the stairs, eager for breakfast.

Except.

Except that as I reached for the door that opened to the stairway, my eyes darted instinctively toward the hallway where Taylor's room was. The fourth-floor halls formed a long U, with the shorter bathroom hallways capping each end of the long main hallway. Taylor's old room was down one of those shorter hallways by the smaller bathroom.

And the door was open.

Again?

I couldn't tell if I was really breathing. Letting go of the stairwell door's handle, I stepped toward Taylor's old room. My boots now made my feet heavy as I moved closer to the doorframe.

When I reached it, I looked in. And the room was mostly empty. On the wood floor was a box of cleaning sprays and a case of brown paper-towel rolls. Next to the window was a vacuum cleaner. I breathed.

And the window was closed.

I stepped closer to it to make absolutely sure. Then I reached back and touched the door behind me. I'd watched enough horror movies to know this was when the door is supposed to slam closed, locking me in.

But the door stayed put. It didn't even squeak at my nudge.

In this moment, I remembered sitting on Taylor's rug one night while she sat on the bed. We were both doing homework, but as she typed, she was singing "Jingle Bells" as a cat would: *Meow meow MEOW, meow meow MEOW, meow meow meow meow MEOOOOOOOOWWWW.*

This had always been one of her more charming eccentricities—that she liked to sing like a cat. I always had the feeling that this was something her family had laughed at too much when she was five or six, and she was still trying to milk it.

I stepped closer to the window. I couldn't help myself. I

hadn't been in this room since we were friends, but I wanted to see the view from the window.

How far down was it? How had everything looked to her right before she did it?

I shook the thought away. It had been dark when she jumped. So it didn't matter. She'd probably just seen blackness, and hurled herself into it. It must have looked completely different than it did now in daylight.

And yet I felt myself moving closer to the window, just to see. Just for a second. And then I'd get out of here. And tell Anna about the open door, *like a good little Windkin.* As Taylor would have put it.

The window was frosted. As I stepped closer to it, a gasp escaped me.

There were letters etched in the frost.

I MADE

I stepped closer. There was a second line beneath it, squished in between the first and the bottom of the window.

It wasn't as clear as the first line. I squinted at it.

HER JUMP.

Before I had time to think or even breathe, I leapt forward and furiously wiped the words from the window.

And then.

Thunk thunk thunk.

I heard my boots against the wood floor before I really understood that I was running back to my room. The white doors of my dormmates blurring before my eyes, terrifying me with their uniformity, their sameness with Taylor's. When I reached ours,

I pushed it open and nearly fell back into the room, slamming the door behind me.

I tumbled onto Star's already-made bed.

"Haley!" she gasped. "What's going on?"

"I don't know," I mumbled into her quilt. "But . . . Taylor's door is open again."

"Oh," Star said uncertainly. "Okay."

"Can you tell Anna?" I asked, my voice calmer than I felt. "I mean, if you think she needs to know. I don't really feel like talking to her."

I wasn't sure why I said that. It just felt like I needed to thrust the burden of my discovery on someone else—quickly. Because I felt significantly less sane than I had five minutes ago.

"Well . . . *sure*," Star replied.

She sounded almost gratified to be given this assignment.

As soon as I had this thought, I instantly felt bad for having it. Star wasn't like that. It was the kind of thing Taylor said about her. The kind of thing Taylor said about *everyone*, really.

"I'll go find her now," Star said, leaving the room.

Sure thing, Star Crunch, a mean little voice called after her in my head.

"Shut up," I murmured, although I wasn't sure to whom. If anyone.

Once I caught my breath, I realized I hadn't even mentioned to Star what I'd seen written in the frosted window. Or that I'd wiped it away. So when Anna went in to check things out and lock the door again, it would be as if the words had never been there.

◆◆◆

The spontaneous evening hall meeting was held in the down-stairs study area—the one with the big maroon wingback chairs and the stodgy lace curtains. The one that parents liked to sit in when they visited because it was pretty—but no one actually liked to study in because it was drafty and uncomfortable and the floorboards groaned at the slightest movement.

Since there weren't that many chairs in the room, most of the seniors sat on the musty oriental rug. Anna stood in front of the old fireplace shouting, "Quiet, everyone. I want this to be a very quick meeting."

I knew where this was going, and I wasn't looking forward to it. Once the chatter in the room stopped, Anna clapped her hands resolutely.

"Okay. So. Look, everyone. Twice this week, fourth-floor students have awoken to the corner room, Room 408—that is, the housekeeper's supply room—having its door unlocked and open and the window open as well."

I felt a few stray gazes being directed at me (the former friend of that room's last occupant), but I tried to ignore them.

Anna hesitated. "Umm, or rather, the window was open the first time. Today it was just the door."

I felt my pulse quicken as I thought of what was written on the window. I probably should've told Anna or had Star tell Anna. But it was so cruel I was beginning to wonder if I'd really seen it.

"It wasn't Ms. Engels," Anna went on. "I've spoken to her

multiple times, and she's as baffled as I am. Now, I don't think I need to explain why this is a problem, aside from the fact that it made the fourth floor extremely cold the first morning. If you're not clear about that, feel free to ask me privately. I will say this: if someone is doing this intentionally, I'm going to ask you to stop."

I was looking down at my hands now, still avoiding the other girls' eyes.

I made her jump.

Those words kept coming back to me—along with the question I'd been turning around in my head last night—about Taylor screaming or not screaming. About the girls who lived in the rooms next to her. Alex kind of knew the one named Lily. The other girl's name I still couldn't remember.

Anna went on: "Ignoring this request will result in consequences—loss of off-campus privileges, to start. And a report to the dean of students. Maybe that's all that needs to be said. I hope so. Because if this is someone's idea of a funny prank, they are seriously mistaken. If anyone knows who might be responsible for this, and has information they'd like to share with me, I'm available in my room. I don't want to belabor this, so that's it. . . ."

Anna sighed deeply and looked quickly around the room, seeming to avoid eye contact with any particular girl. "Unless anyone has comments or questions they'd like to voice right now?"

No one said anything. The floor creaked with the collective shifting of weight in the room.

Ursula Gruber raised her hand. "Umm . . . besides that closet, does someone else have keys to the different rooms? Besides you?"

"Aside from the student keys to each room, I have a copy and the main residential office has one as well. Ms. Engels has a key to the supply room, but she doesn't have keys to any other student rooms. None of the custodial staff have direct access to student room keys, if that's what you're asking. Is that your concern?"

"Uh . . . I guess," Ursula said.

"Anyone else?" asked Anna.

No one spoke or raised a hand. I felt my heartbeat begin to feel heavy and fast again. This question of keys—and who had them—made me uneasy. Taylor was always losing things—phones, jewelry, and even her key. I knew this about her. And I wondered if anyone else in this room knew it, too. Always I'd wondered if it was part of being a rich kid—constantly losing expensive things and not much caring.

"Okay, then," Anna chirped. "I'll let you all get to your studies."

Maylin met me as I came out of the room.

"Want to hang out with me and Alex for a little while?" she whispered.

The advantage of being a senior and living in Dearborn was that the "mandatory study hall" hours were that in name only. We could "study" wherever we wanted in the building, not just the study areas or our own rooms. Which meant we could hang out in each other's rooms.

I was happy to leave the meeting behind and not be alone.

When we got upstairs, Alex was already in Maylin's room—cross-legged on the rug, laptop open.

"You know," Alex said, "I just don't know if Anna should've made a big thing of this. Maybe that old door lock is broken, or maybe Ms. Engels has been absentminded the past couple of days. But now everyone knows, and everyone's going to be all worked up, and everyone's going to think they have to come up with a theory about it."

Maylin shook her head and sat on her bed, pushing aside a pile of laundry that had been dumped there.

"I mean, I really appreciate Ms. Engels and everything she does," Alex continued. "But I think this whole 'supply room' thing is kind of insulting to all of us. It's obvious Ms. Engels actually doesn't *need* that room for anything. The real supply closet downstairs is enough, and that's what she's used to using. She probably left the bogus upstairs one unlocked for a few days by mistake."

This theory would've been perfectly plausible to someone who had *not* seen those grim words scribbled on Taylor's old window.

"But—" I began.

Alex and Maylin both looked at me expectantly.

"Never mind." I shook my head. I wanted to share what I had seen—but not now. Not yet. Not until I could find a way without sounding crazy. And I wasn't ready to tell them about the video from Thatcher, either.

I saw Maylin glance at Alex before picking up a pair of pajama bottoms and folding them slowly.

"Maybe it *is* the Winter Girl," Maylin murmured. "I mean,

I'm not really into that stuff. But Kate Goldberg's older sister was in Dearborn just two or three years ago, and she was good friends with someone who *swore* she saw the ghost. It really freaked her out. She almost had, like, a nervous breakdown."

Alex looked unimpressed. "That's a thirdhand story. All Dearborn stories seem to be like that. Isn't that convenient?"

Maylin folded a pair of pink-and-black polka-dotted underwear until it formed a tiny little square.

"Kate Goldberg's sister's friend is a *real* person," she pointed out.

Alex stared into her laptop screen. "I'd be interested in hearing it straight from her, then."

Maylin rolled her eyes. "Hey. I mean, I'm not saying I believe in the ghost, really. But maybe there's some weird energy in the building, opening and closing doors and windows and stuff."

"Yeah, sure." Alex spoke as she typed on her computer. "Like maybe everybody is getting their period at the same time and it's making the lights flicker."

"*What?*" Maylin said.

"Well, you know . . ." Alex was clearly shifting into informational mode, looking up from her laptop. "I've read and seen stuff on TV about how sometimes poltergeists happen in places where there's like a stressed-out tween or teenager. There's some theory that all the nervous, messed-up psychic energy of a pubescent kid—usually a girl, gotta blame it on a girl—is what's causing the weird shit to happen. Not a ghost."

"But this is a *senior* dorm," I reminded her. "We're all way past pubescent."

"Can we stop saying *pubescent*?" Maylin said.

"Way Past Pubescent," Alex repeated. "Can that be our band name?"

"Stop!" Maylin squealed.

"Maylin hates words that have *pube* in them," Alex told me.

"Shouldn't everyone?" Maylin lay back into her pile of laundry. "I'm officially declaring this a no-pube zone."

"But do you think it's *possible* that the ghost has always been that kind of energy?" I asked. I kind of liked this idea. It was weird, but at least it didn't involve dead people.

"Like all of our nervous little adolescent girl-brains are doing it?" Alex said. "No. No, I don't believe that."

"But there are people who think this is a real thing? A young person's brain causing a poltergeist?"

"Yeah. Look it up. You've never heard that before? There are a lot of famous cases. Of people suddenly thinking there's a ghost in their house. Dishes flying off the shelves. Furniture falling over. But really, it's usually in a house where someone is going through puberty."

"Hear that?" Maylin exclaimed. "*Puberty*. Alex didn't last two minutes."

"But what happens when the kid gets older?" I asked. "Does the poltergeist go away?"

"Usually everyone gets scared and moves out of the house before that, I guess. I don't remember. I read a few stories like that when I was a kid, that's all. I'm not an expert. You should look it up."

"Like, do they outgrow the poltergeist? Or does it stay with them?"

Alex shrugged.

"There are still a lot of things I'm waiting to outgrow," Maylin said, a little dreamily. Probably she was thinking about Wes again.

"Is one of them Taylor Swift?" Alex asked. "Because my vote would be for that."

Maylin pulled a big-eyed, fluffy white stuffed seal off her bed. She tossed it and expertly hit Alex on the ear with it.

"Well, we all know *you* emerged from the birth canal singing dark indie ballads," Maylin said.

Alex was laughing as she tossed the seal back.

"Did you have to say 'birth canal'?" she demanded.

"Yes." Maylin grabbed a metal water bottle off the floor and gulped from it. "Absolutely. I was tailoring my message to my audience, like Mr. Packer always tells us to do."

Alex rolled her eyes and put her earbuds in. Then she pulled one out and said, "And we all know how you feel about Mr. Packer."

"I'm not even going to dignify that with a response," Maylin said.

"I'm not sure if dignity has anything to do with it," Alex replied.

There's no stopping Alex and Maylin when they start in like this. Sitting silently on their rug, listening to them go back and forth, I decided Anthony might be a better bet for showing the Thatcher video. I felt closer to him lately. He'd known Taylor better than Alex and Maylin had. And he might have more of a neutral response, in a way, since he wasn't a Dearborn resident himself.

Someone knocked on Maylin's door.

"Come in!" Alex yelled.

It was the sophomore Alex tutored in chem, a laptop case slung over her shoulder.

"Hey . . . guys," she said softly, apparently embarrassed to be addressing a roomful of seniors. She was petite and urchin-eyed like Alex, but without any of the disarming confidence. I couldn't remember her name.

But it was time for me to get going anyway.

"I'd better go get to work," I said, standing up and gesturing for the sophomore to take my place on the rug. "But Alex . . . there was something I wanted to ask you about."

"Yeah?"

"That girl Lily Bruno, who graduated last year . . . do you keep in touch with her? You were kind of friends, right?"

Again, Alex and Maylin exchanged meaningful glances. No one wanted to address the obvious—that I was talking about one of the two girls who'd essentially witnessed Taylor's death—who'd first seen her lying on the pavement in the moment afterward.

"Not really friends." Alex hesitated. "Just lab partners."

"But do you have a way of getting in touch with her?"

"I might still have her old number to text her with. I'll have to check."

I paused. "Maybe you could send it to me."

I felt like all eyes in the room were on me—except the sophomore's. She was unpacking her laptop—probably trying to look busy.

"When you get a chance," I added.

"Sure," Alex said.

I mumbled that I needed to get to my homework, then said a quiet goodbye before closing the door.

✦✦✦

I didn't go back to my room right away. Instead, I headed downstairs and sat for a while in the empty dining hall.

I texted Anthony:

I have something I want to show you.

It took him only a minute to reply:

Want to talk?

I *did* want to talk. And to show him Taylor's video, which I no longer felt I could keep to myself. But I knew he had a paper due tomorrow. Anthony was a last-minute guy. I imagined him banging away furiously on his laptop, pushing his hair from his face, tucked away in his spare, mostly undecorated dorm room.

Not now, I typed. *But any chance you remember the names of the girls from last year who found/heard Taylor the night she jumped? One was Lily Bruno. I'm trying to remember the other.*

Jayla Martin, he wrote back. *She was in orchestra.*

Did you know her?

Not really. Leo knew her from Afro-Latino Alliance. Said she was funny.

Know anyone who might know her number?

No. Why?

Long story, I typed. *Will tell you in person.*

Dinner together tomorrow?

Sure.

I was grateful Anthony and I had warmed up to each other this year. Warmed-over leftovers.

I switched over from our chat and opened Facebook. There was a Jayla Martin who had a few friends in common with me. I went to message her, but then my fingers froze over the keys.

What to say? Best not to mention murderous words written in window fog, I decided. Keep it straightforward. But not *too* straightforward.

Hi Jayla. I hope you're doing well at college. As you might know, I was a friend of Taylor Blakey's. I was wondering if you would be willing to talk to me about the night she died. There are some things I'd just like to settle for my own peace of mind, if that makes sense? Thanks, Haley

Did it sound reasonable? I wasn't sure, but added my number. I hit Send, then sat and worried about my homework for a few minutes. The calculus problems this week looked especially hard. And the thought of those made my body feel way too heavy to move itself upstairs to tend to them.

After a minute more, the less ambitious act of staring at my phone paid off:

Hi Haley—Yes, I remember you hanging out with Taylor last year. I hope you're doing okay and we can talk if you want. I know you've got classes till 3, and I have a late class tomorrow until 4. After that, maybe?

Thank you, I replied. *Let's try then.*

I added her contact to my phone and saved the number she'd tacked on at the end, finally feeling satisfied enough to get back to schoolwork for the time being. In our room, Star was busy on her laptop. She looked up, gave me a stressed-out sort of smile, and went back to work. We didn't Twizzle.

9

Breathe in. Maybe.

Breathe out. It was me.

In. Poltergeist.

Out. Mine.

Opened that door.

Scribbled the words.

Crazy.

Stop. Being. Crazy.

But maybe.

Maybe. Maybe my brain created the words on the window. Maybe they weren't really there. Maybe I looked fast and just *thought* I saw them?

Lying still, listening to Star breathe in the dark. It's a peaceful noise, at least. As an insomniac, you also learn not to resent your roommates for their sound sleep. Or at least you learn to try not to.

And in the long hours in the dark like this, I forget how old I am sometimes.

I could be nine again, worrying about what might happen if I go to sleep. Or fourteen, worrying about what might happen if I don't.

Nine: If I go to sleep, I might wet the bed again. Or sleep-walk to the edge of the stairs, and tumble down them, awakening with my head cracked open like a smashed pumpkin.

Not that it had ever happened. But I was a worrywart as a kid. And I'd seen my mother slip and fall halfway down them once—on a night when she and my dad had had a little too much gin and tonic.

And fourteen: The first night at Windham, lying in the bed my mother had made before she'd gotten in her rental car and driven back to the airport because she didn't really have the money for a second night in the hotel. Me picturing my mother arriving home just before midnight, passing by my half-empty room. She wouldn't say, "Night, Haley. Try to sleep," because I wouldn't be there. My eyes stung at the thought as I tried to make out the contours of my new room in the dark. That first tiny room with Alex, with the broken sliver of blinds where the light came in. Since Alex's bed was closer to the window, that sliver illuminated her small fingers that lay across her thin elbow as she slept on her back.

I'd worried about all the things I might screw up if I couldn't manage to fall asleep. Failed cross-country tryouts. Failed attempts to make friends. Inability to focus in my new, super-challenging prep school classes. Being called on and looking sleepy and stupid if I couldn't answer the questions.

When I fell asleep that night, I think it was in the comfort of knowing that even if I failed everything, it would be nice, in some ways, to go back home, to not have to think of that room being empty and my mother and little brother eating their chicken casserole dinner without me.

To get to hear that "Night, Haley" for a few more years.

But.

But it wasn't to be. Because I met Taylor a couple of days later. And from then on I didn't ever consider going home.

10

Eleven Nights Left

All of the girls are sleeping soundly.

I used to be like these girls. Beaming and bright-eyed. Moving with light, tapping steps and not this ghostly shuffle. That was Before, of course.

Before.

I never understood what a beautiful and painful word that was.

Before before befoooooore. Stretch and moan the end of that word, and it can go on forever.

Soon enough, they will learn. I will teach them: what it feels like to be in the ugly After.

11

Wednesday, January 30

After French class, I stayed on the Farnswood campus. Upper-class students were allowed to be here until the last shuttle at seven-thirty on weekdays—for library study, activities, meals, or "visiting," which often actually meant making out in an empty student lounge or in the woods behind the athletic building.

I had about forty-five minutes to kill before I'd meet Anthony for dinner, and I knew he was still at orchestra. My plan was to talk to Jayla Martin.

It was really too cold to stand outside talking, but I didn't want to be overheard. I found an empty women's bathroom in the foreign language hall and dialed Jayla's number. She answered and I felt a little unfocused as she asked me a few polite questions about how I was. I did the same. And then there was an awkward silence.

"So you said you wanted to ask about Taylor?" she said.

"Well . . . yeah. I was wondering if you would mind telling me exactly how it happened that night. Exactly what you heard and saw. I know it probably seems terrible, to want to know, but—"

"It doesn't seem terrible," Jayla said quickly.

"I just didn't ask a lot of questions last year, but this year—" My voice echoed over the bathroom tiles.

"You don't need to explain. But . . . where did you want me to start?"

"Umm . . . it was around two or three a.m., right?" I was trying to keep my voice low. "Everyone was sleeping? And then something woke you up? Can you start from there?"

"Yeah. Okay." Jayla hesitated. "Well, I woke up to Taylor screaming. Like, I could hear her through the wall. I jumped up in bed. I didn't run out of my room *right* away. There is this shock when you wake up suddenly sometimes, you know? When you're not sure what just happened?"

"Of course," I said.

"Well, it was like that. But then I heard this other noise in her room, this ruckus like she was freaking out, banging against something or thumping the walls, I don't know. I sat there with my heart just kind of pounding for a minute. But then I got up and went to the hallway and started knocking on her door. And a few seconds later Lily comes out of *her* door, screaming that she just saw Taylor on the ground out the window. And she starts calling 911. And I don't really believe her at first, so I'm pounding harder and then finally I just tried the door, and it opened and we both ran in and looked out the window and . . . Lily was right. She was . . . she was down there."

We were both silent for a moment. I was trying to stay focused on what I should ask next—to keep my brain from forming very vivid pictures of what Jayla was saying.

"And then I left and got the RD, Tricia," Jayla went on. "Lily was still screaming and crying at the window until Tricia and I came back, and Tricia asked me to take Lily into my room . . . and she went down to be with Taylor and called the Barton RD to come be with us while she waited for the ambulance."

"Was Taylor . . . still alive?"

The grim echo of my voice in the bathroom was driving me crazy. I got up and stormed out.

"I don't know. I know she wasn't by the time the ambulance got there, so I'm guessing, hoping, not."

"So when you heard her when you first woke up . . . was she saying anything? What was she screaming?" I tried to lower my voice again as I headed down the stairs.

"Oh . . . she wasn't saying anything. Just screaming. Shrieking. Like you do when you're waking up from a nightmare or whatever. There were no words."

"So why do you think she was screaming?" I asked, pushing my way out of the building's glass doors.

Two youngish-looking boys passed by as I said this. One of them, ruddy-cheeked and bespectacled, paused to stare at me. I winked at him and he scurried away.

"I don't like to speculate, but . . ."

"It's okay," I said, watching the two boys disappear behind a nearby dorm. "Anything you can tell me is helpful."

"I've got to think whatever she was taking might've been giving her some kind of hallucinations or voices or something."

"But . . . does pot do that, though?" I asked, pacing along the side of the building. It was too cold to find a bench to sit on. But at least the crisp air was bringing me back to myself.

"There was a lot of it in her system," Jayla said slowly.

"They found that out later. Probably you knew that. She might've had a whole bunch of those brownies, not just one. That's . . . hard-core."

"Yeah . . . ," I said. A cold gust of air blew over me, practically taking my hat off. "I guess."

"Well . . . it's not a satisfactory explanation to me, either," Jayla said with a sigh. "But it's the one that makes the most sense. I don't think she . . ."

Jayla trailed off. She didn't want to even say *suicide*.

"Did you ever wonder if someone was in the room with her?" I asked, tugging at my hat.

Jayla was silent for a moment. I stamped my feet and wiggled my toes.

"Um . . . not really. No one ever came to her room much. Except . . ."

I drew in a breath.

Except me. That was what she was going to say.

"But the way she was screaming, could it be she was screaming at *someone*?"

"Like I said, there were no words. It wasn't like a *Get out of here, don't touch me* kind of situation. It was like someone waking up from a nightmare."

I considered this distinction for a moment, unsure if it was clear to me. But it felt inappropriate to call it into question. Jayla had been there; I had not.

"I know this might sound a little weird, but did you hear anything else unusual going on in her room before that night?" I asked. "Like, say, in the week leading up to it?"

It seemed odd to me that no one would have awoken the night she took the footage—the way she'd torn out of her room and thrown her phone and everything.

"Umm . . . not that I can remember. But you know, Taylor and I chatted sometimes. In the bathroom, the hallway, whatever. And in that week or so before . . . she seemed a little messed up. Not her same self."

"Oh. Yeah?" I felt like I'd swallowed a paperweight and it was slowly sliding down toward my chest.

"Well, I grabbed lunch with her a few days before . . . because she looked kind of lonely."

I gulped. Lonely, in part, because her shadow had left her.

"Did you guys talk?"

"A little. She said she was failing calculus, and falling behind on all of her homework because she'd lost her laptop. She thought maybe someone stole it in the library. I was like, *Don't you want to report that?* She said no, she hated talking to the administration, maybe she would just order a new one online. But it seemed like she *should* be worried about it."

"Taylor lost things all the time," I murmured.

"When I saw her a couple days later," Jayla continued, "she said a librarian called her after the laptop turned up in the library Lost and Found. She was like, *I guess I have to start doing work again,* like she was disappointed she didn't have that excuse not to study anymore. I thought a lot about that later. That she seemed totally . . . apathetic, I guess. Like how I could have said or done something to make her feel better? But at the time I just thought she was . . . I don't know . . . unfriendly? Checked out because it was senior year? Done with all the Windham shit? I just didn't think she was in serious trouble. And I probably should have, looking back."

"There's no way you could have known," I said softly.

We were both quiet for a moment.

"Umm . . . do you know what happened to the old RD, Tricia?" I asked. "Where she ended up?"

"No idea. I've only kept up with a few kids from my class, even. You might ask someone who was on the soccer team. She was also the coach. Maybe someone kept in touch." Jayla paused. "Did you have any other questions?"

"I don't think so," I said reluctantly. I couldn't feel my face anymore, in any case.

"Well, let me know if you do."

Jayla wished me luck with the rest of the school year, and I wished her the same. After we hung up, I sat still for a moment, staring at the *CALL ENDED* message, unsure how I was supposed to feel.

I headed to Anthony's hall, rubbing my hands against my cold cheeks. First I walked fast, and then I walked slow. But either way, my boots seemed to want to tap out the rhythm: *I. Made. Her. Jump.*

12

Anthony and I brought our trays to a small corner table where we could be by ourselves.

"I'd have come to *you* if you'd wanted," Anthony said after eating a couple of limp vegetables in silence. "I could've used a crisper serving of broccoli tonight. A properly cooked piece of fish."

Anthony always made me smile with his middle-aged sentiments and turns of phrase. The Farnswood dining halls had the same menu as Windham because it was all under the same dining services. But in Anthony's dining hall the food was always mushy and overcooked. He told me recently, *No one wants to complain because the cook is a nice guy and seems kind of depressed.*

"Sorry," I said. "I wanted to get out of there. I need a break from Dearborn."

"Yeah? What's up?"

"Does it ever bother you," I said slowly, "that even if what happened to Taylor *was* all because of a freakishly trippy dose of cannabis, it was also, like, a fulfillment of a prophecy?"

Anthony touched his new chin stubble. "Uhh . . . can you unpack that for me a little?"

Anthony's greatest ambition is to host one of those nightly cable news shows where the various pundits and politicians argue and sputter and generally make asses of themselves while the host stays smart and suave. His personal hero is Don Lemon on CNN. There is no doubt in my mind that he'll get there one day. He acts, half the time, like the cameras are already rolling for him.

"Well . . ." I sighed. "For years, people told a story of the ghost of a girl who jumped from that building. Or hanged herself. I mean, kinda the same thing. And then history buffs like Star are all like, *Nope, no one ever died by suicide in that building*. And then, though, Taylor *does*."

Anthony regarded me sadly.

"Old buildings have ghost stories," he said. "Ghost stories often have a suicide or a murder in them. Boarding school kids fetishize suicide. These are all well-known facts even outside of Windham lore. I have a friend at Harrington Prep and a cousin who went to Mosely. They both have buildings like Dearborn and ghost stories like that."

"But their ghost stories didn't come *true*," I whispered.

"Look, Haley. I'm still depressed about Taylor, too. But we all know she had *so many fucking issues*."

As if to punctuate this remark, his phone emitted a quick guitar riff.

He took it out of his pocket again.

"Who the hell are you texting right now, Anthony?"

He put it back in his pocket. "Sorry. Vince Courtier."

"Huh?" I said. Vince Courtier was sitting two tables away from us. In fact, he was looking at us while he shoveled apple crisp into his mouth.

"He's kind of, like, my new friend."

"Uh . . . huh," I said uncertainly.

It's kind of an open secret at Windham-Farnswood that Anthony is probably gay. He never says so for sure. But girls don't bother having crushes on him anymore, like they did freshman and sophomore years. Last year there was a senior named Leo who he hung out with a lot, at least in the beginning of the year. I'm pretty sure they were together. And then I'm pretty sure they broke up. Anthony was sad for a little while without saying why. Being friends with him was like the opposite of being friends with Maylin. There was a lot, with him, that apparently didn't need to be said.

"Now, what was I saying?" Anthony asked.

"So many fucking issues," I reminded him.

"Oh! Right. Well, yeah. You know what I mean."

"Yeah," I muttered. "We don't need to talk about them all. Not tonight."

Anthony hesitated. "Do you want dessert?"

I shook my head. I knew he didn't want any, either. He almost never ate sweets.

"I want to show you something," I said, taking out my phone and earbuds.

◆◆◆

I studied Anthony's face as he watched the video. It changed from skeptical to curious to anxious.

"Let me rewind that part," he said in the middle.

"What part are you on?"

"Is she whispering something?"

"I don't think it's her, though," I said slowly.

"Then who's with her?" Anthony asked.

My gaze met his.

"Nobody," I said. "It's the middle of the night. In her room."

Anthony was silent, watching the video for a minute more. After Taylor dropped her phone in the Dearborn hallway, he looked up at me.

"It mostly goes on like this for six or seven minutes until she comes back out of the bathroom and picks the phone up and shuts it off," I told him.

"Then I want to hear the whisper again."

He backtracked the video, listened, and backtracked again.

"I think she's saying the name Samuel," I offered.

Anthony nodded. *"Samuel was sixteen."*

"You think?"

"Yeah." Anthony pulled the earbuds out of his ears and handed them to me. "Listen."

I backtracked and listened.

Yes. He was right, now that I listened again.

"Who is Samuel?" he asked softly.

"I don't know," I said. "But the ghost girl of Dearborn, according to the story, had a boyfriend who dumped her."

"Oh God." Anthony rubbed his eyes. "Taylor was probably messing with someone. Someone who believed in that ghost. That's probably why she made this video."

"I don't know . . ."

"You and I know she liked messing with people's heads. I mean, just look at the Jocelyn Rose thing. . . ." Anthony didn't look entirely convinced of what he was saying. We both knew that the Jocelyn Rose video had been an entirely different kind of prank. More Taylor's style. Effortlessly cruel. A prank ghost video was almost wholesome in comparison. And strangely ambitious.

"But *who*?" I persisted. "Whose head was she messing with in this case? She didn't have any friends left. Except you, I guess."

"Well, she didn't show it to *me*," Anthony said.

"Then who?"

Anthony shrugged. "It *is* conceivable that she made friends with some other girls after you . . . after you guys had your . . . friend breakup."

He'd just barely stopped himself from saying something like *after you ditched her.*

"Yeah. Sure. But something about this feels *real* to me. She seems really afraid. Really frantic. And she wasn't that great of an actress."

That was why Jocelyn Rose got cast as Abigail in *The Crucible* last year, and not her. I chose not to add that out loud.

"Well," Anthony said, gazing at the dessert table. I could tell he was holding something back, too.

"Anthony?" I prompted.

"Maybe I should mention one thing. Now that you put it that way."

"Yeah? What?"

Anthony sliced at a broccoli floret with a butter knife, roughly removing its head from its stem.

"Well," he said slowly, "one of the last times I talked to her . . . a couple weeks before she died . . . maybe even less than that . . . she told me she was thinking of spending a night or two in the infirmary. It was kind of random. She clearly wasn't sick. Like she didn't have a cough or the sniffles or anything. She just said she needed a break from the dorm."

The Windham infirmary—like the Farnswood one—was a no-questions-asked place. It was assumed that if you showed up, you were sick. But you couldn't do anything there but rest. You had to stay in bed and do nothing but eat an occasional bowl of broth with toast. You couldn't even bring your laptop or use your phone except to contact your parents. It definitely wasn't the sort of place that would normally appeal to Taylor.

"You've never mentioned that before." I felt myself becoming numb—finger by finger, toe by toe, moving toward my hands and my feet. "Did she actually go?"

Anthony shook his head. "No. I mean, I guess not. I remember seeing her the next day, and figuring she decided not to go. I mentioned it to the dean when they had their little investigation, but didn't think that much of it. It had just seemed like typical Taylor, scheming to get out of a term paper deadline or whatever."

"But maybe she really *did* need a break from the dorm," I said. "If the dorm itself was part of the trouble."

"Maybe," Anthony said softly.

He was scaring me a little. He was supposed to double down on his insistence that the Dearborn stories were just stories, and that I should stop torturing myself about Taylor's death. But the video had rattled him—made him forget his script.

I put my phone in my backpack, out of sight.

"I wonder if some girl killed herself in her Dearborn room a long time ago, a girl broken up about her boyfriend, Samuel, there would be ways the school could cover it up, make sure it didn't appear anywhere in its history, its archives."

"There *could* be," Anthony said, picking up his fork and poking at his dry fish. "And schools like this have their reasons."

"Thank you for your honesty, Anthony," I said.

"No problem," he muttered.

♥♥♥

Since it was freezing, I turned down Anthony's offer to walk me to the shuttle stop.

"Text me when you get back to Dearborn," he said as I pushed through his dining hall's doors. "So I know you're okay."

"Sure," I said. Even though we both knew that just because I got safely to Dearborn would not mean I was okay. "Bye."

I pulled on my gloves as I walked to the shuttle stop. The wind was frigid, and my face felt frozen after only a minute. My hair blew around my face wildly, my ears stung. At the bus stop, I wrapped my arms around me and stamped my feet, feeling too stiffly cocooned to pull off my backpack and find my hat in it. I tried to hum away the cold.

The wind blasted my face. I closed my eyes. In the momentary darkness, I heard my mother's voice shouting the obvious question:

WHY AREN'T YOU WEARING YOUR HAT?

My mother and I had talked a few days ago—only briefly,

about my brother's latest basketball game and her efforts to find me a cheap plane ticket home during the spring vacation. It had felt like a conversation we'd had a hundred times before. Sometime in the middle of last year it had started to feel like my mother and brother weren't my immediate family anymore. More like an aunt and cousin who wished me well from a faraway place. And I spoke to my dad even less.

And the shuttle was here anyway. I boarded it with a huff of relief, then heard a couple of other girls tumbling in behind me, giggly and breathless from the effort of running to catch this last shuttle.

On the ride back home, those two girls—probably sophomores, by my guess—were the only other students riding. They were in the back, laughing and whispering the whole way. I resisted the urge to give them a steely upperclasswoman gaze. They were kind of cute. They reminded me of Taylor and me the time we got drunk one rainy Saturday afternoon, then took the shuttle to the Farnswood campus, sneaking a bottle of Taylor's vodka with us. We met up with a few of her older guy friends and ended up playing drunken football in the muddy back athletic field. I'd never played real football—with tackling—before, and never had since. Taylor had taken photos of us all in the mud but was smart enough not to post them anywhere. We looked obviously drunk in them. We wore borrowed boys' clothes home on the last evening shuttle.

"I've never tackled anyone before," I'd said to Taylor as we sat together on the minibus. "I think I love it."

"Of course you love it," Taylor had snorted. "Josh was being particularly gentle with you, in a manly kind of way."

"Oh, shut up. I mean, guys take this opportunity for granted. That they can just join a sport where they can mow other people down, if they feel like it."

"And be mowed down. Don't forget that half of it."

"I think I'd consider it pretty seriously, if it was an option for me."

"Are you trying to tell me about your repressed anger, hon?"

Taylor was into the idea of anything repressed. She thought a lot of people were repressed. Our English teacher Ms. Tremblay in particular.

"No," I'd said. "I'm trying to tell you that I think I would like an excuse to tackle people."

The shuttle pulled up to Windham's front stone gate, and we all stumbled out single file into the cold. When the other girls reached the sidewalk, they paired up, the first waiting for her friend to hop off the bus before walking toward the dorms. When I stepped onto the curb, I unthinkingly tried to do the same—glancing behind me for a split second for Taylor. And then realizing—in the same moment that I heard one of the girls giggle again—that of course she wasn't there.

As I approached Dearborn, teeth chattering, I thought of what Anthony had said about Taylor: *You and I know she liked messing with people's heads.*

13

Curfew wasn't for a few minutes. I sat outside on the freezing-cold bench next to Dearborn and willed myself to look up at the window of Taylor's old room. It was the only dark window on this side of the building at this still-early hour.

Samuel . . .

My chest and stomach felt hollow. Despite the cold and the wind, I was dreading going into the warmth of that building. It wasn't a warmth I could trust.

I let my gaze widen to the whole building. You could almost call it cheerful, since most of its lights were on. Sturdy and solid, even. Its castle quality could maybe feel safe and protective instead of bleak and menacing. If you really wanted it to. That was how I had tried to look at Windham's stodgy buildings when I was young—especially when I first arrived. But not since last year.

I headed inside and signed in at the front desk but didn't go upstairs. Instead, I turned on the light of the creaky-floored sitting room where we'd had our meeting last night. I couldn't bring myself to head on up the stairs yet—to have to pass by Taylor's door.

Sitting on a claw-footed couch, I considered my talks with

Anthony and Jayla: Taylor's final moments. The window. The screaming. The scatterbrained quality of her last few days—failing classes, a planned escape to the infirmary, her laptop in the library Lost and Found.

I opened my last chat with Alex and hoped she was still awake.

Hey, did you ever have a chance to look up Lily's #?

True to her conscientious form, Alex wrote back almost immediately:

Yeah. Here's her contact info, altho it's a year old fyi. Probably still works, but we didn't keep in touch. Good luck.

Seeing the icon with Lily's name and number pop up made me relieved that she didn't ask what exactly I wanted with Lily.

Laying down my phone, I closed my eyes. The wind outside battered at the room's old windows, and one of them gave out a *thunk*. My eyes popped open, and I thought of something Maylin had said last night.

Kate Goldberg's older sister was in Dearborn just two or three years ago, and she was good friends with someone who swore she saw the ghost.

I hopped up and paced the room a couple of times. The floorboards croaked their approval.

Someone who swore she saw a ghost would not find it so hard to believe that Taylor heard a phantom whisper, or that I saw something written in window frost. In fact, such a person might rate as crazier than me, and thus be comforting to talk to.

I switched over to my chat with Maylin:

Kate Goldberg lives in Barton, right?

Then I waited—having vague second thoughts. She and Alex

81

were probably together right now, reporting my randomly pestering texts to each other, wondering yet again if I was "okay."

Yeah, Maylin wrote back.

Was it her sister who went to UPenn? I texted back, resisting the urge to ask if Maylin was alone or not right now. If she was answering so readily, I decided it didn't really matter.

Maybe? was Maylin's reply, and I didn't want to push it, so I switched gears.

You know what room Kate's in?

Not sure but I think the second floor.

Thanks! I typed, already starting toward the Dearborn dining hall.

Barton Hall—which is a huge dorm and houses most of the juniors and a fair number of sophomores—is connected to Dearborn by the joint cafeteria. It's similar to how the two first-year dorms—Shelton Hall and Gregory Hall—are joined. You can move in between them even after curfew, as long as you're back in your room by ten. (Eleven in Dearborn, so seniors can feel just slightly more like grown-ups.)

Only the smaller junior and sophomore dorms—called Underhill House and Compton House—are freestanding, unconnected to any other dorm, with their own smaller dining rooms. Some girls prefer those to Barton because the rooms are newer and the heat works better.

After passing through the vacant hall, I headed toward the stairwell, where a girl—a smiley junior I recognized from cross-country last year—was about to head up. I asked her if she knew where Kate lived and she gave me directions. When I finally knocked on Kate's room, I saw two names on the door and realized she had a roommate. But it was Kate who answered, already in pajamas.

"Hey, Kate . . . I don't know if you remember me. . . . We were in newspaper together for a little while last year."

"Of course." She opened her door a bit wider and I caught a whiff of incense—which wasn't allowed. Not that I cared, but it maybe half explained the nervous expression on her face.

"My friend Maylin was mentioning to me that your sister is at UPenn. . . . Is that true?"

"No." Kate cocked her head. "Swarthmore."

"Oh! Well, that one is on my list, too. Swarthmore. Does she like it? Do you think she'd be willing to talk to me about it?"

This was a pack of lies, of course. Luckily, Kate didn't know me well enough to know that I wouldn't want to go to a small college, and that I probably didn't quite have the grades to bother trying for Swarthmore, either.

"Yeah, Addison likes it okay." Kate hesitated, apparently deliberating whether to call me on this rather sudden change of heart. "And yeah, I'm sure she'd be willing to talk to you about it."

"That's great. Would it be okay to text her?"

A few minutes later I had Addison Goldberg's number in my phone, and was heading back through the dining hall to my own dorm. I texted as I walked:

Hi there. This is Haley Peppler from Windham-Farnswood. I just talked to your sister and wanted to ask if you would be willing to chat with me about Swarthmore? It's my top choice!

Also, there is someone else from your class I've been trying to get in touch with and was wondering if you could put me in contact with her.

Addison's reply came before I'd even made it all the way up the stairs to the fourth floor:

Sure. Not having the best semester, so I might not be the person to talk to if you want someone all rah rah. I could probably talk Friday for a bit, though. Who are you trying to get in touch with?

As I stepped out of the stairwell, I wasn't able to stop myself from glancing down the side hall that had Taylor's room at the end of it. The door was closed. I exhaled. The hallway was filled with the usual early-evening quiet. Everyone was studying or plugged into a tablet or phone.

I stopped short of my room and texted back.

Thanks! Friday is good. Afternoon? Actually, I don't know the name of your friend, but someone told me she saw the Dearborn ghost? I am doing a project on campus ghost stories.

While I waited for a response, I noticed a single piece of popcorn on the floor by our door.

Maybe around 4, I'll call if I can. Her name is Bronwyn Spruce and tell her I said hi, we haven't talked in about a year. I don't know if she will still want to talk about that, but you can try. Good luck, talk to you Friday.

I saved the number she'd typed at the bottom of her message. Well, I would cancel before Friday. And I'd heard of Bronwyn Spruce. She'd been a senior when I was a firstie—and kind of a campus celebrity. Girls with names like that tend to be. I remembered her wavy blond hair and striking dark eyebrows, her cute ski clothes, her impressive murals in the art department hallway that annoyed me for the reminder that someone who is pretty and rich and fashionable can't always be dismissed as shallow.

I picked up the piece of popcorn before typing *Thanks!!!* And then I went into my room, which smelled like a movie concession stand. Star was sitting on her bed with a purple ceramic bowl of popcorn and there was a matching bowl, piled high with it, on my desk.

It was so like Star to prepare these bowls instead of just eating out of the microwave bag like most other girls would.

"Hey!" Star said. "I thought you might want some popcorn. If you don't want it, just leave it and I'll take care of it. I didn't want to eat the whole bag myself. It's, like, double butter."

"Uhh . . . well, thanks," I said, taking a handful of popcorn.

"I take it you ate dinner . . . elsewhere?"

"Yup. At Farnswood with Anthony."

"Anthony Ripley?"

"Yeah," I said.

"He's cute," Star remarked.

"I guess," I said, not wanting to put myself in a position to explain about Anthony right now. "He's just a friend."

Star turned her attention back to her laptop. I got into my pajamas and then took out my calculus homework. For twenty minutes, our room was silent except for the occasional munching of popcorn. I couldn't get my mind off Bronwyn—and the text I would need to write to her. Still, I willed myself not to take my phone out again yet.

When I finished my calculus, I took out my laptop to work

on my next English paper. But I found myself staring at the blank screen, then took out my phone.

While she was rich like Taylor, Bronwyn had been in a different social circle—the more wholesome and athletic type. The Golden Child variety. She wouldn't remember me, and would probably think I was weird for writing her. But it didn't really matter. Graduates were kind of like ghosts, too. No one thought much about them once they were gone.

Hi Bronwyn, I typed. *I'm a senior at Windham, and I hope you don't mind, but Addison Goldberg gave me your name as someone to talk to about the Dearborn ghost. Would you be willing to talk?*

I stared at the message for a couple of minutes. Star announced that she was tired and going to brush her teeth.

I nodded as she left the room. I took out my European history textbook and read a few lines about Robespierre. Then reread them. My brain refused to absorb anything.

I picked up my phone. I really wouldn't have anything to show for my evening if I didn't contact Bronwyn. I hit Send just as Star came back. She punched her pillow and put on her sleep mask.

"Good night," Star sang—so cheerfully I wondered if it was actually sarcastic. *Is she annoyed with me for something?* I thought before remembering one more thing to text.

btw Addison says hi!

"Good night," I said.

I hadn't gotten through the next sentence about Robespierre when my phone vibrated.

"Sorry," I whispered to Star, turning the phone's volume down.

"No worries," she mumbled.

Wait, what's your name? Bronwyn had written back. *Do I know you?*

Maybe I should've seen it as comforting that things don't change—that snide girls stay snide long after they leave Windham.

No, I'm Haley Peppler.

Did something happen at Dearborn?

I considered my response for a couple of minutes before typing simply:

Yes.

Nothing really bad like last year, I hope? I just looked it up now and didn't see anything.

No, nothing like last year. But Taylor Blakey was my friend, and I would appreciate talking to you.

Bronwyn didn't reply right away. I watched my phone, half listening to the sound of Star breathing rhythmically. She was already asleep.

Bronwyn's reply appeared: *Ah, okay. I don't know how much I can help, but we can talk.*

When? I typed back.

Now works, Bronwyn offered. It was a generous offer, and I wondered if I should feel bad for assuming she was still snide.

Thanks, one sec.

I stepped out of the room and headed toward the stairwell doors.

"Hey," Bronwyn answered. "How is old Windham these days?"

"Oh, I don't know," I said. "It's getting old for me, I think."

"I remember the feeling. Actually, it's pretty late there, isn't it? Sorry, I'm in a different time zone."

I sat on the floor and leaned back against the stairwell doors.

"I stay up late. My roommate's used to it. So . . . where are you now?" I asked.

"UC Berkeley. I'm a junior now."

"Oh?" That sounded lovely, to be somewhere sunny and far out of reach of bitter New England ghosts. "You like it?"

"Yeah. I love it. Now, were you good friends with Taylor Blakey? I'm so sorry."

"Thanks," I said, and bit my lip for a moment. "So, look . . . if you don't mind, I would really like to hear what your experience was in Dearborn. I heard you had a . . . um, paranormal experience there."

"Paranormal. Yeah. It was paranormal, all right."

"What happened? Can you talk about it?"

I heard Bronwyn take a deep breath. "Yeah. I guess. I woke up one night and there was this girl just inside my doorway, staring at me in my bed. Staring at me really maliciously, it felt like. My heart was pounding so fast, it's hard to remember exactly what happened. I started screaming, jumped out of my bed, and then she was gone."

I hesitated, waiting for more. I had questions, but I didn't want to sound skeptical.

"I know she was there," Bronwyn murmured. "Right in the room. It wasn't a dream."

"That sounds so scary," I said.

It did sound scary. Even if it didn't sound real.

"She was pale and had straggly hair. She was wearing an old-fashioned nightgown."

"Oh," I said, just so Bronwyn would know I was still listening.

"The thing is, the night before, and a couple of nights before that, I heard these weird knocks on my door and even, like, in my closet. I didn't think that much about them, really, until I saw her."

"Was it just the one time you saw her?"

"Once was enough. I refused to sleep in my room for a few nights after that."

"What did you do?"

A few rooms down, a door creaked open. Ursula Gruber came padding down the hallway, headed for the bathroom in a pair of teddy bear boxers and a Windham T-shirt.

"I slept in Addison's room for a couple of nights."

I paused, waiting for Ursula to pass. We exchanged insincere smiles.

"And then after that?" I asked.

"I went back to my room because Addison's roommate was complaining. I had a plan to get permission to leave campus for a few days if it happened again."

I heard the bathroom door clunk shut.

"But it didn't," Bronwyn added.

I knew more than a little bit about weird sleep issues since I'd had some when I was a kid. Sleepwalking and some other stuff I outgrew a long time ago—with the lingering insomnia. But I used to read about these things, and there is a common form of nightmare where people are kind of half-awake, half dreaming. They are awake enough to see the room around them, but their brain is still dreaming—maybe producing some image that appears to be in the room—a man in the corner, an animal on the bed. Maybe this was what happened to Bronwyn.

"Did the girl say anything?" I asked.

"No. Just stared. Now, did something happen to you, Haley? Or are you asking on Taylor's behalf?"

"A little bit of both," I offered, unsure how much I should say.

I didn't feel like telling her about the window scrawl. And I didn't think I should share Taylor's video with someone I didn't know very well. But I had an idea of what else I might show her.

"Can I send you something?"

"Okay," Bronwyn said uncertainly.

"Hold on a second," I murmured. I slipped back into my room and studied Star's motionless form in her bed. Her old photo of the girls gathered in front of Dearborn was still on her desk from the other night. I zoomed in on Sarah Chase, the sour, spooky-looking girl, and snapped a quick picture. Then I texted it to Bronwyn.

"The girl in the picture I just texted you . . . Does that look like the girl you saw in your room?"

Bronwyn paused for a second. "Umm . . . my girl was really frail. This girl looks like she's of pretty hardy stock, actually. And darker hair."

"Oh," I said, unsure if I was disappointed. If she'd said yes, I might have had an anxiety attack.

"Are you . . . okay?"

"I . . . um . . . haven't been feeling so comfortable sleeping in Dearborn lately," I admitted.

"I don't blame you. They couldn't let you live in another dorm, considering everything that happened to your friend?"

"I didn't ask to."

It hadn't occurred to me. All seniors lived in Dearborn. No matter what. It was the tradition. And as a scholarship kid, I wasn't in the habit of asking for exceptions.

"There are people who . . . well, I don't know if I should say this."

"What?"

"There are people who . . . and I'm not going to say I'm one of these people . . . who think that there was probably more to your friend's death than Windham wants to say."

"What people?" I demanded.

"Well . . . look," Bronwyn said. "I'm going to send you something. If anyone asks, it wasn't me."

"Uhh . . . okay. What is it?"

"You'll see. I'm going to do it as a screenshot. There was a Facebook group I was part of for a little while. It's mostly older women. Windham alums. They've all had bad experiences in Dearborn. They all believe there's something wrong with the place. Some are more woo-woo about it than others. One of them thinks there must be some noxious mold growing in the building that makes some of the girls go crazy and see things. Anyway, they're like a little club—they chat online about their theories. Not just about Dearborn, of course, but other super-natural stuff or whatever. That's partly why I stepped away from it. It all started to weird me out after a while. Even though it was kind of hard to get into the group, once I was in, I wasn't sure I wanted to be there."

"Oh. Wow. Sure, I'd like to see anything you can send me."

"You can text me your email address after we talk, okay? And like I said, don't tell anyone I sent it to you. I'm doing this because you're a friend of that girl Taylor. I kind of don't want to think about it anymore. But I get it that you do. Since you're still there. Since you're still close to it."

"Okay," I said, wondering if I'd made too much of Bronwyn's expensive clothes and haughty smile when she was at Windham. Or, for that matter, the rumors about girls quitting the swim team because she was such an imperious team captain. She seemed perfectly nice. Exceedingly nice, even.

"Then you can text me if you have any questions about it," she said.

"Okay," I murmured. "Thanks."

"And Haley? Take care, okay?"

After we'd hung up and I'd sent her my email, I dusted myself off, tiptoed back to my door as quietly as I could, and slipped back into the room. Star had flipped from her back to her side and now was scrunched up in a ball, her back to me.

My history text was still open on my bed. I read a paragraph or two more of my assignment and then checked my email on my laptop.

Bronwyn's message had already come through with a screenshot of a Facebook discussion between several people. The discussion seemed to be moderated by a person named Suzie Price, whose profile picture was of a sunflower instead of a person:

Suzie Price: Hi all. Please let me know if you do not want to be included in this, or you can remove yourself from the discussion. I know there has been very little discussion on this group recently—it isn't my intention to frighten everyone or bring back bad memories. But I wanted to alert everyone to some tragic news from Windham. A student jumped (or fell) to her death from the fourth floor of Dearborn the night before last.

Darla Heaney: Oh no.

Jane Villette: I heard about this because I live in Northam—not too far from Windham. It was on the local NPR affiliate, that there had been a student death. Such a tragedy.

Lynette Rakoff has left the discussion.

Darla Heaney: The school's PR is not saying directly, but it sounds like it was a suicide. Prayers for the family.

Darla Heaney: Maybe this will light another fire under the administration's behind about that building.

Laurie Rowell: Never. They never will.

Suzie Price: Let's maybe wait until we hear more about the details before we speculate about that.

Isabella Kaufman: They're saying the girl had a drug problem.

Laurie Rowell: How convenient.

Karen Norcross has left the discussion.

Suzie Price: Who's saying that?

Jane Villette: A friend of mine's daughter is there as a day student.

Laurie Rowell: Someone ought to call Ronald Darkins back for a visit.

Suzie Price: He's dead, sadly.

Laurie Rowell: Oh. RIP. Or . . . probably not. Probably he's haunting someplace or someone or other, just to prove himself right.

Suzie Price: I know we all have our baggage about Windham and Dearborn, but I feel like this is kind of unseemly. Even in the context of this little group.

Laurie Rowell: Windham admitting that a student had a drug problem? Hmm, I think they might be desperate not to have to admit to *another* problem . . .

Jane Villette: Can we take a step back here, ladies? The poor girl. Her poor parents.

Darla Heaney: Well, they definitely aren't poor.

It took me a couple of minutes to take all of this in. They all sounded like Windham girls, actually. But when I clicked on their profiles, several of them looked like they were pretty old. Laurie Rowell seemed to have kids. Suzie Price mentioned grandkids in her profile. Darla Heaney's profile said she graduated from UNH five years ago, so she at least wasn't as old as the others. But here they all were, gossiping about Taylor's death.

For a moment, I wondered if I should consider this discussion malicious. But then—at least they were *angry* about it on some level. At least they cared. And there was a general sense that Windham's administration had something to hide.

I had questions. I reopened my message with Bronwyn:

Thank you for this. Have you ever met or talked to any of these ladies?

Only Suzie. You have to talk to her to get in the group.

Is she (I hesitated, searching for the right word) *nice?*

Yeah. She's nice, but not all of them are. A couple of them seem a little nuts, just go in knowing that. If you want to contact Suzie, friend her on FB, or try to message her. Ask her to call you if you're serious about joining the haunted group. She won't just add you automatically. She's very wary of interloper trolls.

The haunted group. That wasn't a club I was certain I wanted to join.

Okay thanks, I wrote back, at a loss for a more specific response.

Was I haunted? Had Taylor been?

The wind whistled outside, and the sound of it pulled my attention away from my laptop. Star, seeming to hear the noise in her sleep, mushed her face into her pillow. I let my gaze creep upward to the framed poster above her bed—of a smiling beluga whale. I usually tried not to look at it, because the more I looked at it, the more I felt its innocently happy facial expression resembled Star's.

Stop that. I was so startled at the thought that I almost scolded myself aloud. Another mean thought about Star. A Taylor sort of thought.

I picked up my phone and texted again.

How did you connect with this group exactly?

Last year I met another Windy at a party. I was a little drunk and started talking about the ghost. She said her mom (also a Windy) knew someone who'd had a scare in Dearborn, and then she gave me that person's contact info, and that person is in the Facebook group, so she helped me get signed in. I am glad I'm not the only one, but it's all a little weird for me. I'm not suggesting you should join them but thought you'd want to know it's an option.

Thanks, I wrote simply. But then added *Goodnight* so Bronwyn would know I didn't intend to hound her with questions all evening.

How very legacy of Bronwyn to refer to herself as a *Windy.* Only girls whose mothers and grandmothers went here used that affectionate term. The rest of us riffraff all thought it sounded too much like a fart reference.

I put my phone down and read over the Facebook discussion again.

After a few minutes, I Googled *Darla Heaney.* She was likely the youngest of these women, and maybe I could gauge how crazy she was by seeing what kind of dirt I could find about her.

Since she had a relatively uncommon name, it didn't prove to be very difficult. She was an employee at an environmental firm near Philadelphia. And that had kind of a sane whiff to it for sure. Maybe I'd been expecting to find something a little weirder—like that she'd have an Instagram full of pictures of hairless cats, or an Etsy store of cocktail dresses for infants.

I returned to the discussion to see who else in the group I might stalk, but my eyes settled on something else. A guy's name.

Someone ought to call Ronald Darkins back for a visit.

Was he someone's boyfriend? Was this an inside joke?

I clicked back onto Google and typed in *Ronald Darkins.* The first thing that came up was a Wikipedia bio.

Ronald Darkins (1936–1999) was an American parapsychologist, paranormal investigator, and author. He was associated with several well-known paranormal claim investigations, but is likely to have investigated hundreds of additional lesser-known cases. Early in his career, he avoided media attention and quietly investigated cases part-time while teaching general psychology at Weston Community College in Vermont. After the publication of his most well-known book, *Resonances and Reflections,* in 1992, he was in much higher demand for investigations and media appearances. The popularity of such shows as *Unsolved Mysteries* during the early and mid-1990s heightened his public profile, giving him minor celebrity status, with which he was never comfortable, according to close friends and family. From 1978 to 1994, he always conducted his investigations with the help of his wife, Kathleen, whom some claim was clairvoyant. Their marriage and working relationship ended with their divorce in 1994. Darkins continued to conduct paranormal investigations on his own and published *Ghost of the Gallows: Paranormal Encounters in the American West* in 1996. His last book, a work of horror fiction titled *Dew Drop Dead,* about a haunted restaurant inn, was published posthumously in 2001.

The photograph beside the initial paragraph was of a smiling but slightly cross-eyed man in his forties, with a shock of dark hair, a trim beard, and large round glasses.

I sucked in my breath as I scrolled down the page, scanning for any other relevant details about this guy's career. At the end was a long bibliography that listed his books and media appearances. It seemed like he was big in the early '90s. He'd occasionally been on shows like *Unsolved Mysteries* and *Paranormal Detective*.

Ronald Darkins was a ghost hunter. But he'd been dead for more than twenty years. Still, my eyes focused on *Someone ought to call Ronald Darkins back.*

Back? Meaning he'd come to Windham at some point? Or called one of these women at some point? Or maybe he went to Farnswood?

I Googled his name along with *Windham-Farnswood*, and then with just *Farnswood* and *Windham* individually. Then I spent the next half hour scrolling and clicking on page after page where those names came up together. But I found no media reference to him ever visiting the school. It didn't surprise me. Windham-Farnswood had a very stuffy, old-fashioned administration—moneyed academics who'd gone here or to similar schools themselves. There was no way they'd let some cheesy ghost-hunter show film an episode here.

I sighed and minimized my search screen. It was already late, so I started again on my homework. I finished most of it in about an hour. Then, once I'd put on my T-shirt and flannel pants and shut out the light, I tried to ignore the occasional rattle-crack of the window glass shifting with the strong wind outside.

14

In the dark, my brain flirts with sleep but of course comes back to Taylor.

I met Taylor in the first few days after cross-country practice. I felt her watching me in the locker room after the third day of tryouts. She came up and asked me where I'd come from.

"Michigan," I'd said dumbly.

"What brings you all the way to Windham-Farnswood, then? Travel all that way, don't you want to go somewhere a little fancier? Choate, maybe? Exeter?"

I stared at her for a moment, trying to determine if she was making fun of me. The story of how I'd ended up here wasn't one I'd been planning to share anytime soon.

"I'll bet you'll be varsity. You're really good. You've got amazing times, amazing stamina. I was varsity last year, too. I was the only firstie on varsity."

I didn't know what to say. I was trying not to stare—but trying, too, to decide if I thought she was pretty.

"You're a sophomore?" I said.

"Yeah."

Yes, I decided. Pretty. Just not in a conventional way. She had what my mother called a "strong profile." Bigger nose, but she carried it well. Fierce, dark eyes that appeared to be laughing at everything.

Age gap aside, she invited me to have dinner with her and her friends in Barton. I agreed—and ate at a table full of sophomores and juniors who were all scheming how to get off-campus permission to sneak out to a day student's party the following weekend. They were friendly with me even though I said next to nothing. Many of them seemed to defer to Taylor on things—and tolerating my presence was no different. Taylor and I lingered over dessert for a while after all of her friends had left.

She asked me where I was from in Michigan. I told her there was no way she'd heard of my town. She asked me again why Windham "of all places." I answered only that my mother had heard it was a nice school.

Taylor seemed to accept that. Instead of replying directly, she paused and then asked, "Do you know you have a little bit of a sibilant s?"

"What's that?" I asked.

She smiled. "It means you hiss some of your s's. It means there's some snake in your nature, probably."

I had to look up sibilant *on my phone later.*

No one had ever mentioned it before—although I overheard my mother decline for me to be tested for speech services when I was in second grade. And whatever Taylor meant by comparing me to a snake, I decided to take it as a compliment. Taylor seemed like a good person to have as a friend, so I would take what I could get.

And that night I didn't have to toss and turn for quite so long to get to sleep. Because I was starting to feel like this whole Windham idea might work out.

15

Ten Nights Left

Like all ghosts, I have a story to tell. The story of how I got this way. A story that doesn't heal with telling. I've told the story to so many silent rooms, to mirrors in which I no longer see myself.

The story does not belong to those girls.

They whisper some fiction of a Sarah Suicide. They find it delicious.

Winter after winter.

Girls in. Girls out.

Some see and feel a darkness of their own imagining.

But I am the real thing.

16

When Star nudged me awake, her long wet hair touched my elbow.

"If you hit snooze one more time," she said, "you'll be late to your first class."

I sat up. "You've showered already?"

"Yeah. I've been up for a while."

"It wasn't cold in the hall?"

"Not this time," Star said quietly.

"Did you happen to look down the hall . . . at the . . . supply closet?"

Star shook her head. "I didn't think to . . . Do you want me to go look?"

"Uh . . . no, that's okay."

✦✦✦

Reluctant to spend any extra time in Dearborn, I'd decided I'd walk to the library after classes. My plan was to find a quiet, private place to write to the leader of the Facebook group Bronwyn had told me about.

I made my way through the main reference area—with its stained glass windows and eager studiers at the long, shiny tables—and into the closed stacks. My favorite place to work was the fourth floor of the stacks, in the dusty cluster of carrels by the yellowed theology books that nobody checked out anymore. This was where the stacks were the most tightly packed and the oldest-smelling.

Once I was settled in a carrel, I took out my laptop and tapped over to the screenshot Bronwyn had sent. Then I opened up Facebook and looked up Suzie Price, clicking on the option to send a message.

Dear Ms. Price: I am a Windham-Farnswood senior, and someone gave me your name as a person to connect with about disturbing Dearborn experiences. I wonder if you would be willing to answer some questions about your own memories of the dorm and those of some of the other alums you know.

I closed that window and started working on my English paper. If Suzie Price's commitment to social media was anything like my mother's—that is, spotty and unpredictable— I could possibly be waiting a month or two for a response.

My attention to my work lasted about three minutes. I thought about how Taylor used to occasionally track me down here. Usually she wouldn't stay long—she claimed the air wasn't fresh enough and the packed shelves were too claustrophobic. But one time she'd lingered here with me long into a listless Saturday. She'd sat at the carrel opposite me, letting me catch up on homework while she listened to music with her phone and earbuds. I was fairly certain she'd just fought with her boyfriend and was hiding from him, but I didn't make her say it. I never made Taylor do or say anything.

We were there for a while before we heard the door to the stacks open and then slam shut. A few minutes later, the sounds of a girl sobbing came from the opposite end of the stacks. Taylor must've heard it—or seen my surprised expression—because she ripped her earbuds out. And then we both sat silently, listening to some faceless girl blubbering away because she thought she was alone. Because she probably didn't want her roommate to catch her crying, and had come here for the solitude. She had a distinctive gasping way of crying.

The girl's sobbing started to turn to sniffles. I doubled down on my homework, hoping—in vain, I knew—that Taylor would do something similarly silent until the poor girl pulled herself together and left.

But then I saw Taylor throw her shoulders back. Her mouth opened, and out of it came a perfect imitation of the girl's long, gasping sobs—if a bit louder, to ensure that it was heard.

After it echoed through the stacks, I heard myself snigger—from shock or amusement, I wasn't sure. We heard the rush of a body moving toward the door of the stacks, and the inevitable slam. And then we were alone again, and said nothing about it to each other.

Now I wished we had. What had been wrong with me, that I could let her do something like that and say nothing?

I tried to shake away the feeling that I could still hear Taylor's fake sob echoing through the stacks—and tried to return my attention to the second paragraph of my essay. I wrote a lame transition sentence to start the first body paragraph. Then I deleted it. Then I opened up Thatcher's video and hit Play before I could have second thoughts.

My heart thudded at seeing Taylor again. But to hear her say "Say it again, bitch" was strangely comforting. Such a Taylor thing to say, even if I wasn't sure who she was saying it to. But then the sight of her window set my heart racing again.

After watching it once, I played it again with the volume all the way up. I stopped in the middle, after the faint whisper, played it again. Yes, now that Anthony had said it, I could only hear it as *Samuel was sixteen*. It seemed like there was another word or two after that, but it got garbled in the movement of Taylor jumping up and running out of her room.

This time I watched the video to the very end—all eight minutes of the empty, silent Dearborn hallway one year ago.

There was something mesmerizing about watching an empty hallway—so much so that I jumped when a noise finally came out of the phone—a muffled squeak and a bang, and then, a moment later, the groan of the heavy bathroom door opening. Taylor's legs came into view and then the screen image flip-flopped and the video ended.

I pulled the earbuds out and put my fingers resolutely on my keyboard, but could not remember what my English paper was about. Skimming the shoddy introductory paragraph, I tried to steady my breath. Oh yes. *The Invisible Man*.

My computer dinged an alert, and I toggled back to my internet browser. Eager for any distraction, I sat back up and saw I had a new message on Facebook.

Hi Haley. You can call me Suzie. I am happy to talk to you, but can you tell me who gave you my name? Usually I prefer that the group be kept confidential, and send new member requests to the core group of other members before approving. You are a senior, so you're living in Dearborn now? Are you okay?

I wrote a reply right away—vaguely amused by all of this cloak-and-dagger secrecy, but nonetheless grateful for the final question of the note (to which I did not know the answer).

Dear Suzie: Another alum gave me your name and info. I am sorry if my note came as a surprise. She was trying to be helpful. I have some concerns about what happened to my friend Taylor Blakey last year. I'm not sure if you'd heard about that or, at least, what Windham has reported.

I hit Send and waited. The reply came quickly.

Haley, I am so sorry about the loss of your friend. Yes, I and other alums heard the sad news shortly after it happened. I am happy to chat about any questions you have, but I don't know how many answers I can provide. I and the small group of alums I've gathered are seekers primarily. We don't have answers. We hold space for each other and are sympathetic to each other's experiences with things that cannot be explained.

Oh God, I thought. I could see what Bronwyn meant about some of the ladies being more woo-woo than others. I wasn't really into *holding space.* But maybe it was my responsibility to do so for Taylor. Even if she herself would've made gagging noises at the phrase.

Do you want to talk or do you prefer this Facebook messaging? I wrote.

I think it might be good to talk. How about this evening? I am leaving for a doctor appointment now.

Okay. I can talk anytime between 6:30 and 9 (EST). I included the EST so she wouldn't know I'd already Facebook-stalked her enough to see that she lived in Pennsylvania. After adding my phone number, I hit Send.

My stomach was grumbling. I packed up my things, left the library, and started to cross campus toward Dearborn. But once its front doors and castle roof were in view, my feet began to drag. I was cold, but I wasn't ready to submit myself to another evening in the dorm—endless studying, blank screen, cold hands typing near the draft of the window. Afraid to go to sleep. Afraid to *not* go to sleep.

I slipped my phone out of my coat pocket. Struggling to tap at my speed-dial numbers with my gloved hands, I had to try a few times.

My mother answered right away.

"Hi honey," she said. "This is a nice surprise."

"Yeah. I just had a free moment."

I gazed at the Dearborn entrance and wondered what the dining hall was serving tonight. Lately, I thought often of the ham sandwiches my mom used to put in my lunch every day. Sandwiches I used to take one bite out of and then throw away. I hated ham, but I never felt like I could tell her.

"I was thinking it would be really nice to come home for the next break," I said, trying to sound cheerfully casual.

"Oh? Oh. Last time it sounded like you weren't sure. But I can look for a bargain flight online."

"Well . . . I mean, if you see something *really* cheap." I felt myself hedging.

My mother already strained to pay the small portion of the tuition the school had allotted as our responsibility.

"I'm sure we can find something reasonable," she said. "It would be nice to have you home."

The words made my eyes sting. I *wanted* to be home—for the first time in a while. Even though my mother and brother and I had almost nothing to say to one another anymore, and needed lots of Netflix and chips and root beer to fill the silence and the vague but constant hunger. Even though the whole house smelled like our old dog, Lippy, who didn't seem to recognize me anymore; even though the worn kitchen linoleum never seemed clean no matter how much you mopped it.

At home, I could at least hear my mom say, "Try to sleep, Haley." It had never helped all that much when I was a kid, but maybe it would now.

"Do you believe in ghosts?" I blurted, to keep myself from crying.

"What?" It sounded like my mother was sucking on something. Like a cough drop.

"Do you believe in ghosts?" I repeated, gazing up at Dearborn's stern brick facade. Lately, I was also starting to wonder about all of the building's former occupants over its hundred-plus years. How many of them had been as sad as me, as messed up as me?

"Sometimes," she said, smacking her lips. "Why, is there a ghost at Windham?"

"Yeah. A pretty famous one. You didn't know about that, growing up in Heathsburg?"

"Oh . . . we had our own horror stories to deal with, Haley."

I gripped the phone tight, chastened and silent. "Uh . . . yeah, I know."

Life was hard for my mother growing up in Heathsburg—in the shadow of Windham-Farnswood. Her father died when she was ten. Her mother had been a secretary at a local gas company. My mother had two older sisters and a younger brother, and they had to use food stamps. Like a lot of Heathsburg townies, she would never have been able to afford Windham tuition. And she had not quite had the grades for a scholarship, although she had tried for one.

"I just wanted to hear your voice," I said. "But I should go— I'm about to miss dinner."

***

It was after seven p.m. and Suzie hadn't called yet. In the meantime I'd written to Lily Bruno, sending her the same message I'd sent to Jayla, hoping my success rate would carry over.

Hi Lily. I hope you're doing well at college. As you might know, I was a friend of Taylor Blakey's. I was wondering if you would be willing to talk to me about the night she died. There are some things I'd just like to settle for my own peace of mind, if that makes sense? Thanks, Haley

As I hit Send, I crossed my fingers that they weren't friends.

I'd also watched Taylor's video twice now tonight. I felt compelled to watch the long minutes of empty hallway without skipping. Something about the sounds at the very end—the soft squeak and bang before Taylor opened the bathroom door and retrieved her phone—unsettled me almost as much as the stuff in her room. I just couldn't quite say why.

"Star?" I said.

Star looked up from her laptop. "Yeah?"

"How does Ms. Noceno respond when people come into the archives looking for information for nonacademic projects? Just, like, personal interest kind of stuff?"

"I don't think that happens much. I bet she'd be thrilled. Why?"

"I have a few questions I think she could help with, but . . . What if I came in asking about darker topics? Like deaths and other tragedies on campus? Would that bother her? I mean . . . not recent deaths. But stuff *like* that."

The school archives seemed a sensible place to start learning about the people who'd lived here before us. Maybe I could also look up that girl Sarah Chase. And see if I could find something about a *Samuel*.

"She loves it when kids come in," Star said. "And even if you were asking about something morbid like campus deaths, she wouldn't blink an eye. Of course she knows people are interested in stuff like the Windham ghost stories, especially the Dearborn ones. People research that every so often for little projects or the school paper."

Star closed her computer. "You could come with me to archive hours tomorrow. I could help you."

"Well . . . sure. I'd appreciate that."

Star leaned forward and sank her chin into her hand. "How about at two-thirty? That's when it opens, and I usually go right when it opens."

Before I could answer, my phone started to buzz, showing *UNKNOWN NUMBER* on the screen.

"Hello?" I said, giving a little thumbs-up to Star as I slipped out of our room.

"Haley? This is Suzie Price. How are you?"

"I'm okay."

"Are you in Dearborn right now?" Suzie sounded pleasant, motherly.

"Yeah. Umm, in the hallway of the fourth floor."

"Ahh. Well, I'm glad you could talk. How is your final semester going?"

"Not bad," I said, pacing down the hallway a couple of steps and then back again.

"I loved so many of my Windham teachers," Suzie said.

"Yeah," I murmured, even though I didn't entirely share the sentiment.

Apparently sensing my impatience, Suzie said, "Now. Let's talk about your questions."

"I . . . um . . . just wanted to hear what you and your friends' experiences had been in Dearborn that made you feel like there was paranormal activity here."

"Well . . . not all of the women in the group are my friends, per se, and our experiences vary quite a bit. I can start with my own, though." Suzie paused and I slid into a sitting position next to my door. "I lived in a single in Dearborn. Several times I woke up feeling a presence in the room. Oddly, I didn't always feel it to be the *same* presence. Usually it was dark and weighty. But occasionally I'd wake up laughing, and feel for the first few

112

moments that someone was there . . . laughing with me. I would hear it for a few seconds as I was waking up."

I shuddered and pulled up my knees, wrapping my long cardigan around them.

"I never saw the girl . . . but two of the people in the Facebook group have seen her. Two women who graduated more than a decade apart and had never met each other before . . . had remarkably similar stories."

"Can you tell me?" I asked.

"Both of them experienced a couple of nights of waking up to the sound of some slow knocks on their doors. Like that was the portent, or the seeking permission to enter. And then both of them had an experience of waking up and seeing a girl . . . a pale girl in a white nightgown. One of them saw her standing in her doorway, watching her. The other . . . even scarier. Standing right over her, staring down."

"Wow," I breathed. It sounded like Bronwyn had shared her story with the group.

"I know. In both cases, they reported that the girl looked angry. With the one where the girl was standing by the bed, she whispered something. Something like 'sad heart.' And then the girl reached out and yanked the sheet over her face."

I was speechless for a moment. Forget sleeping tonight.

"That's the worst of the stories . . . or at least the worst of the actual *sightings*. I know there is someone who saw the girl in the basement when she was doing laundry at night, but she's not part of the group, so I haven't heard the details. But I've noticed a *heart* theme with some of the hauntings, when you look at them collectively. There was that 'sad heart' thing, but also a couple of women who were haunted in the '80s or '90s say that they found a shape of a heart scratched in their wall or on their door shortly after. And I believe there was one other alum who said she heard some kind of whispering about 'your heart.' Not with a sighting. Just hearing a murmuring."

"*Really?*" I said. Goose bumps started to cover my arms. And then, it felt like, the rest of my body. "So maybe there's a theme of a broken heart?"

"Maybe." Suzie sounded a little skeptical.

"Did anyone ever mention the name *Samuel* in any of these hauntings?" I asked.

"Umm . . . not that I can recall. Why?"

"I just heard something about that once, that's all," I said. "So . . . um . . . how did you all find each other? All you alums?"

"There are several Windham alumnae Facebook groups. That's how I first got in touch with my friend Jane Villette, who graduated a few years after me. We hadn't known each other then, but it was through other social media interactions that we discovered we'd both had memories of visitations in Dearborn. Because of their sensitive nature, we ended up making a separate group just for those discussions. A couple of people had experiences so bad that it kind of developed into almost a mental health issue, I'd say. So we don't want the discussion to be public. Even among other Windham alumnae."

"Okay," I said, wanting to encourage her to talk but feeling weird about the words *almost a mental health issue.* "I see."

"We don't contact each other that often. It's just . . . when you have an unusual experience, it's nice to know there are others out there that have had it, too . . . who know you're not crazy."

"Yeah . . . makes sense," I offered.

"And not all of us have such dramatic stories, either. Some are stories like mine. Feeling watched. Feeling a presence. Hearing knocks or just strange little accidents. A smoke alarm that always went off at three a.m. A lamp falling over spontaneously and breaking. Some books flying off a desk. Stuff like that. Now, how can I help you? Are you wanting to speak to other Haunteds directly?"

Haunteds. I felt my chest seize.

"Is that what you call yourselves?" I asked.

"Oh! Not generally. It's just what we call the Facebook group, is all."

"I guess I'd like to be on the Facebook list in case I have more questions. If you're willing."

"Yes, absolutely."

"And . . . one more thing. Has the building ever been professionally . . . assessed, I guess is the right word . . . for paranormal activity? Because I saw the reference to . . ."

I clamped my mouth shut. I wasn't supposed to have seen the screenshot of the Haunteds' discussion.

"I heard once Ronald Darkins's name mentioned by an alum," I corrected myself. "I, uh, looked him up recently."

"Oh." Suzie sighed and laughed a little. "That's just a little bit of fun. Rumors about Ronald Darkins coming and staying at Dearborn. It was kind of a running joke later, at reunions and things. I'm surprised you've heard of Ronald Darkins. He was kind of a flash in the pan . . . and probably before you were born."

"Oh," I said. "So Ronald Darkins wasn't a Farnswood student or anything like that?"

"Oh *no*." Suzie laughed again. "Is that what the story is now? It's hard with all of these Dearborn rumors, separating the legends from the real stories, of course."

"I know what you mean," I offered. I was distracted by the now distinctly cold feeling in the hallway.

"Well, in any case, I should probably tootle now. But I want you to know you're welcome in the group. So I'll send you an invitation, then. And you can contact me anytime if you have more questions."

"Thanks," I said.

We said goodbye. I decided to go brush my teeth and grabbed my toiletry caddy. Once I was in the bathroom, its heavy door closed behind me with its usual groan and thump. I hesitated before going to the sink—because that sound reminded me of the very end of Taylor's video. Right before she came out of the bathroom and picked up her phone.

Thinking about it now, something bothered me about that. I pulled my phone out of my back pocket and clicked through to the video, skipping to the very end.

Right before Taylor came back to her phone on the floor, there were two sounds. First a muffled *EEEEE* and then a bang. And then the familiar *OARRRR-thump!* of the bathroom door. When I'd watched it before, I'd attributed the whole set of sounds to the bathroom door. But now I wasn't so sure.

I pushed the bathroom door open and let it fall closed again. *OARRRR-thump!* I went into the hallway and pulled it open, then let go. *OARRRR-thump!*

There was no screeching or banging. Maybe that was a separate sound from inside the bathroom before the door was opened. So what had Taylor done in the bathroom right before coming out? Knocked something over? Knocked a soap dispenser off the wall?

After I finished brushing my teeth, I stopped in front of Taylor's door and considered its proximity to the bathroom and her neighbors. Lily on one side of her and Jayla on the other. Only two other rooms down this corridor—one next to the bathroom, the others across from it. These side halls were always quieter than the long main hallway where Star and I lived.

Shivering, I reached out and touched the crystal doorknob of Taylor's room. Maybe I could get into the room sometime, and search for hearts scratched in the walls.

"Haley?"

I whirled around, and there was Anna. She was wearing fuzzy panda slippers with her tights, pencil skirt, and crisp-collared white shirt.

"What are you doing?" she demanded.

I stared at her stupid feet. I hated fake quirkiness. It was the common overcompensation of someone who knew, deep down, that they really shouldn't be working with teenagers.

"It was so cold out here I was worried," I mumbled. "I was worried it would be open again."

It was actually true on some level—so why didn't it sound believable?

"You were her friend, weren't you?" Anna's tone softened. "Star mentioned it."

I looked up at her face. A little too pretty to confide in. I wondered how she managed as a counselor.

"I was just noticing how cold it was out here," I said, ignoring her question. Since she already made clear she knew the answer. "In the hallway."

"The thermostat is set for lower as the night goes on, to save oil," Anna explained, folding her hands in front of her. "Since it doesn't make sense to maintain the temperature all night when everyone is sleeping. It's not a matter of budgeting so much as being environmentally conscious."

I nodded. No, certainly it wasn't a matter of budgeting. One year's tuition here could pay for about a third of my mother's house outright.

"The hallway is always colder," Anna continued. "It's a bigger space and doesn't have as many heating vents."

I nodded.

"Well, good night," I called, heading back in the direction of my room.

"Good night, Haley," Anna returned. When I reached my door, I turned and saw she was still watching me, her hand slithering behind her ear, touching her hair, checking the tightness of her bun.

I half expected her to say *TRY to sleep.* But then I remembered that she wasn't the person who said that to me. And that no one had said that to me in years.

17

I guess I've come to accept that when I lie here in the dark, it's going to be about Taylor.

The way I dumped Taylor all at once last year—probably she deserves my nights. Probably she deserves more than that, even.

Maybe I thought that the sibilant thing made me special. And maybe it did. But I would come to learn soon that Taylor asked everyone questions like that.

That's a tighter shirt than you usually wear. Are you trying a new style?

Oh. You decided not to take AP Bio after all?

Why do you think you're so much shorter than your brother? Is one of your parents short?

Four meatballs! Impressive. Do you, like, really love meatballs?

Questions people weren't sure how to answer. Questions that often had a little jab embedded in them somewhere. But she was generally such a bubbly and engaging conversationalist, one tended to focus on that and try not to be offended. Most of the time, I told myself at first that she didn't know how her questions came across. She delivered them so innocently, so sincerely. And we all had our childish little blind spots.

It wasn't until December of my first year that I started to see it differently.

We were in the locker room, changing together after cross-country. Most of the other girls were in the showers.

She caught sight of my ridiculous stash of Avon deodorants—six identical purple-capped plastic mushrooms peeping out from behind my pile of clothes.

What's that about? Do you have half a dozen armpits?

No. *I laughed.* My mom buys them in bulk. I brought them straight here from the mail room yesterday. She probably forgot that she already gave me a set. I have a few already in my room.

I didn't explain that her friend gave her a deal on bulk Avon deodorants. It was way cheaper than buying them one at a time or in a grocery store.

Can I have one? *Taylor asked.*

I handed her one, not considering why she might want to smell like Avon antiperspirant instead of her usual expensive Chanel aura. She walked over to Kylie Puckett's locker, which was open. Kylie was in the shower still.

She positioned it right in the front.

She needs it, *Taylor said.* I mean, she kind of smells like a dude sometimes. Let's go.

I was stunned for a moment. It was kind of true. Kylie was a sophomore like Taylor—the only other underclass runner on varsity besides Taylor and me. She was faster than both of us. But she did sweat quite a lot.

Let's go, *Taylor repeated.*

I yanked on my pullover and shoved my feet into boots even though I hadn't yet put on my socks. I threw the socks and re-

maining deodorants into my backpack—because after this, I couldn't be seen with that weird old-lady brand deodorant in the locker room. Kylie would know where hers had come from. Or rather who.

That night I told myself that Taylor hadn't really meant to do that. It was a prank of impulse and opportunity. If she had had a chance to really think about it, she would've changed her mind.

18

Nine Nights Left

The story, of course, starts with a girl. This girl was smart, but time would reveal, fragile. She came here from miles away with high hopes and gentle ways. Probably she had some starry-eyed notion that this place would change her — make her tougher, smarter, better. But it did the opposite, sadly. It broke her.

Some girls are built up here, but it can't really happen, can it, without a few being broken along the way.

19

Friday, February 1

The archives were housed in a long glassed-in room on the top floor of the library, separated from the regular stacks with an elaborately carved wooden door. It was open only three days a week for a few hours—every minute of which Star seemed to camp out there with Ms. Noceno, the oldest and least friendly of Windham's three librarians.

As we closed the door behind us, Ms. Noceno glanced up from her computer and pushed her red-framed glasses up her nose.

"You brought a friend," she said to Star—in a tone that wasn't quite approving.

"Yes," Star said, taking off her backpack. "She's doing a little research of her own, but doesn't know where to start."

"Wonderful," Ms. Noceno said, glancing at her computer once more before focusing her gaze on me. "I don't know how much Star has told you about how things operate here. Most of the older materials—letters and journals and original school documents—are kept in the locked files behind the divider wall. We have everyone look at them at the front tables here, and ask that you not bring in any bags or pens—that you work with a pencil, or you can take pictures of materials with a phone. You can request to look at anything you want—and all of these binder indexes here in the front are a good resource for figuring out which original materials you might want to request be brought out. I can give you a quick tutorial on those, but what are you hoping to research today?"

I looked at Star, who was already making herself comfortable at one of the long wooden tables, opening a notebook, looking about as happy as a kid about to blow out her birthday candles.

"I want to research the history of Dearborn Hall," I offered. "Or . . . parts of its history."

"Parts of its history," Ms. Noceno repeated. "Any specific parts?"

"Yes. I would like to research student life in the hall first. Just generally."

I felt like that sounded respectable. I didn't really want to bring up tragedy and ghosts right away. And to start with the vagueness of *Samuel* might make me look a little dumb.

"Okay. Well, there's a great deal of information on that. We're lucky to have a large number of student letters throughout the school's history, and for a time there was this tradition of housemothers keeping a journal of the year's events in the dorm. Like social events and things. Now, what era were you hoping to study?"

"Not one particular era." I exhaled, deciding to come clean. "I wanted to see, uh, among other things, if I could determine when the ghost stories about Dearborn began."

"Interesting." Ms. Noceno's expression looked strained, like she might be holding in a coughing fit or a sneeze. "I think I have a couple of head starts for you on that. Although I doubt anyone could pinpoint the exact beginning of those kinds of stories. It being an oral tradition, of course."

"Didn't you want to research, like, student tragedies in the dorm, too?" Star piped up, tapping her pencil on the table. Then, when she suddenly seemed to realize what she had just said, a dark blush bloomed on her neck and cheeks. "I mean . . . uh . . . *historical* tragedies?"

Ms. Noceno drew a slow breath into her nostrils, considering both of us for a moment. "Star, shall I get you the Bromley papers? You've been working with the third box lately, right?"

"Yes, please," Star said. "When you have a chance."

"I'll be right with you—what did you say your name is?" Ms. Noceno asked.

"Haley," I said.

"Okay, Haley. I'll be right with you after I get Star's things," she said. "And then we can sit down and discuss what materials will be most useful to you. See, Star has it easy. Because Caroline Bromley is one of Windham's most famous alums, there's an extensive set of files on her specifically, organized decades ago. We have about eight files like that, on specific alums."

I nodded. I knew there was a famous poet among the Windham graduates, plus a senator. Fancy ladies, those Windies.

"Is there one on Lucia Jackson?" Star asked. "I've been meaning to ask."

Lucia Jackson was a well-known author who had also gone to Windham. One of her crime novels had been turned into a Showtime series. Alex really liked her books—said they had strong, quirky women characters. I'd never read any of them— never had much time for pleasure reading at Windham.

"She's a little young to have a file," Ms. Noceno said icily. "Maybe she'll get one when she's dead."

Ms. Noceno disappeared behind the wall divider, leaving Star and me to our awkward silence. Star continued to tap her pencil on the table, avoiding my gaze.

"Did I offend her?" I whispered.

Star shook her head with a tiny smile. "She's like that with everyone."

When Ms. Noceno returned, she handed Star a gray box file and set another identical one on the table, closer to me. As Star happily opened her file, Ms. Noceno gestured for me to sit.

"Tell me a little more, Haley," she said, taking the seat across from me. "Is this an academic project? For a particular teacher? If it's a personal project, that's fine, too. I'm just trying to get a sense of the parameters here."

"Well . . . ," I began. "Mostly personal. There is a history of people having frightening experiences in Dearborn. At least in recent decades. I think that's undeniable, based on some conversations I've had with a few . . . friends and alums."

Ms. Noceno tilted her head with mild interest. "Recent alums?"

"Recent and not so recent," I said. "So I'm researching the history of *that* specifically, not whether or not there was some dramatic death in the building long ago, like girls used to like to talk about."

I hesitated. *They liked to talk about it before it actually happened.*

"Because I don't know if that's really the key to when the stories started, or what they're *really* about," I added.

Ms. Noceno nodded. "I think I understand what you're saying. And I think that's a smart way to go about it. Look at the reported experiences first—the stories—for what they are—rather than jumping to conclusions about what kind of incident or history must have caused it. Which is how most students try to approach it, when they come in here with the Dearborn ghost on their mind. They're always looking for something they can't find. A murder or suicide story that doesn't appear to exist, as far as I can tell."

"Does that happen a lot? Students looking for that?"

Ms. Noceno shrugged. "Every so often. Interest in the ghost waxes and wanes. Students tend to leave disappointed when they see that Dearborn doesn't have the kind of history the stories tell them. Yes, it has a history of supposed hauntings. But it has no history of a girl dying there in a white nightgown in the 19th century. That's the jackpot everyone seems to think they're looking for."

"Okay," I said, feeling a little stupid. "I'm just not sure where to start. I've never been to the archives before."

"Now, first of all, each building—at least, each of the older buildings and certainly all of the residential buildings—has its own box of files." Ms. Noceno tapped the other box she had brought out along with Star's. "I took the liberty of bringing it out, because I thought you'd like to see it. Now, there *is* a small independent file about Windham ghost stories, but all the material is relatively recent, except for a few cross-references to other files. I'll get that for you as well. It was only my immediate predecessor who saw fit to give it its own file, so it's a little sparse. I think previous librarians were reluctant, maybe because of the school's religious origins. People have relaxed about these things in more recent decades."

"Okay," I said. "I'd like to look at the file, even if there's not much in it."

Ms. Noceno nodded. "But the bulk of our archives are our letter collections. And finding your topic in those is a little trickier, a little less straightforward. The letters are filed alphabetically by the name of the writer, so to speak. Students and teachers, mostly. The binders list the letter collections chronologically, starting in 1867, which as you probably know is the year Windham opened. The binders contain summaries of most of the letter collections. So if you're looking for specific types of content, you need to read through the summaries. Of course, I'm familiar with what's in a fair amount of those letters. Certainly not all of it. But there are many collections I've read over, or at least whose summaries I've read over. So when a student comes in looking for a specific topic, I often can direct them to letters that I know address it. Like I know that the Mary Trowell Downing collection has a great deal about the early athletics program, just for example. And more relevant to your studies, I know that there is mention of a supposed ghost sighting in Dearborn in the Louise Johnson Riley collection. She went here in the early 1920s, and her family gave us all of her letters in the '60s or '70s, I believe."

"I would love to see that," I said.

Ms. Noceno nodded. "And there *may* be other references to 'the ghost' in other student letters we have in the collection that I haven't read . . . but there is no direct way to find that out. We used to have a volunteer—an elderly local alumna—

who read through all of the letter collections and summarized their contents for the indexes. Since she stopped coming in a few years ago, there is a small amount of material that hasn't been so meticulously read through . . . she didn't quite finish the project . . . and we're still getting new material on top of that."

"More old letters?" I asked.

"Sometimes. I mean, we're not likely to get a lot more 19th-century material at this stage, but alumnae and their families do send things when they surface. Letters or pictures or pennants. I think sometimes it makes people feel better, when they have deceased relatives, to send us stuff like that, rather than to throw it out. It's not all useful to us, but we try to treat it respectfully. Anyway . . . now, to clarify . . . is this primarily a study of the supernatural lore of Dearborn Hall, or a broader study about student life? Because you mentioned student life when we started talking."

"Umm . . . a little of both?" I said.

Ms. Noceno studied me, her crow's feet deepening for a moment. "Okay. Well, as I said, I have a box file for each building. Those don't contain the student letters, but there are pictures and some housemother journals and some other random goodies. Would you like to start with the Dearborn one?"

"Oh . . . yes, of course. That sounds good."

"All right. I'll start you on that and then bring you the Riley letter."

"Thanks," I said, and opened the front snap of the box I'd been given.

The front files were occupied mostly by a few years' worth of housemother journals. The "journals" weren't like diaries in the traditional sense—more like long letters of ten to thirty pages, handwritten on yellowed paper.

I tried my best to focus my eyes and attention to really *read*—not just skim for words like *whisper, haunted, ghost, death:*

School opened Tuesday, September 8. The first day was very busy, with parents helping to "settle in" despite the heavy rain. Upperclass girls were delighted to find the rooms furnished with new beds and the parlor decorated for their arrival. . . .

The "journal" proceeded to describe, in great detail, the Halloween, Thanksgiving, Christmas, and May Day celebrations that occurred in the dorm's dining hall, putting great emphasis on the festive decorations and special foods. (*The tables had red cloths, were strewn with acorns and golden leaves, and apple and nut pies were served after a chicken and gravy feast. . . .*) This sunny account of the whole year seemed to have been written in one go at the end of the year—maybe to ensure another year of employment as a housemother.

It wasn't really a journal of the daily life of the girls—like who got sick, who fought with whom, who was struggling and flunking. It was more of a rundown of all the lovely things that had happened throughout the year. At the end was a list of all the students who lived in the dorm. In some cases, these lists were annotated with things like *Left at Christmas,* or in a few cases, the word *Kitchen* or *Laundry.*

"Why do some girls have the word *Laundry* by their name? Were those, like, work duties?"

"Exactly," Ms. Noceno said, glancing up at Star as she pawed through a file cabinet. "And Star can tell you some things about that, right? Since it pertains to Caroline Bromley."

Star looked up from her work. "Yeah. Caroline was a kitchen girl."

"She helped out in the kitchen?"

"Yeah. Somehow she avoided laundry duty her whole four years here, and that was considered the worst. But these duties were performed by girls who were here on scholarship."

"Oh," I said.

"There was, unfortunately, a tradition of scholarship students at times having to do menial tasks to help pay their way, in a sense," Ms. Noceno chimed in. "Of course, it's nice in any school setting for students to pitch in. To take pride in the school's physical setting, to plant flowers, to keep things swept up and nice. But in the late 1800s through the early 1950s, there was a fairly obvious distinction between 'pitching in' and poorer students earning their keep, so to speak. Doing laundry, say, or doing kitchen work like the dishes and so on. Things the full-paying students weren't asked to do. From our modern-day perspective, it feels rather punitive, doesn't it?"

I nodded. The way she was peering at me over her red-framed glasses, I felt like she wanted me to say something more. Could she tell just by my demeanor that I was a scholarship kid? That in the days of old, I might have been washing Star's bloomers for her?

"It's *awful*," Star said, and I wondered if her exaggeratedly mournful expression was for my benefit.

But the truth was I *liked* being part of the scholarship contingent at Windham-Farnswood. It made me feel scrappy. And I felt like it absolved me of any of the white-glove embarrassments of the school's past. I've always felt like having a lot of money would make me feel guilty. And I'm not a person who deals well with guilt.

"Was Caroline Bromley poor?" I asked.

Star looked surprised at my blunt use of the word.

"Well . . . no. Just of relatively modest means compared to most of the other girls who came here in the early years. Her father ran a small general store in Maine. Her mother was a teacher at a one-room schoolhouse. The story is that Caroline attended the school, when her mother taught there, from age three. That's how she got to be so smart and precocious."

Star seemed to realize that she was falling into one of her typical Caroline monologues.

"But anyway, yes, her position as one of the students of lesser means . . . that's one of the big issues I'm trying to work with in my project," she added.

"Here you are, dear," Ms. Noceno said, approaching my table with a binder of laminated materials. "Now, normally you'd have to flip through and read it and find it yourself, but I recalled roughly where it was in the two years of Louise Johnson Riley's letters. Winter of the second year."

"Thank you," I said, and leaned over the letter, pushing the Dearborn file aside.

February 12, 1920

Dear Robert,

I hope you are feeling stronger now. I have been worrying since Mother's latest letter. Please write me as soon as you are able.

My chemistry studies are proving more difficult.
I spend hours each night on my science texts. It is a
welcome respite from other worries. But all the while that
my brain is engaged, my heart is praying that you and
James will get well and stay well.

I tried to take some delight in the snow yesterday. A
fire was built in the living room hearth. We had spiced tea,
and one of the lovely kitchen ladies made apple fritters.
Happily, attention has turned to Valentine's plans, and
there was none of last week's talk of the restless spirit
that is said to haunt the upstairs halls in this, the shadow
season. My friend Harriet has recovered from her fright
at seeing the specter in the dark dress. We have all vowed
not to ask her about it. The subject seems to put her into a
terrible state. Perhaps forgetting is best.

Do not tell James I write to you about these things. He
will say that I am silly.

I am eager to hear news from home. Please give
Fletcher a pat on the head from me.

Your loving sister,
Louise

" 'This, the shadow season,' " I murmured. "In 1920. That's pretty far back for the ghost stories."

"It's quite something, isn't it? It proves that the stories didn't start in the '70s and '80s because of all the horror movies that were coming out then."

"Oh. I wouldn't have thought of that."

Ms. Noceno pushed her red glasses up her nose. "I've heard it discussed . . . since I don't think the stories were particularly active in the '60s, from what I've heard from alums. I think the stories were frequent and maybe a little more nefarious by the '70s and after. Pop culture was perhaps helping it along. Movies like *Carrie, The Exorcist, Poltergeist*. But this letter shows that the background was already there."

I nodded. I knew some of those titles because my father liked horror movies and watched them sometimes on nights my mother was working. He wasn't as tuned in to my insomnia as my mother was; he didn't know that sometimes I'd get up and sneak out of bed and sit on a step about halfway down the carpeted stairs—and quietly watch TV along with him. He never seemed to know that behind his back he had a little ghost peeking through the banister, ready to flee up the stairs if he started to rise from the couch.

"Dearborn was built in 1879." I glanced back at the building dedication documents to check. "So there are still several decades in between when we don't know if there were any stories."

"And I wonder if they were calling the ghost 'Sarah' then," Star said. "I mean, around 1920."

"I wish she'd given that kind of detail in her letter," I said. "It feels like she had talked to her brother about the ghost before, so she doesn't really have a reason to lay it all out."

"Yes." Ms. Noceno settled back into her swivel chair. "Sadly for us, their initial discussion of it was probably face to face, not in letters. You're welcome to look at the whole collection, of course. It's about forty letters—mostly to her brother, and mostly from 1920 and 1921."

"Hmm . . . okay, I'll look at the letters that came before it and after it."

"You can try that if you wish. But my recollection is that she never references the 'spirit' in any other letters. Otherwise Doreen—the volunteer who used to write up the letter summaries—would've referred to that in her index. This is the only reference, unless she missed one. Which is unlikely. Doreen was meticulous."

"And you don't have the brother's responses?"

"No, sadly."

"Okay," I said.

I turned my attention back to the Dearborn box. There was a file of boring documents about the financing and building of the dormitory in 1879, and a program for an inaugural ceremony for the official opening of the dorm.

"Oh," I said, looking up. "I meant to ask. Can I see if there are any letters by a student named Sarah Chase? She was here around the same time as Caroline Bromley, like late 1880s, early 1890s?"

"We can certainly check the letter index after you're through with that."

I nodded and kept going through the box. According to a newspaper article that occupied its own file, there had been a fire in 1978 and students had to stay in other dorms and a converted classroom space for a month while repairs were done. A student had been smoking, which was of course against the rules. The article didn't say whether she was kicked out.

Behind that were three files full of photographs. One file had only sepia photos of the building itself—and primarily from 1891. The building hadn't changed much since then. It was still a fortress-like mass of brick, lined with prettily small-paned windows. There was a tree to the right of the entrance that was gone now, replaced by a few bushes that now hid half of the dining hall windows. Otherwise, Dearborn stood fast as it always had.

The next two files were all of students in the dorm—mostly arranged group photos, but with a few random candids from dorm functions mixed in.

The very first photograph was the one Star had shown me a few days ago—with Caroline Bromley and her classmates. The next one showed more students, and was from a few years later—1897. Then it seemed like group dorm photos had fallen out of favor—because the next one was from 1919.

"Is there a reason why so many photos are missing?" I asked Ms. Noceno.

"What do you mean, 'missing'?" She wrinkled her nose.

"There's a Dearborn group photo from 1897 and then none until 1919," I told her.

"Well, we're lucky to have the ones we have. I doubt they were taken each year. And there was no official way of collecting and filing them. The school archives didn't exist in an official capacity until the early 1950s, when one of the librarians decided to gather everything in one spot and give it its own space. And several of the group dormitory and athletic photos are posted in the cases outside the admissions office. At least there, lots of people will actually look at them."

I nodded and opened the last file of photos, which were the most recent ones—mostly in color. It was interesting to see the change of style of the girls in the '70s—when decades of tweedy skirts and torpedo bras gave way to jeans and T-shirts and generally less coiffed, more colorful hair.

It seemed like there was unusual enthusiasm for the group shots in the '80s and '90s—or at least someone was paying more attention to giving copies to the archives. There was one for every year—usually taken in the creaky sitting room, but sometimes outdoors. And with a good amount of participation—the crowds looked large, as if photo participation had been mandatory. In one they were all in costumes. In another they had wrapped themselves in streamers and a few were holding balloons.

I paid special attention to the photos from those years. This was the time when my mother grew up in Heathsburg. She might have encountered some of these girls—in the grocery store, at the 7-Eleven, at the occasional party with her own public high school classmates—as bored Windham-Farnswood kids sometimes managed to insert themselves into weekend townie activities.

In most of the early '80s photos, there stood next to the girls a plump, severe-looking woman with a short, gray bowl cut. She was never smiling for the shot. Even in the photo in which she was wearing a cheerful red Windham sweatshirt (an odd pairing with a long denim skirt), she looked miserable to be there. A bona fide housemother, so unlike our fashionable and decidedly sympathetic Anna, or Tricia, Dearborn's RD from last year, who sometimes smelled faintly of smoke and favored billowy muslin blouses without a bra. I smiled to myself. I probably would've liked this housemother. Sometimes I liked things to be old-school. According to the name key, her name was Sharon Finneran.

When I flipped from the 1985 photo to the 1986 one, I noticed that the bowl-cut lady was gone. In her place were a man and woman standing alongside the group of girls—this time a smaller group, arranged in front of the Dearborn fireplace.

The woman was in her thirties—blond and smiling. The man looked quite a bit older, and had round glasses and bushy dark hair. I stared at him for a moment. Then I flipped over the photo. Someone had typed up the names of the students in a list. Below that it said *Cathy and Bob Rawls, Dormitory Parents*. I started getting a funny feeling in my stomach as I took out my phone and found the Wikipedia page for Ronald Darkins that I'd read the other night. I looked from my phone to the photo and back again.

The resemblance was uncanny. It wasn't just about similar hair and similar glasses.

Ronald Darkins and Bob Rawls had the same nose. They had the same puckery half-smile. Bob Rawls had slightly shorter, more conventional hair than Ronald Darkins, who had a salt-and-pepper mane. But they had the same face.

I put my fist over my mouth to keep from making a noise very unbefitting for the archives.

Ronald Darkins and Bob Rawls were very likely the same person.

What the hell was happening here? Why the different name? And had Suzie been lying to me about Ronald Darkins?

I flipped to the 1987 dorm group photo. Next to the students was an entirely different couple—a short bald man and a petite woman with curly strawberry-blond hair. Both smiling broadly. They appeared in the 1988 photo as well. Their names were John and Charlene Stiber.

I flipped back to 1986, took out my phone, and snapped a close-up of Bob Rawls in the group photo.

Star looked up at the snapshot noise my camera made. Closing the binder, I stood up.

"I have to go," I said.

"Now?" Star asked.

"I'm not . . . feeling so well. I think I should go lie down."

In a flash, Ms. Noceno was at my side, whisking the Dearborn box away from me. It took me a moment to realize she was afraid I might puke on the precious historical documents.

"I'd love to come and read more of Louise's letters next time," I said, heading toward the door.

"Feel better, Haley," Ms. Noceno said, waving me out.

20

There was still an hour before dinner. I settled myself in one of the spongy brown chairs of the dank "Student Lounge" basement in the campus center beneath the mail room. Girls tended not to hang out there since the carpet smelled weird and the snack machine offerings were usually old and picked over.

First I Googled *Ronald Darkins* and *Bob Rawls,* to see if the names came up together in any meaningful way. I didn't find anything.

Then I went into YouTube and searched for Ronald Darkins there.

A few shows from the '90s came up—with names like *Paranormal Detective* and *Unsolved Mysteries.*

I popped my earbuds in and clicked on the first video. Some creepy synthesizer music played, then a deep-voiced male narration: *A colonial house with a cheerful exterior but a dark history. An upstairs bedroom that a child refuses to sleep in. A typical child's imagination for monsters? Or is there a troubled supernatural presence lingering here? We sent in our guest investigator, Ronald Darkins, for a look.*

I watched as the show got started. A little boy saying that

he hoped his parents would sell their house. I was tempted to fast-forward to where Darkins appeared, but waited to hear the whole story. The parents knew that a strangling death had occurred in the house two decades earlier, but said that their son would have no way of knowing that.

Ronald Darkins seemed pleasant. He had a nervous habit of rubbing the aquiline bump on his nose with his middle finger—like he was constantly checking to see if it was still there—while he spoke to the beleaguered homeowners.

He asked the mom a few questions and then led her up the pea-green carpeted stairs.

"It's possible Gregory senses your apprehension about the history of the house, don't you think?" he asked.

It seemed like an unexpectedly sensible question for this hokey show.

Darkins's voice was deep and comforting, contrary to the bizarre, insect-like appearance his glasses gave him. And I sat mesmerized by him for a moment, watching him mount the creaky old stairs of the house. He spoke very sweetly to the scared little boy, and I began to wish he still lived in Dearborn.

I paused the video and reminded myself that Ronald Darkins was dead. He'd been dead for nearly two decades. He wasn't going to help me. He wasn't going to save anyone. And even if I could talk to him, Taylor would still be dead.

Was it his apparently brief stint as a houseparent here that had made him a paranormal enthusiast? I looked at his Wikipedia page again. Nope. His paranormal publication credits began in the 1970s.

I clicked on the second video. It was the same early '90s show, with the same awful synthesizer intro. This time Ronald Darkins was investigating a sandwich shop that supposedly had loaves of bread and kitchen implements flying off the countertops. The shop owners had a hard time keeping the place open, because terrified employees kept quitting.

This all took place in a run-down strip mall in Arizona, and I found it all kind of hard to take seriously. But Ronald and his wife listened solemnly as the earnest potbellied shop owner described the night when a container full of freshly cut lettuce flew off the counter and slammed into the wall, narrowly missing his head.

"Was that the first time something like this happened?" asked Ronald's soft-spoken blond wife.

"No," the owner said. "The first time it was a tomato flinging around the room. Kind of funny. This second time was much scarier, more violent."

I paused the video.

Ronald Darkins was dead. But maybe his ex-wife wasn't.

Returning to his Wikipedia page, I copied her name again and then pasted it into the search bar.

As I started to scroll through the results, I murmured "Please be alive" a couple of times. My heart sank when I saw there was an obituary from 2004. But that Kathleen Darkins had been born in 1920 in Kansas City and lived her whole life there. So she wasn't my Kathleen Darkins.

A few results down were the words *Kathleen Darkins, proprietor.* I clicked on that link and found myself in an *About us* section of a website for something called New Moon Wellness Emporium.

KATHLEEN DARKINS, PROPRIETOR

Kathleen has worked as a teacher, a massage therapist, and a life coach. She owns the New Moon Tea company, as well as the Essential Herbals soap line. She opened New Moon Wellness Emporium in 2003. She is available for wellness consultations Tuesday and Thursday evenings as well as Saturdays—by appointment preferred.

I clicked to the home page. The shop sold "Teas, essential oils, crystals, candles, herb soaps, herbal supplements, and other wellness essentials." It also advertised classes and workshops on crystals, which some other lady—not Kathleen—taught. It was located in a suburb of Boston—just about an hour from here. I took in a breath and held it for a moment.

There was no picture of Kathleen available. But I had a hunch that running a "wellness emporium" was exactly what a woman who'd been doing ghost hunting in her thirties would be doing in her sixties. Also, a person who owned such a shop would be more likely to keep the last name from a marriage that brought her a little bit of mystical notoriety, wouldn't she? I was certain I had the right Kathleen Darkins. What I wasn't sure of was what to do with this information.

Under *Contact us,* I found a phone number and an email address.

I hesitated before typing *Dear Ms. Darkins.*

Windham-Farnswood had swept Taylor's death under the rug—or shoved it into the cleaning supply closet, to be exact. And it looked to me like this wasn't the only thing about Dearborn Hall the school had decided to keep quiet over the years. I wanted to know more.

Holding my breath, I finished a quick message inquiring if she had any time available for a consultation on Saturday. I didn't have a car, but Maylin and Anthony did. Only seniors could have cars on campus—and with stringent restrictions. But Maylin in particular was often looking for an excuse to get off campus on weekends. At this point, we still had time to get permission—if I could convince her. That is, if Ms. Darkins wrote back.

◆◆◆

"I'm having a little trouble understanding." Maylin poked at her salad, frowning at her hard-boiled egg. "Why can't you just order your mom something from Amazon?"

Maylin wasn't really looking at me as she spoke. Instead, she was staring at Alex's chocolate ice cream and peanut butter, which was quickly disappearing into Alex's mouth. We were sitting at one of the corner dining hall tables with two other girls—Rhea, a friendly junior I knew from newspaper, and Alex's sophomore tutoring charge, whose name I was still hoping I'd remember sometime.

"It's not as weird as it sounds. We went shopping at this little place this one time my mom came to visit last year. She loved this lady's candles and soap. And she doesn't have a website you can order from or anything."

Alex raised her eyebrows and licked peanut butter off her spoon.

"That's funny," she said. "I thought you told me once that your mom hated hippie shit."

Damn that Alex and her steel-trap memory. I wondered what else about me she'd never forgotten. I was beginning to regret that I'd not asked Anthony. I had thought Maylin would be an easier sell since she loved shopping.

"Not really," I said. "I mean, she's not like 'spiritual' or whatever. But she likes a nice-smelling candle as much as the next middle-aged lady. Or she liked *these* ones."

"I bet if you called the shop owner and told her the situation, she'd be willing to send an order to your mom," Rhea pointed out.

"Well, I want to smell and pick out the stuff myself. And I don't have a credit card or anything. I can only go and pay cash. Besides, wouldn't you like to get out for a few hours and away from Windham? I looked up the town. They've got some really cute shops."

"Just drive her, Maylin," Alex mumbled. "You've got that car, you might as well use it."

"You want to come?" Maylin asked Alex. Rhea and the sophomore couldn't come since they didn't have senior privilege.

"Well, no. I can't. I have a lot to do at the greenhouse. And I have to rewrite my chem lab."

"There's still time to get permission if you put in for it tonight," I reminded Maylin.

When Maylin wants to go for a weekend joyride, she gets her mom to write to the administrative office to tell them she

145

has permission to go visit her aunt Grace in Amherst. Aunt Grace *does* exist, but Maylin has only seen her once since her first semester at Windham.

"Okay," Maylin said reluctantly. "Wes has a basketball game anyway."

I thought I saw Alex rolling her eyes as she got up to get seconds on ice cream.

"Did she roll her eyes at me?" Maylin hissed.

"No," Rhea said quickly, blowing her red bangs out of her eyes. "I think she just had wicked brain freeze."

We went silent as Alex returned to the table.

"So you two decided if you're going?" she asked.

"Yeah," Maylin said. "We are."

"Good," Alex said.

She ate the ice cream quickly, in big bites. When a gob of peanut butter fell into her lap, she picked it up with her fingers and popped it into her mouth.

"See you later," she said, picking up her bowl and spoon as she stood. "I've got a ton of work tonight. Oh! Shit. You and I have a session tonight, right?"

She was looking at the sophomore, who nodded.

"My room this time," Alex said. She left the dining hall, and her sophomore followed moments later.

"What's that girl's name again?" I said.

"Chloe," Rhea replied. "She's my roommate."

"She's really *shy*," Maylin observed, stating the obvious.

"Well . . . yeah," Rhea admitted. "But she's nice."

I was slightly embarrassed by Maylin, who had a persistent

and inexplicable habit of calling out shy people. Like they were rare birds, to be spotted and proudly pointed out.

"Hey—guys," I said, eager to change the subject. "I've got something I've been wondering about."

"Yeah?" Rhea said. "What?"

"Either of you ever noticed any hearts carved in the walls of this building?"

Maylin snorted. "What're you talking about?"

But Rhea's big brown eyes seemed to pop.

"Rhea?" I said. "Is that a yes?"

"I *have,* actually," she said. "Why do you ask?"

"An alum I know mentioned it, that it was a thing, years ago. Where have you seen one?"

"Well . . ." A look of doubt came over her delicately freckled face. "I don't live in Dearborn."

"So you saw one in Barton?" I asked.

"No. In the joint laundry room in the basement. Do you want me to show you? It's kind of hidden."

"Sure," I said.

Maylin waved at me as we got up. "Have fun with that. I'm thinking about nine-thirty or ten tomorrow?"

"Great," I said. "Thanks. My mom will appreciate it."

♦♦♦

"Here," Rhea said, pointing behind one of the dryers. "I found it when I was searching for a lost sock back there."

I looked where she was pointing. There was indeed a heart

carved into the wall there—a little smaller than my hand. Inside it were scratched letters:

"Oh," I said, slightly disappointed. A standard lovers' heart with initials. Like you'd carve on a tree. Maybe there was some slim chance that the *S* stood for *Samuel*. But probably not. I had been thinking of *Samuel* as a first name, not a last name.

"Was that not what you meant by a heart?" Rhea asked.

"No, that's definitely a heart," I said dumbly. "Thanks for showing it to me."

"Who was the alum who mentioned it?"

"Oh . . . um . . . a friend of my mom's," I shot back—unsettled by how fast my brain could produce the weird lie. I hoped she didn't ask more. I didn't want to have to build the lie, or bring my mom into it any further.

Rhea nodded, apparently sensing my reluctance to say more.

"This reminds me of the time we all snuck Reggie Brooks into the girls' room," she said. "In the English hall to see the graffiti that had been written about him."

"I forgot about that," I said. That had been a particularly slow day in the school newspaper room. Someone had scrawled, *Reggie Brooks is yummy*, perhaps sarcastically, but Reggie had seemed tickled regardless.

"I miss Reggie," Rhea said. "Is he still around?"

"Yeah. He's in my calculus class. I think he just got sick of newspaper. Joined robotics or something instead."

It felt like Rhea wanted to stay and talk. I knew the feeling—not wanting to go up to your room yet. Not wanting to face all the books and term papers and your roommate's boring but well-intentioned face. Just not yet.

"Are you on the soccer team?" I asked her. I seemed to remember seeing her out on the fields.

I was wondering about Tricia, last year's soccer coach and Dearborn RD. The only adult present when Taylor had died.

"No," she said. "Last year. But I wasn't very good. I didn't try out this year."

"I was just wondering if you know what happened to the old coach."

"Tricia?"

"Yeah."

"Someone said she's a bartender now or something."

"Serious?" I said. That sounded made-up, but I thought it might be rude to say so.

Rhea shrugged. "Probably beats babysitting at rich-kid camp."

And then there was that awkward moment where I wasn't sure if I was dealing with a fin-aid kid like myself, or one of those self-effacing well-off kids like Star.

"True," I said.

21

"Hey, why did you run off like that?" Star asked.

She was already sitting cross-legged on her bed, laptop open, when I came back from dinner.

I rummaged through my backpack, uncertain which home-work assignment to start on first. "I wasn't feeling so great."

"I think Ms. Noceno was disappointed. She was happy I brought in a live one for her. She gets tired of hanging out with just me."

"I'll go back sometime," I promised, plugging in my laptop.

"There aren't any letters from or to a Sarah Chase, in the letter archives, she said. But she photocopied some of the stuff from the ghost-story file for you to look at."

"Really?"

"Yeah." Star got up and fished in her own backpack. "She must have liked you. Either that or she's working on getting the archive use numbers up. I think there might be a budget issue with keeping it open."

Star handed me a thin packet of stapled papers. "She and I looked through that ghost file together. Most of the stuff was kind of silly—like the occasional student newspaper article about the ghost. Filler for Halloween or whatever. Someone does an article every few years. But we both thought you might want to see this. A student in 1994—her name was Melanie Obringer—put together a collection of stories she was able to gather from alums, going several years back. It looks like it wasn't a school project . . . just like a casual compilation. She didn't write a report or introduction or anything."

"Cool," I said, looking at it. It seemed like it had been photocopied from an old dot-matrix printout.

I had a single room, and I liked it that way. Until the night I saw her and heard her. I woke up in the middle of the night. I have no idea what time it was. Everything was quiet—it must have been past midnight, at least. I heard a low, whispery laugh. I looked up from my bed and saw this silhouette behind my curtain. She was pale and small with big eyes and long hair, wearing white. A white nightgown, like. I'm shivering just telling you this, all these years later. She was fuzzy because of the curtain, but I think she was staring at me. She said, "He sees." And then it seemed like she was coming toward my bed. I closed my eyes. I was screaming. And when I opened them, she was gone. The next day my next-door dormmate did say she heard me screaming, but of course everyone told me I was dreaming. To this day I don't think I was dreaming. She was there. In the room. I refused to sleep alone for weeks. It was against the rules, but I slept on my friend's floor with a sleeping bag for a while. When I finally felt ready to sleep in the room again, I slept with the door wide open. Which was also against the rules. But I kept opening it whenever the housemother would close it. Till she gave up and let me sleep with it open until I graduated.

    —Sheila Hahn, '74

I sucked in a breath as I read this one. *He sees.* Who sees? Samuel?

"What?" Star said.

"So . . . creepy." I tried to sound casual, and to keep the paper from shaking in my grip. Taylor had been wanting a break from her room. But she'd been out of close friends by then. No one left to ask if she could sneak onto their floor with a sleeping bag. Would she still be alive if she'd had someone to ask? I exhaled and let my gaze move on to the next accounts:

I heard three knocks on my door two nights in a row. The following morning I awoke just at dawn, feeling unsettled. There was a dead bird, slightly rotted, at the foot of my bed. I brought it straight to Miss Finneran. She interviewed every student in the dorm trying to find out who had done it. She asked me if I had any enemies in the dorm. I think she had probably watched *The Godfather* recently, and was thinking of the horse head. But I felt then—and feel now—that there was something malevolent in that building. I didn't have enemies at that age. I was the quiet, studious type who just went about my work, minded my own business.

    —Diane, '80*

I woke up at three a.m. and heard a whispering coming from my closet. I bolted out of my room. Nobody believed me. It was terrifying. It only happened the one time. I slept with my lights on for the next few nights. I tried to convince myself it was in my head—that it was part of a dream. But I know it wasn't. A couple of days later I found a heart shape scratched into the side of my closet. I know it wasn't there before that.

—Karen Norcross, '90

I steadied my hand again, noting not just the whispering but the familiarity of the name. She was one of Suzie Price's "Haunteds" in the Facebook group. It was likely from this Karen that Suzie got her information about the hearts.

I woke up in the dark and felt a presence pressing on my chest. I thought I was going to die. Something blackish was over me, over my bed. I tried to scream. I couldn't. It was like my mouth was full of sand. I tried and tried. When I finally managed a wail, it scared the shit out of my roommate. Excuse my French. When she woke up, the dark presence was gone. I was afraid to go to sleep the next night. But it didn't return.

—Anita, '92*

*Last names were left out upon alumnae request.

I let all of these stories sink in for a minute. I could feel Star's eyes on me as I rested the papers on my knees.

"You know what's weird?" I said slowly.

"Well, there are a lot of things that are weird here," Star said, sinking onto her bed.

"That old letter that Ms. Noceno showed me from Louise what's-her-name. She said the ghost wears black. The girl here who saw the ghost in the '70s said she was wearing a white nightgown. And other stories I've heard also say she's in a white nightgown."

"Well . . ." Star pulled up her feet and sat cross-legged. "Who's to say a ghost can't change clothes?"

"Or maybe there's more than one ghost."

"Yeah." Star smiled a little. "Maybe they fight for our attention."

"This *is* prime haunting ground, I bet." My gaze instinctively crept upward at the crack above Star's bed. "What better real estate for a ghost than a building that looks like an old insane asylum?"

"Filled with potentially hysterical young ladies," Star added.

"What else have you got there?" I asked, pointing to the other folder Star had offered—which was now on her bed by her feet.

"Oh! Ms. Noceno took the liberty of also sending along some information about campus deaths. Since ghost curiosity-seekers always want to know about that. She reiterated that there's no record of anyone dying in Dearborn before last year."

Star reached over and handed me the folder.

"Uh . . . thanks," I said, taking it.

"She said it's easy information to access—campus deaths—because she said someone researched the question a long time ago."

I flipped through the grim file. The first thing in it was a stapled set of papers on which Ms. Noceno had stuck a neon-green sticky note. *Josephine Lewis, Thrown from horse.*

"Did you look at this stuff?" I asked Star, showing her the sticky note.

Star shook her head. "I figured I'd let you look first. She says that in addition to what's there, there was a cafeteria worker who had a heart attack in Shelton Hall in the '90s, and there was a day student who died in a car accident around 2004. Which wouldn't count as an on-campus death. And because those were recent things, it's not the kind of thing they'd have much about in the archives. She just mentioned those."

I flipped to the next page in the folder.

"*Stella Roper, Influenza,*" I read. "I feel like from her handwriting Ms. Noceno was enjoying this way too much."

Star's eyes went wide. I worried for a moment that I'd offended her, talking that way about Ms. Noceno.

"Let me see," she demanded, grabbing the folder. A couple of other sheets fell out. "*Damn,*" she said, reading the top page.

"What?" I said.

"I just . . . I've heard of Stella Roper before. I've come across her name in my Caroline Bromley research. I was . . . curious about her."

I watched Star sigh and then start to riffle through the papers in her desk drawer—most of them photocopies of old letters and other archival materials.

"A kindred spirit?" I said softly.

I'd forgotten that Star's real name was Stella. She hated it, she told me last semester. When her parents told her in first grade that it actually meant "star," she begged them to just call her that instead. And they eventually relented.

"I thought maybe, yes." Star shrugged, pulling out a sheet of paper. "I hadn't had time to research her yet, since I'm really focused primarily on Caroline."

The paper Star had pulled out looked like a photocopy of an archive document—a list of names and dates. *Caroline Bromley* was the first name on it, with the date *1890* next to it. The next name on the list was *Minnie Gardner,* with *1891* beside it. The next name had *1892* next to it, and so on. I squinted at the words scrawled across the top.

"You can read it better on the original in the archives," Star said. "It says, 'Our silence is not eternal.' I found this list in one of the Caroline Bromley files."

"Our silence is not eternal," I repeated. "Is that . . . religious?"

"I don't think so. What's really exciting about it is that it kind of resembles something Caroline Bromley said and wrote later in life, when she was a leader in the women's suffrage movement. *Our silence, forever broken.* There's even a picture of her and another woman holding up a sign that says that."

I'd heard that phrasing before. Most Windham students probably had. The portrait of Caroline Bromley that hung in the administrative building—also called Bromley Hall—said that beneath it.

"Wow," I said. "Did Caroline herself write that at the top, you think?"

"I like to think so. The handwriting doesn't quite match the few documents of hers we have from later in life, though. It might have been someone else. And you can see that the handwriting changes over the years as different girls participated. There was apparently kind of an underground women's suffrage group here at the school, and this is the list of the student leader of the group for each year."

"Was that the year she graduated, or what? I don't remember."

"No," Star said. "It was the second year she was a student here."

I scanned the list of names. It went all the way up to 1921.

"They dissolved the group a little while after women got the right to vote?" I said.

"I assume, yes." Caroline shrugged. "It seems like maybe they could've kept it going and fought for other women's rights, but maybe they didn't think of it that way."

The handwriting changed over the course of the list—clearly it wasn't all written by one person, but many people over the years. Some names had a little symbol next to them—a flowery-looking star. Caroline Bromley's name had one next to hers.

"Do you know what that little star means?"

"No idea. I feel like someone might have gone in later and put a star next to the names of the women who were actually active in the suffrage movement later in life. I'm not sure. Ms. Noceno says this has been in the archives for only about six years. It was Ms. Holland-Stone who actually figured out what it was, when it came in with a box of other junk. Because the third name on the list, Helen Driscoll, is *also* someone who became a suffragette—someone less famous than Caroline, but who was active with her in the movement when they were adults. Her name has a star, too. And she'd apparently made reference to the student group in a letter that's in a different archive somewhere. Seneca Falls, probably."

Ms. Holland-Stone, my Western Civ teacher, was also Star's senior project advisor—and the chair of the history department.

"Anyway, someone brought this list in," Star continued. "Along with a Windham diploma and a few old schoolbooks and papers and other stuff that someone found in an attic after their grandma died. A great-great-aunt had gone to Dearborn, or something."

"Oh. Is the great-great-aunt's name on the list?" I asked.

"Yeah. Paulina Nielson. The last one on the list. But the family didn't know much about Paulina as a person or her history at Windham. They weren't a legacy family or anything."

"Stella's listed here for 1916," I pointed out.

"And she died two years after that. She didn't live to see the women's suffrage amendment happen. That's so sad."

"At least all the other girls on this list did, probably," I said. "Including Caroline."

Star frowned at the list when I handed it back to her.

"This list is a big part of my project, in a way," she said. "I've been researching some of the names on it when I have time. I'm not able to find information about everyone, but I'm finding that a few of the girls, including Caroline, most importantly, were scholarship girls."

"Why is that *most* important?" I asked.

"Well . . . it's interesting. Sometimes people downplay the role of working-class women in the suffrage movement. It's interesting that here on campus the girls most interested in that didn't necessarily fit the mold."

"But . . . why would that be?" I asked.

"I've actually given this some thought. And I think maybe that not having so much money and power earlier in life would

158

naturally lend itself to envisioning having more power, more of a voice, in your adult life as a woman."

"Is that your thesis?" I asked, trying not to sound skeptical.

Star shrugged and blushed a little.

"How much suffragist activity could the girls really have participated in while they were stuck here in Heathsburg?"

"At the time, I guess it was the thought that counted. And Caroline certainly put the thoughts into action later."

My gaze crept down to the name *Stella Roper*.

"Was Stella Roper a scholarship girl?"

"I don't know. I haven't gotten to researching her yet—otherwise I'd have already known she died."

"Mmm," I said, and tidied up the papers in Ms. Noceno's Death Folder. "So Stella died in 1918, and the first mention of the ghost that anyone knows about is from 1920."

Star shoved the student leader list back in her drawer and wove her head back and forth.

"Stella . . . Sarah . . . Stella . . . Sarah . . . kinda similar. Is that what you're getting at?"

"Maybe," I said. "I dunno."

"I don't think the overly academic girls of the early 20th-century Windham would mix those up. *Stella* is Latin for "star." *Sarah* is Biblical, Hebrew. They're totally different."

"Just a thought," I said.

Star glanced at her phone.

"Maybe I should try to get some homework done," she said.

I agreed. But when I opened my laptop, I saw I had a new email—from Kathleen Darkins.

Dear Haley,

I don't have any appointments scheduled on Saturday. Did you have a particular time in mind? Would this be a crystal consultation or a general wellness profile?

I didn't know how to answer that question. I was tempted to write Kathleen back and ask her point-blank if she was at Windham in 1986. But I felt I already knew the answer, and over email it was too easy for her to avoid the question. Best to leave it alone until I arrived in her shop tomorrow and asked her face to face.

22

Once we were friends, Taylor never quit asking me why I was here. Here at Windham. She was curious like that. She could sense where there was a story. And she was relentless about getting to hear it.

It wasn't until the very end of my first year that she got me drunk enough at a party to tell it. We were in the basement of Charlie Bronner's house, lying on a soft, colorfully flecked carpet that seemed expensive even though it reminded me of the time my brother puked up half of his Halloween candy—all Twizzlers and Nerds and Skittles, which he favored. Jackson Pollock rainbow puke.

She asked me if I missed my brother, and I said yes, sort of. And that led to it. Why I was here.

I told her that it all started—probably, as far as I could tell— with sixth grade. My parents got divorced when I was in sixth grade. Which didn't have to be all that remarkable. But they'd fought about custody. Fought viciously, if we were going to be honest. There was some judge my mom wanted me to tell about how crazy my dad acted when he was drinking. But the worst of it had been when I was like eight or nine, which had felt like forever ago, and couldn't she tell about that herself? And was *she going to mention that at the time she had often gotten pretty wild and angry, too? And she wasn't making my little brother say much of anything—so why was it all on me?*

There were different grown-ups—lawyers, judges, some kind of weird therapist who kept wanting to play Jenga—who wanted me to say different things. There was my mom running out of money to be able to pay her lawyer, and not being able to buy a Christmas tree. There was the night my dad came and pounded on the locked door—THUNK THUNK THUNK— screaming for us to let him in, until the cops came. And then there was the not knowing if we were supposed to pretend that never happened when my brother and I visited my dad a week later. Mostly, there was fear of what would happen next. The next day, the next hour, the next minute.

It was that stuff that started it, I think. This feeling I had when I was twelve—this feeling like I was sinking. Not drowning. Just sinking. Like into sand. Deeper and deeper down. The feeling accompanied me into seventh grade, even after my parents seemed to have settled on a cold, angry truce.

Life felt generally terrifying then. I couldn't possibly do gymnastics at the Y anymore. I'd been on the tumbling team with my friends Fiona and Nelly. But I could no longer get my brain around a layout or a roundoff, much less my body. I felt too heavy for any of that. Up to my thighs in sand.

When I announced to my mother that I wouldn't be going back to the gym, she didn't argue with me. I understood that with all of the divorce legal fees and the other financial burdens of now being a single parent, my quitting was likely a relief to her.

Some of the sleep stuff came back. The sleep stuff from when I was younger. My mom caught me sleepwalking one time and on two horrifying mornings I woke up to wet sheets. (This part I'd managed not to tell Taylor. Even when I was drunk, my brain guarded that, refusing to transmit it to my tongue.)

Sometime at the beginning of seventh grade, a girl came up to me in the hall before gym—a girl unknown to me in the sea of middle schoolers, who hadn't gone to my elementary school.

"Do you ever brush your hair?" she asked, looking back at the two girls who had followed her over. One of the girls I recognized as a new friend of Nelly's.

They must have been applying lip gloss together right before approaching me. All three sets of lips looked so slippery that I couldn't stop staring. The girl had to repeat her question.

"Yes," I said absently.

"Oh. Okay. I was just wondering."

But it occurred to me later that my hair had indeed become rather unmanageable lately. There was a large knot in the back that I'd been pulling up into a sort of half ponytail. But doing that didn't entirely hide how large it was getting. I did brush my hair, but now that I thought about it, it felt like maybe I only brushed the front and had forgotten about the back for a while. When you're distracted by the general act of keeping yourself from sinking, other stuff tends to get only half done. So now the knot was bigger than I remembered it. Puffy. It had drawn those wet-lipped girls like flies to a corpse.

I tried for a couple of days to work the knot out. Eventually I cut it off, leaving a sort of thin spot. I thought it wasn't noticeable, but I was apparently wrong. Some girl—a different girl,

*but friends with the original girl—pointed it out, asked if some-
one had put Nair in my shampoo. After that I wore my hair up
in a ponytail for a year. But at least that gross knot was gone.*

*Somehow in all of this I stopped seeing Nelly and Fiona
much. I went to Fiona's birthday party, but I could tell I was just
there because her mother made her invite me. Nobody talked to
me, so I ate caramel corn the whole time.*

*With few friends, I had a lot of time for homework and I
did okay in school. Sometimes the sinking feeling would over-
whelm me and I'd drop the ball with this class or that. But I
always aced math. Math came naturally to me.*

*And I would run after school, up and down the hilly streets
of my neighborhood. Put on sneakers and run and run and run,
because you can't sink while you're moving fast.*

*On Valentine's Day my mother dragged me to take a PSAT
test. She didn't say why. She just said, "Let's see how you do."
So I took it without any stress. I did okay on the verbal, but
freakishly well on the math. I should have known something
was up when her eyes popped as she opened the test scores. But
I had no idea that my mother was sending the results, along with
my school records and a writing sample, to her friend Michelle,
who'd never left Heathsburg and worked in the main administrative office at Windham. Michelle helped get my application
to the top of the pile of financial aid hopefuls.*

*My mother didn't breathe a word of it to me until the ac-
ceptance letter and scholarship notification arrived. She didn't
want to get my hopes up. But she presented me with both on a
rainy April evening, over a humble dinner of salad and English
muffin pizzas.*

"I'm not trying to get rid of you," she said. "I will miss you with all of my heart if you go. But I wanted you to know that you can have something else—if you want it."

I could tell she'd probably planned and practiced these words, and I burst into tears at hearing them. I didn't know if I was happy or sad. But I remember understanding, gratefully, that it didn't matter how I felt. I was going to Windham either way.

My mother had, in her own good time, noticed I was sinking. And this was the best way she could think of to save me. Because it was how she herself had always wanted to be saved. By going to that beautiful old pie-in-the-sky school just down the road from her parents' little Heathsburg bungalow.

When I'd finished telling all of this to Taylor, she didn't ask about my mother. She didn't ask about gymnastics. She just said, "Fiona and Nelly. Sound like shitty friends. And how did they get such stupid names?"

"I love the name Fiona," I'd said defensively.

Taylor shook her head and was quiet for a minute or two.

"One time my brother locked me outside all night," she said after a while. "My parents thought he was old enough to babysit."

I didn't know how this was connected—except in the spirit of mutual drunken confessional. Or maybe because we both had brothers we hardly ever saw.

"Which brother?" I asked, because I knew she had two. One three years older than her, one five.

She didn't answer. Her eyes were closed. She'd passed out.

23

Eight Nights Left

Of course she hoped this place would change her—improve her. But it didn't change her enough. We can't really blame that all on a place, though, can we? Places don't break people—not usually. But rather the people who occupy those places.

It was those golden girls who broke her with their cruelty. That's how the story goes. Those beautiful, lithe, smart, rich ones. Girls like that are timeless, aren't they?

24

Saturday, February 2

Maylin and I started out early, with coffee and muffins from the dining hall. Still, we decided to stop at the Heathsburg gas fill-up for chips and sour candy straws. One hour didn't make for much of a road trip, but we could pretend.

As we made our way down the main drag of Heathsburg, I remembered something my mom told me about growing up in this town. You'd often see Windham and Farnswood students walking up or back from the Rite Aid or the doughnut shop on weekends—you could tell them by their preppy clothes. When my mom was a senior at the public high school, she had a boyfriend who liked to pretend they were in a video game in which they'd knock down the "Windyfarts." He'd jolt his steering wheel just slightly in the direction of the sidewalk when he'd see one, and say softly, *Plink!* And my mom would giggle in spite of herself.

So be careful if you ever walk on that main drag, she concluded. As if her old mouth-breather boyfriend was still gunning it up and down that street thirty years later.

"I tried to get Alex to change her mind and come with us," Maylin said, putting her blinker on for the highway ramp.

"She's got a lot on her plate," I said. "As usual."

"Yeah, well. She keeps saying she's falling behind on things."

"Could that really be true?"

"Umm . . ." Maylin glanced at me, then stared back at the road. "She actually does seem stretched a little thin. Or just, like . . . disinterested."

"Is her mom okay?" I asked with a sinking feeling.

At the end of our freshman year, Alex's mom was diagnosed with breast cancer. She had gotten intensive treatment and was okay now, but we both knew that her family worried about the cancer returning.

"I feel like she would have told me if it was that."

"But one of us should ask, just to be sure. Alex might not offer information like that if you don't ask her. And she might need our help."

"She might not want our help," Maylin said. "The thing is, I think she's getting help from somebody else."

I hesitated, curling another sour straw into my mouth and chewing it as quietly as I could.

The thing about Maylin was that it was easy to get information out of her. But I didn't feel comfortable digging for dirt about Alex.

"I think she's going to a therapist or something," Maylin said conspiratorially.

I kept chewing, looking out the window, unsure if I wanted her to go on.

Even as firsties, when Alex and I didn't necessarily like each other very much, we'd respected each other's privacy. Neither of us came from the cushiest of backgrounds, like some of the other girls. We didn't ask each other too many questions, and we gave each other some silent slack. I wasn't sure I wanted to mess with that.

"She had her laptop open on her desk the other day," Maylin continued. "And I saw that she had looked up therapists in Derby."

"Derby?" I said. Derby was twenty minutes from Windham-Farnswood. But there was an occasional school shuttle to the shopping center there. "Can't she . . . use one of the school counselors?"

Maylin shrugged. "I've heard they're all pretty lame."

"There's one named Brenda who's okay," I offered. "She talked to me the day after Taylor died. I was still kind of in shock, so I don't remember it that well. And I didn't follow up like she wanted me to. But she wasn't . . . terrible. It would be kind of like Alex, though, to want to talk to someone entirely off campus."

"I guess," Maylin admitted.

Not that it was any of our business.

"Maybe none of this would be an issue," I said, "if you stopped looking at the shit on her desk."

I opened a bag of chips and offered them to her. My words had maybe come out a little harsher than I intended.

"Well, I can't unsee the stuff now." Maylin kept one hand on the wheel but buried the other in the chip bag. "I'm not a bad person for worrying about a friend."

No," I said. "You're not."

I wondered silently how Alex could afford a private therapist. It seemed unlikely that she could. Maybe Maylin had misread what she'd seen on Alex's desk. Unless it was a list of private providers that the school had relationships with—for kids who needed some sort of specialist. I thought about Alex cramming in the chocolate ice cream and peanut butter last night, then leaving dinner before the rest of us. Bulimia? I doubted it. But it was *possible*.

"That might even be why she seemed eager to get rid of us today," Maylin continued. "Maybe she's taking the shopping shuttle today for an appointment and doesn't want to have to talk about it."

Maylin scowled at the road in front of her. My phone chirped and I looked at it. I was startled to see a text from Lily Bruno, finally responding from a few days ago:

Hi Haley. Hope all is well at Windham? Sure, we can connect sometime. I don't really like to talk about it, but I understand if you feel like you need to.

I wasn't sure how to reply. Lily wasn't offering a particular time. She was going to leave it at "sometime," seemed like, and force me to press the issue.

Are you free tonight? I texted.

"But how many therapists do you know that work on Saturdays?" Maylin asked before adding, "So maybe she just wanted to get rid of me in a general sort of way."

"Maybe we shouldn't worry about it until we have a chance to talk to her about things," I mumbled.

Maylin was quiet for a moment.

"Put the address in the GPS, would you?" she said.

As I did what Maylin had asked, I heard my phone chirp again.

Yes, Lily had written back.

***

The New Moon Wellness Emporium had an impressive storefront—with a moon and stars on its overhead sign and white Christmas lights snaking around the tiers of displayed goods in the windows.

Maylin had begged off at a clothing boutique a few doors down, as I'd kind of been hoping she would. She had also caught sight of a cute coffee and pastry shop she thought she'd like to try, and we'd promised to text each other in a half hour or so.

A bell on the door jangled as I entered the Emporium. Once the door was shut, I was enveloped in the sounds of flute music and water trickling—and clashing smells of cloves and lavender. The slender, gray-haired woman at the desk near the back didn't look up immediately. She was pulling some cloth-wrapped items out of a box. As I got closer, I saw that they were probably soaps.

"Hi," I said, approaching her. My palms were sweating.

I'd been expecting someone wearing a long floral muumuu, or maybe an organic hemp sack dress. This lady had on jeans and a pink sweater with little fake pearls studding the sleeves.

When she looked up, I asked, "Are you Kathleen?"

"Yes." The woman put a soap to her nose and took a long sniff. "I am."

"I wrote to you about Saturday appointments."

"Oh! I see. What can I help you with, honey?"

"I . . . um . . . thought I might get a couple of candles for my mother. And . . . I had another question for you."

I could feel my pulse quicken as I heard the words leave my mouth. I wasn't used to confronting people.

"Sure. What kind of candles does your mom like?"

I glanced quickly around the shop to see if we were alone. It appeared we were. And it occurred to me that I wanted to get the awkward part over with before Maylin might decide to come looking for me early.

"Umm . . . I don't have a question about the candles." The words tumbled out. "I was wondering if you have ever been to Windham-Farnswood Academy in Heathsburg. If you've ever worked there or . . . anything like that? Like, um, in 1986?"

Kathleen's mouth went slack. She stared at me.

"Windham . . . yes. But . . ." Kathleen leaned against the stool behind her desk. She didn't look angry. "How did you know that, honey?"

"I . . . um . . . I saw a picture of you and your husband in an old dorm photo. But . . . you were a houseparent? With your husband? And you went by different names then?"

"Yes. Ex-husband." Kathleen smiled a little. "In the '80s. For six months. Long time ago. Ron's been gone for many years now. Where did you come from, honey? Are you local?"

"No. I drove here this morning from Windham. Or, my friend drove me. I'm a student there. Can I just ask . . . Did you and Ronald go to Windham *knowing* that Dearborn was haunted? Is that why you were there? Or was that just a coincidence? And why were you using different names?"

"That's a lot of questions at once. What's your name?"

"Haley."

"Haley. It was a long time ago, as I said."

Kathleen reached out and touched one of the sets of wind chimes hanging next to her counter. They bonged gently.

"But can you explain why you were there?" I asked.

Kathleen rubbed the back of her neck and smiled. "Oh dear. Do you want to sit down?"

"I'm not sure," I said flatly.

"Okay, then. How about some water?"

"I'm okay," I said.

"Did someone at the school tell you about this?" Kathleen asked.

"Not really. I heard something from an older alumna. Not something for sure, it was just like a rumor."

"Okay." Kathleen gazed at me, the sides of her mouth tightening. "And you drove all this way to confirm an old rumor?"

Kathleen didn't wait for me to answer. She took a glass from under the desk and drew water from the water cooler against the wall.

"I don't use little paper cups," she said. "But I keep these glasses clean for customers."

I nodded and she watched me take a sip.

"I had a friend . . . a year older than me," I said. "Last year she died. In the Dearborn building. Well, she jumped and died, I mean."

Kathleen murmured "Oh no" under her breath, but I kept talking. Surrounded by flute music and gentle smells, I suddenly felt compelled to confess.

"I don't know exactly what happened," I said. "But I think there's something wrong with the building. Something maybe made her do it. I don't know how to explain. But I'm wondering what you and your husband were doing there and what you thought of the building."

Kathleen put up one finger to signal me to stop talking. Then she walked to the front of the store and turned the *Open* sign to *Closed*.

"I'm sorry to hear about your friend," she said. "I really am so sorry."

"Thanks. Can you tell me anything about what you were doing at that dorm?" I asked. "You were using different names. Were you hiding from the school that you guys were . . . ghost hunters?"

Kathleen shook her head. "The school hired us. Or rather, the headmistress did. No one else knew. Just her."

I hesitated, taking this in. "So she knew you were ghost hunters?"

"No. We studied parapsychological phenomena. We never called ourselves ghost hunters. We weren't advocates of 'hunting' anything. Mrs. Bradford wanted the dorm to be studied . . . diagnosed, in a sense. She hired Ron because she understood he took a very careful, hands-off approach. That he considered himself primarily an observer, and avoided sensationalism."

"None of the girls knew who you were?"

"Not at the time. A few years later, Ron was on TV more. So I imagine a few girls from that senior class probably saw him and noticed a resemblance. He told me he got a letter once, inquiring, which he didn't respond to because he didn't want to get the headmistress in trouble. But you're the first person who's come and asked me."

"So the headmistress at the time . . . She hired you and Ronald." I had to repeat this to help it sink in.

"Yes. Her name was Betty Bradford. She's dead now, I imagine."

I nodded, stunned silent for a moment. I'd heard the name before. There were some funny stories about the Betty Bradford era of the school. She was a spinster who fancied herself an Emily Dickinson type. Supposedly she left baskets of muffins or cookies for students on the dormitory doorsteps. She had a bunch of dogs, and would always bring a chronically barking beagle to stuffy school functions.

"Did you find what she hired you for?" I asked.

"She was concerned about the building." Kathleen pulled another bar of soap from her box and sniffed it. "She'd been a student herself and knew girls who'd had frightening experiences there. And the year before we came, there was a serious incident. . . . A student who thought the place was haunted had a mental breakdown. Betty was concerned about things escalating. She'd read our names in an article about poltergeists and poltergeist study, and she contacted us and proposed we come and study the place."

"Disguised as houseparents?" I said, thinking back to the dorm photo of the Darkinses with the girls.

"Not disguised . . ." Kathleen put down the soap on her counter. "Just doing two different jobs at once."

"What did you think of the place? Was anything done? A blessing, an exorcism? A ghostbusting of *any* kind?"

"No . . . We were there primarily to observe, and we were never sure that was what the place needed. Ron and I were a little more . . . agnostic than some of the paranormal investigators of our time."

"Aren't you a clairvoyant or something? I thought I read that on the Wikipedia page."

Kathleen studied me for a moment and then picked at one of the little pearls on her sleeve.

"More like 'something,' " she said quietly.

I hesitated. "Well . . . how did you feel living in that building? Did you feel like it was haunted?"

Kathleen drew herself a glass of water, pulled up a stool, and sighed before she took a drink.

"I definitely felt unsettled at times," she admitted. "But *haunted* might not be the word I'd use. I felt a conflicting convergence of energies."

"What does that mean?" I demanded. It sounded vaguely like bullshit.

"It means I couldn't identify one distinct spirit occupying the place. And Ronald had some theories about mass hysteria, mass delusion. But they were very tentative theories, because the place and the incidents didn't really follow any of the usual patterns of either of those things. It was a very confounding place."

I exhaled, realizing I'd been holding my breath through her last few sentences. *Conflicting convergence of energies . . . hysteria . . . delusion . . . a confounding place.*

"Be right back," Kathleen said.

Kathleen went into her back room for a moment and came out with a tall stool.

"Please have a seat," she said, positioning it near her own.

"Look," she said. "I have some things from that time that might help us both . . . might jog my memory, and might clarify things for you. They're in boxes in my basement at home, though."

"I'm not sure how long I can . . ." I trailed off. Maylin was expecting me to text her soon. And while this lady seemed nice, I didn't really think it was a smart move for me to accompany her to a basement. There was a fractional chance she might boil me in a giant kettle and use my melted fat to make some kind of healing emollient.

"Well, maybe I could send you some things if I find them," she offered. That sounded very tentative. "Although . . . I'm not sure I want to part with them. They're some of the files from my and Ronald's time there. Maybe I could make copies, but . . . before we figure that out, can I ask you a little bit about your friend?"

"I guess," I said, feeling a wave of relief at the question. I knew she'd been eager to ask it, and I didn't want to have to anticipate it any longer.

"You said she jumped from a window in Dearborn. Can I ask from what floor?"

"The fourth. The top floor. Does it matter?"

"The upper floors have a little more negative energy, I believe."

I didn't ask her to clarify.

"And they're sure she jumped?" Kathleen wrapped her hands around her water glass like it was a steaming cup of coffee. "She wasn't pushed? It wasn't an accident with alcohol or anything like that? Were there any witnesses?"

"She was alone in her room. No one really thought she had been suicidal, but maybe she was without anyone knowing. There was also some strong weed involved. I don't really buy any of those explanations. Especially since . . ."

"Since what, honey?" Kathleen coaxed.

I closed my eyes for a moment, taking in the gentle flute music. "Since now that I live there, I feel like there are signs that it was more complicated than any of that."

"Suicide and strong weed are both complicated," Kathleen said softly. "But . . . what *kind* of signs?"

I hesitated, listening to the flutes again—and the trickle of the little fountain. I breathed in the weird, guilty comfort of knowing I was in the presence of the sort of woman my mother usually hated.

"She was maybe hearing whispers in her room right before she jumped," I said, taking out my phone.

I showed her Thatcher's video and told her about the open window and door last week, and then the writing on the window glass. Kathleen listened carefully but expressionlessly.

"I'm glad you found me," she said when I was finished.

"Do you think there's something wrong with the place that might have killed her?" I whispered.

"Well . . . I can't say *that*. I don't know near enough to even begin to say that. But I think you're right to ask questions."

Kathleen tapped her fingertips along her chin, thinking. The

178

flutes warbled. The fountain trickled. My phone chirped and I glanced down.

Where are you? Maylin had texted. *This place has killer cupcakes!!*

"How about this," Kathleen said. "I have your email address. I'll scan what I have and send it to you by tonight. Then you won't have to wait long for them. And then I could keep the originals, which would make me feel more comfortable."

"That would be perfect," I said, pocketing my phone.

"I hope it will help you. I'll also give you my number for when you're done reading."

I took down her number as she dictated it to me. Before I was even finished, the phone chirped again.

You still picking out candles?? You are a very devoted daughter. The coffee place is called Common Grounds. It's like three doors down from your candle shoppy place.

"My friend is wondering where I am," I said. "She's my ride home."

"That's fine." Kathleen went to the front door and turned the sign to *Open.* "You should catch up with her. I promise I'll send those things tonight."

"Thanks."

"Ron worked hard on them. It will be good to see them going to someone who finds them useful."

My phone chirped again.

"You'd better go, sounds like," Kathleen said.

"Yeah, I guess." I plucked two votive candles from a display by the register. "I'll buy these first, though."

I needed them in case Maylin asked me what I'd bought.

Kathleen waved me away as I took out my wallet.

"On the house," she said.

I thanked her a few times and then headed for the door. As it jangled, Kathleen called out, "Haley?"

One of my feet was on the sidewalk and the brisk February air had already hit my face.

"Yeah?"

"It's not in your head," Kathleen said. "Or rather . . . not *just* in your head. It's real. There's something real happening in that building. I felt it . . . before you were even born. Remember that."

"Okay," I said, then let the door close behind me.

25

I was alone in my room—about a half hour before curfew—when Kathleen's scans arrived.

REPORT:
WINDHAM-FARNSWOOD ACADEMY CONSULTATION

INTRODUCTION

My first contact with Ms. Elizabeth "Betty" Bradford, headmistress of the Windham School, the all-female half of the larger Windham-Farnswood Academy, was in August 1985. In her initial call, she explained that she had read some of my research and comments in a publication about the Tina Resch poltergeist case, and asked if I would be open to being a consultant for her school, which has been experiencing potentially paranormal activity for many years. The site of the activity is the Dearborn dormitory, occupied currently only by senior students. The building was erected in 1879, and has always been a student dormitory—although in the first few decades, it housed students of all grades.

Mrs. Bradford was clearly versed in the Resch case as well as other publicized paranormal cases from recent decades (Amityville house, Lindley Street poltergeist, etc.). She shared that she was attracted to my "open-minded approach" (her words) to paranormal activity (in particular that I've studied mass hysteria and mass delusion as well as paranormal phenomena), and that I always work alongside my female consultant (that is, my wife Kathleen). She asked if either of us had experience working with teenagers, and was interested to hear that Kathleen had worked as a camp counselor throughout her summers in college and has occasionally substitute-taught when we aren't traveling for consultations. One week after our initial conversation, Mrs. Bradford contacted us again to propose a long-term contract consultation.

She asked that, if agreed upon, the terms of our consultation be absolutely confidential, no matter what the findings or outcomes, and never be referenced in any future CVs or media engagements. Pseudonyms would be used for our residency at Dearborn Hall, so the wider school community would not be aware of our history as paranormal investigators. She offered a generous compensation that included full room and board at the academy for the months of January–June 1986.

Mrs. Bradford had us sign two separate contracts—one for our official employment as houseparents, the other for our paranormal-parapsychological consultation. My understanding is that the former was submitted as part of the school's general budget and the latter kept in her personal files to ensure against any breach of the strict terms of that contract. It is also my understanding that we are receiving the standard houseparenting stipend from the Windham-Farnswood HR department, but the additional, confidential paranormal consult compensation is being paid by Mrs. Bradford herself. Copies of both contracts are included herein.

Mrs. Bradford explained to us at the outset that Dearborn Hall has had a long history of paranormal phenomena—or at least the perception of paranormal phenomena—throughout her long personal history with the school and the dorm. She was a student at the academy in the late 1930s, and her mother attended from 1905–09. While Mrs. Bradford herself never experienced a haunting, a friend of hers did. She saw the young ghost girl in her doorway, and said she uttered words to her that were mostly inaudible, but for the two words "sick heart." Unfortunately, that friend of Mrs. Bradford's is now deceased. Mrs. Bradford says that she recalls that in the 1930s her friend and their peers referred to the ghost as Sarah or occasionally Sarah in Black, at times shortened to Sarah Black. She was said to appear in the upper hallways in black clothing, although Mrs. Bradford says she cannot recall if her friend confirmed that detail when she experienced an actual sighting. Most reports of sightings, according to Mrs. Bradford's recollection, are of a pale, petite, undernourished-looking young woman.

I paused in my reading, lingering on the words "sick heart." Like a broken heart, perhaps? Like I had suggested to Suzie Price? Maybe. She had claimed someone had heard "sad heart," which wasn't all that different. But *sick heart* sounded more sinister.

Glancing around the room, I missed Star's cheerful presence.

Her mobile of delicate paper umbrellas revolved slowly, as always, above her bed. Her beluga smirked at me from behind it.

Mrs. Bradford claims that she reported her friend's sighting to her mother, who admitted she had heard rumors of similar encounters in her day, but made it clear that she didn't think her daughter should engage in study of—or even discussions of—the occult. "My mother was very religious and traditional. She didn't care to talk about such things." Mrs. Bradford recollects that her mother said that the ghost was, in her student days, rumored to quote Scripture during her visitations. But she believes that may have been her mother's pious embellishment of a topic that otherwise made her uncomfortable.

Nonetheless, Mrs. Bradford maintains a personal curiosity about paranormal phenomena, and confesses a rekindled interest in the Dearborn ghost when she'd still hear students mention it in the 1950s, when she came back to her alma mater to teach history for three years. After that, Mrs. Bradford taught at a small college for many years, and didn't return to Windham until she was tapped to be headmistress of the school in 1982.

"I wasn't terribly surprised to discover that the ghost girl had stayed on all that time. Windies are nothing if not tenacious. And I have to assume the ghost is a Windy."

Mrs. Bradford explains that disturbances don't occur every year. Sometimes they're minor, e.g., noises or drafts, but every few years, or at least once a decade, it seems—there are more serious incidents, with more serious consequences.

Last year was one such year.

A senior student and Dearborn resident, who will hereby be referred to as Student X, was hospitalized in February after displaying symptoms of mental distress for several weeks. As I am not a mental health professional and have not seen this young woman's medical records, I cannot describe her condition in detail here. I am limited to what Mrs. Bradford reported to me, which was thus: The student refused to sleep in her own room, and was often found in the early mornings sleeping in her sleeping bag on the common area couches. When threatened with administrative consequences, she began sleeping in out-of-the-way places in the building in which she was not likely to be caught, such as the floors of other students' rooms, and, when that wasn't possible (apparently her friends got tired of her insistence on keeping the lights on), the kitchen storage room on the ground floor. When asked why she wouldn't stay in her room, Student X would repeatedly say, "I have to sleep where she can't see me."

Student X's grandparents are generous donors to the school. Mrs. Bradford explained that the administration delayed action on this problem in order to avoid upsetting a legacy family. But when the student's sleeping habits began to affect her performance in classes (she was starting to fail several), as well as the housemother's observance of her eating poorly and growing thinner, action had to be taken. The student was taken into the infirmary, and the nurse there, feeling the student's condition beyond her treatment capabilities, recommended hospitalization, to which the student's family agreed reluctantly. After a hospitalization of about two months, the student was allowed to complete her coursework and exams through a tutor at home, and eventually earned her Windham-Farnswood diploma.

Mrs. Bradford's proposal was that we come to Dearborn as temporary houseparents. We agreed that my and Kathleen's initial role should be that of observers.

"Damn," I breathed as I came to the end of the introduction. Eccentric old headmistress Betty Bradford had hired an *undercover* ghost hunter to study Dearborn and its students. Was that legal? I wondered. But more importantly, it confirmed not only that there *were* school administrators who believed that something was wrong in the building—but also that the place had rumors of hauntings potentially as far back as 1905.

And Student X's troubles seemed to resemble Taylor's before her death. The recording of the whispers, for one. But also Anthony's suggestion that she was looking for ways to avoid sleeping in her room.

I glanced at the time. Ten minutes to curfew. Maybe Star was back in the building and had decided to hang out in someone else's room.

"Oh!" I muttered to myself, suddenly remembering that I was supposed to call Lily Bruno—and that privacy would be best for that. Better to do it before Star returned. I quickly took out my phone and tapped Lily's number.

No answer—which didn't really surprise me.

I tossed my phone on my bed and returned to my file, scrolling through. It had several more sections, with headings like

Arrival and First Days, Impression, Logged Events, Relevant Historical Background, Student Interviews, Student X, Student Y.

Student Interviews was by far the longest part. I glanced over the summary at the top.

> Student interviews were conducted informally, and transcribed in summary/from recollections, not recorded or transcribed verbatim. There were 84 senior students living in the hall, but meaningful interviews were not possible with every student since a systematic interview process was not possible with the confidential nature of our role/study, as prescribed by our client. Informal interviews/discussions were conducted with 52 students.
>
> 2 reported recent experiences that they describe explicitly as paranormal.
>
> 1 reported an experience that her peers think was of a paranormal nature but she does not.
>
> 8 discussed the details of Student X's mental breakdown as they had heard them and/or theorized about the cause of this incident.
>
> 7 reported second- or thirdhand accounts of paranormal activity in the dormitory in previous years—4 of a poltergeist-type description, 3 more distinctly a spirit entity.
>
> 3 appear to show signs of possible mental distress, although no formal clinical assessment has been made.
>
> All students interviewed had known of the dorm's reputation as a haunted place before residing there, and all had heard of "Sarah" throughout their earlier years at the school.

Roughly half claim belief that there might be some truth to the stories.

Students X and Y have been given letter designations and are addressed in their own portions of the report, due to the special nature of their cases. They are not among the numbered interviewees.

I stopped here to take a breath. Closing my eyes, I thought guiltily of my abandoned correspondence with Taylor's brother, Thatcher. If I were to write him right now, what would I say?

Dear Thatcher,

I am still not sure who or what was whispering to your sister in that video. But it's looking more and more like there's some sort of paranormal problem here. Taylor was apparently not the first girl to lose her shit in this dorm. In fact, it was happening before she was even born, and lots of people seem to know about it . . .

The door squeaked and I opened my eyes as Star strode in, smiling as she tore off her red wool coat.

"It's official!" she said.

"What's official?"

"Mark and I are together."

I dragged my gaze off my laptop screen. "Mark who?"

"Mark Byrne." Star grinned.

"Oh. I *think* I know who he is. Plays baseball? Does he have brown hair and sideburns?"

"Yep. That's the one."

"I didn't know you were a sideburn girl," I said.

Star made a little claw with her hand, and a growling noise in her throat—I guess to indicate that sideburns drove her wild.

"Uhh . . . congratulations? I didn't know this was going on."

"Oh . . . there's a lot people don't know about me."

There was still a goony smile on Star's face. I decided not to ask if she'd had a drink or two. I glanced at my laptop, debating whether I should share this stunning cache of dark campus history. I decided against it, not wanting to steal her thunder. And Star was in rare form right now. Maybe, for once, she didn't want to talk about long-dead Windham girls.

My phone chirped for attention.

Sorry to miss your call, Lily Bruno had texted. *I'm out with friends right now. Try in the morning? I don't have anything going on.*

"Me too," I said absently.

I congratulated Star again and then went back to Kathleen's files.

♦♦♦

I was still reading after Star had turned in and fallen asleep. She'd offered to use her sleep mask, but I had told her I didn't mind reading in the dark if she didn't mind the computer glare.

At first, I started with the section called *Student Interviews.* They were kind of boring—because as Darkins had pointed out, they didn't amount to much. One was a lengthy interview in which a student who didn't know Student X speculated at length about her having multiple personalities. The student had just read the book *Sybil*. Another said that she heard of a girl a few years ago who kept feeling a cold hand on her in the night. But it was a thirdhand story.

Most of the girls had simply heard the same things about the Winter Girl over their years at Windham that I had: that her name might be Sarah. That she haunted in January or February. That she knocked on doors or could be seen in a white nightgown in the hallway if you got up and ventured to the bathroom after midnight. That she was to blame for the various weird noises in the building on winter nights. That she had been spurned by a young man and killed herself in her room. One girl said something I hadn't heard before, though: *Some girls say that she's looking for her replacement. That she's tired of being a ghost, that she'll strangle or smother you in your bed if you're not careful. And then* you're *the ghost.*

I stared at that line for a moment, then read on. When asked where she'd heard that, the girl said her older sister had told her, when she was a freshman and her sister was a senior. Since it sounded like the sort of thing an older sister would say to freak out a sibling, I decided to try not to worry much about it, for now.

I skipped over some of the interviews to the parts called *Student X* and *Student Y*:

STUDENT X

As Student X wishes for her story to remain confidential, she spoke to us by phone on the condition of anonymity. Her words are reported here verbatim, with her permission. (X is Student X and Darkins, D, is myself.)

X: *It started with the whispering.*

I felt my breath catch at this, but continued reading:

It came from somewhere in my room. Two different nights. It was a female voice. After a couple of nights it went away, and I felt like I must have been dreaming.

D: Can you tell us what she was saying? The female voice?
X: *The first time, she said, "I see you when the lights go out." The next time, I couldn't hear what she was saying. I think I heard the name "Samuel," but it was too soft to really say for sure.*

My eyes blurred for a moment, and my heart jumped.
Samuel. Like Taylor's Samuel. It was a real thing. Student X had heard the *same damn thing* that Anthony and I had heard. And that presumably Taylor had heard.
Same ghost. Thirty years ago. Or a different but similar ghost? Who had selected Taylor as her replacement?
I was shaking. I wanted to turn on a light to calm my nerves. But I didn't want to wake up Star. I reread the lines and then kept reading:

X: *The first time, she said, "I see you when the lights go out." The next time, I couldn't hear what she was saying. I think I heard the name "Samuel," but it was too soft to really say for sure.*

191

I was too terrified to really listen, since I was jumping up and turning on the light, and then left the room. But just as soon as I thought it was going to be over, I heard it again. A week or so later. And I think it was two or three nights of silence after that. Just enough for me to be tricked into thinking I could relax. And then I saw her in my doorway. While I was sleeping.

D: Was your door open or closed?

X: *Closed. A sort of sound woke me up, like someone taking a breath, and there she was.*

D: Did she speak?

X: *No.*

D: Did she appear to see you? Make eye contact with you? Gesture at you in any way?

X: *I cried out, I think. And hid under the covers for a second. And there was a knocking sound on my door, then on my window. It was terrifying, like everything was coming apart. And when it stopped, she was gone.*

D: What did she look like?

X: *Sad. Long face. Like a horsey face, kind of. You know how some girls sometimes look like horses?*

I paused here without knowing quite why. Of all of the strange things that Student X had said, this struck me as particularly curious—that she would assess the attractiveness of a ghost's face.

D: I suppose. Do you remember anything else about how she looked?

X: *Not really.*

D: Her hair . . . her face . . . what she wore?

X: *Oh. She wore white.*

D: So let's go back to her looking sad. Not angry?

X: *I don't remember. Empty, blank, but sad.*

D: Okay. So why did you decide to start sleeping in other rooms?

X: *Wouldn't you?*

D: Hard to say. But yes, I'm sure I'd have my reservations about it.

X: *I started to feel out of control, not knowing when I might see her or hear her again. I didn't want to sleep in that room, by myself. Anywhere was better than that room.*

D: Did you see her anywhere else in the building, once you stopped sleeping in your room?

X: *Yes. When I slept on the couch in the sitting room on the first floor, I saw her slip by. I felt like she was pursuing me. That she wasn't just sad. She was targeting me for some reason.*

D: Did you ever think of talking to her?

X: *No. I don't want to talk to a dead person.*

D: Why not?

X: *I just don't want to. It scares me. Like it scares most people.*

D: Okay. That's fine. I understand.

X: *After that it felt like I couldn't sleep anywhere.*

D: Why didn't you go back to sleeping in friends' rooms?

X: *They kept making excuses why I couldn't. They didn't want to get in trouble.*

D: Would Ms. Finneran have punished them for it?

X: *Yeah. Ms. Finneran is a bitch and a freak of nature.*

D: Okay. Well, did you share with Ms. Finneran your concerns about the ghost?

X: *No. Not at first. Only when things got really bad. I was really tired, so I was probably babbling at that point. It scared the old battle axe.*

D: How do you know?

X: *She sent me to the nurse right away. We didn't have a long conversation.*

D: Okay. And now, about a year out from all of this . . . do you still believe you saw and heard a ghost? Or do you believe something else was happening?

X: *Since Mrs. Bradford says you're trying to help the school, the girls in Dearborn, I'll tell you the truth. Yes, I still believe I saw a ghost. I still believe she meant me some kind of harm. I had to say something different to the nurses and therapists, so I could go to college. My parents and I don't discuss it, and if they asked me, I would lie. But I'm telling you what I still feel. I wasn't crazy. Except until the ghost drove me crazy. And since I'm not there right now, she can't get at me. She can't make me crazy again. But I remember how it was. She was there. She was real. I don't know what she wanted, but I'm glad I got out of there.*

If I stopped reading, I would have to think about this *Samuel* consistency, which I could already tell was terrifying me before I had even let my mind fully process it.

So I kept reading:

STUDENT Y

Student Y came to Kathleen's attention early on in our stay at Dearborn Hall. From the beginning of our stay, we noticed Student Y's behavior was markedly withdrawn, to the point of being concerning, given last year's incident. When asked how she was, or asked about her schoolwork and activities, she gave minimal answers. According to other students and faculty, she had a reputation of being a high academic achiever in previous years but seemed less engaged this year. Having ascertained this early on, we watched Student Y carefully for signs that residence in Dearborn was affecting her adversely.

One of our challenges was to observe and check in on the wellness of students throughout our stay. Kathleen's attempts to befriend Student Y eventually bore fruit. The interview roughly transcribed below occurred on March 31, 1986. This is the discussion that took place between her and Student Y when Kathleen brought up Student X's incident last year. (Y is Student Y and K is Kathleen.)

Y: *I hope she's okay now.*
K: We hear she is.
Y: *Good. I've heard that, too.*

K: Did you have any concerns about living in Dearborn, after hearing what happened?
Y: *Not really.*

K: Have you experienced anything here yourself?
Y: *Yeah. I've experienced a lot of things.*

K: I mean, have you observed anything you couldn't explain . . . anything that felt like it could be supernatural?

Y: *Yeah, actually.*

K: Yeah? I'd love to hear about it.

Y: *(After some hesitation and coaxing) Well . . . I saw her.*

K: Saw who?

Y: *The ghost.*

K: When? Where?

Y: *A few weeks ago. In the hallway.*

K: How do you know it was the ghost and not just some other student?

Y: *She was there and she was gone. She was wearing a white nightgown. She didn't look like anyone who lives on my floor.*

K: What did she want, you think?

Y: *What most ghosts want, right? Just to be . . . seen? To let us know they exist?*

K: You seem remarkably calm about this.

Y: *Everyone makes way too big a deal about the ghost.*

K: You say ghosts should be acknowledged. . . . What makes you say this?

Y: *Well, isn't that what everyone says? And it's not like this is the only ghost I've ever seen before.*

K: When have you seen others?

Y: *In my house growing up. There was a ghost who'd stand near the couch and make faces at me. I stopped seeing him after I was like five.*

K: You weren't scared?

Y: *I think I was a little too young to realize this was something that should freak me out.*

K: What do you think he wanted?

Y: *I think he was bored. I think ghosts come out and play with kids for the same reason some living people kind of light up when they see a kid. It's a chance to be fun, to get something besides a regular humdrum grown-up reaction. Ghosts get used to being ignored, but know they might get something more out of a kid.*

K: If the ghost you saw was the same ghost that (Student X) saw last year, why do you think it had such a profound effect on her, while for you it just feels like a casual encounter?

Y: *Probably she was denying to herself that she even saw anything. The more she denied it, the more she pretended she didn't see it, the more the ghost wanted to get something out of her.*

The ghost probably didn't mean to freak her out that much. She probably wanted to have a civil interaction. By freaking out, it was like running from the ghost. So the ghost chased her, I guess, in a way.

K: Do you think you're clairvoyant, perhaps?

Y: *No. I don't think you have to be clairvoyant to see Sarah. So many people have talked about seeing her, I don't think it's a matter of clairvoyance.*

K: So how do you know Sarah saw you and was satisfied with your interaction?

Y: *Well, I haven't seen her since. I don't think anyone else has, either. This year, I mean.*

K: Did you say anything to her?
Y: *No, just kind of nodded and smiled.*

K: But she'll come back next year.
Y: *Yeah, maybe. That's what they say.*

K: Why do you think she keeps coming back?
Y: *I don't know. Maybe she can't help herself. Or maybe she just likes tradition. Windham girls are like that, I guess.*

It was too late to call Kathleen, but I wondered if Kathleen had Student X and Y's names somewhere. Or if maybe I could track them down. Maybe they were in the Haunteds Facebook group. They would be about my mother's age now—or just a little bit older. I wondered why one was so much more frightened of the ghost than the other.

I was intrigued by Student Y's casualness.

But I had a feeling I—and Taylor—could relate more to Student X's terror.

I was too tired to read on. Or just afraid I'd find something further in that would scare me even more than what I'd already read, and I'd never sleep again.

I closed my laptop and slid into bed. And then I started counting goats. I hadn't tried this since I was a kid. Even then I always counted goats instead of sheep because I thought goats were so much cuter. This time I named the goats as I counted:

Luna, Odysseus, Brawny, Harriet, Mathilda, Nibbles, Nugget, Thor, Johnny, Gloria.

Cool names, dumb names, cute names. After a while I was just thinking of names and not picturing any goats. Since a few minutes in, I knew it was all just an exercise to keep one particular name out of my head until the morning:

Samuel.

26

Once I was Taylor's friend, I couldn't change my mind.

Because if I was not her friend, I would be in her sights.

And I could not bear to have that sinking feeling again.

I was better at Windham than I'd been at home. And yet I didn't know how to swim on my own, not really. Taylor helped me stay above the surface. Not so much Taylor herself, consciously—but the fact of being Taylor's friend.

So when Taylor posted a selfie of herself and me in which Layla Lawson was in the background digging up her nose with a tissue, I had to assume she'd chosen that out of twenty other shots because she liked our smiles in that particular one.

When Taylor privately called Hannah Fort a "blobfish," I did laugh, because she does in fact have a morose resting face.

And when Taylor asked Toni Escobar, right after her big history presentation, if she'd had tuna fish for lunch, I figured it was some kind of private joke between them.

And so on and so forth.

I was used to Taylor's casual meanness by the end of sophomore year. And still I was a little stunned when she showed me that video right before the summer.

The footage was of Jocelyn Rose making out with Charlie Bronner in his room the night he'd had a party.

Charlie Bronner had the most parties of any day student. Technically his house was in walking distance to campus— although it was a long walk. His parents went away a lot, and he didn't have any siblings.

Taylor had been with him a little while when they were sophomores—until she got an older boyfriend. But they'd stayed friends, and she was always at his parties.

I'd been to a couple of his parties, but I hadn't gone to the one where she'd gotten the footage. Taylor hadn't mentioned it to me, saying later she knew how swamped I'd been with work that weekend. It was probably a lie. Sometimes she just didn't want me around. Or just neglected to invite me to things occasionally to make sure I would never assume, never take her power of invitation for granted.

The thing was—she knew Charlie and Jocelyn had been flirting with each other.

But Taylor had never liked Jocelyn much. And when she saw them cozying up on the couch early in the evening at the party, she told me, she knew Charlie's MO well enough that she had a hunch what was going to happen next. He was going to sneak Jocelyn up to his room and lock the door.

Taylor herself had been behind that locked door a couple of times.

And no, Taylor never explained the impulse very well— the impulse to go up there first, prop her fancy new iPhone up against his desk lamp, and hit Record. It was not an impulse I understood.

The party had gone on for several hours. But of course, Joce-lyn had the same curfew time as all the other boarding students. When the couple left Charlie's room, Taylor retrieved her phone before rushing out so she could catch curfew, too.

What she ended up with was three and a half hours of foot-age. More than half of it was of Charlie's empty room. But some of it was of Charlie and Jocelyn on Charlie's bed. Kissing at first—and then with both of their shirts off.

In the video, Charlie assured Jocelyn that he liked big nipples.

And Jocelyn told Charlie that no one had ever touched them before.

I watched it in Taylor's room. My mouth was hanging open by the end of it. Not so much because of what I'd just seen but the sheer audacity of Taylor managing to film it.

"Taylor," I said. "You need to delete this."

"Well, of course I will," she snapped. "What do you think I'm going to do, make a YouTube remix of him saying he likes big nipples?"

I was too stunned at these words to speak.

"But why . . ."

"I was bored, Haley. Why do I ever do anything?"

"Why did you even show me?" I put her phone down on her bed, screen down, horrified.

It took her a while to reply. She was busy scraping gray wax from her radiator. She'd accidentally left a bar of snowboard wax there and it had melted.

"I thought you might find it kind of interesting."

Typical Taylor. A twenty-dollar bar of wax and she'd let it melt. Oopsie!

"Why would I?" I demanded.

"Never mind," she mumbled. "I should just delete it."

"Yup," was all I said.

It was obvious later—the following fall—that I should have said more. But I don't think it was obvious then.

27

Seven Nights Left

And so.

Whatever fight she might have had left in her before Windham — that was gone by the end.

She was bitter and depleted by the night she died.

She was only sixteen.

So young, so tragic — how could she not become a ghost?

28

Sunday, February 3

THUNK THUNK THUNK!

I sat up. My heart raced.

"Star!" I gasped. Was that a knock at the door?

"Mmm . . . huh?"

"STAR, DID YOU HEAR THAT?" I yelled so she would wake up.

Despite the darkness, I could see Star stirring.

"What?" Star sounded groggy. "What is it, Haley?"

I tried to catch my breath. "Someone was knocking on the door."

"Then . . . shouldn't we answer it?" Star asked, still sleepy.

I'd found my phone under my pillow by then. "It's three a.m.," I hissed.

"Yeah." Star was getting out of her bed. "Only Anna would knock in the middle of the night. Like maybe this is . . ."

Star was almost at the door.

"Don't open it!" I gasped.

"Hello?" Star said to the door.

When there was no answer, she opened it. There was no one there.

"I was going to say that maybe it was some kind of drill." Star stepped out into the hallway and looked around.

"A drill? Then they'd use the alarm system."

"Well, I don't know. A lockdown drill? Anyway. No one's in the hall. Didn't you say you haven't been sleeping very well lately?"

"You didn't hear the knocking?" I said.

Star closed the door.

"Do you want me to turn the light on?" she asked.

"Maybe you should," I said.

The instant our beds and messy desks and Star's beluga whale poster were all in bright view, I felt dumb for being so scared.

"Maybe somebody needed, like, a tampon or something," Star said.

"There are a lot of obnoxious girls on this floor, Star, but no one obnoxious enough to consider that a three a.m. emergency."

Star shrugged. "If you say so. Do you know that houses make more noise in the coldest months? It has something to do with the dry air, and the contracting of the wood, or something. Houses make more pops and groans and maybe you just thought you heard knocking?"

My heart was no longer pounding in my ears.

"Where did you hear this?" I asked. "About noisy houses in the winter?"

"My dad told us that once, when we were staying at a rental

house in New Hampshire where we used to ski. My sister said she heard pops."

"That's brilliant," I said. "Maybe that's the reason there's a ghost in Dearborn only in January and February."

We were silent for a moment.

"Also, I used to dream of someone pounding on my door," I admitted.

Long ago, when I was eleven or twelve or thirteen. When I was a different girl.

Star looked puzzled for a moment, then looked away.

"Well, then that's probably what it was," she said.

Star was staring at her feet, scrutinizing the chipping purple paint on her toes. It seemed like I needed to say something more.

Earlier, I had been considering showing Anthony the Darkins papers first. But I felt an urgency in this moment. I was still shaking, and I didn't want to have to try to go back to sleep yet.

"I have something I want to show you, Star," I said.

◆◆◆

It was a relief to have an excuse to keep the light on.

Sitting up on my bed with my fleece blanket wrapped tight around me, I watched Star scrolling through the paranormal report on my computer, her lips moving and her eyes widening.

"This is *amazing*," Star said. "Is there any chance that it's a joke?"

I had to admit I hadn't thought of that.

"Umm . . . the lady who gave it to me . . . I don't think she would have a reason to mess with me."

Star grunted and kept reading.

"Did you see the part about the headmistress's mother yet?" I asked. "It shows that the ghost story was already circulating between 1905 and 1909."

"Yeah, I saw that," Star murmured. She didn't take her eyes off the screen.

"So your girl Stella, who died in 1918, probably wasn't the ghost. Or the original one, anyway."

Unless the original ghost selected Stella as her replacement, and then . . . I pushed the thought away.

"Right," Star said softly.

I had the feeling she wasn't listening to me.

"I'm really interested in Student X and, actually, even more, Student Y," I said. "I wonder if there's any way to find them. We know at least that they graduated in 1985 and 1986."

Star didn't reply. She got up, put my laptop back into my hands, and opened one of her desk drawers.

"They called her Sarah in Black," she said, snatching a couple of overstuffed manila folders out of the drawer. "And maybe sometimes *Sarah Black*."

"Yeah, I saw that," I said. "The ghost who does wardrobe changes."

"That's not what I was thinking about." Star knelt on the floor and scattered the contents of one of the folders across the rug, plucking out the Dearborn group photo we'd been looking at a few days ago.

"Sarah in Black," she said, looking from me to the photo. "Sarah *in* Black? Or Sarah Black?"

"Both, I guess. Like it says."

"I'm thinking they meant *Sarah Black*. That that came first, and then it turned into *Sarah in Black*, or a Sarah wearing black, or whatever. I'm thinking that's the one to pay attention to. A *name* that got adjusted or misunderstood over the years. *Sarah Black*."

"There's no Sarah Black in that picture," I pointed out—as I would have remembered. "Even if you're right."

"But there was a Leonora Black, remember?" Star jabbed her finger at the photocopied picture. "Caroline Bromley's friend? The one I don't know as much about?"

"Leonora is a pretty different name from Sarah," I said.

"I wasn't thinking Leonora is the ghost. I don't know much about her, but I think she lived to around the 1940s, just like Caroline Bromley. But that's not the point. There's a letter . . . actually, two letters . . ."

Star opened the other folder and started flipping through pages.

"Now, I don't have *all* of Abigail Ashton's letters photocopied, but I thought I had all of the ones that said anything related to Caroline. And there were two that mentioned someone named Sally. I hadn't known exactly what she was talking about, but—oh. I think this is it. Or this is one of them."

Star lifted a sheet up to her face and read, " 'Leonora is still distressed and missing Sally. Her latest letter from home reports that she is doing better, content to be back home, baking and keeping house with her aunt.' "

"Wait," I said. "Back up. This is a letter from Abigail Ashton, Caroline Bromley's friend? The one from the picture you showed me?"

"Yes. I had wondered who Sally was, and I had seen another letter that made me think it was Leonora's sister. I'll have to find it. I hadn't pursued it, of course, because it wasn't all that relevant to my project about Caroline. Just a curiosity, since I'd wondered about Caroline's friends."

"You think her friend Leonora had a sister Sally."

"Yeah. Remember, she was mentioned in the letter about Halloween? She was too shy to dress up as Alice?"

"Yeah. But her name was *Sally* Black."

"Sally was a nickname for Sarah. Back then. I mean, it still can be. But now it's usually a separate name. But anyway, if there was a Sally Black, she might have also been Sarah Black."

"Okay," I said.

"And doesn't it sound to you like this Sally was maybe a student with them here at the school, but went home?" Star handed me the photocopied letter.

"Yeah, maybe," I said, skimming the slanted script of the letter. "Probably."

On the photocopy, Star had at some point highlighted a line of the letter. It said, *Caroline has been trying to cheer Leonora— gathering her flowers and leaving small gifts. I don't think it is having much effect, sadly.*

"Do you highlight stuff that mentions Caroline?" I asked.

"Sometimes."

I nodded, hoping I'd someday have the same amount of passion for something—anything—that Star did for Caroline Bromley.

I read the rest of the letter, which was mostly about weather and a difficult French class.

"This isn't the only letter of Abigail's in which Sally is mentioned," Star said. "But I don't have copies of *all* of her letters, of course. I only copied things directly relevant to Caroline Bromley, but I could go back and try to find the ones where I saw Sally come up."

"If you think a Sally . . . or Sarah . . . Black was a student here during Caroline's time, how do you confirm that?"

"It might not be all that hard. Aside from Abigail's letters— the archives has student rosters for almost every year."

"Even that long ago?"

Star nodded. "They're just lists of names, mostly. But they're better than nothing. The archives are open on Monday. Oh my gosh, my heart is pounding. I can't wait."

"Me neither," I said. "But what do we do *now*, then?"

Star took a deep breath. "Maybe we Twizzle? And try to forget about it until we can get into the archives?"

"I guess."

Star took her king-size Twizzlers bag out of her desk drawer. Watching her, I said, "How's Jocelyn? Are you guys still in touch?"

Star hesitated, then extended a Twizzler to me. "Yeah. Not a real lot, but yeah."

"You just haven't mentioned her all year," I said softly.

Our eyes met as I reached for the candy.

"You haven't asked," she said in a low voice, hesitating before she let go of the Twizzler. "But she's okay. Not great."

"Is she at another boarding school or . . . ?" I peered casually out the blinds. There was a gentle flurry coming down, pretty in the lamplight.

"No. She's at a public school in her hometown."

"Which is where?" I turned from the window to look at Star.

"Connecticut," she answered.

"Oh." I nodded and nibbled the end of the Twizzler.

"Apparently it's a good school. It's just not where she expected to be this year, you know?"

"She could have stayed here."

I pictured Jocelyn—raven-haired, petite, perfect in the Abigail role in *The Crucible*. Becoming the character so convincingly that you forgot that she wore ill-fitting pastel baby doll dresses, that she made humming noises when she chewed food, that she followed Mr. Packer around like a puppy dog sometimes.

"She didn't feel she could." Star paused. "And it would've been pretty hard, I think. Did you see the video last year?"

"Yeah," I admitted, though a little stunned by the bluntness of the question. "Uh . . . did you?"

Star shook her head. "I heard about it before it got to me. Once I knew who and what it was, of course I wasn't going to watch it."

I shouldn't have brought up Jocelyn if I didn't want to talk about the video. But I had wanted to ask for a long time. I had wanted to hear she was doing okay.

"What colleges is she applying to?" I asked.

"Art and design places, mostly. Like there's an art college in New York she wants to go to. She's afraid of how the school switch will look on applications, though. She has some new guidance counselor who had to write a letter explaining that it

212

had nothing to do with academics. She's worried that will draw even more attention to it."

"That does sound kinda . . . tough," I said. "Tough to decide."

"I don't know what she decided to do, in the end. I didn't ask. I think she found even the dilemma kind of horrifying. Anyway, one way or the other, it seems she doesn't like to talk to me much anymore. Like, nothing personal. It's just that everything Windham is kind of shitty for her to think about."

I was quiet for a minute. Star and Jocelyn had been such good friends last year—this all seemed hard to believe. They ate together, walked to class together—always hunched close together conspiratorially, giggling at something or other.

"She'll feel so much better when she gets into that school," I said. "I bet she gets in wherever she applies."

"Yeah, well. I hope so. I'll be happy for her when she figures out where she's going, when she can feel relieved that no one cares she switched schools. Then she'll really be able to say she's put it behind her, you know?"

"Yeah," I said, and tied my Twizzler into a knot.

"Can we turn the light out now?"

Star sounded tired. I nodded, flipped off the light, and felt my way back to bed in the dark.

29

Star was gone by the time I woke up. It was past Sunday break-fast time, and I wondered if she was off somewhere stroking Mark Byrne's sideburns. Wherever she was, I hoped she was in-doors. My old boyfriend, Jake, and I used to only ever make out outside—because it was really the only place you could avoid getting caught. I got used to rolling around in wet, nearly fro-zen leaves, and having numb hands and face at the end of an evening.

I couldn't remember now if I ever really liked Jake that much. I pulled myself up in bed, hugged my knees, and watched the late-morning sleet through the window. I kind of enjoyed the sound of it pattering on the glass. It was one of those weekend mornings when Dearborn never seemed to get warm enough, and the minutes didn't seem to want to pass. Wrapping myself in the fleece blanket my mother had bought me, I considered calling her. I missed her, but everything I said to her was always just code for *I'm okay now. Don't worry. I'm okay now.* Some-times I got tired of talking in that code. And sometimes—like now—it felt like lying.

Since I'd missed breakfast, I found a protein bar and nibbled it while I reached for my laptop. I opened up the Darkins file and scrolled up and down, trying to find the parts I hadn't read yet.

SUMMARY/CONCLUSIONS

As always, I am hesitant to draw any conclusions in matters of the paranormal. In this case, I am doubly so.

Dearborn Hall appears to be a place with multiple afflictions—a ghost, an intermittent poltergeist, confused adolescent psychic tensions, with possible telekinetic results—or none, in which case the student population has a peculiar talent for storytelling and imaginative self-deception. Either way, it is a place of convergence of much tension and conflicted psychic energy—that much is clear. The unique problem of this setting is that so many of these usually isolated phenomena appear to be occurring in one place—intertwining with each other, almost competing with each other.

What is most stunning to me is the possibility of a unique form of group delusion that appears to span over more than a century. The unusual persistence of the Dearborn ghost stories appears to have brought about consistent—almost yearly—experience of the paranormal within the student population in this dormitory. Whether that ghost story tradition makes some individual students more sensitive to actual paranormal activity, more apt to interpret uncomfortable or unusual experiences as paranormal, or more susceptible to mild to moderate delusions of ghostly experiences is undetermined.

In drawing tentative conclusions, one cannot ignore the

curious factor of the portrait of Sarah Dearborn that hung on the wall for several decades, and which appears to have resulted in the ghost stories about a young woman in a black dress—Sarah in Black—until years after its removal. It is indeed a severe and arresting portrait—Kathleen and I viewed a photograph of it. Interestingly, in the years after its removal (due to water damage), stories about "Sarah" appear to more often feature a girl in a white nightgown. This suggests that the student population's stories—and their experience of the ghost—were influenced by the portrait. This indicates that over the years, the ghost has changed along with student lore.

I paused here. I'd heard of this portrait, which had hung in the front hall of the dorm for so many decades. What had become of it? "Water damage," obviously. But when it had been damaged, was it simply tossed in a dumpster? Maybe there was a photo of it somewhere.

I kept reading:

> I am not arguing here that all of the paranormal "Sarah" sightings and experiences have been solely imagined ones— although evidence indicates that some are fabricated—but that this setting might contain an unusual collective psychic energy that influences and intensifies student experiences of a ghostly embodiment. This possibility is fascinating and worthy of further study.
>
> It is undeniable that each year or two or three, an individual student has an intense personal experience of the paranormal—ghost, poltergeist, or some pairing of the two.

As in my writings about Tina Resch—which Mrs. Bradford knows well—I believe here that the more problematic elements of the phenomenon are exacerbated by the mental and emotional distress of the victim(s). This is not to say that mental and emotional distress is the cause of the phenomenon. But it is my firm belief that a victim of psychic disturbance is most likely to be harmed if he or she is not secure and supported in other aspects of his or her emotional life. In those cases, the ghost or poltergeist is given more psychic space in which to wreak havoc.

The difference in response from Student X and Student Y to their paranormal encounters speaks to this problem. One student became very ill as a result of her experience with the "ghost." The other was mentally equipped to see it, to acknowledge it, but not cede any emotional power to it.

With that in mind, I turn, with some concern, to my general observances of the students in their day-to-day lives. Life in Dearborn is, for many students, isolating, exclusively academic, stressful, and cold. While many of the students are very mature, the depressive effects of being separated from one's family take their toll. The occasional small poltergeist is likely to find a carnival of opportunity here, and develop more power and energy than it would otherwise, in another setting.

Given Dearborn's long and persistent history of ghost stories, it appears that whatever paranormal energy afflicts the building—a lingering and unsettled spirit, perhaps—has been given more force and collective energy by the (mostly negative) attention paid to it by its residents over the years. There is not a single student who lives here who does not know who "the Winter Girl" is. Students fear her—and even anticipate living in fear of her as they move their way up through the grades and then reside in Dearborn for their final year.

I believe the most effective remedies here might be regular cleansing activities (such as sage burning) and, more importantly, closer attention paid to the emotional well-being of all students housed in this dorm. Mental and emotional strain appears to make individual students vulnerable to the myriad paranormal influences—both real and imagined, I daresay—that have converged in this unique place, and to exacerbate it. It is also the element over which school staff and administration have the greatest control. We have limited powers over restless spirits and unruly poltergeists. But our ability to limit their influences is strong when we recognize the need to take care of the members of the community most vulnerable to them.

I skimmed the Student X material again, my eyes stalling at the words *Student X's grandparents are generous donors to the school.* Whoever she was, she had this in common with Taylor. In Taylor's case, it was her parents.

And I considered Bronwyn Spruce for a moment. I was pretty sure she was a legacy student. That didn't mean her parents or grandparents or any relatives gave money to the school. But it seemed likelier for her than for some.

I couldn't think of a tactful way to ask this in a text to Bronwyn, though. And it seemed unlikely to me that a ghost would care much about money. Generous financial contributors to the school, however, were more likely to end up in the larger, more desirable single rooms in the side hallways.

It was a little tricky, how this happened. Technically there was a housing lottery at Windham. But there were all kinds of exceptions to that rule—and a lot of the most financially well-off students seemed to have vague and self-identified "special needs" that required them to be closer to the bathroom, or by themselves in a big room, or have more windows because of their seasonal affective disorder, or whatever. And so they had ways around the lottery system.

Maybe one of those more desired rooms was where the ghost resided? Or maybe the ghost just preferred those parts of the dorm—down the shorter, quieter hallways where the rooms were bigger? Maybe the ghost didn't care how a girl ended up in her space—like through money and influence. Maybe she just happened to haunt anyone who ended up there.

Although Kathleen Darkins had mentioned the upper floors having more psychic tension, I had never heard any Dearborn lore that identified a particular floor or room that was specifically haunted. But maybe "Sarah" still had her favorite spots in the building. Maybe she liked the same rooms the rich girls did?

It seemed too early to text Bronwyn, but at some point I'd ask her which specific room she lived in senior year. And it might be worth asking the Facebook "Haunteds" the same question.

I went back to the report, read a couple of student interviews, and then looked at the introduction and conclusion again. Both mentioned a case of someone named *Tina Resch*—related to something Darkins had studied before and that also apparently interested Headmistress Bradford.

I clicked out of the Darkins file and onto Google, where I typed *Tina Resch*. Up came a Wikipedia page, an article from something called "Murderpedia," and countless articles with names like "Paranormal Files: The Curious Case of Tina Resch," "Tina Resch: Telekinetic Mom or Deceptive Killer?" and "The Real-Life Poltergeist of Tina Resch."

Settling against my pillows, I began to read.

The first article clarified the difference between a ghost and a poltergeist. A ghost, it said, is generally thought to be the lingering spirit of a dead person. A poltergeist is a somewhat more mysterious entity that causes flying or moving objects, loud noises, or other disturbances—usually in the presence of a particular person. A poltergeist was often, though not always, thought to be caused—unconsciously—by telekinetic energy from the person it plagued.

Tina Resch was a teenager from Ohio who supposedly had a poltergeist. In her presence, plates would smash into walls; lamps would spontaneously fall off tables; radios and other household appliances would turn themselves on and off unexpectedly. In 1984, when she was fourteen, her story hit national news and the media descended on her parents' home.

Before this all began, Tina had had a very troubled and difficult life. Abandoned as a baby, she was adopted by the Resches when she was two. They were strict parents, and she rebelled. She did poorly in school and was often in trouble. When she was thirteen, her best friend died in a car accident. Shortly after that, the poltergeist activity began to develop around Tina. It got to be so unsettling and dangerous that the Resches had to send some of their foster children away to stay in different homes.

The media was in and out of her parents' house for a while—that is, until a camera she didn't realize was rolling caught her pulling a lamp off a table, causing most previously interested observers to conclude she had faked the whole ordeal for attention. She fell out of the public eye, left her adoptive family, had a string of abusive boyfriends, and then gave birth to a daughter, Amber.

Tina Resch was in jail now—because in 1992, Amber died at age three, probably at the hands of Tina's boyfriend, and Tina was thought to be involved. She'd gotten a plea deal to avoid the death penalty.

I slammed the laptop shut, wishing I could unread the words, unknow about Tina Resch. Plates flying around a kitchen was one thing. But the dark place where her story ended—I didn't even want to think about that. Ronald Darkins knew she was a person whose mental health needed attention, poltergeist or no poltergeist. He had no idea how right he was.

How strange that Betty Bradford had been so interested in Tina's story. Then again, it was not such a dark story in 1986. Back then, it was just a story about a girl who might have a poltergeist or might be a faker.

Faker.

I got up and got dressed to shake the word, shake Tina Resch, shake the knocking I'd heard in my dreams last night. When I headed out for the bathroom, I was startled to see someone kneeling in front of Taylor's old door in a red flannel shirt. Stepping closer, I saw it was the maintenance man who occasionally came into the dorm to tinker with the old radiators or fix a broken showerhead. He was hunched over his toolbox, muttering *"Shitdamn."* All one word. I bit my lip to keep from giggling. Something about his delivery reminded me of my dad. I crept up behind him as he pulled out a piece of sandpaper.

There was something scratched in the door above him.

I MADE HER JUMP.

I gasped and the guy turned around.

"Yup," he said. "Not pretty. They called me a half hour ago. But I'll have it all painted over in no time."

I nodded. "That's good," I said.

I knew I should leave him to get back to his work, but I couldn't quite move yet.

"So don't worry about it," he added, watching me, scratching his brown beard.

"Um, were there any hearts carved with that?"

"Hearts?" he repeated.

"Uh . . . ," I said. "Never mind."

"Okay," he said, and started sanding.

"They pay you overtime for this?" I asked. "It's Sunday."

He smiled, surprised. "Yeah."

"Good," I said, and went into the bathroom to catch my breath.

Standing at one of the sinks, I stared into the mirror.

I MADE HER JUMP.

JUMP.

JUMP.

JUMP.

The word echoed in my ears until it was indistinguishable from the *thunk thunk thunk* I'd thought I'd heard in the night, and then from the pulse of my heart. The carved heart in the laundry room flashed in my head, and then I had to grip the edge of the sink to steady myself. My vision was feeling spotty, my knees a little weak.

I had not imagined the words.

The words were really there this time.

I bumbled into a stall, locked the door, and sat on the closed toilet. After a few slow breaths, I felt better. And then my phone buzzed. A group text:

Mandatory hall meeting before dinner, 5:15. Have a good Sunday, all. Anna

Well, it was clear what the meeting would be about. Anna thought someone was fucking around, vandalizing Taylor's old door.

Anna probably didn't believe in ghosts. But Anna didn't know about Student X and Student Y and all the rest.

My phone buzzed again. I jumped. This time it kept buzzing. Someone was calling me.

"Hello?" I said.

"Haley? This is Lily Bruno. Weren't we supposed to talk now?"

"Oh!" I said. "Right."

"I decided to call instead because I have an appointment in like an hour and I didn't want to keep playing phone tag."

I unlocked myself from the bathroom stall. "Well, thanks for being willing. I know it's a hard topic."

"I'm sure it's just as hard for you." Lily paused. "I know what good friends you were. I remember seeing you together all the time."

"We were on-again, off-again, but yeah," I admitted, pushing through the bathroom door and scurrying back to my room.

"Everyone is," Lily offered. Which sounded a little weird to me. Because I didn't think it was true.

"So, you wanted to hear about that night?" Lily prompted. "Do I have that right?"

"Yes. I know it's kind of strange. I wasn't ready to hear the details last year . . . It was just too hard. But now that I live in Dearborn, right on the same floor . . ."

"They have you living on the *same* floor?" Lily asked incredulously.

"Yeah. I'm here . . ."

Entering my room, I breathed a sigh of relief to see that Star was still gone.

"What the fuck is wrong with those housing people?" Lily demanded.

"It's not their fault. . . ." I pulled my fleece tighter around my shoulders. "I could have requested a different floor. I just . . . didn't. I didn't think of it. My friends Alex and Maylin are on this floor, though, too."

"Oh," Lily said absently. "So then . . . what did you want to ask me?"

"Just what you remember about that night," I murmured. "That's all."

"Okay. Well, I didn't see her that night at all. I can't even place the last time I saw her. Like if I saw her at dinner that night, it didn't register in my head."

"Okay," I said. Tears were forming in my eyes as I watched the sleet stipple my window. I decided not to influence her story with any of the things I'd seen, read, or heard in the past few days.

"But then that night, I woke up . . . It was after two . . . I

224

woke up when I heard something in her room. Um, like a struggle, like a bang. Like her struggling in there."

"Screaming, too?" I offered—even though I knew this was
the wrong thing to say. I was leading the witness.

"No. I heard Jayla said she heard screaming, and maybe she
did. But I didn't."

"Okay. So . . . struggling. Like maybe someone else was in
there with her?" I asked.

"Well, I've had that thought before, but . . ." Lily was silent
for a moment. "No, it wasn't like a fight. I think it was all just
her at her window, like trying to get it open. You know how
those old windows are heavy, and get stuck. The struggle seemed
at the window end of the rooms, although I can't say for sure.
I heard a bang at that end of the room, and then a sound . . . a
screechy sound . . . the old window opening, I guess."

Lily's voice was a little shaky as she continued.

"And I looked out. That's when I started screaming. And I
ran out of my room, and I was calling 911, and then Jayla was
there in the hall, too, knocking on Taylor's door, and Jayla just
pushed her way in and the room was empty and cold and we
both ran to the window. The next few minutes are a blur because I was just there at the window, still screaming, and Jayla
at least was able to keep her head on enough to go get Tricia—
the RD. I feel like Tricia had to drag me out of there, I was in
such shock."

"I can imagine," I said, and paused, hesitated. "Were you
and Taylor ever friendly?"

"No, not really. We were never really in the same classes."

Lily, from what I remembered, was an overachiever, like

Alex. Taylor never knocked herself out with a ton of studying or AP stress.

"Do you think it was more the drugs or more of a suicide?" I asked.

"I really can't say," Lily said softly. "I wasn't in the room. I wasn't . . . in her head. I don't think anyone can answer that question. All I can tell you is what I heard from the next room."

"But the idea that she was having some kind of hallucination . . . that's a reasonable explanation to you?"

"Reasonable . . . well . . . it's about as close to reasonable as anyone could get, I guess."

"Did you see or hear her acting weird at any time before that night? Like, in the week before? In the middle of the night, or anything?"

I was wondering if anyone along that corridor had heard her shout and drop her phone and run into the bathroom the night she'd filmed herself.

"No . . . not that I can remember. But like I said, I didn't really know her."

I stared at the papers covering Star's desk.

"Do you believe in ghosts?" I asked.

Lily was silent.

"Are you there?" I asked.

"Yeah . . . I just . . . I don't know. Sometimes. When someone would tell a really scary ghost story in the dark, maybe when I was younger . . ."

Tap tap tap.

Someone was at my door.

"Just a second!" I called.

"Sounds like I should let you go," Lily said.

"I guess," I admitted.

Lily was so soft-spoken and calm, I wished we had a reason to stay on longer. But I had a feeling this conversation was painful for her.

"Thanks for talking," I said.

"Anytime," she replied. "Good luck with everything."

We hung up and I opened my door. Alex was there, poking at her phone.

"Was there French homework?" she asked, looking up and stepping in.

"No," I said.

"Okay . . . great." Alex looked like she was weighing whether to say something more.

"So—dorm meeting tonight, huh?" I said.

"Yeah," Alex said, sighing—probably with relief. That I had brought it up, and she wouldn't have to. "Are you okay? I was wondering if you saw what . . . happened. You weren't at breakfast."

Alex looked tired. Since she was pale, she always looked slightly anemic—even at her most energetic. But today it seemed a little worse.

"I'm fine," I lied.

Alex looked skeptical.

"Hey . . . I've been meaning to ask how your mom is," I said gently, sitting on my bed.

It would be very much like Alex to get bad health news from home, not tell us, and then just try to plow on through with her crazy-ambitious schedule as if nothing was wrong. I felt bad that it had taken me this long to ask—given what Maylin had told me in the car yesterday.

"Very good, actually," Alex said, brightening a little. "She's going on a little trip with her sister. To the Grand Canyon and Las Vegas."

"Oh, nice. When?"

"Umm . . . a couple weeks." Alex moved aside a few books and a pair of jeans to sit on my bed. "I don't remember the exact dates, since I'll just be here anyway."

Alex glanced around the room—taking in my messy desk and Star's even messier desk—piled up with overstuffed manila folders of archive photocopies.

"Did you ever end up talking to Lily?" she asked.

"Yeah. I was just getting off the phone with her when you knocked."

"Did that . . . help?"

"Not really," I admitted.

Alex nodded.

"My AP physics grade is going to shit," she mumbled, still looking around the room, this time letting her gaze settle on Star's beluga poster. There was something irresistible about that thing. Mesmerizing, even.

"I'm sure that's not true," I offered.

"It is true. You know what's frustrating? That people get this idea of you in their head, and they can't let go of it. So they can't ever see it if you're struggling. It's not real to them."

I sucked in a breath.

"I'm sorry," I said.

"It's not your fault," she snapped, so angrily it felt like she meant the exact opposite.

I stared at her in spite of myself. Her face crumpled a little.

"I'm sorry . . . ," she said, shaking her head as she looked away from me. "I've had a couple of rough nights."

"Rough how?" I asked. "If you're having trouble sleeping, at least we can commiserate."

"Oh . . . no. It's not that. I would *love* to sleep. I've just been up late catching up on stuff."

"Really? You didn't by any chance knock on my door in the middle of last night, did you?"

Alex looked startled by the question, then shook her head. "Uh . . . no."

We were both silent for a moment. I felt like I had to offer something more.

"Do you ever feel like when you leave here," I said, "you're going to have to deal with a bunch of stuff you left hanging before you came? Like leaving here isn't just a whole new chapter, but going back to all the shit you forgot when you came four years ago?"

Alex gazed at me for a moment, expressionless.

"No," she said. "But maybe that's just me. Whatever I was doing or thinking four years ago feels very far away. It's the *next* few things I need to do that I can't really seem to manage."

I saw now that there were tears forming at the corners of her eyes. I didn't know whether I should look away or get closer to her. Alex and I were always like this. Even when we were fourteen. We gave each other respectful distance.

"I know what it's like to feel like you're sinking," I said slowly.

"Sinking?" Alex wiped her eyes with the sleeve of her black cardigan and sat up straighter—already recovered or feigning recovery.

I hesitated. *Sinking* was a word I used in my head when I was younger, before I came here. Before I knew the word *depression* might actually apply.

"To feel, um, overwhelmed," I said.

Alex looked like she was considering this.

"Have you ever taken sleeping pills?" she asked suddenly. "Like Ambien?"

"No," I replied, surprised. "I don't think doctors like to prescribe that to minors."

"So you don't have anything like that?"

"No . . . why?"

Alex shrugged. "Just curious."

"Do you . . . feel like you might *need* something like that?" I asked. Maybe that was what the therapist appointment had been about—if there had been one. Alex going looking for a little chemical help sleeping. Which likely no one would honor without permission from her parents or the school or probably both.

"No . . . I just wondered if it had ever gotten that bad for you. Since we've never really talked about it much."

"Well, I've never thought to ask a doctor for something like that. They always tell me to try soothing teas, to not drink coffee, to not be on a screen before bed." I rolled my eyes at the last one.

"That all sounds kind of lame," Alex offered.

"Yeah," I agreed. "It is. But the coffee one is probably a good idea."

"I guess I should get back to work." Alex looked reluctant as she got off the bed. "See you at lunch, maybe?"

"Yeah," I agreed. "Later."

After Alex had closed the door behind her, I waited for a few moments, listening to her footsteps recede down the hallway. I wondered what had been the real purpose of her visit. It seemed unlikely that she'd really forgotten what the French homework was—and she should know by now that I wasn't the most reliable source of academic information. More likely she was checking to see if I was okay after seeing or hearing about Taylor's door. Or she'd come specifically to ask "casually" about sleeping pills.

I sat on my bed and closed my eyes. A rush of recent sounds and words washed over me.

Thunk thunk thunk

Life in Dearborn is, for many students, isolating, exclusively academic, stressful, and cold. . . . The occasional small poltergeist is likely to find a carnival of opportunity here. . . .

I heard a bang at that end of the room, and then a sound . . . a screechy sound . . . the old window opening, I guess. . . .

Have you ever taken sleeping pills?

I made her jump.

Those last ones drowned the others out.

I made her jump.

Over and over again. I leapt up from my bed, hoping

movement would break the repetition in my head. Then, scrambling to the closet, I yanked the pull string.

In the back left corner of the closet, I had four purple plastic bins. One was filled with random junk: papers I couldn't bear to throw away from last year (like the only A grade Ms. Garrison had ever given me in English), old candy I didn't like much but might need when pulling an all-nighter, a couple of random things from Jake, hair elastics, a purse I rarely used—black with a starry brocade. My mother had gotten it for me at a second-hand store. I loved it, but there was no occasion to use it here at Windham-Farnswood.

I pushed my hand into the front pocket of the purse, and there they were: my key to Taylor's old room and her burner phone. Where I'd left them last October. Was it October? Yes, it was. Taylor had left a little early for October break. I had stayed behind because I always did. No cheap flights, and *Thanksgiving will be here before you know it.* That's what my mom and I would say over the phone, anyway.

And it was that last day before Fall Break that the dean's message hit everyone's box. Dr. Ivins was disturbed at the circulation of a certain video on students' cell phones and social media—not by its contents, but by the gross violation of privacy. She would be conducting a thorough investigation, effective immediately. And anyone who had information about the incident was advised to come forward. Failure to do so would result in expulsion.

It was kind of serendipity that I'd had Taylor's key. Kind of not. She always left it with me when she got to go away and I didn't. She would let me hang out in her room if I wanted a break from my roommate, Maya—and let me play with her fancy devices, since she wouldn't always take them all with her.

So I had the key when she called from New York. I had it when she asked me to go to her room and find the burner phone and get rid of it. The one she'd sent the video to—of Jocelyn and Charlie—before she'd then texted it anonymously to a bunch of kids we knew.

If you have any doubt, just throw all the damn phones away. She had enough money to cover them all.

They're not going to break in and search your room, or anyone's room. I'm pretty sure that's illegal, I had assured her.

I would still feel better knowing that it's gone. I'll be able to enjoy my vacation a little better.

It was that line that broke me—that made me decide I hated her.

This wasn't like the Avon deodorant incident or the girl she called *Blobfish* or the time she was wailing in the library stacks. This didn't make me frightened for my fragile self. This made me *angry.* She'd tried, when I'd first found out that she'd distributed the video, to say that it was a stupid impulse. But the fact that it required her to go into Derby to purchase a burner phone—that proved it had taken some forethought. And while I understood about being jealous—God knows, I understood *that*—I did not understand how the fact of a nerdy and unassuming girl getting a stupid school-play part over her could bring out such cruelty, or such determination. Since when did she even care about things like school productions?

That weekend I got lots of studying done—and took long walks, crunching endless leaves underfoot, going over my words—my plan—for Taylor so intensely that sometimes I could feel my lips moving dramatically, my eyelids fluttering. I was giving a speech to the biting autumn wind.

But when Taylor returned, I surprised myself. I actually gave the speech to *her.* And then we weren't friends.

I thought of these things as I gripped the key in my fingers. We weren't the kind of friends who wore each other's clothes— she was way taller, and my clothes were all from Target anyway. We weren't the kind of friends who gave each other birthday gifts—hers was in the summer, when we were apart, and I always insisted I didn't want anything when mine came around in March. So I had very little to remember her by, really.

I pulled my coat on, shoved the key and phone into my pocket, and zipped it forcefully. After grabbing my hat, I closed my door behind me and didn't bother to lock it.

It was still sleeting when I got outside. The tiny ice specks felt like pinpricks on my cheeks.

At first I took a couple of steps toward north campus, intending to walk to Upper Pond. But then I thought better of it. I wanted that key and phone to be farther away—off school grounds, never to be found. I turned in the other direction, heading for the campus gates.

☙❧

Cars shushed by on the main road. I thought of my mother's warning about her old boyfriend and townies like him. I think Heathsburg had become more suburban since then. Practically everyone had a Subaru or a Volvo, it seemed like. Everyone drove respectfully.

I blinked against the driving sleet.

I won't tell anyone about the burner phone, okay? I told Taylor when she returned at the end of Fall Break.

And then there were my words to Assistant Dean Wickman when she questioned everyone who was at the party—or associated with anyone from the party—two days later:

Well, the party was a long time ago. I remember I wasn't invited to the party. I remember being kind of sad about it. But Taylor came back early so we could watch a movie. Told me it was lame and I hadn't missed much.

Cold-blooded. I could lie quite well when I had a lot riding on it. And what I had riding on it was freedom from Taylor.

And then, that night, to Taylor—

This is the only time I'm going to lie for you. Don't worry about the burner phone. I'm not going to show it to anyone, but I'm keeping it, for now. But I need to take a break, Taylor. A break from all of this. I'm going to eat at my own dorm tonight.

And I'd slithered on home to Barton, feeling bloated with pride—as if I'd just swallowed large prey. Never mind that whenever I saw Taylor after that, I froze and often broke into a sweat—reminding me that I'd been the prey all along, and always would be.

Yes, I'd blackmailed and dumped her. But I was still terrified of her. It had been a gamble. And Taylor jumped before I found out if I'd won.

Yes. Cold-blooded.

So cold-blooded, the words *I made her jump* just might apply.

✦✦✦

When I got to the 7-Eleven, I fished the key and burner phone out of my pocket and tossed them both into the trash by the front entrance. Then I went inside and bought a hot chocolate— the kind that sputters out of a metal machine. It was too sweet, but it kept me half-warm for the long walk back to my dorm. As I sipped and walked, I thought about what Jayla had told me about Taylor's temporarily lost laptop, discarded in the library Lost and Found. Was it possible something was on that laptop that someone wanted to get their hands on? Some proof of something? Well, if it was the original Jocelyn and Charlie footage they were looking for, they didn't find it there.

And no one would ever find it now.

Not that it much mattered. Taylor couldn't get in trouble anymore.

30

Hard to sleep after the words on Taylor's door.

No denying them now. No blaming them on my overactive imagination. Half the floor had seen them, and Anna, and the maintenance man.

Shitdamn.

And then there was Anna's circus of a meeting.

Vandalism of school property is a serious offense. Vandalism in the dormitory is especially egregious because this is a safe space, a sanctuary.

Fuck your sanctuary. My friend died here.

And Anna didn't say exactly what the punishment would be. Which was odd. She just basically said "No more funny business" in ten different SAT word-salad ways.

But forget all that. Forget ALL of that, for now, Haley.

Try to sleep.

You need to go to sleep.

You know what kind of things happen when you don't sleep.

The sleepwalking was bad enough. But the bed-wetting was the really horrific problem. My frantic online research had informed me that this problem was extremely uncommon in girls. And that nonetheless I would probably outgrow it. When I arrived at Windham-Farnswood, it had not happened in over a year. And still, the possibility terrified me.

Possibility became reality one October morning of my first year, when Alex was my roommate. I woke up to the shamefully familiar sensation of a squishy bed. I did some panicked calculations in my head. I had three full sets of sheets. So I could maybe throw these ones out if that was the easiest way to get rid of them quickly. I could have my mom send another set, or I could catch the next bus to the shopping center on the weekend. But what if I wet the extra sheets in the meantime? It was only Monday, I didn't really want to involve my mother, and these things seemed to happen in bunches.

No, I would need to wash them. I would skip dinner to do it discreetly, if I had to. For now, I just had to get them hidden away and sealed somewhere they wouldn't smell.

I hopped up and changed my pajamas. Then I tackled the sheets, balling up the top sheet tight and cramming it into a plastic grocery store bag since I didn't have a larger garbage bag. I started to do the same with the fitted sheet when I heard movement behind me—the rustling of Alex's sheets. My crinkling of the plastic bags had awoken her.

With my heart thudding, I finished shoving my second sheet into a plastic bag before turning around. Alex's gaze was fixed on my bare mattress, but then darted to the wall, avoiding eye contact.

"What . . . time is it?" she murmured, stretching in an exaggerated way. It felt for a moment like she was a cartoon character, delivering a predictable line.

I stared at her, paralyzed by indecision, uncertain of the meaning of her groggy expression. We could both ignore the reality of what I was doing, and go on with our morning as if nothing had happened. We could. But there was no way to be sure Alex would. And her silence rattled me.

"Please don't tell anyone," I whispered.

"Tell anyone what?" She looked genuinely confused. "Bad period?"

I glanced at the plastic bag hanging from my hand. I didn't know what to say. Were we both pretending she couldn't pick up the pee smell in the stale air of this tiny room? Was a heavy period less embarrassing? Yes. A little.

"Just . . . don't tell anyone," I repeated.

"Of course I wouldn't," Alex said, her voice lowering almost to a growl. "What the fuck do you take me for?"

"Thanks," I murmured, stunned. I had never heard her talk that way before then.

We barely spoke for the rest of the week.

31

Six Nights Left

But the story doesn't stop there.

Because I am her and she is me.

I used to know the difference. Until that window opened and that cold gust of death swirled us together.

32

Monday, February 4

Star and I got to the archive room early on Monday, and waited for Ms. Noceno to come and unlock it.

"I'm glad to see Star is making a believer out of you," Ms. Noceno said to me, pulling her keys out of her sensible corduroy skirt pocket with a forceful jangle. "I wasn't sure if I'd see you again."

"We're looking up that girl together," Star said, talking fast. "The girl I mentioned in my email to you yesterday? Did you get it? A girl named Sarah Black or Sally Black. From Caroline's time."

"Yes, dear. I got it." Ms. Noceno turned the key and pushed the door open. "You mentioned you were both curious about the old Sarah Dearborn portrait, too, no? Let me just get settled here. Was this Sarah Black person in Caroline Bromley's class? Class of 1892?"

"Probably. We're not sure. Maybe a different class, but attending roughly the same time."

After we'd waited a few minutes at the long tables, Ms. Noceno came out from behind the partition with two binders.

"Well, here are the student registration rosters from 1880–1890. And here are the lists from 1890–1900. That should pretty much cover it."

We started with the first year that Caroline had attended—which was the 1888–1889 school year.

I let Star look in the first binder while I sat twirling my pencil.

"Ms. Noceno," I said. "Did you go to Windham?"

Ms. Noceno looked up from her computer and smiled broadly.

"Oh no," she said. "I'd sooner eat glass."

I wasn't sure I'd heard her answer correctly.

"What?" I murmured.

"*Black, Leonora Rose, freshman,*" Star read, ignoring us both. "And look! Come here!"

I hopped up and leaned over the binder. The names were all written in black pen on yellowed paper, encapsulated in plastic protectors.

"*Black, Sarah Georgetta, sophomore,*" I said, reading the next line as Star slid her finger down.

"So that was the year Caroline was a freshman?"

"Yeah. Along with Leonora." Star flipped ahead to the 1891–1892 school year registrar's book. "So Sarah was one year older than them. Let's see . . . Caroline's there as a senior, of course. And Black, Leonora . . . still there."

"Sarah wouldn't be there anymore either way, anyway. She'd have graduated by then. She'd have graduated in spring of 1891."

Star and I checked the books for all of the intervening years.

While Caroline Bromley and Leonora Black had both attended the school for four years, Sarah had only attended in 1887 and 1888—for her freshman year and half of a sophomore year. Hers was one of a handful of names that had *Left at Christmas* written next to it in 1888.

"Well, there we have it," Star said brightly. "A girl named Sarah Black. Who lived in Dearborn. But didn't stay and graduate like her younger sister, Leonora."

"I wonder what old Ronald would've had to say about that," I mused softly.

Star shook her head, rolling her eyes pointedly toward Ms. Noceno. Apparently she was committed to keeping the Darkins report our little secret.

"Star?" Ms. Noceno said loudly, as if to telegraph that she knew Star was trying to get something past her.

"Yeah?"

"Ms. Holland-Stone is coming to join you today, correct?"

"Oh! Yeah."

Star turned to me. "Ms. Holland-Stone and I sometimes have our project advisory meeting in here. It makes it easier because then I can show her some of the stuff that I'm finding. But she won't come for like twenty minutes, so we've got time."

Star turned back to the old registration book. "It's sweet that the listing has both of their middle names. If I'd realized the registrar's lists had that, I'd have looked up Leonora sooner, since I've been curious about her. That might help us find other stuff. You'd be surprised how many long-dead people come up in Google searches. Genealogy records and census records and stuff."

"With a name like Sarah Black, don't get your hopes up," Ms. Noceno piped up from her desk. "Such a common name, it might be difficult to come up with reliable information."

"With a middle name like Georgetta, it might not be so hard," I pointed out.

"If she ever married, that might muddle things, too," Ms. Noceno chimed back.

"You're such a party pooper, Noceno," Star sputtered.

I waited for Ms. Noceno to look stunned, but her face didn't even twitch. It occurred to me that this was actually how she and Star spoke to each other most of the time, in the quiet familiarity of the archives, just the two of them. They were apparently just breaking me in the last time. And I had a feeling that "Noceno" might even consider *party pooper* a compliment.

"Let me see," Star said, typing on her laptop. "Ancestry.com comes up right away . . . surprise, surprise. And we've got something here already. From the public family trees, looks like."

"I'm going to leave you two to that," Ms. Noceno said, "while I take a peek in the listing of all of the larger portraits and art pieces on campus. I know the old Sarah Dearborn portrait was damaged—I can't imagine it's still on campus, or I would know where it is. I think it was probably damaged beyond repair. Unfortunately, the administration didn't keep track of these things very well until the 1950s or '60s, as I've mentioned."

She said this with a sniff of disapproval. While both she and Star were working, I took the registration book and flipped through the pages, admiring the elegant sloping handwriting. And then I remembered someone else I had wanted to look up—someone I'd forgotten about for a few days.

Chase, Sarah. She was class of 1892, like Caroline. And next to her name it said *Laundry*.

She was one of the hard-luck laundry girls. No wonder she had such an unhappy expression in that old picture. I started to feel a little shitty for blaming all the haunting on her. Now that we had our sights on Sarah Black instead.

Beside me, Star sucked in a breath as she read something on her laptop. I watched her scroll, shake her head, exhale.

"What is it?" I asked.

"She's giving us a dramatic pause," Ms. Noceno said to me.

"Fuck," Star muttered, gaping at the screen.

"Star!" Ms. Noceno snapped, this time genuinely shocked.

Star shook her head and spun her laptop screen around so it faced me.

Below the Ancestry logo were the words **Sarah Georgetta Black**.

And beneath that:

Born 12 November 1872 in Rochester, New York
> **Daughter of Joseph Black and Lucinda (Langworthy) Black**
> **Sister of Thomas Black, Daniel Black, Leonora (Black) Post, and Angelina (Black) Willis**
> **Died 10 February 1889 in Rochester, New York**

I gasped at the sight of the death date.

"February of 1889." Star looked almost as stunned as I felt. "She must have died just a few months after she left the school."

It took me a moment before I felt like I could breathe again. And a moment more to find my voice.

"I wasn't really even looking at the year," I said—so softly only Star could hear.

"Girls?" Ms. Noceno said. "Something interesting?"

Star scowled for a moment, confused. But then I saw her face tighten and then blanch with understanding.

The month and the day.

They were the same as the date Taylor had died.

33

Star and I were still gaping at each other when the heavy archives door swung open and Ms. Holland-Stone walked in—immediately filling the room with the smell of perfume. An expensive Chanel type, like Taylor used to wear.

"I'm a little early," she announced, dropping her black leather messenger bag in the cubby area before walking to the main tables.

Ms. Noceno's nose seemed to twitch as she nodded acknowledgment.

"Are you okay?" Star whispered to me.

"What're we whispering about?" Ms. Holland-Stone asked, smiling as she approached us.

Star closed her computer.

"Star is being modest," Ms. Noceno said. "I believe the girls have just made a discovery about one of Caroline Bromley's peers. They were just about to tell me what it was."

Star stared at me, apparently paralyzed. Neither of us wanted to bring up the Taylor connection, clearly.

I glanced from Ms. Holland-Stone to Ms. Noceno. Ms. Holland-Stone was wearing black leggings and boots and a fluffy gray poncho, with her hair swept up in a mother-of-pearl hair clip. Looking at their expectant faces, I noted that they weren't actually that far apart in age. It was just that one tried very hard to look young—and the other perhaps the opposite.

"She died young," I offered. "She was sixteen."

"What was her name?"

"Sarah Black."

"Oh." Ms. Holland-Stone dropped into the chair next to Star's and stared blankly at the closed laptop. "Not Leonora Black?"

"No," Star said softly. "Her sister."

"We're going to try to find out more about her," I said.

I nudged at Star's elbow, and she opened her laptop. As Ms. Holland-Stone read about Sarah Black, Ms. Noceno got up, walked over, and read over their shoulders.

"This *is* sad, that this young woman died. Leonora's sister. But is she directly related to your studies of Caroline?" Ms. Holland-Stone asked.

Star glanced at me. "Well . . ."

"Sarah Black is more my project than Star's," I said. "Sorry to distract her."

"You're doing a senior project?" Ms. Holland-Stone looked skeptical. "History? Who's your advisor?"

"No," I said. "It's a personal project."

"Which we encourage, dear," Ms. Noceno put in, patting me on the shoulder. "If you want to find out more about this girl, though, it appears that our resources at Windham might be somewhat limiting. She apparently only spent a year or two here. Most of her life was in Rochester, New York. You might want to see what kind of resources they have there."

Ms. Noceno stepped away and disappeared into the back glassed-in portion of the archives. Some of the Darkins report was coming back to me now in pieces. About the tricky difference between ghosts and poltergeists. About how one tended to stay in one place, and the other had a tendency to follow people wherever they went.

"We ought to see what they've got, yeah," Star said. "They probably have death records, newspapers?"

"Is your primary concern her death?" Ms. Holland-Stone asked. She raised an eyebrow at me, then shifted her gaze to Star.

"No," Star replied. "But she *was* sixteen. Naturally we're curious how she died."

We were all silent for a few moments.

"Let's speak honestly," Ms. Holland-Stone said. "Since you mentioned this to me earlier, Star. This is related to the Dearborn ghost stories, right?"

Star glanced at me. I watched Ms. Noceno returning to her desk, frowning, file folder in hand.

"Right," I admitted.

"Excellent," Ms. Holland-Stone said, folding her arms. "I was curious about that myself, when I was a student at Windham. Especially my senior year. Unfortunately, there have been so many Sarahs at Dearborn through the years . . . as students and teachers, actually . . . that it seems nearly impossible to get to the bottom of the story."

"But there haven't been many Sarahs who died this young," Star pointed out.

"Well . . ." Ms. Holland-Stone rearranged her fluffy poncho

to drape over her thighs and looked at her watch. "You might be onto something there."

"Speaking of Sarahs *and* Dearborn," Ms. Noceno said, "I found something odd in the art collection listing. As we all know, the Sarah Dearborn portrait no longer graces the walls. Since the 1950s. But apparently the damaged portrait stayed on campus—probably in a basement somewhere—until 1975 because there is a bill of sale and agreement here that says an alum purchased it with the intention of restoring it and return- ing it to campus. A woman named Norma Fleming. I guess she never did, because there's no documentation about it after that. And we obviously don't have the portrait, so I suppose she never got around to it. Or found it too badly damaged to restore."

"Huh," I said.

"Sad," Ms. Holland-Stone offered.

"Weird," Star added.

"I've got an appointment after this, ladies." Ms. Holland- Stone looked at her watch again. "So, Haley, if you'll excuse us? We'll go to that table so you don't have to move."

"That's okay," I said, hopping up. "I was about to leave anyway."

It was true. The date February 10 was still echoing through my head. I doubted I'd be able to concentrate on anything else.

As I started to gather my things, Ms. Noceno gestured for me to come to her desk and I followed.

"I took the liberty of looking this up for you. Rochester is a fairly large city, so I suspected this would be the case." She turned her computer screen so I could see it. Beneath the heading *Rochester Public Library* were the words *Rochester News-paper Index* written in purple.

"If you give me your email address," she said, "I'll send you the link. They don't have all of their old newspapers scanned and online, of course. But they have a very nice index of all of the article headings and topics that you can look up alphabetically online, see? Going back to 1818."

She clicked on the heading *AAB-ACC* and it brought us to some scans of old-fashioned catalog cards. She scrolled down. The cards said things like:

ABBEY, E. WINIFRED
    —Married John F. Corris
    UA, Je 28, 1876, 3 – 5

ABBEY, JOSEPH (BRIGHTON)
    —Obituary
    UA, My 22, 1879, 2 – 2

"You look up what you need," Ms. Noceno explained, "and then you request the actual article from the library staff. A small fee for each article. But it says here they can scan and send material. So you don't have to wait for snail mail or go all the way to Rochester."

"Thanks," I said, writing down my email for her. "I'll definitely give that a try."

"Good luck," she said, turning her screen around again. "Come back if you need anything."

I tried to wave to Star, but she and Ms. Holland-Stone were deeply engaged in Caroline Bromley talk.

34

Hi everyone. I am the latest member of this group and I am doing some research. Was wondering if any of you who had supernatural experiences in Dearborn can recall the exact date it happened? I would really appreciate your responses.

I wrote the Facebook message to the "Haunteds" group as soon as I'd gotten back to my room, before I'd even taken off my coat. Then I turned my laptop volume all the way up so I could hear if any responses came in while I got settled, crammed some potato chips in my mouth, and got out some calculus homework. Within a few minutes, two replies came in.

> **Laurie Rowell:** Hi Haley. Sorry, it was 20+ years ago. Only remember that it was winter of second semester.
>
> **Penny Sidorski:** I'm old. Don't know the date. It was over the course of a week, though. Not just one day. Noises. No sighting for me.

I suspected most of the responses would be like this. I closed my laptop and texted Star:

You going to be back soon?

I was eager to talk with her about what we'd found. And I didn't like being alone in Dearborn right now. This feeling had

252

been creeping up on me since the fright I'd had the other night with the knocking on the door.

To distract myself, I picked up my phone and typed a text to Anthony:

What are you up to right now?

His reply:

Hanging with Vince. We have become study buddies.

Damn. He was with his new crush. Good for him, but this meant he wouldn't be available to talk and dull the feeling of aloneness in this room.

Have fun, I wrote back reluctantly, then refreshed the Facebook page to find a new message.

> **Jane Villette:** I'm pretty sure mine was on Valentine's Day—the night of. My boyfriend and I had a "romantic" outing before dinner, and then I thought the whispering I heard later was my punishment from hell. I was a very dramatic and guilt-plagued teen. 😊

I exhaled. This felt like good news. I turned back to my calculus homework and managed to finish a problem. As I started the next one, another message notification dinged.

> **Darla Heaney:** Mine was right after my birthday, which is February 9. I can't remember if it was one or two days after. I think one. So probably the 10th, but maybe the 11th.

My chest tightened. I had to remind myself to breathe as I dove for the keyboard.

Darla, can you tell me what kind of experience you had?

I typed fast, worried that Darla would log off before she saw my reply.

Darla's reply took less than a minute.

A face in my window.

What kind of face?

A girl. It was terrifying.

More than once?

No, just once. Which was enough.

I wasn't sure what to ask next, but I wanted to keep Darla from walking away from this conversation.

Did the girl look angry? I typed.

Darla was silent for a few minutes, but I saw the little texting dots appearing and disappearing.

This is bringing back really bad memories, someone named Lynette Rakoff interjected.

I think I was too frightened to see it to say. Her face wasn't clear. Like she had a veil or a shroud over her face.

The back of my neck prickled. Where the hell was Star? By the pond somewhere, getting hickeys from Mark Byrne the Sideburn?

I positioned my hands over the keys. They were shaking, and I didn't know what to type next. What did it mean that the ghost seemed to come back often on the same day? What did it mean that Taylor had died the same day as Sarah Black?

What year was that? I typed.

2010.

Star walked in, flushed and smiling.

"Hey!" she greeted me.

She'd definitely been with Mark after the archives.

Okay, thank you for all of the info, everybody, I wrote before slapping my laptop closed.

"We need to get ready," I told Star in a low voice.

"For what?" she said. "Dinner?"

"No," I replied. "For February 10th."

♦♦♦

Star and I sat by ourselves at dinner—for the first time ever.

"Okay," she said. "We know that Sarah Black died young, the same day of the year that Taylor died. That feels . . . significant. Significantly scary and horrible."

I nodded and nibbled on a piece of lettuce. I never used words like *horrible,* but was grateful for people like Star who were willing to.

"Especially since that's just six days from now," I murmured.

"But then the rest of the hauntings are fuzzy, in terms of dates," Star pointed out. "You only got *one* confirmation that a haunting occurred *maybe* on that date."

I shook my head. "Doesn't matter. Two deaths on the exact same day . . . Whatever Sarah Black's ghost did to the other girls, it feels like she . . . or it . . . killed Taylor. Or at least . . . was *involved* in her death. I mean, is there any way around thinking that?"

Star shuddered but then took a big, enthusiastic spoonful of mac and cheese.

"We know that Sarah Black didn't die in Dearborn, though," she said. "She left at Christmas, it says. Dropped out. She wasn't a student here anymore. That makes me inclined to think that she didn't become the Winter Girl."

"So you think it's a requirement for a ghost to haunt the exact place they died?"

"Well . . . no," Star admitted. "Look . . . why don't you forward me that Rochester Library link that Ms. Noceno gave you. Maybe we can find out how she died. I'll work on that for you. That might help us a little."

"Maybe she caught some kind of illness here and then went home and died?" I said. "So in a sense she blames her death on this place? Either way, it looks like the dorm has a February 10th problem."

"I wouldn't go straight to that, though," Star said slowly, bringing a spoonful of pasta up to her face and staring at it for a moment. "I'd say hold off until we can figure out more about what *happened* to Sarah Black."

Normally I enjoyed mac-and-cheese night, too, but tonight I didn't have the appetite for it.

I chased a slippery cherry tomato around my plate, trying to spear it with my fork.

"Sure, we should find out more about Sarah Black. But beyond that, we know enough to be afraid of what might happen on February 10th. And we probably ought to try to *do* something about it."

"What *can* we do, though?" Star asked, lowering her spoon without taking a bite.

I gave up on stabbing the tomato. I was thinking of that creepy thing one of the girls had said in the Darkins report: *Some girls say that she's looking for her replacement.* Was Taylor the replacement? Was Taylor the ghost now? How many replacements were there? With Sarah Black dying in Rochester, that could be just the tip of the iceberg. I didn't want to say this out loud to Star, though—for fear that speaking it could make it more possible, more true. My hands were starting to go cold.

"I'm thinking about Students X and Y," I said, trying to rub some warmth back into my hands. "About how they were so different. Did Student X encounter, like, a murderous ghost? And that's why she went sort of crazy, she was so scared? And then Student Y seemed to be able to acknowledge the ghost quietly, without much trouble."

"Maybe they encountered entirely different ghosts?" Star replied. "I mean, why doesn't the report focus on that? It seems like Ronald Darkins just tries to say it's all about the girls' different psychologies. Why does he go straight to that?"

"Well, that's another thing I can ask Kathleen about, I guess. I was waiting until I had the whole report read. But I've got about a hundred questions now."

"You sure that lady's legit?" Star asked.

I shrugged. "No. But she's participated in tons of paranormal investigations, she remembers Dearborn pretty well, and she seems interested and willing to talk to me about it, no strings. Know anyone else like that who can help us with these . . . supernatural issues?"

"Well . . . no," Star admitted.

We were both silent for a minute. I picked up the cherry tomato with my fingers and popped it into my mouth. When I chewed it, a slightly foul taste filled my mouth. The tomato had looked nice on the outside, but on the inside it had started to go bad. I forced myself to swallow it anyway.

"I just had a thought," I said hoarsely. The thought was

just as rotten as the tomato. Almost as rotten as the previous thought about Taylor, but not quite.

"Yeah?" Star was corralling her last couple of pasta elbows onto her spoon.

"What if the problem isn't Sarah Black at all? It was just blamed on her, over the years, because she'd died young? But what if she was the victim of the problem, not the cause?"

Star glanced up from her plate. "How do you mean?"

"Bad things happen on or around February 10th," I said. "Sometimes *really* bad things. We're assuming that if Sarah Black died on February 10th, 1889, she was the start of it. But maybe there is something older and darker than her. That was here before her? A spirit or a poltergeist or a curse or something. It followed her home and killed her. It's still here, ready to mess with us. It messed with Taylor."

Star put down her spoon, abandoning the two little elbows left in it.

"I don't like where this is going," she whispered.

"Me neither," I said, feeling my stomach begin to sour—from the tomato or the weight of my own words, I wasn't certain. "But you have to admit it's a possibility."

Star glanced around the room, scanning the other tables, but then focused her gaze on me.

"Are you trying to decide who to tell that your roommate is going crazy?" I asked quietly.

"Not at all," Star said. "I'm wondering if you can call that Kathleen lady as soon as we get upstairs."

35

It was 7:59. I'd texted Kathleen in the dining hall and we'd agreed on eight p.m., but I didn't want to be obnoxiously punctual. While I waited for a couple more minutes to pass, I glanced over the first few questions Star and I had jotted down when we'd gotten back upstairs.

Ronald seemed unsure if there was a ghost or a poltergeist. How did YOU feel?

Did the date February 10 ever come up as an especially problematic or dangerous time?

Tell me more about Students X and Y. Can you tell me their names?

Star helped me come up with these questions before she'd left so I wouldn't feel weird and self-conscious on the phone.

I scribbled *Do you think girls here are in danger?* below the other questions and dialed Kathleen's number.

"Haley?" she said, instead of hello.

"Yes," I said, feeling a wave of relief that she'd answered.

"Have you read the whole report?" she asked.

"Pretty much," I said.

"It's a lot to take in."

"Yeah . . . I've got some questions."

"I figured you would."

"I'm curious about Students X and Y," I said. "Can you tell me what you remember about them?"

"Okay. Sure. I vaguely recall Ron using those mysterious labels in his report. He liked to keep things kind of cryptic even when it wasn't really necessary. But since I didn't read the whole thing before I scanned it for you, you'll have to remind me which girl is which."

"Student X is the one who had a breakdown before the headmistress hired you. Her breakdown seems to have started it all off, in a sense."

"Oh. Okay. Yes, but we never met her—she'd graduated. We only ever managed to talk to her on the phone. Mrs. Bradford arranged it—at some risk to her, because I believe that she kept the student's family out of the loop. She was over eighteen, but that still involved some risk. Anyway, we never saw her face or knew her name. And it was a brief conversation. Ron did the best he could with the report."

"What was your sense of her, from the phone conversation?" I asked.

"Mmm . . . it was a long time ago. My general sense was that she wanted to put the whole thing behind her."

"Do you think there's a way to find her?"

Kathleen was silent. But as I listened to her breathe, I realized there were all kinds of ways to find Student X. I knew her graduation year—1985—to start.

"I'm not sure," she said. "You could start with a senior class roster for that year, start calling the graduates, and see if someone remembers her name."

"You met Student Y," I said. "Do you remember her name?"

"I do, yes. I barely remember the names of any of those girls. Thirty years takes its toll. But I remember hers. I might not have, if she hadn't become kind of . . ." I heard Kathleen sigh. "Kind of famous."

"Famous?" I repeated.

"Her name is Lucia Jackson."

I gasped. "The writer?"

The one Alex liked. The one who might merit her own file in the archives when she was dead, according to Ms. Noceno.

"Yes," said Kathleen. "Are you a big fiction reader?"

"No. But everyone at Windham knows who she is."

"Yes. Well, that's Student Y."

"Are you sure?" I asked.

I sat down at my desk, noticing that I was breathless from pacing the rug.

"How could I not be sure of something like that?"

"Did you ever talk to her again?"

"Of course not. I liked her book *Stormchaser,* though. But the movie wasn't as good."

"I wonder if she would be willing to talk about what happened," I mused.

"I suppose there's only one way to find out," Kathleen said, rather cheerfully.

I was silent for a moment, scribbling *LUCIA JACKSON!* on my list of questions.

"Do you know anything about contacting famous people?" I asked. "Since you used to be married to a semifamous man?"

Kathleen laughed. "He wasn't *that* famous. And we separated right around the time he was becoming kind of cult-following famous."

"Okay. Well, I had a couple of other questions. Not just about Students X and Y."

"Sure. Go for it."

I nervously poked my pen back into its holder, then pulled out the fake white tulip I'd stuck in there with the pens.

"We've identified a girl who went here in the late 1880s, named Sarah Black, who died young," I explained. "We—my friend Star and I—think she could very well be the ghost. I don't know if you remember in the report that in Headmistress Bradford's time, and before that, some girls called her *Sarah in Black*. We think originally it was Sarah Black."

"Okay. Sounds reasonable."

"She died the same day as my friend." I stared at the fake tulip. It was yellowing now. I'd had it since I was twelve. "February 10th."

I heard Kathleen suck in a breath.

"Oh God," she said.

"What?" I asked quickly, tossing the tulip onto the desk, standing up instinctively. "Do you know what that might mean?"

"I . . . no. I'm just shocked. That's very unsettling."

"She didn't die on campus." I was pacing again. "She died a few months after she dropped out. Her sister Leonora stayed a student here, though. We kind of figured it out through that."

"This is very impressive, Haley. That you've made all of these connections. I wish Ron and I had known about this girl."

"So, um . . . we're a little worried about February 10th."

"I see."

"We're not sure what to do . . . I mean, my roommate and I."

I went into the closet and tugged at the pull string. The dim light of the closet—with its cheap, low-wattage bulb—felt mildly calming.

"I'm not certain you need to *do* anything, necessarily."

"But . . . have you ever dealt with a really *angry ghost?*" I persisted. "Or, like, a demon?"

"I don't really believe in demons, dear."

"Well, a ghost that was really scaring people or trying to hurt them? Like a ghost who clearly had ill intent?"

Kathleen hesitated. "Are you certain that's what you have here?"

"I'm thinking of my friend Taylor, still. Of what happened to her."

I am afraid she might be the ghost now. I couldn't bring myself to say that part. It felt like a sick thought.

"Okay. I understand. Well, to answer your question, yes. We had a couple of claims of ghosts like that. In one case the family eventually moved away from the house. In another, acknowledging the ghost had a surprisingly positive effect. Apparently that spirit was just misunderstood."

"But what if acknowledging doesn't work?" I demanded. I tugged the pull string again and left the closet.

"It seemed to work for Student Y . . . or rather, Lucia Jackson."

"But it didn't keep the ghost from coming back . . . from still being angry."

I sat on my bed and opened my laptop.

"Well, maybe the ghost is on a bit of a loop," Kathleen

suggested. "Comes back angry—in the coldest winter months, for whatever reason—needs to be acknowledged year after year—like it or not. I think that Student Y . . . or, Lucia, rather . . . had a point when she said that Student X's responses to the ghost probably made it a whole lot worse."

"Student X didn't do anything wrong, though—like try to perform an exorcism or anything aggressive. She was just trying to stay sane."

Just like Taylor. Just like me.

"Of course. I'm not saying it's her fault. I'm just saying that some spirits feed off negative energy. And that something can clearly be learned from Lucia's attitude and experience."

So I was going to have to write to a famous author and ask her for ghostbusting advice. My whole anxious life of avoiding little humiliations had led up to this. I *deserved* this.

"Right," I said softly, glancing at Darkins's report on my laptop screen. "Why . . . why was Ronald so interested in the Tina Resch case?"

Kathleen was silent for a few seconds. "You've heard of that case?"

"I looked it up because it was mentioned in Ronald's introduction and conclusion."

"Yes, well. At the time of the report, it had been in the news, at least, in the couple of years before we were at Windham. It was still on people's minds, or at least his mind, and the head-mistress's. First of all, you should know that Ron was never directly involved with Tina, although the case bothered him, and he wrote about it. An acquaintance of his, a parapsychologist named William Roll, was highly involved with her case, even took her in as a kind of foster father at one point. Tina was *very* troubled, whether she had a poltergeist or not. Ron always thought not enough attention was paid to that obvious matter. That the poltergeist was perhaps a secondary issue."

"Did he think that there was some sort of similarity between her case and what was happening in Dearborn?"

"Oh, I don't know. Maybe just in the potential dark power of repressed female adolescent energy."

Those words made me feel icky.

"Um, okay," I breathed.

"Kind of a sexist idea, perhaps. But it was something Ron spoke about sometimes. Not that I was ever certain it had much merit."

"Don't poltergeists happen around boys, too?" I asked.

"Sure. But that boys' school you have down the road . . . They don't have a problem like this, do they?"

"Well . . . no." I hesitated. "Do you think Tina was faking it?"

"I never met Tina, so I can't say for sure. More than likely, I think. But then, imagine being *that* troubled, to fake that? Imagine how much Tina was probably suffering, as a young girl? Wasn't *that* worth paying attention to? Rather than abandoning her at the first sign of fakery? Make a circus out of her and then dump her when the obvious fact that she needs serious, serious help makes itself so sadly clear? When she was fourteen, Tina probably still could've been rescued from herself. That's what's kind of sad about it, either way.

"But . . ." Kathleen exhaled. "That was an entirely different case. It's not likely that any of you at Windham would be quite as troubled as she was," she said. "At least without someone noticing."

"I disagree," I said. *Heartily.*

"Well . . ." I heard Kathleen sigh. "You're right. You have a point there. Excellent point. I stand corrected. I should know better. Do you have someone in mind when you say that?"

The question took me by surprise.

"I'm not sure," I murmured, letting my eyes settle on the dollar-store tulip on my desk. It had grown sort of rubbery and gross-looking over the years. I didn't know why I still had it—and couldn't remember how it had traveled here to Windham with me. In a pencil box? In a suitcase? It's weird how random shit like that can follow you around, refusing to be thrown away.

"Are you really clairvoyant?" I asked. "We didn't talk about that much at your shop."

"Oh . . . I never said I was for *sure.* I sense presences, energies. I'm not one to say if I sense them any more or less than anyone else."

"I see," I said, deciding not to pursue the question further.

Kathleen had answered my questions openly, and asked nothing in return. It probably wasn't my business if she'd been a bit of a charlatan thirty years ago. That was between her and the long-dead Betty Bradford. And I'd done things in the much less distant past that I wasn't proud of, either—so who was I to talk?

"Now, I'm not sure why you asked that, but the thing about acknowledging a spirit is that you don't need an expert to do it," Kathleen added. "Anyone can. Take Student Y, for example. She just went ahead and did it. If you know a ghost is there and you have something to say to her, then say it. And by the way, burning sage might help. It doesn't get rid of ghosts, like people think. But it cleanses the air of negativity and might bring some clarity to your communication with the ghost, if you wish to have that."

I sat down on my bed and glanced around at our walls, trying to process my response to this. Maybe my eyes were always drawn to Star's umbrellas and enigmatic beluga because I hadn't bothered to put anything on my own wall this year.

"Haley?" Kathleen prompted.

"Yeah, I'm here. You said not to be aggressive, though. Not to feed the negative energy."

"Well, right," Kathleen replied. "Don't be accusatory. Just let the ghost know you know she's there. If you have a favor to ask her, go for it."

And then my eyes were drawn toward my window.

"A favor—like, please don't push any more girls out the window?"

Kathleen was quiet for a moment.

"I don't believe that the message you read on the window said anything about pushing," she pointed out.

"*Making* her jump? Kind of the same thing, isn't it?"

"No . . . because it brings up the question . . . how does one *make* someone jump?"

I felt my breath catch at this question. I didn't like to think of Taylor in the moment before. Looking down at the pavement below.

"Haley?"

"A ghost or spirit could have all kinds of powers that we

don't understand," I said softly, still staring at the window. "Possibly even the power to make someone jump."

"I suppose . . ." Kathleen sounded uncertain.

I didn't feel like talking anymore. My mind was on Taylor again. Taylor at her window, alone.

"Maybe I could call you back another time," I murmured. "I'm sure I'll have other questions."

"Of course, Haley."

"I should let you go."

"Okay. Keep me updated, all right? Take care of yourself."

"Yeah," I said. "Goodbye."

"Bye now."

After we hung up, I lifted my blinds and sat cross-legged on my bed, looking out the window. Two girls were coming toward the dorm in the lamplight, chatting. One was clapping her mittened hands together. The other was wearing a cute knitted beanie that looked like an intricate basket. They both looked so perfectly preppy in their boots and snug wool coats, their hair stylish even under their hats.

They were exactly how I pictured myself—or aspired to picture myself—when I first left for Windham-Farnswood. I'd taken endless trips to Target and Goodwill in search of clothes that would match my picture. Sweaters and boots that looked like the girls' sweaters in the welcome brochures. Sweaters and boots of girls so cozy and confident, they could never sink.

Sometimes, when I would be flitting around with Taylor in the winter, I would think, *Here I am! I'm one of those girls.* It would be like I'd stepped outside myself, and could see myself coming down the walk. See myself toss my hair. See myself walk in that swaying, confident way I had never used before. Hear myself laugh at Taylor's jokes.

I reached out my hand and unlocked the window. The old metal lock was stubborn, but I pushed hard and it snapped free. I forced the window up and a blast of winter air came through the screen.

Taylor always kept her screen up because occasionally she liked to perch near the window and smoke. But I didn't need my screen up for this experiment. I wanted to hear what it sounded like when a Dearborn window closed. I'd heard it before—in the fall, when it was still warm enough to open windows—but wanted to hear it again now. It was a thought that had preoccupied me for the final part of my conversation with Kathleen.

I slammed the window closed. It made a rusty-sounding *EEEE-BANG!* Just as I thought it would. I took out my phone and clicked on the video that Thatcher had sent me, skipping to the very end, right before Taylor comes out of the bathroom. There's a muffled *EEEE-BANG!* And then the *OOARRRRR-thump!* of the bathroom door closing behind Taylor as she comes back for her phone.

My heart was in my throat as I slipped out of the room and headed down to the bathroom.

OOARRRRR-thump! went the bathroom door behind me as I entered. I looked up at the bathroom windows. Along the tile wall—up so high that only the tallest girls could reach them— was a row of narrow, rectangular windows with cranks for opening and closing. The bathroom windows were completely different from the student room windows. Still, I stood on tip-toe to crank one open and closed. It made a soft, low *thump thump thump,* like a heart beating.

The night Taylor had freaked out in her room and filmed it, right before she came out into the hall from the bathroom, a window was closing somewhere nearby. In Taylor's room? And her phone had picked up the sound because her door was still open from when she'd fled the room?

Possibly.

But it couldn't have been Taylor closing the window. Because she was still in the bathroom. It was someone or something else.

◂▸▾

"How was it?" demanded Star, who was waiting in our room when I returned.

"Interesting," I said. "I don't think she's going to help us figure out what to *do,* exactly. But she's got some useful information. For example—Student Y is Lucia Jackson. The writer."

"You're kidding."

"Nope." I glanced up at my window, making a mental note to lock it. I'd forgotten to do so after my experimental slam.

Star sat on her bed, her mouth hanging open. "I'm going to have to process that for a little while. That kind of takes the air out of what *I* found."

"What's that?"

"That Rochester database." She slipped her computer out of her bag. "There's an article in the catalog. *Black, Sarah*

Georgetta. Death. 1889. And then the reference numbers. I've already written to the contact to scan and email that article."

"I don't think that's free," I pointed out.

"I already used my mom's credit card. It's only a few dollars. But it says it takes two to seven days to process these requests."

I nodded. "We'll see what it says."

"Yes, we will. So, Lucia Jackson, huh?"

"Yeah. I'm wondering if I should try to talk to her."

Star got up and picked up a pair of pajama bottoms from a heap of clothes by her bed. "Why not?"

"She's a celebrity."

"Not really." Star changed from her jeans to the pajama bottoms, which were covered with cats wearing Santa hats. "It's not like she's a movie star. She probably doesn't have an entourage. Most people wouldn't recognize her on the street."

Star settled on her bed, pulling her computer onto her lap.

"She's got an author website," she said after typing a quick Google search. "With a contact email. You could just write to her."

"Her email probably goes straight to an assistant or publicity person or something," I mumbled.

"So what? It doesn't mean they wouldn't forward it to her. Say you want to interview her for the Windham student newspaper or something. She might find it charming."

"Yeah, maybe."

"What else did Kathleen say? Any advice for February 10th?"

"No," I said flatly, realizing I'd never really asked that specific question.

"Nothing?" Star looked skeptical.

"Well, burning sage," I offered. "It doesn't get rid of ghosts, but it cleanses the space of negativity."

Star snorted. "Good luck with that working here."

I nearly did a double take, I was so unaccustomed to Star being cynical about Windham. Maybe she'd always been, and I'd just been too caught up in my own stuff to notice.

"Let's see what more we can find out about Sarah Black before we start breaking the fire code," Star said with a shrug—signaling that she was done with crazy roommate shenanigans for the evening.

While Star did homework, I looked up Lucia Jackson, who of course had a fancy website showing all of her beautiful book covers. The *About Lucia* section had only a small black-and-white photo of her. She was leaning against a desk, looking slightly uncomfortable and put out—like someone had stopped her on her way to the bathroom to make her take this stupid photograph. She was wearing a scoop-necked black T-shirt and dark-framed glasses, made slightly less severe by the soft-looking blond hair that curled gently around her chin.

I tried to imagine her about thirty years younger, saying, *Everyone makes way too big of a deal about the ghost.*

I clicked on *Contact*. There were email addresses there for Lucia's literary agent, film agent, publicist, and assistant. Seeing all of those different fancy names made me feel dumb. But I clicked on her assistant, since that was the most humble-sounding of the bunch. A blank email template came up. I poised my hands on the keyboard.

Dear Ms. Jackson,

I am a Windham-Farnswood student and a huge fan of your work. Snapdragon Drive *is one of my favorite books. I was wondering if you have time to do a quick interview about your time as a student here. I'm interviewing artist and writer alums and would love to include you.*

Thank you,
Haley Peppler

It was mostly lies, but now was not the time to pretend I wasn't capable of lying. I hit Send before I could change my mind.

I doubted I would get a response. Lucia Jackson probably got a lot of dumb kids asking her dumb questions. For now it would have to be enough to know that she probably saw the Dearborn ghost once, but seemed to have turned out okay.

Before getting ready for bed, I checked the Facebook "Haunteds" group once more. Two more people had replied to my inquiry about dates of hauntings:

Anita Simons: Pretty sure it was in January, right after holiday break.

Lauren Calhoun: I've kept all my high school and college journals. Scratching on my window. Faint whispery moans and humming in my room. It was February 10.

36

It *was easy to end my friendship with Taylor. Too easy.*

"No one will ever see the burner phone," I assured her. "You don't need to worry about that."

I'm trying to remember now the look that was on her face when she realized that I had not necessarily thrown it away. That I was not necessarily ever going to—that I was using it as insurance in case she was thinking of punishing me somehow.

"I think we shouldn't hang out for a few days, though," I'd said.

I wonder now if my s came out sibilant when I said "days."

The truth was that I wasn't trying to be mean, or even to wield this rare power I had. The truth was I just needed to get out from under her. I needed to know who I was without her. I needed to know if I was cruel or kind or neither. I had come here desperate and broken, and my friendship with her had made me feel pieced together again. With a toxic kind of glue, yes, but it was better than being in pieces, nonetheless. The relief at that vaguely whole feeling had made me accept everything about her. Things I hated. Most of all, that the relief was always actually laced with fear. Fear she'd turn on me and treat me like she treated almost everybody else.

I could no longer remember the face of the girl back in Michigan who'd asked me if I brushed my hair. Whenever I thought of it at Windham, her face was Taylor's.

But no matter, I'd thought, after I'd said those final words to Taylor.

I was studying more now. I was talking to other girls—girls like Star—without wondering what Taylor thought of them. I could put whatever I wanted on my dinner tray without worrying that Taylor might remark about my unhealthy passion for pasta, or the fundamentally gross nature of anyone who eats meatballs, ricotta cheese, hot dogs, cauliflower, or mayonnaise.

When I would see her in the stairwell of the science building, or coming out of the locker room, her face was neutral—if a little tired. Not angry or vindictive or even a little sad. It was like I was one of her already-graduated friends. Just gone.

After she jumped, I began to wonder why I had been so desperate to get out from under her that I had not felt I could wait until June—when she would have been gone anyway. She'd have graduated, and I'd have been free of her.

I told myself it had nothing to do with revenge or cruelty or power.

If I'd really wanted those things, I'd have taken her burner phone to the dean and turned her in. She'd been out of chances by then. She'd have been kicked out of Windham. But I'd never wanted that kind of trouble for her. I just didn't want to have to be her friend—her shadow—anymore.

37

Five Nights Left

It is true what some of the girls whisper. A ghost looks for her replacement. That is how she breaks free.

I am Sarah, I am Taylor, I am all of the girls who came before.

I bear their anger, their frustration, their sadness, their collective vengeful wish.

38

Tuesday, February 5

"Haley. Haley!"

Star's exuberant form was heading in my direction as I left the humanities hall after the last class of the day. I tried to focus, and ran my palms up and down my face as if that might wipe the exhaustion away. Ms. Holland-Stone had just given me dagger eyes for forgetting to hand in my Western Civ paper—and then reminded me of her strict twelve-points-per-day penalty for lateness. Everyone had stared at me as I'd told her I'd have it tomorrow. I hadn't even started it yet.

Star was breathless.

"They came through," she said. "The Rochester Library. They already sent the Sarah Georgetta Black article."

"What's it say?" I demanded, waking up slightly at the news.

"I don't know yet. I saw it on my phone but couldn't open it. We should go to the room and try on one of our laptops."

"Okay," I agreed.

We ran to Dearborn—my scarf falling off and trailing behind me, Star's hands raw and gloveless as she clutched her phone the whole way. When we arrived, flushed and thumping up the stairs, we probably seemed a little giddy.

Anna looked bemused as she was coming down the stairs opposite us.

"Hello, ladies," she said sharply, her gaze darting from me to Star and back again.

We were all quite suspect to her now—since the latest vandalism. Indeed, Star and me looking breathless together—or me looking enthusiastic at all—was maybe an unusual sight.

"Hello!" Star called back, not slowing down. I looked down at my boots and followed her lead.

A few seconds later, we were behind our closed door and Star was shedding her coat, taking out her laptop.

"Okay!" she said, flipping it open and making a few clicks. "It's opening."

I didn't bother to take off my coat and hat as I leaned over her shoulder. The type of the old newspaper article was small, crowded, and slightly faded in spots.

"It's too small to read," Star cried.

"There must be a way to zoom in," I said.

"Oh. Umm . . ." She scanned the page. "Here! Oh my God! There's a picture!"

She struggled to center the page on a blurry photo of a girl. Above the picture was an article in tiny print, and above that a bold headline: *Death of Local Girl, Niece of Mr. and Mrs. Charles Hannaford.*

It wasn't a formal photograph. It was taken outdoors. Sarah Black was standing outside in some grass in a stiff plaid dress, with a fence and a tree behind her. Her pale hair was long, formed into a few thick ringlets—except for a front piece pulled back away from her face. She was looking demurely upward at the camera, heavy-lidded, not exactly smiling, but not exactly frowning, either. She looked impatient—maybe uncomfortable. She also looked about twelve. Maybe she was a very young-looking sixteen. Or maybe more likely this was the only photograph of her the family had.

I dragged my gaze away from the photo to read the article above it.

Death claimed Sarah "Sally" Georgetta Black, 16 years old, at the home of her uncle, mayoral candidate Charles Hannaford, and his wife, Katherine Hannaford. Miss Black was taken sick on Tuesday and was found to have pneumonia. She died on Friday. Her death was a shock to her family and friends.

"That's the whole article?" I said.

"It's not an article, really. Just like a . . . death notice, I guess? Like an obituary."

"Almost like filler," I said. "Kind of sad. I wonder if it would have even made the papers if her uncle wasn't . . . involved in local politics, looks like."

"So she died of pneumonia," Star said. "That's . . . terrible."

"I guess I was expecting something different," I admitted.

"Like . . . ?" Star asked.

"Like something *worse*."

"Dying that young is pretty bad, no matter how it happens."

"I was expecting a murder or a suicide, I guess," I admitted. "Or a freak accident."

Like a freak accident you could blame on a poltergeist. A fire or a flying piano.

"Well . . . of course you can die a quiet death and still be angry, or have unfinished business," Star pointed out. "Maybe it's even worse that way."

"How's that?"

Star lowered her voice. "Because no one's paying all that much attention. Not like they would with a dramatic death."

I moved my face closer to the screen. "At least now we know what she looked like."

"Is that how you imagined her?" Star asked.

Sarah Black was small and kind of frail, like most of the accounts of the Winter Girl described. But then, it was hard to tell if the photo was taken when she was still very young—in which case, of course she was small. And she *was* pale—but in the way most white people looked pale in washed-out old 19th-century photos.

"Can you forward me the article and picture?" I asked.

"Of course," Star said, clicking her email icon. "And now that we've gotten this, I'm thinking we should look up her parents, her siblings, her aunt, and her uncle in the Rochester database. See if we can find out a little more about her through them."

"Good idea," I said. "This is great. But I . . . should do some work now, really. I've been falling so behind."

"Okay." Star looked uncertain, but retreated back to her mountain of archive photocopies.

♦♦♦

Dear Darla: Can I email you something? I have a question for you.

I wrote to Darla Heaney, who was certain she'd seen the ghost in her window on February 10 or 11. I repeated basically the same message to Lauren Calhoun, the lady who'd kept a journal and also cited February 10 as the date of her haunting.

And although Bronwyn Spruce had never mentioned dates, I also texted her the same basic question.

Sure, she texted back.

I studied Sarah Black's photo some more before I sent it, trying again to determine the emotion on the girl's face. Impatience, yes. And if such a girl was stuck here in Dearborn forever, could I blame her for being impatient?

"You want to go to dinner?" Star asked, closing her laptop.

"You go ahead," I said, minimizing the photo. "I'll be going down in a few minutes."

Star looked reluctant, but then left the room wordlessly. I wondered if I'd hurt her feelings—since we'd had a pretty collegial first dinner together yesterday.

Does this picture of this girl remind you of anything? I wrote as the text of my email, and attached the picture of Sarah Black. In the meantime, Darla had sent her email address, so I sent the same thing to her.

An email came in just as I was finishing up—so fast that I thought it was a delivery failure notice. But I was stunned to see this message instead:

Hi Haley,

I'm Gwen Hildale, Lucia's assistant.

Lucia is home from LA this week and would like to help.

Were you looking for a typed Q&A or a phone call? Due to Lucia's tight schedule, a phone call would be preferable—if you can keep it to about 10 minutes?

Best,
Gwen

I was typing an enthusiastic reply when someone tapped on my door.

"Who is it?" I shouted.

"Maylin."

"Oh." I hit Send, closed my laptop, and opened the door.

"Come down and eat with me?" she asked.

"Sure," I said, shoving my feet into sneakers and closing the door behind me. "Where's Alex?"

"I don't know. She's been flaking out on me lately. And . . ." As we headed to the stairwell, Maylin raised her eyebrows at me, clearly wanting me to notice.

"What?" I said.

"Do you think of me as closed-minded?" she asked.

"Umm . . . no. Why?"

"Say you were attracted to women, like, if you were a lesbian or bi, would you tell me?"

I was startled. "Uh . . . I'm *not* attracted to women, so it's a hard question to answer."

"But if you *were*?"

"Umm, I guess I would tell you . . . eventually?" I was feeling a little too exhausted for this kind of conversation. "When I *felt* like telling people, I would tell you, too? If that makes sense?"

"Do you think *Alex* thinks I'm closed-minded?" Maylin demanded.

"No," I replied. "You guys are good friends. And Alex usually isn't afraid to tell people what she thinks."

"But is it possible she would think she couldn't tell me something, because I'm, like, immature or prejudiced or something?"

We were at the bottom of the stairs now, but Maylin wasn't reaching for the stairwell door.

"She didn't sleep in her room last night, I don't think," she said softly, glancing up the stairs for eavesdroppers. "And Kaylin Highfield says she spent the night in that sophomore Chloe Schuster's room."

"Well, good for Alex," I said, shrugging. "She never *did* have any patience for those smelly Farnswood boys."

"Chloe's the girl she *tutors,*" Maylin pointed out, as if this made the matter particularly scandalous.

"Well, that's fine. And maybe, actually, they were busy studying and she got tired and fell asleep."

Maylin shook her head. "Chloe's roommate, Rhea, slept on Kaylin's floor. She said Rhea didn't really say much, just that she and Chloe needed a little break from each other. But then Kaylin's roommate saw Alex sneaking out of the room at like five-thirty or six in the morning."

I hesitated before replying—thinking about the therapist thing Maylin had noticed. And now this. Alex not sleeping in her own room.

"Where do you get all of this information, Maylin?" I asked, trying to keep a neutral tone. "Why don't you just ask Alex if you're curious?"

Maylin made a face. "Wouldn't that be rude?"

"Maybe," I admitted, pulling the stairwell door open for her.

When we got to the dining hall entrance, I scanned the room for Alex but didn't see her. I saw Maylin doing the same. Star was at a corner table, digging into a plate of spaghetti, flanked by other friends.

"Looks like it's just you and me tonight," I said to Maylin.

I'd just barely put my tray down when I saw that Bronwyn Spruce had texted back.

No. *The picture doesn't do anything for me. What's this about?*

I just wanted to get your reaction. We have reason to believe this girl, who died at age 16, might be the Winter Girl.

Who is "we"? Bronwyn wanted to know.

"Who're you texting?" Maylin asked.

"Oh. Uh . . . sorry. Just a friend."

Maylin raised an inquisitive eyebrow. Although I never really told anyone point-blank that I had no friends from back home, I think it was fairly obvious to anyone who knew me.

I sucked up a strand of spaghetti and replied to Bronwyn.

*My roommate and me. Does this look *anything* like the girl you saw in your doorway?*

"Are you upset with me for saying those things about Alex?" Maylin demanded. "Do you think I'm a bad friend because it bothers me that she might be keeping that from me? Do you think that makes me self-centered?"

"What? No, Maylin. Of course I'm curious, too."

Bronwyn replied:

Not really. Maybe a little? Photo doesn't strike me.

I was a little disappointed with this tepid reply.

Okay, thx, I typed. I was staring at the Sarah Black photo again when Maylin nudged me hard.

Alex and Chloe were approaching the table together. Alex dropped her tray of spaghetti and salad with a clumsy clatter. A dinner roll bounced off her tray and onto the floor.

I put down my phone and bent to pick up the roll.

"Want me to toss it?" I asked.

"Five-second rule," Alex said, taking it from me. "Thanks."

"What've you been up to?" Maylin asked after the two girls settled in seats next to each other.

"Just running around trying to take care of shit," Alex mumbled. "Among other things, I think we timed about half the bulbs wrong in the greenhouse."

"Can you change the date of the bulb show?" I asked.

Alex didn't reply—and she didn't look that great. Her eyes were glassier than they'd been when she'd visited my room the other day, the circles beneath them a deeper purple.

I glanced at Maylin, who didn't seem to notice.

"Are you okay, Alex?" I said.

"Yeah. Just hungry," Alex said, taking a bite of the dirty roll.

I didn't know if I should point out that she didn't *look* okay. That rarely helps, in my experience.

"You need to take it easy," I said, as gently as I could.

"Good advice," Alex said, picking up her fork and stabbing at a piece of lettuce. "I *love* advice."

I made another concerned face at Maylin. Lesbian or no,

this was not a girl who was caught up in a romance. More likely, this was a girl who might be having a little bit of a nervous breakdown. And who, for one reason or another, *was not sleeping in her own room.*

"What's this?" Maylin said. I looked up to see she was holding my phone, staring at Sarah Black's picture.

The sophomore Chloe was leaning in, gazing at it with Maylin. I was a little too stunned to snatch it away from them right away.

"It's . . . uh . . . just an old picture. Of a girl who used to go here."

"When?" Maylin asked. "Looks really old. Why do you have it on your phone?"

"I just . . . Star got me into looking at these old pictures."

"What's that teeny-tiny type below the picture?" Chloe asked.

I was surprised to hear her speak, because she so rarely did.

"Death of Local Girl," Maylin said.

"No, not there," Chloe said. "Below the picture. *Really* tiny. See how blotchy it is?"

Alex crammed a cucumber slice into her mouth, watched me for a moment while she chewed, and then barked, "For fuck's sake, give the girl her phone back!"

Chloe looked wide-eyed and remorseful, recoiling from the phone. Maylin glared at Alex but silently dropped my phone into my hand.

"It just caught my attention," Maylin murmured defensively.

"As these things do," Alex said pointedly.

Maylin and I exchanged a look. Yes, somehow Alex knew

about us gossiping about her therapy contacts. Somehow Alex knew everything. She always did, somehow or other.

Maylin and Alex were glowering at each other. But I was more interested in the picture on my phone. Chloe was right. There *was* a minuscule print below the picture of Sarah, squashed below the bottom of the photo, presumably to fit above the bottom border of the newspaper. I had to zoom way in to even start to see them as distinguishable words.

I was not focused, as the others were, on the silence that had fallen over our table. I think we had all—even Chloe—registered the same thought at once: an unaccustomed nastiness had accompanied Alex to dinner. *There was something wrong with Alex.*

But I couldn't fully digest this because my fingers were still sliding over the screen of my phone, zooming further in until I could make out the first word. *The.* Slide to the right. *Lord.* To the right again. *Seeth.*

I kept sliding across the screen. Slowly, slippery, refocusing. Until I'd read the whole thing:

The Lord seeth not as man seeth; for man looketh on the outward appearance, but the Lord looketh on the heart. 1 Samuel 16:7

A Bible quote.

I eyed *Samuel,* and felt myself floating above the dining hall table for a moment, vaguely hearing Alex apologize for snapping, and then Maylin saying sorry for being nosy.

"Haley?" Maylin said.

Maybe Samuel wasn't a bad boyfriend after all. *Samuel was sixteen.* That was what Anthony and I had thought we heard on

Thatcher's tape. But was it really something like, *Samuel one sixteen*?

"Umm," I said. "It's no problem at all."

I threw my phone onto my tray and stood up. "I'm not feeling so great. I have to go."

39

In my room, I Googled *1 Samuel 16:7*.

I used to go to church with my mom before she decided she didn't have time for it anymore. So I didn't know all that much about the Bible.

What came up was a more modern translation than the one that had appeared below the picture in Sarah Black's death notice, but essentially the same thing: "The Lord does not see as mortals see; they look at outward appearance, but the Lord looks on the heart." And it was often quoted simply as "God sees the heart."

I rifled through my desk drawer until I found the old '90s printout Star had given me of the ghost story accounts. I scanned quickly to confirm. The ghost had said "He sees" to a student named Sheila Hahn in the 1970s.

Breathless, I opened my laptop and reread the opening of the Darkins report until I found the line I was looking for: *Mrs. Bradford recollects that her mother said that the ghost was, in her student days, rumored to quote Scripture during her visitations. But she believes that may have been her mother's pious embellishment of a topic that otherwise made her uncomfortable.*

"Pious embellishment," I scoffed. Mrs. Bradford should have listened to her mother after all.

And then there were the hearts. The hearts Suzie Price had spoken of.

I slammed the laptop closed and raced down the stairs to the laundry room. Thankfully, it was empty. Everyone else was still eating.

Behind the dryer where Rhea had shown me, there was the heart with the letters:

God sees the heart.

"Uhhhhh," I exhaled.

Mrs. Bradford's mother had attended roughly around 1905.

This Bible-quoting ghost had been around for more than a hundred years. And that particular bit of Scripture clearly meant something to Sarah Black, or her family, or her history. The ghost, if there was one, was almost certainly Sarah Black.

Had Sarah Black been in Taylor's room whispering to her a few nights before she died?

And quoting the Bible? I knew that students at Windham used to be way more religious in the 19th century—even had religion classes and mandated church attendance. But it seemed like the ghost was barking up the wrong tree, quoting the Bible to Taylor.

God sees the heart. Sad heart. Sick heart. He sees. I see you in the dark.

And hearts scratched in the wall.

Was this a consistent message? I wasn't sure. The ghost was preoccupied with the heart, that was clear. But what did she *want*?

My phone buzzed in my pocket. I had two emails that had popped in at the same time.

First, Darla had written back:

Hi Haley,

All I remember from that night was a shrouded, scared sort of face. This picture doesn't really jar my memory one way or another.

Darla

So much for my idea that the Haunteds would all immediately recognize Sarah Black as their ghost. Unless, maybe there *were* two ghosts, like Star was saying. One who wore white and one who wore black. One who quoted the Bible, and one who said darker things like *I made her jump?*

I quickly thanked her for the reply and hit Send.

My next message was from Lucia Jackson's assistant:

Haley, Tonight actually works for Lucia if you can please remember to keep it short. 7:30 to 7:40. Thanks.

♦♦♦

At 7:31, the call came from an area code I didn't recognize.

"Hello?"

As if I didn't know exactly who was calling. As if this wasn't intimidating at all.

"Hello, Haley? This is Lucia calling."

"Yes. Hi. Thank you so much for agreeing to talk to me. I bet a lot of Windham students ask."

"Actually, no." Lucia's voice was cheerful, almost youthful. Not what I was expecting from her author photo. "You're the first one in about ten years."

"Oh."

I didn't know what to say. I tried not to think about how rich and famous Lucia Jackson was.

"But all one has to do is be a squeaky wheel," she said.

"Um . . . since we only have ten minutes, I should cut right to the—"

"Who said we only have ten minutes?" Lucia laughed.

"Your assistant."

"Oh. I see. Well, maybe that's all it will take. But I'm not setting an egg timer here."

I was silent for a few painful seconds, which, in spite of Lucia's words, I felt I could almost hear ticking away.

"I actually wanted to know about the Winter Girl. I mean, you know, the ghost that haunts the senior dorm?" I said, hearing my own words rush out with the same sort of helpless dread you feel when you watch something fragile—and just out of reach—falling and breaking. "About your experience with it. That's the main thing I'm researching. Do you know what I'm talking about?"

An even longer silence followed this time. I stared at the door, praying that Star would not choose this moment to come through it. I hadn't seen her since dinner.

Lucia cleared her throat. "Of course."

"Okay, great." I hesitated. "Because your name came up when I started researching this question."

"Can I just interrupt you for a moment, Haley?" Lucia's voice seemed to soften a little. "Are you the scholarship student?"

I hesitated, momentarily stunned by the relatively personal question.

"I'm . . . uh . . . on financial aid, yes."

"No, I mean the Fleming scholarship."

"I . . . don't know what that is."

In the silence that followed my words, I thought I heard Lucia sigh.

"Oh. Never mind. Someone contacted me recently about this one particular scholarship." Lucia's words were tumbling out now, similar to how mine had been seconds earlier. "If I'd make a contribution, or something. Sorry to interrupt. I didn't mean to be rude. So, we're talking about the Dearborn ghost here, and you're interviewing artist and writer alums about that specifically?"

"Yeah," I said. "Your name came up in particular because when you were a student here, when you were a senior, someone interviewed you about it."

"Someone?"

My mind went blank. I couldn't remember how I'd told myself I'd skirt around the peculiar details of how I'd come across her interview.

"Your houseparents. They, um, kept a cool sort of journal of their year at Dearborn. I found it in the archives."

Good, Haley. Straight up lying to the celebrated writer. *Go for it.*

"Okay. This is sounding familiar now. They were kind of into the ghost thing, I remember. They liked to talk about it."

"They wrote down what you said." I hesitated. "That you saw the ghost but she didn't scare you."

"I see." Lucia paused for a moment. "Now, why are you researching this, Haley? Are you a senior?"

"Yes."

"Have you been visited by the ghost recently?" Her voice was sharp again—disapproving? I couldn't tell.

"I don't know. I'm researching this because of my friend. My friend who died in Dearborn last year. I don't know if you heard about that?"

Lucia sucked in a breath and didn't speak for a moment.

"Oh no . . . I didn't. I'm . . . sorry."

"She jumped out of the window of her room on the fourth floor," I said. After a moment, I added, "Her name was Taylor."

"I'm . . . *so* sorry," Lucia repeated, her voice almost a whisper now.

"Thank you. Now . . . do you remember those houseparents sort of interviewing you? Your senior year, when you lived in Dearborn?"

Lucia was silent for a moment. Then she cleared her throat.

"I remember talking to them about the ghost a lot, yes. Oh my goodness. That housemother that year was a trip. Her big hair and her advice for the lovelorn. I don't know where the hell Windham found those two. It was an odd year at Dearborn—my understanding is that they were gone by the next year. Rumor had it the lady was Headmistress Bradford's hippie niece or something, that she was basically putting them up in Dearborn for a year until they got on their feet."

Interesting that Lucia and the other girls had found the Darkinses odd enough to come up with a rumor like that. And that the reality was far weirder.

"Just . . . um . . . a couple more things about what you said about the ghost?" I prompted.

"Oh. Sure."

"You said that you saw the ghost but she didn't scare you. That you just kind of acknowledged her and moved on with your life."

"That . . . sounds like me, I guess."

"So it's true? You saw her?"

"Well . . . yes."

"And it didn't scare you?"

Lucia was quiet for a moment.

"Haley . . . your friend . . . Please tell me if this is an inappropriate question, and if it is, I apologize. But can I ask what this has to do with your friend?"

"Well, I'm getting around to that. The ghost you saw . . . Did you get a bad feeling when you saw her? Do you think it was a ghost capable of doing something evil?"

Lucia didn't make a sound for about a minute.

"Hello?" I said.

"You think your friend's death had something to do with the ghost?" Lucia asked quietly.

I tried not to overthink my answer. About how what I was saying might in fact sound a bit like a potential Lucia Jackson novel. Or just sound crazy.

"Maybe," I admitted. "Umm, are you in front of a computer? Do you mind if I email you something, while we're on the phone?"

"Sure," Lucia replied. "But my assistant forwards me all of my email from my author account. So here, use this address instead of what you used before."

She rattled off a different email address from the one I'd gotten off her website.

As I started to prepare the attachment with Sarah Black's photo, I asked, "You saw her in the hallway?"

"Yes. The housemother reported that I said that?"

"Was it true?"

"Yes, but . . ."

Lucia paused for a moment before continuing.

"But it's . . . *fuzzy*. High school wasn't a great time for me. Maybe I didn't see what I thought I did. Maybe it's best not to . . ."

She trailed off.

"Did the ghost say anything to you?" I asked.

"Um . . . no."

"Do you think there was something special about you, that made you be able to see the ghost and not be scared of it?" I asked, growing concerned that my ten minutes would soon be up.

"Oh, now . . . what would give you that idea?" Lucia asked.

"Did you really see ghosts when you were a little kid?" I could feel now that I was fighting back tears of frustration.

"No," Lucia admitted. "That part's not true."

"Why did you say that, then?" I demanded. "To those house-parents?"

"I was seventeen," she said quickly. "I can't remember exactly. I mean, I was shy. I did weird things for attention. I might have had a little crush on that househusband or whatever they called him."

Her ability to admit to a lie so casually took my breath away for a moment. Then again, it was a teenage lie from thirty years ago.

"It was his wife who interviewed you, not him," I reminded Lucia.

"Oh. Well, of course I don't *really* remember what was in my head then. I'm sorry."

"But you saw the ghost, and she didn't scare you."

There was a brief silence.

"That's true," Lucia said quietly.

Please tell me how not to be scared. Please tell us all.

"There was a girl the year before you who got really freaked out by the ghost . . . had to leave campus?"

"Yes. Yes, that was sad. How did you know about that?"

"The houseparents wrote a bit about her, too. Do you remember her name?"

"They wrote down my name but not hers?" Lucia asked.

"Umm . . ."

I sucked in a breath. What was a little white lie between liars?

"Yeah," I said.

"Probably they wanted to protect her privacy. It sounded

like she had such a terrible time. I . . . wouldn't feel comfortable sharing her name, even if I remembered it. She . . . she's probably suffered enough."

I felt slightly embarrassed for asking. Now the famous author thought I was an insensitive snoop.

"You should have gotten my email by now," I murmured.

"Oh! Yes. Here we are. This is kind of fun."

There was a click and then a pause. And then I thought I heard a little gasp.

"*Where* did you get this, Haley?" Lucia demanded. "You're a Fleming girl, aren't you?"

The Fleming scholarship. A Fleming girl. Why did she keep bringing up *Fleming*?

"Is that the ghost you saw in the hall?" I asked, my pulse quickening.

Fleming. I grabbed a pen and scribbled down the name on my hand. I had heard that name before. Now, where had it been?

"Where did you get this?" she said again.

I wasn't sure exactly *what* I'd gotten over on Lucia, or why it felt so satisfying to do so.

"From the Rochester Public Library archives. Is that the ghost you saw in the hall?"

"Yes," Lucia snapped. "But I was probably a little crazy. Windham brings that out in certain girls. And you can quote me on that, if you like. I'm afraid I need to go now."

"You *do*?" I said dumbly. I underlined *Fleming*, pressing my pen hard into my palm.

"I'm afraid so. I have a conference call with the West Coast in a few minutes, actually. But Haley—please do accept my condolences about your friend. I hope you find the answers you're looking for. Truly, I do."

"Thanks," I said.

"Bye now," she said, her voice softening—probably with relief.

And then she was gone. *CALL ENDED* flashed on my phone screen.

I put the phone down and looked at Sarah Black's picture. I tried to decide if the uncertain look on her face frightened me. But really, it just made me sad. There was something familiar in the sadness of her expression, but I couldn't say from where.

I'd shown that picture to a few different "haunted" alums, to little avail until now. And while emailing Lucia the photo had been kind of weird, she'd been fine—even delighted—with the weirdness of it all until she'd *seen* the actual photograph of Sarah Black. And then she'd stonewalled.

What did it mean that the strongest reaction to the picture of Sarah Black came from the girl who had supposedly been the least afraid of her? And what did it mean that she was suddenly in such a hurry to get off the phone?

40

Between Lucia Jackson and Bible sleuthing and cram-writing my late Western Civ paper, I was too distracted to think much about Alex. But now she's on my mind.

Sleeping in someone else's room. Looking exhausted. Snarling at Maylin and Chloe. Was it just my imagination that she'd caught a glimpse of the picture right before she'd snapped? That something about the picture set her off?

A line from the Darkins report comes to mind: "According to other students and faculty, she had a reputation of being a high academic achiever in previous years but seemed less engaged this year."

That's what he said about Student Y—Lucia Jackson. And it feels true of Alex now, too.

I've spent so much time worrying about being haunted myself—and about what might happen come February 10. But maybe it's not really me who's haunted. Maybe it's Alex. Alex, who's trying to pull herself out of it with therapy or pills, but who doesn't know what she's dealing with. I need to warn her. Or at least talk with her?

Would she ever say so if she was experiencing something

scary, something potentially supernatural? I keep coming back to Alex's little speech about people making assumptions about her. I'm probably guilty of those assumptions, too. She's been so steady, so self-sufficient, for as long as I've known her.

Like the night of the second peed bed. Freshman year. About two weeks after the first. But it was also the last. Last one forever, fingers crossed.

It was the night before Halloween. That time I awoke in the middle of the night—from a dream that I'd fallen into a giant fish tank and was half-heartedly trying to swim to its surface, admiring a few koi on the way up. Half-awake, and then, with the oh-no-not-again realization, out of bed, on my feet, heart thumping with dread.

I glanced over at Alex's bed to see if she was awake.

But she wasn't there.

My heart raced even faster at this discovery. She was in the bathroom, surely to return at any second. Way worse than her being asleep—and me just having to make sure I didn't wake her up—was her coming into the room just as I was pulling apart my bed or changing.

What would I do if I heard her come to the door? Jump back into the wet bed and then pickle there until I was sure she was asleep?

No no no. It would NOT go that way.

It was with—I felt—almost superhuman speed that I got those sheets into a plastic bag, throwing my pajamas in with them and tossing it all into the back of the closet. I had another set of each out in a few seconds, and struggled to get the fitted *sheet on the mattress. New pj's were thrown on backward. And then I was dressed and the bed was suddenly made, and I was in it.*

And I was still alone.

And it was the night before Halloween.

Or rather, three a.m. in the early hours of Halloween.

Now that I was safely back in a clean bed, I puzzled over Alex's long absence. I wondered if I should check the bathroom. Even though that might be weird since we weren't friends— since we weren't supposed to notice things about each other.

I couldn't go back to sleep. Did Alex disappear like this often? And I usually slept through it?

It was about an hour before I finally heard the door ease open. I shut my eyes. After it closed, I opened one eye just enough to see Alex changing from jeans to sweatpants in the dark. And then she was in her bed.

After a minute or two, I heard her sniffling. A whimper or two accompanied the sniffles, and then there was silence. But it was enough to know Alex was crying.

I wanted to say something to help.

But I was supposed to be asleep.

I vowed to be really nice to her the next day.

And I was. I really was. But she acted the same as she always did. Quiet and studious and self-sufficient. Whatever had taken her out of the room—whatever had upset her—she clearly didn't want to talk about it. At least not with me.

It was not until months later that I learned of her mother's diagnosis. It was terrible to think that I could have helped just a little, somehow. But instead, Alex had been all alone.

41

Four Nights Left

Not much longer now. It feels different. It's almost time.

Time for someone else to know, to carry the burden, to feel this same slippery blood on their hands.

42

Wednesday, February 6

When I woke up, *Fleming* was still written across my palm in blue ballpoint ink.

And I swiped right to read a new email alert on my phone:

Dear Haley,

I apologize for having to get off the phone so abruptly, and I want to say again how sorry I am to hear about your friend. I am not terribly connected with Windham-Farnswood anymore, am not a very active alumna, so I had not heard until now.

You say you are a fan of my fiction, so I wonder if you have read any of my stories? If you will send me your Windham address, I would like to send you something—my first collection of stories, which was published when I was very young. It is out of print now and I doubt that the Windham Library has a copy, so will have Gwen FedEx it to you.

If you wish, perhaps when you are finished reading it, you could donate the book to the school. In the meantime,

*I believe you will find the story titled "The Snow Angel" of
particular interest.*

*Call me again sometime if you'd like. I am again sorry I
had to go so quickly.*

Kind regards,
Lucia
(212) 555-0009

The message had been sent just after one a.m.—again, from
her personal email address instead of the one I'd been using to
communicate with her assistant. *LuciaJ272.* Should I feel honored? I wasn't sure. I really didn't know what to think of Lucia
Jackson.

I knew I'd end up missing breakfast if I tried to compose a
meaningful reply or dig up info on Fleming. Besides, I found her
sudden warmth confounding. I wasn't sure if I trusted it.

♦♦♦

In the afternoon I finished my lunch early and went to Taunton
Hall, where the guidance offices were, on my way to my next
class.

When I got to the main counter, I didn't bother to ask for
my counselor. The front desk secretary was generally nicer and
more helpful anyway. When she looked up from her computer,
smiling expectantly, I said, "I was wondering if I could get some
information about the Fleming scholarship?"

"The *what* scholarship?"

"The Fleming scholarship."

She frowned. "I'm not familiar with that."

"Can you please look it up? Someone told me I would be a good candidate for it."

I tried not to notice the ease with which the lie came out of my mouth.

The secretary hesitated, fingering a curl behind her ear. "You're currently on financial aid?"

"Yeah," I said. "And I'm a senior."

"I'm pretty familiar with all of the endowments for students, as well as the scholarships for outgoing students, and that one doesn't ring a bell."

"Do you have like a listing of all of the scholarships?"

I knew this secretary was relatively new—the old one had retired when I was a junior.

"Just a moment." She clicked and typed for a few seconds. "We do, but I'm not seeing anything under that name. Who told you about it?"

"An alumna," I murmured.

Someone contacted me recently about this one particular scholarship. If I'd make a contribution. That was what Lucia had said.

"Maybe it's a new scholarship?" I offered.

"Perhaps you can check with her and see if she's misremembering the name?" The secretary tapped her pen and shrugged. "Did she receive this scholarship herself?"

"I don't know," I said. "I'll have to check with her. Thanks. I'd actually better get to class."

"Sorry I couldn't be more helpful!" the secretary called after me.

✦✦✦

Fleming scholarship

 Fleming scholarship Windham Farnswood

 Fleming scholarship Lucia Jackson

I was Googling these things on my way out of my last class even though I knew it wouldn't be helpful. Before I got back to the dorm, I remembered someone else I could ask: my mother's old friend Michelle—who worked in the main administrative office, and who'd put in a good word for me when I was originally applying. She and my mother had not been best friends growing up together in Heathsburg, but had been neighbors and classmates from kindergarten through high school, and had always been friendly. Their moms had borrowed cups of sugar from each other, bought Girl Scout cookies from each other's kids, that sort of thing. My admission to Windham-Farnswood had apparently been an extension of that neighborly spirit.

I didn't see Michelle much—although every December I brought her a little box of chocolates or cookies and a handwritten note. My mother had asked me to do it the first year, and every subsequent year I'd done it on my own.

I asked the front office receptionist for Michelle—who I knew had a cubicle in the farther-back offices.

"Hey, Haley," Michelle said, emerging about a minute after the receptionist had summoned her. "Everything okay?"

She gestured for me to sit on the plush red couch in the reception area—the one that was usually for visiting prospective students and their fancy parents.

"Yup," I said, leaning against it rather than sitting. "I just had a quick question for you."

"How's your mother?" Michelle sat and pulled her pilling purple cardigan tight over her chest and smiled.

"She's good."

"She must be so proud of you. You know where you're going to college next year?"

"Not yet. Crossing my fingers. I think I want to go to University of Wisconsin."

Thankfully, she didn't ask me why I wanted to go there. I felt I had good reasons, but I knew they probably sounded vague to the sensible adult ear.

"I'm sure you'll find the right situation. So much to look forward to."

I nodded. "So if you could help me with something—just a quick question. Have you heard of something called the Fleming scholarship?"

"Hmm . . . no. A Windham scholarship? Or something from an outside institution?"

"I was under the impression it was something directly related to Windham."

"That doesn't sound like anything I work with, in terms of the endowments for financial aid students. You might want to check with Guidance if it's a college scholarship."

"I'm not sure which it is. I was talking to an alumna, and she made reference to a 'Fleming scholarship.'"

"Are you sure this person wasn't being sarcastic?"

"Why would that be sarcastic?"

Michelle glanced at the receptionist and made a sheepish face at me.

"Because one of our richest alumnae is Ms. Fleming," she said quietly. "She's sort of local. And as valiantly as the alumnae association has tried, they've never gotten her to give a penny to the school."

"Really?" I said.

"Yes. I hadn't heard her name in years. . . . My understanding is they gave up trying at least a decade ago. It's kind of funny. The tight-wadded old bird must hate this place. She's got a couple of charities in her name. But she's never given anything to Windham."

"Maybe she figures Windham doesn't need it?" I pointed out.

There were plenty of rich ladies and gentlemen willing to give donations to their alma mater. Windham-Farnswood wasn't really suffering.

"Maybe. Anyway, her name is Norma Wozniak Fleming."

And hearing the name *Norma,* I remembered why Fleming had sounded familiar to me when Lucia Jackson had first said it. *Norma Fleming.* Ms. Noceno had mentioned the name. She was the alumna who had bought the ruined picture of Sarah Dearborn, saying she'd have it restored.

"How'd she get so rich?" I asked slowly. "Family money?"

Sarah Dearborn in the black-dress portrait. The *Sarah in Black.* Not to be confused with Sarah Black—who appeared to the girls wearing white? Quoting the Bible?

"No. She and a business partner had a frozen baked goods

company. You probably never heard of Orchard Hill Farms cakes and pies, but they were big in the '70s and '80s. They sold the company for millions of dollars. By then I think Norma was married to a CEO of someone in fast food. I think they invested really well, too. And they didn't have kids."

"You know a lot about her," I said.

"Just Windham gossip, you know. My friend Gina in Alumnae Relations used to talk about her all the time—it drove her crazy that they couldn't make any headway with old Norma Moneybags. But . . . Norma was more of a hot topic ten or twenty years ago. Now she's an old lady. I'm waiting for the inevitable news story that she's died and left her estate to her cats."

I smiled at this. It made me think of Taylor—of the stray calico cat she'd tried to house in her room the year before last. When she was a junior and I was a sophomore. I hadn't thought about that in a long time.

"Okay," I said, pulling on my backpack. "Thanks. Oh! One other thing."

I remembered something that had been on my mind—since Michelle seemed to know all of the hidden Windham gossip.

"Do you know what happened to Tricia, the old soccer coach, who was the Dearborn RD last year?"

"Yeah. Actually, she got a coaching job here in town, at Heathsburg High. She stuck around because she's engaged now—to the guy who owns Cosmic Comics."

"Really?" I said. That comic store was just about a mile farther than the gas station I'd walked to on Saturday. I'd always seen it from the shuttle window when I'd go shopping in Derby.

I'd always been curious about it—since I read comics occasionally when I was a kid—but the shuttle didn't make special stops.

"Yeah. I believe she helps him run the shop now, too. She was there when I went in for stocking stuffers for my son. Seemed happy. No love lost between her and Windham."

"Huh," I said. Tricia sounded way cooler than Anna. "Thanks."

"My pleasure," Michelle replied. "I ought to get back to work. Say hi to your mom for me."

On my way back to Dearborn, I wondered what had become of that old cat of Taylor's. Taylor had never been very clear about where she'd found it or how she was sure it was a stray. She'd named it Dottie and bought it organic cat food and let it sleep in her bed. She got away with it for three weeks because it didn't meow much, but Dottie went for a stroll once after Taylor didn't fully latch her door closed when she went for a shower, and the resident director had seen her.

The next day, she made Taylor take Dottie to the pound. Taylor had cried so bitterly I'd wondered if she was putting on an act, her face so wet and shiny it looked like plastic. Like the dollar-store imitation Barbies my dad used to buy me after long days together raking leaves.

I hadn't hugged Taylor that afternoon because we weren't the hugging kind of friends. I'd told her that Dottie was so sweet I was sure she'd end up in a good home. Taylor had kept crying, and didn't reply. She told me she wanted to be by herself that night, and we never discussed Dottie again.

43

In the late afternoon after classes had finished, I went back to my room and searched *Norma Fleming*.

A website came up for something called the Fleming Foundation. It appeared to be an organization that gave money to medical research and special camps and activities for children with various medical issues.

I found and clicked on the tab that said *Our Founder*.

There was a photo of a woman with tight white curls, red lipstick, and a warm smile.

Norma's philanthropic work began in 1975, when she started the Healing Hearts Foundation. In 1983, she purchased an eight-bedroom home and had it fully remodeled to serve as a rooming house for families of children being treated at St. Catherine's Hospital. The Robin Hill Family House in Covington, Massachusetts, is funded exclusively by the Healing Hearts Foundation, an arm of the Fleming Foundation, and is run with the assistance of a committed team of volunteers. Norma, who lives intermittently on the home's property in the Robin Hill Cottage, is still on the volunteer team to this day. Her oatmeal chocolate-chip cookies are a guest favorite.

Below this segment of the bio was a photograph of a large yellow Victorian house with lots of lilies and petunias growing out front and a white swing on the porch. I looked up the town of Covington. It was about twenty-five minutes from Windham-Farnswood. Sort of local, just as Michelle had said.

> Norma went on to open six more free and sliding-scale family rooming houses for patient families near several different hospitals in New England and New York State.
>
> In 1987, Norma began the Healing Hearts Scholarship Fund, which provides tuition assistance to families of children with medical issues. In 1990, she began the Brian Drayton Scholarship Fund to help college students whose medical needs require additional funding, accommodations, or equipment.

Sounded like a nice lady. I could imagine her thinking that compared to these causes, Windham really didn't seem like a worthy recipient of her money. Even if girls without money—like me—might be the trickle-down recipients. Her attention was understandably focused elsewhere. I didn't think Windham could really begrudge her that.

It didn't entirely explain why she'd never gotten the Sarah Dearborn portrait restored, but maybe she was just a busy person and had other priorities.

And she wasn't dead yet. So she couldn't be the ghost.

But Lucia Jackson must've brought her up for a reason. I wondered if Lucia knew about Norma Fleming's connection to the portrait. Or if there was another reason why she kept bringing up her name.

I knocked on Alex's door.

"Come in!" she yelled.

As I opened the door, I saw it: a tiny heart. Scratched in the outer doorframe. Just slightly bigger than a quarter, it was carved low, almost at doorknob level. I sucked in a gasp as I saw it, my gaze meeting Alex's as she sat up on her bed. Her hair frizzy, a flushed crease across her cheek.

"You okay?" she asked groggily.

"I'm sorry—were you sleeping?" I asked, trying to compose myself, making a split decision not to ask her about the heart first thing. I'd come here to check on her, after all—not make her feel worse.

"I was just trying to take a little nap."

The carving was so tiny, so low, that perhaps it had always been there and I'd never noticed. We generally convened in Maylin's nicer, more spacious room, so I didn't know every nook and cranny of Alex's. I exhaled.

"A nap a couple of hours before bed?" I said slowly. "That can really mess with your sleep."

"I figured if I didn't wake up till morning, that would be okay."

"Um, Alex?" I pulled her desk chair closer to her bed and sat on it. "Is there a reason you've not been sleeping in your room some nights?"

"Oh." Alex rolled her eyes. "So that secret's out."

"Well, *is* it a secret?" I asked.

"Not really. I don't see why anyone should care."

"Neither Maylin nor I care where you sleep. Or . . . we *care* because we *care* about you. Just . . . it doesn't make a difference to us . . . in case you were wondering."

Alex smiled and shook her head. "Is that what you two think? You guys are cute. No, Chloe's not my girlfriend."

"Then why did you sleep in her room?"

As the question left my lips, it felt vaguely obnoxious. Normally I would leave it all alone, like I always did with Anthony. But I felt like I had to ask—because her behavior was starting to resemble Student X's. It scared me.

"She's having a lot of trouble with chemistry." Alex sighed. "So I was helping for a couple of hours. I got so tired I went down for a micronap on her floor, but then I didn't wake up for the rest of the night, and she was too shy to wake me up, I guess."

"Okay," I said.

This didn't explain why Chloe's roommate, Rhea, had made herself scarce all night, but I decided to stop pressing. Maybe there was some truth to Maylin's theory after all. But it really wasn't any of our business.

"Hey . . . you're a big Lucia Jackson fan, right?" I asked. Awkward segue, but I was eager to divert the conversation away from Alex's private life. I was starting to feel like a creep for bringing it up.

"Well . . ." Alex shrugged. "Kind of. I used to be more into her, like, sophomore year. I don't have time for that kind of reading right now."

"You ever read her story 'The Snow Angel'?"

Alex turned away from me and plumped her pillow—as if she was wishing—even hinting—to get back to her nap.

"Don't think so," she said, smoothing the pillowcase. "I prefer to read whole novels."

Alex curled up on her bed and rested her head. Clearly I was supposed to take the hint now. In the fetal position, with her tired eyes pleading, Alex looked about twelve years old. The vulnerability in her face struck me deep. It reminded me of something I couldn't quite name.

"I want to tell you something," I said, my voice dropping almost to a whisper.

"Yeah?"

I swallowed the impulse to ask her about the heart.

"If you ever feel like you can't be alone in your room at night, you can come hang out with me and Star. Even if you want to crash on our floor."

"Well, I appreciate that offer." Alex curled up and rested her head on the pillow. "I don't think it will be necessary, though. I like my room."

"Really, just . . . if you ever don't feel like things are right in your room . . . please go to someone. Even if it's not me."

Alex's gaze shifted away from me, and her mouth went slack. I felt like she had suddenly recognized something in what I was saying—something that matched her experience.

"Why would things not feel right in my room?" she asked quietly.

I hesitated. Was I scaring her? Was I making things worse?

"I don't know for sure," I said. "I just think that's what happened with Taylor. That she started to feel like being alone in her room was getting to her. That the . . . um . . . energy of that was weighing on her . . ."

I figured if I said *ghost,* then Alex would shut down this conversation completely. Let alone *Bible-quoting ghost,* or *ghost who changes dresses,* or *dueling white-dress, black-dress ghosts.*

But while I tried to decide on my next words, I was stunned to see a big tear was rolling down Alex's cheek. Then another. They splashed down on the crew neck of her black sweater.

"But I don't think she was crazy," I said softly, unsure if I should keep going. "I'm really starting to think there might be something that Dearborn does to people. That we all need to be careful that nothing like that happens to anyone *this* year. We need to take care of each other, watch out for each other, and make sure no one's too isolated like Taylor kind of was. Especially between now and February 10th. That date might be . . . important."

Alex's shoulders were shaking a little, but she wasn't making a sound. Just quietly wiping away a steady stream of tears.

"There's really *something* here. Something . . . bad. It might not be a ghost, it might be some other force or tension, but whatever it is—"

Alex covered her face and an actual, audible sob tore through her.

"Why are you crying?" I asked gently.

Alex sniffled and wiped at her face with her fingertips.

"Because I'm tired. And because I'm sorry about what happened to Taylor," she said. "And I'm sorry you have to live in this building after all that. I don't think I've thought before about how fucked up that really is. That they even let you live on the same *floor,* for fuck's sake."

"It's okay," I said. "I'm okay."

"No, it's *not.* And *you're* not. Do you hear yourself?"

I had never seen Alex so torn up. And the only time I'd ever seen her cry before was that one time our first year—when I wasn't supposed to have seen.

"Did you know there's a little heart carved in your doorframe?" I whispered.

Alex was silent for a moment.

"Yes," she hissed. "It's been there all year. What does that have to do with anything?"

"It's a sign of the . . ." I trailed off. I *did* maybe sound a little crazy.

"There. Is. No. Ghost. *Haley.*" Alex's voice was low and feral.

She was staring at me, her face wet with fresh tears, her expression strained with a fear she was trying but failing to hide.

Fear for me? Or fear for herself that she was unwilling, still, to admit? Either way, she looked so young and so scared. That familiar twinge her expression had given me a few minutes earlier—I understood it now. I remembered where it came from.

"Okay," I whispered. "Okay."

Alex wiped her face with her sleeve, sniffled, and looked at her phone.

"I know things have been hard for you here sometimes. Like they've been hard for me. This place isn't *us,* but we endure it for all of the opportunities it'll supposedly give us, right?"

"Right," I said, still whispering.

Tap tap tap. There was a barely audible knock on Alex's door.

I got up and opened it so Alex wouldn't have to. Rhea was standing there.

"Hi," she said. "I was just wondering if Chloe was here?"

"Nope," Alex said quickly, sitting up. "We don't have a tutoring session this afternoon."

Alex's words were stilted. Her use of the phrase *tutoring session* was kind of weird, like she had to reiterate why she and Chloe spent time together. Nothing romantic. *Nothing to see here, folks.*

"Oh." Rhea looked puzzled. "Okay."

"I've got a couple of things to do alone before dinner," Alex said, the pitch of her voice unusually high.

Both Rhea and I started. Alex really wanted us both to leave.

We said quick goodbyes, and I stole one more glance at the little heart before Rhea and I headed down the hall. When I reached my door, I turned to Rhea before she continued to the stairwell.

"Alex spends a lot of time in your room lately, doesn't she?" I asked.

"Yeah . . . kind of." Rhea looked a little sheepish. "She and Chloe . . ."

She seemed unsure how to finish the sentence. I thought I heard the stairwell door creak, but then no one came out of it.

"If you ever think Alex needs help, will you let me know?" I said, lowering my voice. I was trying to shake the feeling that the little carved heart—among other things—meant that Alex was marked somehow.

Rhea hesitated. "What do you mean?"

"She's my friend. I lost a friend last year. And I'm trying to be a better friend."

Rhea looked at the floor, embarrassed by my awkwardness. I didn't care. I wasn't sure what to do for Alex, but it seemed like doing something—*anything*—was better than doing nothing. I couldn't tell everyone about the ghost, about my fear of the looming February 10. That would look crazy. But I could at least make sure there were other girls looking out for Alex.

"Okay," she whispered.

◆◆◆

Once I was back in my room, it took me a few minutes to find the picture on my laptop. It wasn't in my main photo file, as apparently I'd never downloaded it from my email.

My mother had taken it on my very first day at Dearborn—when Alex and I had become roommates sight unseen. The housing office must have figured we'd get along—two scholarship kids from the Midwest.

Alex's parents had gone back to their hotel and would see her the next day. But since my mom had to say her official goodbye that evening, she'd lingered. Her suggestion that Alex and I pose for a "new roomies" photo had embarrassed me even though I understood that it was one of several last-ditch strategies to extend the goodbye.

Alex and I had stood awkwardly next to each other in front of her bed. We didn't know each other well enough for someone to drape an arm over the other.

My mother sent it to me with a short note:

Hope you are having a wonderful second day. You'll do great!

Alex seems like a sweetheart.

Indeed, Alex did seem like a sweetheart. You could tell from the picture. Doe-eyed and uncertain, trying to smile. Her long light brown hair was sort of lifeless from a long, humid day of moving our stuff up the freshman dormitory stairs. Several inches shorter than me, her face not yet matured as it was now, she looked way younger than our fourteen years.

I clicked back to Sarah Black's photo.

Since it was a black-and-white photograph, of course I couldn't tell exactly what color Sarah Black's hair was—but it was on the lighter side, like Alex's. They both had eyes so big they didn't quite fit their thin faces. They both had a skinny vulnerability that made you want to cook them a cheeseburger or brew them a cup of hot cocoa—fatten them up, make them smile.

That was what had startled me, seeing Alex curled up in her bed—looking very much her younger self, reminding me of this picture:

Sarah Black and young Alex looked strangely alike.

44

I minimized the photo when Star walked in.

"Hey," she said softly. And then stood there gazing at me for a moment.

"You okay?" I asked, to prevent her from asking the same of me.

"Well . . . yeah."

"You look like you have something to say."

Star eased her backpack off her shoulder and sat down on her bed.

"I was wondering something," she said.

"Sure?"

"Are you friends with Rhea?"

"Um . . . not really . . . we were just talking. You saw us?"

That would mean that it was Star who'd started to open the stairwell door when Rhea and I were in the hall together. But she maybe hung back when she saw us talking. And listened to me talking about Alex?

"No," Star said quickly. "I was just wondering."

"Yeah, no. She hangs with Chloe, who hangs with Alex, so she's usually around. I just was asking her something random. Why?" I pressed.

Star reached into her coat pocket, pulled out some M&M's, ate one, then offered me the bag.

"You know how there are some people who you get the feeling hate you?" she asked.

I hesitated, taking a single piece of candy. "Uh-huh."

Certainly I had had that experience. Particularly when I was friends with Taylor. Lots of secondhand death rays came my way. But I had a feeling it was different for Star. Like she got it in her head that this or that person hated her without there being much evidence, just to make herself feel bad. Or that for her, *hate* meant something more like *thinks I'm a dweeb.*

"We . . . uh . . . weren't talking about you, if that's what you're worried about," I said.

But then it occurred to me that Star had overheard Rhea's and my entire conversation and was hoping I would confide in her. She and I talked about history and ghosts, but there were a bunch of real-life things that I always left out.

"Well, of course you weren't . . . I didn't mean it like that," Star said quickly, blushing. "I just wondered if you guys were friends."

I shrugged and popped the M&M in my mouth. "We're not."

Star sucked in her lips for a moment, then pulled her laptop out of her bag.

"I have something for you," she said. "Something pretty good."

"Yeah? Will it be served with a Twizzler?" I was trying to lighten the mood, help us both shake off the embarrassing conversation that had just occurred.

"Well . . . that's what I brought the M&M's for. It's something from the Rochester Library. Something kind of juicy."

"About Sarah Black?" I asked.

"Well, kind of. About her aunt. The one she was staying with when she died. There was one article listed about her when I went in for more the other day. They just sent it to me. Look." Star plopped her laptop in my lap.

December 13, 1889

Sirs and Madams—

I write in support of my dear old friends Kate and Maggie Fox—and to shine a light on Maggie's recent recantation, which I believe deserves more public attention than it has received.

Hungry reporters were eager and present in abundance on that terrible day at the New York Academy of Music last year. Maggie was coerced to announce that her mediumship— and that of her sister—was a sham. Naysayers laughed and gloated and had great fun. None of them understood the terrible circumstances Maggie was in at the time, that made her feel she had no choice. Now that she is recanting her statements, where are all of the eager reporters? Few have been circumspect enough to consider that Maggie had fallen victim to opportunists who wished to take advantage of her poor health and destitution. Even close friends did not realize the desperation of her situation, or we would have come to her aid.

Kate's and Maggie's gifts are delicate, and have always made them vulnerable to reprobates who wish to take advan-

tage. This forced denunciation of spiritualism was the most egregious. Now that Maggie's friends have come to her aid, she is no longer in such personal and financial straits, and has taken back up her spiritualist roots in earnest.

I do not expect everyone to believe in Maggie's and Kate's powers. I do believe, however, that the Rochester area press has a duty to tell their whole story—and not end it on their worst, most misguided, day.

My sisters in spiritualism deserve better, as do all of us.

> *Sincerely,*
> *Katherine Hannaford*

"This is really exciting, isn't it?" Star squealed. "Leonora and Sarah's aunt Katherine was a friend of the Fox sisters!"

"Who are they?" I asked, too tired to care if it was a stupid question.

"They're famous. They were these two women—well, girls when it all started—who started the spiritualist movement in the 1800s. Remember I was talking about the spiritualist movement a few days ago? When we were first talking about the ghost?"

"Oh . . . yeah," I lied, and waited for more.

"So, these two girls lived near Rochester, New York, in the mid-1800s, and one night they claimed to hear a mysterious knocking in their room. They told their mother and she heard it, too, and got scared and then . . . well, let me find a little summary for you."

Star took her laptop, typed a few words, clicked a few times, and then handed it back to me.

THE FOX SISTERS AND THE RISE
OF AMERICAN SPIRITUALISM

The Fox sisters' story began in 1848 in Hydesville, New York. Sisters Kate and Maggie, ages 11 and 14, alerted their mother to some mysterious noises they were hearing in their humble home. They convinced their mother that the sounds "responded" to them—such as answering with a requested number of knocks. Their mother and some of her friends became convinced that they were communicating with the spirit of a peddler who'd been murdered in their house. Friends and neighbors soon descended on the house, followed by curiosity seekers and reporters.

Kate and Maggie's sister Leah (who was several years older than them, and raising a family on her own after being abandoned by her first husband) took them to her home in Rochester—and found that the mysterious "rappings" followed the girls. The sisters' story garnered the interest of several local religious leaders and intellectuals. Soon, under the direction of their older sister, Kate and Maggie performed the phenomenon in a public hall in Rochester, and then at several different venues in New York City. Still managed by their elder sister, Kate and Maggie became well-known mediums, and traveled extensively, giving séances in many US cities. They drew the attention of public figures such as James Fenimore Cooper, William Lloyd Garrison, Sojourner Truth, and Horace Greeley. Sometimes they summoned important historical figures in their séances: the spirit of the late Benjamin Franklin was a frequent crowd-pleaser.

There were many skeptics, but still the Fox sisters' popularity grew, and so did spiritualism generally. Numerous copycat mediums began to emerge—many of whom hailed from the Foxes' native upstate New York.

Maggie became involved with a Catholic man, Arctic explorer Elisha Kane, who discouraged her from her spiritualist activities, which he considered fraudulent. Maggie stepped away from spiritualism during her common-law marriage to Kane (whose family rejected Maggie), but returned to mediumship after his untimely death in 1857. Kate married a fellow spiritualist, Henry Jencken. As Kate and Maggie aged and the pressures of public and family life mounted, both women began drinking heavily. There was frequent tension with their sister Leah, who had parlayed her spiritualist prominence into surprising societal respectability. She remarried a Wall Street banker and had a more stable life than her younger sisters—whose relationship with spiritualism became conflicted over the years of personal struggles.

In 1888, Maggie made a public confession at the New York Academy of Music, claiming that spiritualism was a sham. Supported by Kate, she admitted that the initial knockings on that fateful night were made by an apple on a string, and that later she and her sister perfected the skill of cracking their knuckles and their toe joints to make the mysterious rappings. Maggie was paid $1,500 to make this statement, a fact that spiritualists often point out to discredit it (along with the fact that she recanted about one year later). While Maggie tried to resume spiritualist activities, they were never as popular as before. Leah remained a prominent spiritualist until her death in 1890. Kate and Maggie died in 1892 and 1893, respectively—both penniless.

"So an early instance of poltergeists showing up around teenage girls," I offered.

"Oh . . . it's so much more than that, though. Those two girls were huge for the tradition of, like, séances and things like that in 19th-century America . . . and other countries, too, as it spread. They pretty much started that whole movement. They were famous mediums while they were still teenagers, even. I wonder if Sarah and Leonora's aunt knew them when they were girls, or just when they were older."

"But what does that mean for Sarah Black, you think?" I asked.

"I don't know, exactly. But I'm starting to develop a theory. If their aunt, who at least partially raised them, was *friends* with the Fox sisters, and very clearly a big believer in spiritualism, then that probably rubbed off on them. Maybe then Sarah or Leonora—or both of them—had spiritualism in their upbringing. Maybe they brought that *here*."

"Okay." I nodded. "Makes sense."

"Then . . . well . . . I'm not sure where we go with this . . . but if Leonora was sort of a spiritualist, maybe she, like, did séances and stuff. Tried to conjure her sister after she died. Which could have started the whole Sarah Black anxiety that got people thinking about a Sarah ghost haunting the halls."

"Or it really *did* unsettle Sarah's ghost and set her to haunting the halls," I offered. "Or unsettled some other spirit by accident."

Star hesitated, stretching her mouth downward with exaggerated skepticism.

"Let's not go there immediately," she said.

"Well, what if *Sarah Black herself* was big into spiritualism? What conclusions do we draw then?"

Star thought about this. "I don't know."

"Would a spiritualist be more inclined to *become* a ghost, you think?" I persisted.

Star smiled nervously.

"I can't tell if you're serious, asking that question."

"I can't either," I admitted. "It just felt like the natural next question, to me."

I turned back to the laptop article and stared at the picture of the young Fox sisters. The one on the right wore white, and looked sad and troubled as she looked directly into the camera. The one on the left had on a darker dress. Her gaze was shifted sideways, looking away from the camera. She appeared more bored and preoccupied than her sister. It was sad to think of what their charade—or their ordeal, depending on how you looked at it—did to their lives eventually.

"Star?" I said, without looking at her.

"Yeah?" she replied.

I looked from one sister to the other. I couldn't decide which girl was more painful to look at. Whether the pain came from lying and faking or genuine ghostly experiences, it was clear to me they were both suffering there in their pretty dresses. I closed the laptop and handed it back.

"I haven't told anyone this," I said quietly. "It was Taylor who took that video of Jocelyn."

Star slid her laptop onto her desk, avoiding my eyes.

"Yeah," she said softly. "That's not a surprise. Why are you, uh, bringing that up *now*?"

"You're saying you knew that?"

Star shrugged. "Most people kind of knew. I mean, who *else* would do something like that? Even Charlie was mortified, right? It probably wasn't any of *his* close friends."

"Did Jocelyn know?" I asked.

Star sat on her bed, cross-legged, looking at her hands. "Of *course* Taylor was definitely one of her main guesses. But she was so upset, catching the person wasn't really at the top of her list of priorities. It was hard enough for her just to get through the day, those first few days."

"Yeah. I can imagine."

"But . . ." Star's voice lowered almost to a whisper. "*Can* you?"

I hesitated. I'd suffered lots of small humiliations at home before I'd come here to Windham. And then spent a few years scared to death of repeating them somehow. And yet—

"Probably not," I muttered.

"And you didn't answer the question," she said flatly. "Why are you asking me about that now?"

I couldn't tell if there was a little anger in her voice.

"Because something about seeing those girls . . . that picture," I stammered. "Um, thinking about what could have been in their hearts when that picture was taken."

Sad heart. Sick heart. God sees the heart.

Star stared at me for a moment, then shook her head.

"Do you know there were a few days there when I was worried about Jocelyn hurting herself? Like, for real?"

Star seemed to be waiting for my reaction to this, but I couldn't find words quickly enough. It wasn't surprising, but Star seemed to think it was. She got up and started to rustle aimlessly through the papers on her desk.

"I'm sorry," I said.

"I was kind of relieved when she went home," she mumbled. "Relieved that it wasn't me who would have to be watching her, worrying. Isn't that so terrible?"

Star's hands came to rest on top of a manila folder. I thought she was going to show me yet another old piece of paper from her endless supply—but then realized she was only waiting for me to reply.

"No. It's not terrible. You knew she was safer at home. With her family."

Star shrugged. "I don't know if that was really true. Some of us are safer with our families. Some of us are not."

"You?" I whispered, because I felt she wanted me to ask.

"Yes. Definitely safe. But Jocelyn . . . there were issues. I won't go into it. She wasn't thrilled to go home to them, I'll just say that." Star paused before glancing up at me. "And you?"

"Me what?"

"Your family? Safer than here or not?"

"I don't know anymore," I said. The more pressing question for me had always been whether *I* was safer for *them*.

Star studied me for a moment. "And Taylor's?"

"I wish I knew," I answered. "I've wondered that a lot. I wish I knew more about her family. I know that her mom came here for high school, that both her parents made a ton of money, that her dad was an investment banker and her mom was a lawyer.

That she had one brother who was nice to her and one who wasn't."

"How *not nice* was he?"

I shook my head. "She never elaborated much. She used the word *asshole* a lot. I wouldn't overthink it."

Star considered this, then nodded.

"I could have proven it was Taylor that did it," I said. "To Jocelyn. I had the evidence."

Star fell back into her desk chair, letting her arms hang. "What evidence?"

"The burner phone she used to send out the video."

Star looked around the room—presumably so she wouldn't have to look right at me.

"That's where she stored it?" she murmured.

"Yes," I said.

"But you didn't want to snitch on your friend," she said slowly, charitably.

"It wasn't so much to do with being a loyal friend," I said. "I blackmailed her with it."

Star looked skeptical. "Blackmailed her . . . to do what?"

"To leave me alone. To let me ditch her without her doing something like that to me."

Star breathed. "Ohhh."

"Isn't *that* so terrible?" I said, repeating her words. I didn't mean the repetition as mockery, but I wondered how it sounded to Star.

Her face was blank. In her hesitation, I considered her odd question a moment ago: *That's where she stored it?* Like this was a question she'd considered before. Could Star have stolen

Taylor's laptop—temporarily—to look for concrete evidence of what she'd done to Jocelyn?

"Oh, no, *no,*" she said, her second *no* and her exuberant head-shaking giving away her polite insincerity.

No wonder poltergeists hang around teenage girls. We lie, lie, lie about everything, all the time, out of the absolute necessity of being *nice.* The tension is probably like candy to them.

Star and I were both silent for a minute.

I didn't feel bold enough to ask her the question that was on my mind. So I switched gears.

"Star," I whispered. "Why did you ever agree to be my roommate?"

Star glanced at her phone and sighed.

"Star?" I prompted.

"Because I was lonely," Star said. "And my best friend was gone. Same as you. Now . . . are you hungry?"

"Not really," I said. The words *best friend* seemed to linger in the air between us.

"I'm going to see if there are still any Doritos in the machine."

"Fingers crossed," I said, so fake-cheerful I think it startled Star.

She left and didn't come back. And I didn't see her at dinner.

45

Come on, now.

Of all the weird and crazy things.

Star is not a thief, for one. She doesn't have it in her.

And Alex is not a ghost.

Waifish girls are a dime a dozen here at Windham. And everywhere, really.

Alex isn't Sarah Black. Alex most certainly isn't dead. With the exception of these last few days, Alex is one of the most "alive" people I know. And the resemblance is vague. Like when you see two girls with the same color hair together, and assume they're sisters. Like that. Mostly just like that.

And there's no real pattern of Sarah haunting girls who looked like her. Because Taylor had been the visual opposite of Sarah Black. She was tall and muscular with dark hair.

And I think that I was studying Alex in that picture way too hard—because the alternative would be to study the other girl in the picture.

Haley. Fourteen-year-old Haley.

No fear in her eyes. She hides it well. No smile. No frown. She can't decide how she feels and isn't willing to commit. Because to commit would be to lie, no matter what.

And there is no feeling worse than lying.

Even emptiness of any feeling at all.

46

Three Nights Left

February 10.

They want me to sleep through it, those girls.

I hate those girls.

But they cannot make me sleep forever. They will see.

Come that dark night, another girl will fall.

47

Thursday, February 7

I was awake before Star.

I watched her sleeping for a moment, wondering if I'd thanked her enough for all of the sleuthing she'd done about Sarah Black. She seemed to enjoy it. But was I taking advantage of her? She seemed a girl people could easily take advantage of—what with her worrying everyone hated her at the drop of a hat. I hoped Mark Byrne wasn't taking advantage of her. I hoped the romance was a real thing.

These were the thoughts that were bouncing around in my brain as I shuffled to the shower and back. When I returned, I wondered if she was awake yet. I started to push through the door when something caught my eye.

A small heart—slightly smaller than my hand. Carved in the front of the door. Off to the left, opposite the doorknob. With letters scratched inside:

I stood frozen, my heart pounding. It didn't take a lot of fancy code breaking to figure out those letters. *I Made Her Jump.*

On *my* door. Overnight.

In only a matter of minutes, everyone would see this: Star, Anna, Alex, Maylin. *Everyone.* I flew back into the room.

"Morning!" Star said, pawing through her sock drawer.

"Morning," I mumbled, trying to keep the panic out of my voice. I raced to the closet, nearly wiping out on the slick hardwood floor in my socks, yanking the pull string of the overhead light.

Stickers. Stickers! That was the solution, for now. I knew I had some somewhere. Yes. In the purple plastic bins with the old hair accessories and other junk.

"You okay?" Star called.

"Um. Yup. Yeah," I stammered, seizing upon a large square World Wildlife Federation sticker with a panda on it. I couldn't remember where I'd gotten it. Probably a free bumper sticker, and of course I didn't have a car.

I rushed back out, closed the door, peeled the sticker off its backing, and slapped it on the heart. It just barely covered it. Exhaling, I entered the room again.

"What's up?" Star said, staring at me, a single sock hanging out of her hand. The sock was blue with sea turtles on it.

"Just kind of scatterbrained this morning," I said. "I don't think I'm really awake yet."

I figured I could explain about the sticker later. I'd come up with something—say my tree-hugging brother had sent it to me, or whatever. For now I couldn't think of a good fake reason why I'd done it first thing in the morning.

✦✦✦

Morning classes were a blur. Thankfully, Mr. Cortes didn't call on me. I wouldn't have been able to answer. My body moved from class to class, and my face kept on its practiced look of obedient intellectual curiosity.

But my mind was reassessing everything I thought I knew about the ghost.

Sarah Black. Yes, I thought the ghost was Sarah Black. I thought Sarah Black might be haunting Alex this year, even if I could never get her to admit it.

But then why was she at *my* door?

Was she haunting *both* of us now? Was my theory—about Alex being singled out—entirely incorrect? Was the ghost less discriminate than I'd thought?

Or—two ghosts? One in a black dress, one in white?

Like the Fox sisters. But they had no direct connection to Windham, aside from the Black sisters' aunt knowing them. They were older ladies by the time the Black sisters were teenagers at Windham.

Maybe the ghost had been Sarah Black but was no longer. If Taylor died the same day, Taylor could be the ghost now. I had to stop denying that possibility.

And who would Taylor want to harass in Dearborn?

Me, of course.

But—no. Rationally, no. Someone was just trying to terrify me. And they were doing a great job. The question was, who would want to do that?

I'd covered the heart and letters with the same kind of impulse that I'd wiped the words away from Taylor's window. I was scared of them. I was ashamed of them. It was almost as if *I* could have written them.

I had thought those words deep in my head a hundred times.

Who but a ghost would know that?

Who but Taylor would know that?

48

Just before lunch, I got an alert that a package was in the mail room for me. I picked it up right away—a FedEx envelope with a book inside and no note.

The Last Dollhouse: Stories by Lucia Jackson was engraved on the cover. I opened it and saw it was published in 1999. I was curious about the title story, but flipped to "The Snow Angel" as Lucia had instructed. It was only about seven pages.

In the campus center cafeteria, I sat by myself reading while I nibbled a piece of cold pesto pizza.

It was about a girl—an only child—named Evie Fleming. *Fleming* again. Whatever it was with this Fleming woman, Lucia Jackson really wanted to hammer it home.

As the story begins, Evie lives in a village of somewhat vague geography and time period. At the start of the story, Evie is eleven.

Her mother wakes up on the morning of the first snow and squeals and points out to her that there is a snow angel in the backyard, under the ancient oak tree. She explains to Evie that this snow angel mysteriously appears to the family every year, on the first morning of the first long snow. Evie has obviously heard this story before and loves it. As her mother cooks at the stove, Evie stares out the window at the blanket of snow, the weighted-down trees, the snow angel and the squirrel prints running across it. She sings to herself, eating her porridge. Her father comes down the stairs, bellows happily at the sight of the snow angel before going off to his job, which appears to be in a coal mine, although that's not said explicitly.

The next scene is the following year—where a similar incident unfolds on a December morning: the appearance of a snow angel, delighted parents, Evie quietly taking it in.

And the next scene is an evening the following year. Evie is thirteen and her aunt is visiting—her father's youngest sister. Snow is expected that night, and Evie and her aunt stay up reading and knitting long after Evie's parents go to bed.

They seem to be waiting for the snow to deepen. And then Evie goes out and climbs the oak tree without a hat or mittens. There's an old rope tied to one of the limbs—tied by her aunt. After staying there for a couple of hours, she lowers herself into the snow and pumps her arms and legs furiously, "fighting against the cold, but losing. Until she could no longer feel her little hands—and no longer knew if they were moving anymore."

There is apparently nothing magical about the snow angel at all—that the snow angel is always made by one of the youngest girls in the family, starting at age eight or nine and ending whenever she passes it on to a young daughter or niece.

It is unclear why or how this tradition started. But Evie is simultaneously ecstatic and resentful that she has this role—the last snow angel. She does not imagine herself passing this role on to a daughter. She wants sons or no children at all. She imagines her parents dying old and happy, with snow angels appearing to them and comforting them in their final moments.

And she is so cold and delirious that it's uncertain if she's frozen to death in the end—although I preferred to presume that her aunt would eventually go out and save her.

I closed the book, vaguely unsettled, vaguely agreeing with the Darkinses' long-ago suggestion that there might be something not quite right in Lucia Jackson's head. But vaguely feeling, at the same time, that I could relate to that not-quite-right thing. I knew how it felt to have to pretend something was magical that really was not. For the sake of my elders. Or at least, *one* maternal elder. It was like being a reverse Santa Claus. I had, in some ways, been in that role since I was about twelve. But especially since coming here to Windham-Farnswood.

A shudder went up my spine. Could Lucia Jackson really tell so much about me from one short, weird phone conversation?

I shook the question away.

Maybe more Windham girls could relate to that sentiment than were willing to talk about it. It didn't need to be just about *me*. Maybe it was a scholarship kid thing. (But was Lucia a scholarship kid?) And maybe what she thought I could relate to—any Windham senior could relate to—was simply the coldness of it all. Dearborn's high ceilings and drafty windows and relentlessly inadequate heating system. After the warm, cocoon-like underclass Windham experience, it was like Dearborn was designed to cool you down for your exit—acclimate you to the cold reality of the world outside this strange, coddled collection of girls.

After classes, I headed to the library.

The archives were closed, and I doubted that there would be much there about Norma Fleming—since the bulk of the archives was 19th and very early 20th-century stuff.

The main library did have a cheesy "alumnae corner" that students rarely visited—with alumnae books (almost half of them Lucia Jackson's), photo albums of recent school trips or student projects, and a large collection of yearbooks going back to 1940.

Michelle had mentioned Norma's maiden name, and I remembered that it had started with a W. She hadn't said exactly how old Norma Fleming was—although she had implied she was elderly. She *had* said that Norma Fleming's cake and pie business was big in the '70s and '80s. She'd have to have been at least in her twenties then, so that would put her as a teenager . . . well, anywhere from the 1940s to the 1960s. Probably not the '40s, or she would be in her nineties—or dead—by now. The picture on her website was of a woman roughly in her seventies, but it might be an old picture.

I slipped out the yearbook for 1950. Only seniors were pictured. There was no Norma in the W's. Same for 1951. And 1952 and 1953.

But then—1954. *Norma Wozniak.* As I looked at her photo, I felt my chest tighten and my breath catch. She was willowy, pale, bony-faced. Her smile was tentative. Her light hair curled stiffly around her face, like an old Hollywood starlet's. She was the only girl on the page not wearing pearls.

And what was it that was making me hold my breath?

Was it her skinniness, her half smile, her pallor?

Was it all three of those things, or something more intuitive and emotional that made me feel this way? That if you ignored the hair, she looked kind of like Sarah Black?

Was I just seeing it that way because I wanted to?

The passage below the photo, like all of the others from that era, was spare:

French club, Blue ribbon typist, Honor roll, "Sunny," Betty Crocker Award

Betty Crocker Award? I guess that was something they didn't give out anymore.

♦♦♦

As I came out of the library, I worked up the courage to try Lucia Jackson again. There was no answer. I couldn't bring myself to leave a message. What would I say? *Were you trying to tell me something about Norma Fleming?* Obviously she was. I felt inadequate for not figuring it out. Because if Lucia was inclined to explain it to me straight out, wouldn't she have done it by now?

I wandered aimlessly for a few minutes, considering going to the student center, but not certain what I'd do there. I pivoted, reluctantly heading back toward Dearborn for some much-needed studying. But then I saw Anthony waiting near one of the shuttle stops—and had an idea.

"Anthony!" I shouted, and ran up to him. "Hey."

"What's up?" he said cheerfully.

"Not much. I need you to let me borrow your car."

"What? When?"

"Mmm . . . now? Or tomorrow?"

We both knew that I wasn't a great driver because I'd only gotten one summer of practice, not to mention that weekday car trips weren't *really* allowed. But Anthony's residential director was notoriously blasé about seniors bending the rules.

"You know we can't do it now. How about Saturday?"

"Tomorrow? Please?" I said. We could get permission for Friday after class because technically it was the start of the weekend.

"What's this about, though? Can you tell me?"

"Not yet. I can tell you it's important to me. Is that enough?"

"Important how? Give me a category. Important for school, important for family, important for personal life?"

He raised his eyebrows, waiting for an answer.

I sighed. "*Important,* like in the way that if your friend uses that word, you trust their use of it in a general way."

"Oh, *please.*" Anthony made like he couldn't bear the weight of his backpack—as if it was somehow filled with pounds of my bullshit.

"Important for school," I said. "There's this lady, this alum, I want to interview for the paper. I'm on deadline."

Anthony studied me skeptically. I decided to double down.

"Now, do you want to be my rich-boy friend who lords his car keys over my head, or do you want to be a different kind of guy than that?" I asked.

His eyes sort of glazed over. I didn't feel great about it, but I knew I had him.

"Tomorrow after classes," he mumbled. "If we can get permission. But *I'll* drive. Maybe you'll explain in the car."

In my room before dinner, I clicked onto the "Haunteds" group and typed:

Any of you ever heard of something called the Fleming scholarship?

I was getting behind on homework, so I closed my laptop and worked on calculus for a while. When I finished, I found my question had sparked sudden interest:

Jane Villette: No. A Windham scholarship?

Laurie Rowell: Not familiar with it, I wasn't on fin aid.

Darla Heaney: Me neither.

Katherine Van Kamp: Fleming as in the famous Norma Wozniak Fleming?

Laurie Rowell: Norma Fleming is an ungrateful b*tch.

Well, *that* was a stunning assertion. About a nice old lady who gave lots of money to sick kids and their families. Apparently Suzie Price was taken aback as well:

Suzie Price: Hey now. As the admin, I can't condone language like that about any alum.

I heard a couple of sharp knocks. I jumped and grabbed my phone before my brain had a moment to process that knocks don't come from phones.

When I opened the door, Anna was standing there.

"Hey, Haley," she said. "Just wanted to let you know so you wouldn't worry . . . Star's in the infirmary for the night."

"What? Is she okay?" I demanded.

Anna seemed startled by my questions. Maybe I sounded inappropriately panicked.

"Oh . . . yeah, she'll be okay. She said she was feeling suddenly worn down, like she might be getting the flu. Actually, probably for the best for her to take a night off, then. Keep those flu germs out of your room, out of the dorm."

"I see," I said uncertainly.

"You feeling okay yourself?" Anna wanted to know.

"Oh, sure," I said, feeling a vague sarcasm accompanying my words—and dread creeping in behind it.

"Great," Anna said, smiling. "Have a good night."

"You too."

I closed the door gently and turned to stare at the inside of my room. Star's neatly made bed and slightly tidied area around it—absent the usual pile of clothes. Her decorative umbrellas overhead circled slowly, like pretty little vultures.

It seemed Star had known in advance she was going to leave—or saw fit to clean up the space while feeling sick with the flu. The first possibility was a little unsettling. The second was typical Star.

The beluga grinned at me, challenging me to decide which made more sense.

The room felt different now that I knew I would be alone in it for a whole night.

I settled back on my bed and opened up Facebook again.

Karen Norcross: What I think Laurie might be referring to is that she got a free ride to Windham for four years— that townie scholarship, do they still have that? Excellent education that helped her get her start, and whenever anyone asks her about it, she says how much she hated it. Like here: UWClibrary.donorscelebration.3story. And don't get me started on how the alumnae association courted her for years, and never got a penny back.

Suzie Price: I think we are getting off topic. Haley, why were you asking this question?

I typed quickly.

Haley Peppler: Another "haunted" alum—who is not on this forum—mentioned it.

Suzie Price: Probably not really relevant to this discussion, sorry.

Jane Villette: And people who wish to gossip about Ms. Fleming should do it elsewhere. She has done a lot of good for others, that's probably her way of paying it forward, we should leave it at that.

I wondered if I should write that I was sorry I'd started this. Even though I wasn't sorry.

I clicked on the link that Karen Norcross had included in her complaint. It was an article about a generous donation Norma had made to her alma mater college's library. Skimming through, I saw that she mentioned that her college "was a refuge for me—of warmth, acceptance, and intellectual curiosity. It helped heal some of the psychic wounds I'd suffered at a rigid elite girls' school during my high school years."

Ouch. She didn't elaborate, as she went on to describe how she made friends for life in college.

I closed my laptop and went to dinner.

49

So I have to try to sleep in this room by myself.

Star didn't seem sick this morning.

But it is flu season. And the flu can hit you fast—collapse you.

I've only been sick enough to go to the infirmary once. It made me sad; it made me think of the raspberry sherbet my mother used to buy me whenever I had a bad cold.

I should write Star a text saying hi. Even with the phone restrictions in there, she will at least know I care.

But maybe she doesn't want me to care.

What I told her about Taylor and the burner phone and the video of Jocelyn—maybe it was too much. Maybe she hates me now. Which I could understand. And maybe she's kind of hated me all along? I would kind of understand that, too, actually.

I checked the panda sticker right before I went to bed. It seemed like it was wrinkled on one side. Like maybe Star had tried to peel part of it off and see what was underneath.

I'm not certain.

That would have freaked her out for sure. But wouldn't she have asked me about it?

I can't help but feel this has nothing to do with the flu.

And I never realized how much I relied on the rhythm of my roommate's breath to lull me, eventually, to sleep.

50

Two Nights Left

Sometimes it seems to happen in an infinite loop.
    Out the window.
    Out the window.
    Out the window.
    Her face.
    Her scream.
    My trembling hands.
    Please make it stop.

51

Friday, February 8

Anthony's phone GPS had found Norma Fleming's place without any problems.

The yellow Victorian house didn't look as cheerful as it had in the photographs—but about as cheerful as it could be in early February. It didn't have flowers, but it had charming icicles.

"What *is* this place?" Anthony demanded.

I rubbed my eyes and took a long sip of cold coffee. After a night of little sleep—and a long day of classes—I didn't have a lot of energy left for explaining.

"It's called the Robin Hill House," I said, yawning and then pointing out the sign. "Isn't that such a cozy name?"

"I guess," Anthony said, killing the engine. "If you like birds."

As we gazed at the porch, a couple and a small child came up the path from the back driveway and entered the front door. Instantly I felt uncomfortable with my own presence there.

"I mean, I don't *mind* birds," Anthony continued. "As long as they don't get too close. I don't like to be up close to their little dinosaur faces."

"Please drive a little down the street," I said. "I don't think Robin Hill Cottage is on the side we came from. It must be farther down."

"Robin Hill Cottage," Anthony murmured, starting his engine purring again. "Do these people think they're in a Winnie the Pooh story?"

"The lady I'm interviewing . . . she restores old houses and runs some charities out of them," I said quickly, as if this explained everything. "There!"

Indeed there was another ornate yellow house, about half the size of the first but still substantial for a single person or family.

"You're going to wait in the car, right?" I said.

"I guess." Anthony picked up his phone and opened one of his many brain-exercise apps.

"She's only expecting a girl. I don't want to startle her."

"You're right." Anthony didn't look up. "My beard stubble might be too threatening."

I didn't look back at Anthony as I walked the brick pathway and steps to the glossy black door. I rang the bell immediately, like someone who thought she belonged here. About thirty seconds later the door opened slightly. A bright-blue-eyed elderly face peered out.

"Hello. Are you Norma?" I asked cheerfully.

"Yes." The woman smiled and opened the door a bit wider. "Are you the new girl? Are you here for the laundry?"

She was tall but hunched over slightly, with shiny white curls that looked freshly set. She looked several years older than the photograph on her website. Which would put her well over eighty.

"Oh . . . no. I'm a Windham-Farnswood student. I'm here about the Fleming scholarship?"

"Oh. Umm . . you *are*?"

I hesitated, noticing that her soft pink cardigan was buttoned one off, with a lone button hanging loose near her neck.

Was I officially harassing a doddering old lady? Was I crazy?

"Yes," I said.

"Oh, dear." Norma suddenly looked uncomfortable on her feet, and I felt bad for making her continue to stand.

"Do you want to come in?" she asked. "You're Lily, I assume?"

"Umm . . . no," I said. "But . . . I am here about the scholarship. And . . . well, one other thing, but first about the scholarship."

And then I could have kicked myself. Why would she assume my name was *Lily*? I should have let her keep assuming that, to find out.

Norma looked puzzled but then nodded and led me through a fancy marble-floored entryway to a surprisingly spare living room. She lowered herself onto a green velvet sofa and gestured for me to sit in its matching chair.

"It is . . . I'd offer you a cup of coffee, but . . ."

"That's okay."

"At your age, you shouldn't drink much coffee."

"I guess not," I agreed, hoping she couldn't smell my last cup on my breath.

A bell sounded in my ear and I jumped. It was the mantel clock positioned behind me, striking the half hour. Four-thirty.

"So you're on the Fleming scholarship?" she asked, looking slightly amused by me.

"Umm . . . yeah. Or . . . I was told I would be a good candidate for it."

"You're not on the scholarship *now*?"

I hesitated. I didn't like to lie. But then, I knew I wasn't above it.

"I just . . . had some questions."

"Ohhh. I see. You're not Lily. You're the other one. Right? I've gotten your letters. I had hoped we could talk things out sometime, somehow."

"Letters? Oh . . . I think you must be . . ." I hesitated, swallowing the words *thinking of someone else*.

"There were some good questions in your letters. I sent them to my lawyer, and he thought it best to wait until there was a way to talk all together sometime. Or just . . . wait and see. He wants to wait and see first. These things have a way of calming down on their own as time goes on."

"Which questions did you think were good ones?" I said softly.

Norma laughed, her eyes shining, her attention seeming to come into focus.

"I see what you're doing," she said sharply.

"You do?" I said weakly.

"Yes, I'm glad you came, but I can't discuss anything at length without my lawyer here. Maybe I should call him now. See if we might set something up."

I steepled my hands in front of my mouth, trying to hide my panic.

"So you're giving out more scholarships?" I asked, as evenly as I could.

"Well. Yes. Every year. Of course. Are you a freshman?"

"No . . . ," I said. "But I was wondering how I might qualify."

Norma's eyes narrowed. "Wait . . . What did you say your name was? You're not a Sunny, are you?"

I exhaled, unsure what her second question meant. Lily? Sunny? Was she just throwing out cheerful names at this point? Did she maybe have Alzheimer's?

"Haley," I admitted.

"Oh," Norma said, and sat back against the couch cushions. "Haley. I've not heard that name before. Why don't we start over? You seem to be under the mistaken impression that I give out scholarships willy-nilly. But that's not how it works— coming to my door."

Suddenly Norma seemed quite sharp again, and I felt my face starting to burn.

"I . . . well . . ." I decided to try an entirely different angle. "I'm actually writing an article for the Windham school paper. It's about Sarah Dearborn. About her portrait, and what happened to it."

"Oh." Norma looked bewildered. "Then . . . why didn't you say so?"

"I was just . . . curious about the scholarship, but I mainly wanted to talk about the portrait. Did you ever have it restored?"

"No, dear." Norma touched her curls, then folded her hands. "I didn't."

"Will you ever, you think?"

"No," Norma said with a placid smile. "Would you like to see it?"

"Uhh . . . yes. If it's not too much trouble. Yes."

"It's upstairs."

"Oh . . . ," I said, feeling tentative. "I don't want you to have to . . ."

"Nonsense," Norma said, lifting herself shakily off the couch. "I have one of those old-lady roller coasters that gets me up the stairs."

"Roller coasters?" I repeated.

She led me into a hallway with a sweeping staircase. It had a motorized chair lift affixed to it.

"Right," I said.

"You go up," she ordered. "I'll meet you at the top."

I did as she instructed. Waiting on the balcony as her chair whirred her slowly up the banister, I hoped Anthony wasn't getting too anxious.

"It's in the second guest room," Norma said, lifting herself up and grasping the metal cane that was waiting for her at the top of the steps. "Which is the one that never has guests."

She tugged the arm of my coat as she passed me, leading me past one floral-decorated bedroom and then another. The room she led me into was smaller and darker. Its shades were down, and in the corner was a single bed with a silky maroon spread.

"Come in," she said, stepping into the room. "She's right here."

Norma stood in the middle of the dark-stained hardwood floor of the room. I stepped into the room to join her. And then we were both staring at it: the painting of Sarah Dearborn.

Except that it was barely a painting at all anymore. It had an ornate gilt frame, and you could see that it used to be a painting of a woman in a black dress. But she didn't really have a face—

just a washed-out white blot where a face would be, that seemed to drip into the chest of her dress. You could see part of one of her eyes and a chunk of her hair.

"Would you like to know how it was destroyed?" Norma asked softly.

I gazed into the goopy remains of Sarah Dearborn's eye, wondering if she'd been smiling or frowning for her portrait sitting. Her mouth was gone entirely.

"Yes," I said, feeling my chest tighten.

"Well. There was a girl there the same years as me. The early '50s. Her name was Virginia. Came from old money and made sure everyone knew it. She was like the queen of campus. So imperious. But winter senior year, something started to happen to her. Heard voices in her room. Said that messages were appearing on her walls. She never got a good night's sleep anymore. She started to lose her mind a little. She was certain that Sarah Dearborn was haunting her—in her black dress. *Sarah in Black.* And then it happened, late one night."

"*What* happened?" I whispered.

"Virginia threw a glass of water at the painting. And then another. And then another. By the time the housemother found her, she was on probably her fourth glass, going back and forth to the washroom faucet. Screaming at this poor painting. At poor Sarah in Black."

"But this was Sarah Dearborn," I squeaked. "Not Sarah Black."

"It was all the same to poor Virginia," Norma said evenly. "Since she'd lost her mind."

"What happened to Virginia?" I asked, fear rising in my throat.

"She had to go home, sadly," Norma replied.

Like Student X. I nodded, averting my eyes from the white space where Sarah Dearborn's face had once been. Almost an illustration of what Norma was saying. A washed-out blank where someone's head had once been. Crazy girls driven out of themselves. I was maybe getting there myself.

"I have a confession to make," Norma whispered.

"Yeah?" I said, looking at my hands.

"I never intended to have it restored. I like it just the way it is. There is a certain truth to it, a certain twisted beauty. Don't you think, Lily?"

I looked up at her. Watching her smile contentedly at that washed-out face, I decided I had never felt so creeped out in my life.

"So you believe in the Dearborn ghost?" I asked hoarsely, my pulse quickening. Norma was old and frail and maybe borderline senile, but her tone and facial expression were setting off alarms deep in my core. *Sinister. Toxic. Twisted. GET OUT.*

"Oh, dear," she replied. "Absolutely. With all of my heart."

"I have to go now," I said. "My friend is waiting in the car."

"So soon?"

"Yes," I breathed. "Should I help you down the stairs?"

"No. I think I'll actually stay up here and rest awhile. You can let yourself out. My bedroom's just the next one over."

"You sure?" I said.

"Yes, honey. I'm glad you came to see the painting, though. No one asks about it anymore."

"Of course," I offered.

I smiled as I backed out of the room.

"Bye now," Norma said, following me out and heading into one of the floral bedrooms.

"Bye," I chimed, and held my breath as I walked quietly down the stairs.

✦✦✦

I raced down the brick steps and tumbled into Anthony's car, catching my breath and coughing from the cold.

"Why are you breathing all over me?" Anthony said, pulling away. "Didn't you say your roommate has the flu? Cover your mouth, will you?"

"We need to leave now," I said to him. "Please start the car. I want to get out of here."

Anthony scowled as he tossed his phone into his cup holder. "What happened? You knock over a priceless urn?"

"Don't even joke about it."

Anthony started the car. "What's going on, Haley?"

"I . . . I don't know. It was super creepy. I can't explain. I shouldn't have come here."

We made it back to the highway. I breathed a sigh of relief as Anthony accelerated off the ramp. I wondered if maybe Ms. Fleming was afflicted with some early-stage dementia that made her act so weird with that ruined painting.

And yet—I was apparently not the only Windham girl in contact with her. And whatever the Fleming scholarship was, Norma still seemed to have some involvement with it, despite her obvious health limitations.

There was only one Lily I knew who went to Windham in

361

recent years. It made me shiver, remembering that name on Ms. Fleming's lips as she'd stared eerily at Sarah Dearborn's ruined portrait.

Lily Bruno had been present when Taylor died.

I didn't know what the connection was—if any. Still, I took out my phone and found my old exchange with Lily.

I would like to talk to you again, I typed.

About Taylor? was her surprisingly quick reply.

About the Fleming scholarship, I typed back. *About Norma Fleming.*

It took her a few minutes to come back with a one-character reply:

?

I hesitated, but wasn't going to give up that easily.

I know Norma Fleming knows you.

My heart thudded harder and harder as I waited for a reply.

"Hello?" Anthony said. "You're supposed to entertain the driver."

"Yeah, I appreciate the ride. I just . . . don't feel very entertaining."

"You don't have to *feel* entertaining to *be* entertaining. What's going on with you?"

"I don't want to go back to Dearborn," I murmured.

"Infirmary?" he suggested.

"I can't," I said. I didn't explain that I couldn't because I was afraid to face Star.

Anthony shrugged, watching the road.

"Does it ever bother you how beautiful our school is?" I asked. "All of the brick and ivy . . . When I first came, I thought

I would *be* it somehow. That it all looks so smart and beautiful and classy, that if I was here, I would kind of melt into it . . . lose myself in it. But I never really felt that way. I was just . . . *there*. It's just a *place*."

"Yeah? What else did you expect it to be?"

I expected it to redeem me, I thought. *I expected it to make me into a different girl than the one I'd been.* But I didn't say it, because particularly in Anthony's presence, it felt like a stupid thought.

Is this a scholarship I could qualify for, too? I texted to Lily.

"Haley?" Anthony prompted.

"I expected it to be . . . transformative," I admitted.

"Pffft," Anthony scoffed.

"Exactly," I said.

I'd felt the same way about being friends with Taylor. Maybe even more. She had been a part of the beautiful scenery that I wanted so much to embody. Until her flaws made it impossible to see her that way. Which was exactly when I'd decided to ditch her. And that was probably meaner than anything I'd ever seen *her* do. Which was saying a lot.

My phone buzzed with Lily's reply:

Ms. Fleming occasionally helps out Windham alums with college tuition, but she prefers it not be public. Different from her other charities. Please don't share this information or you might put other girls' scholarships in jeopardy. She likes it quiet. She's quirky.

I typed furiously: *Could I qualify? Does the school have info about it?*

Probably not, I'm afraid, Lily answered. *And no, not directly.*

How did you qualify? I insisted. *If it's so private, how did you know to apply?*

Word of mouth, a few different personal connections.

I would like to apply, I typed.

You can't was the lightning-fast response.

Why not?

This reply took almost ten minutes:

One applies by invitation only through the Honor Society.

Lily might have guessed that I never quite had the grades for the Honor Society. But she probably didn't know that for sure.

Great! Then I do qualify. I'll ask about it Monday, I typed.

The Honor Society advisor doesn't know about it. Don't bother asking.

Hmm, I thought. That was definitely suspect.

? I shot back.

It's done through an alumnae group, not through the school administration.

What alumnae group?

This time, Lily didn't reply. Probably because she'd run out of ways to put me off.

I was pretty certain she was lying. And if she would lie about this, what else might she lie about? I thought again of the things the girls had said about the night Taylor died. Jayla said Taylor was screaming. Lily said she wasn't. If someone was going to lie, did it make more sense to fabricate screams or to deny them?

Probably the second.

52

Anthony and I got back to the Farnswood campus in time for me to have a last-minute bite at his dining hall and then hop on the last shuttle back to Windham.

I wasn't in my room for five minutes before there was a knock on the door. It was Anna.

I sucked in a breath when I saw her.

"Oh, hi," I stammered, feeling my cheeks burn with guilt. Had Norma Fleming possibly contacted the school, telling the administration a strange student was harassing her?

"I need to talk to you, Haley," Anna said. "Can I come in?"

"Sure," I said, as innocently and enthusiastically as possible.

She closed my door quietly. I led her in and sat on my bed. She sat on Star's.

"Look, Haley." Anna started to fold her hands, changed her mind, clapped them once, and settled them on her lap. "I wanted to talk to you because I've been told today—by a somewhat reluctant witness—that she saw you carving letters in the front of your door."

"*Who?* Who said that?"

Anna held up a hand. "Did you?"

"What . . . *no!*"

"So you're telling me that witness was mistaken?"

"Yes. Of course. Why would I do that?"

Anna paused for a moment, regarding me sadly.

"Is there *anything* you want to tell me?"

"No," I muttered.

"I saw what was underneath the sticker you recently put on your door," she said.

"Oh." I felt my face go hot, my pulse race.

"Do you have anything to say about that?"

"I . . ." I hesitated. "I would never do that. I just . . . I put the sticker up because I panicked. It scared me."

"So who carved those words in your door?"

A ghost. Taylor. Not good answers.

"I don't know," I said softly.

"I understand that you lost your friend." Anna lowered her voice. "I understand that it has to be difficult for you."

"Yeah," I said quickly. "It is."

"I'm here if you want to talk. Or there are the counselors from the health center, too. If you would prefer that."

I breathed slowly, trying to stay calm and will the heat off my cheeks.

I hated Anna. I hated people like her. Sweet-talking fake people like this who wanted to make you *say* things.

"I'll keep that in mind," I said, smiling at her contemptuously.

Anna glanced away from me but continued speaking. "I hope you understand that if you had something to do with the repeated door vandalism . . . the one on Taylor's old door and your own . . . and it was a result of something you're dealing with regarding Taylor . . . there are people who are here for you, who can help you. And if it *was* you, I would rather you deal with it up front, right now. Because the consequences will be a lot more severe if you deny it and then get caught."

Hate hate hate.

"That's not going to happen," I murmured.

"That's not going to happen?" she repeated.

"I wouldn't do something like that."

Anna sat there for about a minute, saying nothing. I stared at her defiantly.

She got up.

"Okay," she said, exhaling. "I'll let you get to your studies."

I was shaking when she closed my door quietly. I took a breath.

I grabbed a pen and notebook off my desk and carefully wrote the words *I MADE HER JUMP.* Taking another breath, I stared at what I had just produced. I pictured myself carving those words into a door. What would I use? A nail file? A pocketknife?

I owned neither (I used emery boards, not a nail file). And yet, I could *see* myself digging those words into white paint, leaning in hard till my hands hurt.

Hurt like the girl in Lucia's story. The girl snow-angeling so hard her hands were raw.

Like that?

Hurt like the faces of those Fox sisters, those poor sad fakers who probably pretended to be haunted.

Like *that*?

Like both.

Because I *felt* those words. I'd felt them from the first second I'd seen them scrawled on Taylor's window:

I felt I could have written them.

I MADE HER JUMP.

It was true. In a sense.

I wasn't there in the room that night, so I didn't literally *make her jump.*

But I *wasn't there.* Exactly. I was not there for her.

I had discarded Taylor. After all those years of being afraid that *she* would discard *me.*

I MADE HER JUMP.

If anyone did, it was me. No wonder Anna believed I'd carved those words. No wonder someone thought they saw me do it. If anyone would write them, wasn't I the most logical candidate? And Anna didn't even know I had a history of sleep-walking.

I could almost convince myself I had done it. *Almost.*

But I had to ask myself, too: If Anna thought I had done it, why now? She'd not thought it was me yesterday. There'd not been any suspicion in her demeanor then—when she'd come to tell me that Star was in the infirmary. Unless I'd missed it. So whoever the "reluctant witness" was, she'd gone to Anna in the last twenty-four hours.

Why now?

I narrowed my eyes at Star's bed. Again I had to wonder if she was really sick, or just didn't want to face me. Did she maybe know Lily Bruno?

Why now?

53

I haven't been that girl in six years, so why do I feel like she'll be right there waiting for me after graduation? Like she might link me by the arm when I walk out of here in June, and still be hanging there by my elbow when I head off to college?

She's as persistent as any ghost—wan and needy and not knowing whether to scream or smile. All she wants is attention, and that is what I so desperately don't want to give her.

She's strong in her weakness, in a sense.

She is the one who sat in my mom's second lawyer's office— the one that was costing my mom a fortune. Even at age eleven, I understood that. I also understood that this lady—this lawyer—had really nice shoes.

I was staring at her black pumps with the single thin silver strap—dressy, but not flashy—when I promised myself I would grow up and out of this. Be a woman who could afford those kinds of shoes. A woman who could afford them through smarts and strength and never have to lie or cheat or weep to get by.

But I was weeping in her office, while I stared at her shoes. I was saying that the reason I was so scared when my dad was pounding on the door was that "I didn't want to have to think about him hurting her again."

What I was worried about was the time on the stairs—when they had been fighting and it had not been clear who had really hurt who. There had been several times like that. And I was talking more about not wanting to think about any of it again. Not wanting the responsibility of having to describe or judge what I had seen. Because . . . I had never really seen him hurt her for sure. There was no "for sure" between my parents. I knew that now, but had not known it then.

But I knew that this thing needed to end somehow. Everyone was running out of money and patience. I was running out of something less identifiable. Or had I already run out?

And then she had questions, and I gave her answers. Solid, clean answers instead of the messy ones that roiled in my head. My spoken answers told a story that was a little more straightforward, a little more violent, than the one I struggled to remember. It was a story with an ending. I could tell it was the story she wanted, at long last, to hear.

I knew the power of my words—of my exact arrangement of words, which I knew was not quite true. Maybe I did not know it in that moment, but I knew it immediately after—the next time I saw my father for a pizza visit and it felt like the fight had left him and he was going to be happy with pizzas and monthly weekends because he could not bear the things I might say next.

That girl who did that—and then started sinking after she'd done it—I don't hate her.

I just want her to disappear.

And yet, when I imagine myself carving those words on that door, it is her I see doing it, her tangled hair falling in her face, her fingers trembling before they tighten around her utility knife, her nail file, her screwdriver, her whatever. Holding on tight to keep from sinking.

54

One Night Left

All the whispers. All the voices.
   They all say the same thing now.
   Haley Haley Haley.
   It all comes down to her.
   The voices might get to her, in the end.

55

Saturday, February 9

THUNK THUNK THUNK.

I sat upright.

"Star!" I whispered when I'd recovered my breath, eyes adjusting to the pitch black.

But then I remembered that Star wasn't here. I was alone.

"Who is it?" I called dumbly, like every nearly dead horror movie victim on my dad's TV.

I was shaking. I didn't want to get out of my bed. I was afraid that darkness would swallow me while I was between its warmth and the light switch.

I grabbed my phone. It was 2:18 a.m. Tomorrow was the 10th.

The ghost was letting me know she was coming for me.

I breathed in and out and told myself that wasn't true. Seriously, maybe Star had pumped me full of ghost research to put me on edge, maybe to distract me. It was starting to feel a little suspicious, how helpful she had been. Now that she was gone.

So probably the knock had been in my dreams, and I had awoken afraid it was real. It wouldn't be the first time. When

I was younger, I used to dream of that time my dad pounded at the locked front door, yelling for my mother to let him in. Except hadn't that always been more of a *BANG BANG BANG* than a *thunk thunk thunk*?

What difference did it make now?

I thought about what Star had shown me—about the Fox sisters. About their knuckle cracks and their apple on a string.

I typed *the Fox sisters* into my phone and found the picture of them I'd seen the other day—in which they were young—about my age. One in a black dress, the other in white. I imagined *them* knocking on my door. And it helped me relax.

Those girls weren't scary to me at all. I could relate to them. It felt understandable—inevitable, even—that they'd messed with people's heads. They'd said what people wanted them to say. They felt the adults around them wanting it—their parents, their older sister, the newspaper people who swarmed around them. It was how they survived. Or even, for a while, how they had thrived.

I steadied my breathing and turned on the lights. If I heard another *thunk thunk thunk*, I would imagine one of those girls' faces attached to the ghostly fist delivering it. So if I heard it again, it would feel sad, but not scary—and maybe even familiar in its intention.

I took out my phone and tapped on Contacts. My father wasn't one of my quick-dial numbers.

"Haley? Is everything all right?" was how he answered.

We hadn't spoken since Christmas. We'd talked on the phone, but it was my mother's year to have my brother and me for the holiday.

"Kind of. I mean, yeah. I just wanted to talk to you."

"It's one in the morning."

"Two in Massachusetts," I offered.

"They don't have, like, a lights-out time there?"

"Sort of. But they don't really enforce it for seniors. We're supposed to be old enough to figure out when we need to go to bed."

"Ah. That makes sense."

"I used to stay up way past my bedtime even when I was a kid, remember?"

"Umm . . . I guess."

"When you would watch your scary movies downstairs . . . did you know I would sometimes sneak part of the way down the stairs and watch them through the banister?"

I heard my dad running a faucet, then a clatter of what I assumed were dishes in a sink.

"Hmmm . . . I think one time I remember you doing that."

I felt a tear fighting its way out of the corner of my eye.

"It was because I couldn't sleep," I said. "Same as now."

"Ah. Okay."

"I'm sorry," I whispered.

"Don't be sorry," he replied. "It didn't bother me any. And it was probably a good cultural education for you, those movies. Classic horror."

I was silent. *Not for that, Dad. I'm not sorry for the movies. That's not what I'm sorry for.*

"How's Patsy?" I asked.

Patsy was my dad's beagle mix.

"She's good. She's here curled up by the pellet stove."

It occurred to me that my father probably would've been interested to hear about the Dearborn ghost, if I'd thought to tell him about it earlier, when things had first started. What with his old horror-movie habit and all. But it was too late now to explain everything. The story was too crazy, and I was too tired.

"Sounds cozy," I murmured.

My dad told me a story about Patsy's latest encounter with the mailman. Then he asked me how school was. I gave a rote answer about it being a lot of hours of studying, but I was doing okay.

"It sounds like a lot of hard work, but you're lucky to be there," he reminded me.

I decided not to tell him he was lucky to be by a woodstove with a sweet dog named Patsy. That I often wished I was there, too.

We said goodbye.

56

Thump thump thump went my heart and my memory all morning long, its tone alternating between scary and familiar. I ate my Cheerios like a zombie, by turns trying to shake the noise from my head and then trying to access it again.

Thump thump thump.

Did I imagine it? Because tomorrow was February 10?

Probably.

Was I crazy?

Maybe a little. But not crazy enough to carve those letters on my own door. So the question was, who could hate me enough to say that I did?

It was Saturday. So after breakfast, I got back into bed and stayed there for a couple of hours to think on it.

Jocelyn Rose kept coming to mind. But she was long gone. So Star, of course, came to mind next. Jocelyn's close friend. *Best friend?* I had not thought of them that way until she'd said it the other night.

I needed to get to the infirmary to grill Star. But first, I had someone else I had been meaning to talk to. Especially now that I didn't trust anything Lily had said—which brought the night of Taylor's death back into question. It was Lily's account versus Jayla's—and I needed a third account to confirm Lily might be lying.

According to the Cosmic Comics website, they were open from one to five on Saturdays. I called after one o'clock and asked if Tricia would be in.

"This *is* Tricia," said the woman who answered. "And I'm in till five. Can I—"

"Okay, great," I said, and hung up, not wanting to waste another minute.

I bundled up and walked the two and a half miles to Cosmic Comics. I could have asked Anthony for another ride, but I didn't want to burden him again. And I felt like being alone anyway. I walked as fast as I could, focusing on the fog of my breath and the steady THUNK THUNK THUNK of my boots on the sidewalk.

✦✦✦

Cosmic Comics was cooler than I'd imagined—painted black with little decals of stars and galaxies and posters of super-heroes. Behind the front desk was Tricia, with her familiar baggy-blouse look and long, loose brown braid. I'd seen her a lot in the joint Dearborn-Barton dining hall last year.

She nodded at me as I came in, barely looking up, and at first I busied myself in the store, pretending to be browsing. Eventually I found some *My Little Pony* comic books—which I used to read when I was nine or ten. The *Friendship Is Magic* series was still going after all these years. I picked up a copy of the latest one and brought it to the counter.

"Hi there?" I said. "Tricia?"

"Yes. You look familiar. Are you a Windham girl?"

"Yeah. I'm a senior now." I ran my hands over the clear plastic protective cover of the comic book. "My name is Haley. You probably recognize me because I hung out with my senior friend there sometimes. Taylor Blakey."

"Oh." The easy smile fell from Tricia's face. "I'm sorry."

"Yeah," I said. "Um. Thanks."

My phone buzzed. I looked down at it, meaning to be quick, but my heart caught in my throat. The text was from Anna:

Hello Haley. I just looked for you in your room. I need to meet with you at 4:00 to talk. I assume you can accommodate that since you did not put in for any off-campus car trips today or the Derby shuttle. Let me know? Thanks.

Ugh. *What now?* I thought. But I typed a *K* in response before I returned the phone to my back pocket.

"It was just about a year ago now," I said. "Exactly a year tomorrow."

"Oh." Tricia pulled her braid forward, smoothing it against her chest, petting it like a kitten. "You doing okay?"

"Kinda. I don't know. I've been talking to Jayla and Lily. The two girls who were there when she died, you know? Her neighbors."

"Yeah?" Tricia studied me. "Does that . . . help?"

"I don't know if I'm looking for help," I replied. "I'm looking for the truth. They have different stories. Jayla said she heard screaming before the jumping. Lily says she didn't."

"Mmm-hmmm. Yes, I remember that. But—"

"Who do you think is right?" I interrupted.

Tricia sighed.

"Jayla," she admitted.

"Yeah?" My voice cracked with surprise. I had expected her to be diplomatic, to be noncommittal, to say that everyone processes trauma differently.

"Yeah," Tricia said softly.

"Why?"

"Well, I think Lily was so shaken she doesn't remember things exactly as they were."

There it was. Different memories. Everyone telling their truth. But I didn't buy it.

"What makes you say that?" I asked gently.

"She said that the first thing she heard was Taylor's window screeching open. But that's probably not true."

"Why not?"

"Well, maybe you know Taylor's little secret about her window? Since you hung out with her so much?"

Tricia raised one eyebrow. I shook my head.

"She was constantly opening and closing it to sneak a puff or two," Tricia said. "I definitely smelled the weed on more than one occasion. And you don't need to pretend you don't know that, Haley. I don't work at Windham anymore."

"Yes, but . . . that was the secret?" I asked.

"No. Her window. The snowboard wax was the secret. The police investigators noticed it. She had it on there pretty thick. Probably applied it regularly."

Taylor's snowboard wax. I'd thought she'd kept it around to remind everyone what a cool hobby she had, or rather, could have if she tried. Apparently, it had multiple purposes.

"She put snowboard wax on her window?" I asked.

"On her window frame. To keep it from squeaking, I'm sure."

"Are you sure it was her?" I said. "Could someone else have done it? Like, right before she died?"

"No. It was her. She'd done it for months before that. The custodians went into the rooms over the holiday break to re-seal the windows to help with the heating. They noticed how slippery-smooth her window was, and the wax she kept by the window. They mentioned it to me, thought I'd want to know. Like, they thought maybe this meant this girl was sneaking out her window sometimes, something like that. But I didn't say anything to anyone about it. I knew it probably had something to do with her smoking. But it didn't seem worth making a thing of. Especially . . . you know . . . Taylor's family."

I nodded. We all knew why Taylor got away with little things at Windham. Another thing Tricia could admit now that she didn't work there anymore.

"But it *does* make me think Jayla's account was more accurate, I think," said Tricia. "I said as much to the administration and the police. But in the end . . . what did it matter, really? She was either screaming or not screaming before she jumped. If she was screaming, she might have been suffering from some kind of hallucination from all of the THC. If she wasn't, it was maybe more of a suicide. If Jayla was right about the scream-ing, then they could blame it more on the drug. Which I guess is a tiny consolation for the family, in a way. But minimal con-solation, really. I agreed with the administration that it wasn't worth pressing the issue. Jayla and Lily were clearly both pretty traumatized by what they saw that night. Why make it worse by questioning the details?"

"Uh-huh." I nodded.

Traumatized . . . or *lying*. And it seemed like someone would have more of a reason to lie to *deny* screaming than to confirm screaming. Especially someone who seemed to be lying about—or obfuscating—other stuff. Maybe about the Fleming scholarship? Which sounded more like a weird under-the-table thing than a real scholarship. Could Taylor have been connected to it somehow? Her family had so much money, after all. But somehow it didn't all connect.

"Do you think it's possible someone pushed Taylor out the window?" I asked.

Tricia regarded me sadly.

"I . . . no. Nobody could have, I don't think. Everyone was asleep. No one came into the dorm from the outside."

"We all know that it's easy to get from Barton to Dearborn. It's not like breaking in from the outside."

"Yes . . ." I saw Tricia's jaw tighten. What I was saying was scaring her. It took me a moment to realize that she thought I was maybe confessing something.

"I just mean if Jayla really thought she heard screaming," I hurried to say. "I'm just thinking about that part."

The bell on the door of the shop jangled, and two college-age guys walked in.

"I wonder if we should continue this discussion another time?" Tricia asked.

"It's okay," I said. "I shouldn't talk about it, really, but thanks."

I plopped *Friendship Is Magic* on the counter.

"Just this, please," I said.

♦♦♦

All the way home, I thought about Taylor's window. She had quieted the daily opening and closing of her window. Which maybe meant that on the night she'd filmed herself in her room with the whispers—it wasn't *her* window closing I'd heard at the end, as she came out of the bathroom. It was probably someone else's window. Someone nearby. Jayla's or Lily's?

And in all likelihood: Lily. But why? Had it something to do with Ms. Fleming and her secret scholarship? Had Taylor maybe found something out about Lily, or about the scholarship itself, that put Lily's access to it in jeopardy? With that kind of money on the line, could Lily have threatened Taylor? *Even pushed her out the window?*

I was considering this question—and nervously gnawing my nails off—when I walked into Dearborn and saw Anna was sitting at the front check-in desk instead of the usual part-time desk aide. My hand dropped and my heart sank at the sight of her. I knew she was there waiting for me. This was serious.

It felt so natural, like something I'd dreamt a hundred times but only now remembered. Like this had been waiting for me all along, really. Since the day I'd arrived here at Windham-Farnswood, pretending I could somehow be one of these shiny-penny prep school girls.

Anna stood up when she saw me pushing through the front doors.

"I need to talk to you, Haley," she said. "Dean Ivins would like a word with you in her office in the administrative building, and I told her I'd escort you there."

I had no choice but to do a 180 and walk straight back out of Dearborn with Anna, back into the bitter winter air from which I'd just come.

✦✦✦

Within ten minutes I was shuffled into a conference room with tall arched windows and a long, glossy wooden table. This room was so beautiful I wondered what usually happened here. Could this really be the room they used to tell kids they were kicked out? It felt cruel and excessive. Why not do it somewhere humble, like the dank student lounge below the mail room? Or did the dean not even know of the existence of such places on campus?

Following behind Dr. Ivins was Ms. Holland-Stone. I was surprised to see her but kept my mouth closed, my face as neutral and focused as I could make it. I was relieved, at least, that my mom's friend Michelle wouldn't be here on a Saturday.

"Hello, Haley," Dr. Ivins said, sitting at the head of the table, studying me for a moment.

I'd always been an admirer of Dr. Ivins's rather severe style—thick glasses, boxy clothes, a streak of gray hair at her temple that she didn't bother to dye. But I had never had to look her straight in the eye before. I'd only ever encountered her in a group. She surely hadn't known my name until today.

I looked away from her and at Ms. Holland-Stone. She nodded, placing a blue folder before her as she sat, then straightening her silky maroon cardigan around her collar.

"Hello," I replied, letting my gaze bounce between them.

"Thanks for coming in," Dr. Ivins added, as if I had a choice. "Have a seat."

I shrugged my coat off automatically and sat down.

"You're probably wondering why we've called you in, and I imagine you've guessed it's related to the vandalism on your dormitory floor. . . . I understand you and Anna have already discussed that briefly. The vandalism on the vacant room door as well as your own."

I nodded.

"Today we've heard some additional concerns, related to that, and wanted to ask you in here to give you a chance to clarify matters."

"Okay," I murmured, refusing to break eye contact with her.

"The issue now is not only that a fellow student says she saw you carving something on your own door . . . but also there is the issue of the specific *content* of the vandalism."

I waited, holding my breath.

"As I imagine you know, the words were *I made her jump*," Dr. Ivins said. "And then subsequently the letters *IMHJ*."

All three women stared at me, waiting for my reaction.

"Yes," I said softly. "I know."

"Now, Anna has reported to me that you say you're not responsible for the vandalism. Is that correct?"

"Yes," I said carefully. "That's correct. I didn't do it."

Dr. Ivins nodded and scribbled something down.

"Okay," Dr. Ivins said. "With that out of the way, I wanted to switch gears for a few minutes. Do you mind if we talk a little about the night of your friend Taylor's tragedy?"

Her *tragedy*. As if Taylor had written a play.

"Okay."

"I know it's probably a difficult subject, so I appreciate your willingness."

I nodded again.

"There was the question of there being some screaming or arguing right before Taylor jumped. We wondered if you had any information about that."

I took a breath. "All I know about it is what Jayla and Lily have told me. They say different things about it."

Dr. Ivins and Ms. Holland-Stone glanced at each other.

"The question isn't about what those young women have to say about it so much as *your* direct experience of it. What did *you* witness or experience that night with Taylor?" Dr. Ivins asked.

I took a breath. I was really starting to wonder what Ms. Holland-Stone was doing here at all, if she wasn't going to say anything.

"I didn't live in Dearborn last year," I reminded them. "I wasn't with Taylor that night."

"Yes, but of course we all know that students can move freely through the dining hall from Barton to Dearborn and vice versa, even after curfew."

"But I didn't then."

Dr. Ivins sighed and put her hands on the table, stretching

her fingers out flat. They looked elegant on the shiny wood. She had a thick platinum wedding ring and sapphire engagement ring surrounded by tiny diamonds. I wondered what kind of shoes she was wearing, but it would be weird to look under the table right now.

"We have a witness for the vandalism, Haley. And our questioning about the vandalism has led to some other information, concerning the night Taylor died. Someone who was present that night, who was previously reluctant to come forward earlier, *has* come forward in light of all of this."

Someone. Someone *else* now? More than one girl hated me that much? I felt like I'd been punched in the stomach. It took me a moment to recover my voice.

"Who?" I gasped.

"That's not the question at hand. The question is . . . *were* you present, in or near Taylor's room, on the night she died?"

"No. We weren't even friends anymore by then. Taylor and me."

"Why weren't you friends?" Dr. Ivins asked softly.

"We'd just grown apart." I shifted in my chair. "It's a long story."

"We have time. We'd like to hear the story."

I tried hard not to roll my eyes. *Sure you would,* I thought.

"Were you two angry with each other?" Dr. Ivins persisted. "Had you been fighting?"

Fighting? Fighting wasn't the right word.

"Look, can we skip over the preliminaries?" I blurted. "What *exactly* is it that you're trying to get me to say here?"

Dr. Ivins looked startled by my words and tone. She bit her lip and then nodded at Ms. Holland-Stone, who opened her blue folder.

I could just make out the typed page on top. It was the first page of my Western Civ paper. Ms. Holland-Stone was one of the teachers who made us print our pages out of Google docs to save her eyes from too much screen reading.

Ms. Holland-Stone flipped to the final page of the paper. I'd written a pretty awkward conclusion, but I didn't see how that would be relevant here. Shoddy work did not equal guilt.

Ms. Holland-Stone folded back the front pages of the paper and pushed the final page onto the middle of the table. At the bottom of the page someone had scribbled in black marker: *I MADE HER JUMP.*

I felt my mouth drop open. Then I closed it.

"I was concerned," Ms. Holland-Stone said softly, "when I saw this on your paper."

"I didn't write that," I breathed.

"Then who did? Did someone have your paper before you handed it in? Did someone else *write* your paper?"

"No," I snapped.

I pulled the paper toward me.

"It's not even my handwriting," I said.

I stared at the words. The capital *M* had rounded humps instead of pointy peaks—like a lowercase *m*. Which is how I do my capital *M*'s. But the rest of the letters didn't *feel* like my handwriting at all. And somehow I couldn't find my next words.

We all sat there in silence for a minute. I could blame Star, but I didn't want to if I wasn't absolutely certain. Or I could blame Lily Bruno, but that would sound crazy since she was in college now, in a different state.

"In my experience," Dr. Ivins said gently, "sometimes students do things like this when they want some help. We're here to help you, Haley. We know things have probably been rough this past year."

All eyes were on me.

"If you knew that, then why is this the first we're talking about it?" I mumbled.

"Is that a yes?" Dr. Ivins asked. "Yes, you're asking for help?"

Then I closed my eyes. And pictured Taylor. Taylor, when we were still friends. Not broken, but whole. *Taylor.* Equal parts nasty and sparkle.

"Haley?"

What would *that* Taylor say to all of this?

"No," I whispered. *"No."*

I opened my eyes to all three women watching me, waiting for more.

I pushed the paper away. I really didn't know how to explain it. Either someone very clever was out to get me or I was going crazy. Neither felt like possibilities I should mention.

"And I'm not going to answer any more of these questions without a lawyer," I snarled. I was so startled to hear my own words, I half expected my head to spin, maybe some cinematic green vomit to fly out of my nostrils. Like in my dad's old horror movies.

Forget my ticket home, there was no way my family could afford a lawyer for a school dispute. I'd learned at a young age how much lawyers cost.

"This isn't a police investigation," Dr. Ivins said evenly. "It's just a clarification."

A *clarification*. I tried not to laugh at the euphemism. We were officially trying to achieve "clarification of the tragedy," and nothing more.

"It doesn't feel like it," I snapped.

I was trying to remember now if I had handed in my Western Civ paper before Star had disappeared into the infirmary.

We were all silent for a moment. I decided I wanted to be the next to speak.

"I've said multiple times that I didn't carve those words in the door, and I wasn't in Dearborn at all the night she died last year," I said sharply. "What other questions do you have for me? Because I've answered *those* questions."

Dr. Ivins glanced at Ms. Holland-Stone, who raised her eyebrows.

"That's all for now," Dr. Ivins said, then paused for a moment. "But I'm making a special appointment for you to speak to one of the health center counselors tomorrow morning, and then I think we should regroup on Monday. Given tomorrow's sensitive date, can we agree to that?"

"Okay," I murmured.

I tried not to let my face react to this vague verdict. They had clearly not come into this conversation with a plan. They'd expected me to cave—to admit to everything, to admit I wanted "help." Indeed, I probably did need help. But not from them.

"I'm going to ask that you stay in your dorm this evening. Anna mentioned that you occasionally dine at Farnswood, which is fine. But we'd like you to be in Dearborn tonight in case anything comes up."

I nodded.

"We'd also like to bring your parents into the conversation. I'm planning to do that tomorrow. I figure that will give you a chance to talk to them first, this evening. On your own terms. And then perhaps we can all come together tomorrow."

"Awesome," I said. "Thanks."

After Dr. Ivins let me go, I ran downstairs so I wouldn't have to walk out of the building with Anna. And tears of rage were streaming down my face by the time I got outside.

♦♦♦

I headed to the infirmary instead of back to Dearborn. I was going to see Star now because I wasn't sure about the visiting rules at the infirmary in the evening. The nurse let me in to see Star because she was "mostly recovered."

Star had a tiny bedroom to herself. When the nurse opened its door, Star was sprawled on the bed, reading a biology textbook. The room had a light blue–checkered bedspread and curtains that reminded me of Dorothy's dress in *The Wizard of Oz*.

"Where've you been?" I demanded when the nurse had gone back to her desk.

"Well . . . right here." Star shrugged. "I thought Anna was going to tell you."

"I know you're here . . . I mean, but . . . *why*?"

"I wasn't feeling great. Not the flu for sure, but I had a fever. So that was my ticket in."

391

"Oh," I said. We both knew that students usually endured minor illnesses in the dorm.

"Was that the only reason?" I asked.

"Well . . ." Star looked down at the gingham bedspread. "There was definitely a mental health aspect to it, I guess."

"Why mental health?"

"Oh, you know how it is. . . ." Star blushed a little as she smoothed a wrinkle in the bedspread.

"Have you spoken to Anna, or to Ms. Holland-Stone, about me recently, by any chance?" I asked icily.

Star looked up. "I haven't really spoken to Anna about anything significant, ever."

"But Ms. Holland-Stone?" I pressed.

Star's mouth opened slightly, but she didn't say anything.

"Did you write something on my Western Civ paper?" I asked. "Did you try to make it look like my handwriting?"

"What? No. What are you talking about?"

"But Ms. Holland-Stone . . . you've been *talking* to Ms. Holland-Stone."

"I talk to her almost every day." Star bit her lip. "She's my senior project advisor."

"And has the subject of me ever come up?" I demanded.

"Yes. Yes, um, since you joined me at the archives, she's asked about you sometimes."

Star glanced out the window at the darkening sky.

"And what did you say?"

"Not much. Just a little about your interest in the ghost, and . . . well, stuff related to that."

"Did she ever ask you if it was *me* who carved the words in Taylor's door?"

"What? No!"

If Star was feigning confusion, she was doing a pretty good job.

"No," she repeated. "She mostly has said that I'm not being a good friend to you, feeding the ghost thing when you talk about it."

"Really?" I said.

If Ms. Holland-Stone had really been concerned that I was going too deep into the ghost business, why had she not brought it up at the meeting? On the other hand, maybe she didn't feel the need to pile on. The Western Civ paper on which I'd supposedly scribbled those incriminating words—she probably considered that damaging and disturbing enough.

"Because of Taylor." Star sighed. "Because my 'encouraging' you to ask these dark questions about the dorm—and Taylor's room in particular—is disruptive of your grieving process."

"Were those her exact words?" I asked.

Star pulled up her knees. It was odd to see her in plain black yoga pants and an olive hoodie—rather than her usual jolly animal prints.

"Close," she muttered. "I don't remember for sure."

I didn't know what to say to this. I hadn't sensed that level of concern from Ms. Holland-Stone in the conference room. In fact, Dr. Ivins had seemed more sympathetic. Ms. Holland-Stone had been rather blank as she simply presented evidence.

"Did you at any point tell Anna . . . or anyone . . . that

393

you saw me carving up our door? Or Taylor's old door?" I demanded.

Star's face contorted in confusion. *"No."*

"Did *you* do it?"

"Of course not. What the fuck, Haley?"

"That's not why you're here?"

"No. I'm here because I felt shitty, first of all. And . . . there is something I should tell you. If we're going to live together. I mean, I think maybe someone already told you."

"What's that?"

"I stole Taylor's bag from the library last year. With her laptop in it. After Jocelyn left."

I nodded. "You were looking for the Jocelyn and Charlie video. To prove she'd taken it."

"No. Not really. I mean, not *just* that." Star wound her sweatshirt drawstring around her forefinger—so tight it looked like it hurt. "Everyone knew she'd taken the video. I was looking for something—anything—to humiliate her with. To give her some of what Jocelyn had gotten. Emails, pictures, videos. Anything personal. It was a spur-of-the-moment move. I was watching her in this little corner spot of the library, and she just got up and wandered off, leaving her stuff. And I just couldn't help it. I grabbed it and brought everything back to my room. I checked her trash folder first, thinking that was where she'd put stuff like the Jocelyn video."

"And did you find anything?"

Star shook her head. "Not what I was looking for, no. Not the Jocelyn video, and no embarrassing pictures of her without a shirt or whatever, or incriminating emails about term papers she'd bought online—everyone knows she did that kind of stuff, too. I thought there might be something—anything—like that. To burn her with. And I might have if I'd had a little more time. I only had that laptop for an hour."

Star bit her lip, then peered up at me.

"There was a video of you, though. In her trash folder."

I sucked in my breath. A familiar sensation started to come over me. *Sinking*.

"You were lying on a bed singing a little, wearing your track uniform, saying the room was spinning," Star continued. "Pretty drunk, I think. And then you were like, *Fingers crossed I don't pee the bed*."

"*What?*" I said, stunned. I had no recollection of this.

"And then you were like, *Hey, did you know that? I was so fucked up in the head I used to pee the bed. Hey, that's a poem!* And Taylor was just like, *Oh God, Haley. You are soooo drunk!*"

"You seem to remember this video very well," I remarked.

Star pulled the hood of her sweatshirt over her head—hiding, it seemed, from vicarious embarrassment.

"I watched it a couple times. I thought it was interesting that she'd put it in the trash. I couldn't find the Jocelyn thing in the trash folder."

"I . . . see," I muttered.

"It's strange to me that you never talk about Taylor like she was your best friend. Because she obviously was. You guys were in a fight and she kept that god-awful video to herself."

I was quiet for a minute, considering this.

"My very own pee tape," I said.

Star, surprised, cracked a smile. "Yup."

"And you returned her bag to the library Lost and Found?"

Star shook her head. "No. Like I said, I only had her laptop for like an hour. Then someone came knocking and told me they saw me steal her bag, and said they wouldn't tell the administration and get me expelled as long as I handed it over right then and there."

"Who was that?" I demanded.

"You really don't know?"

"No," I whispered. "Tell me."

I was waiting for her to say *Lily Bruno*.

"Rhea," she said.

"Rhea," I repeated, stunned.

Laid-back, pulled-together Rhea with the red hair. Who'd shown me the old heart in the laundry room and asked me gently *why I was asking about the hearts, who I'd heard about them from*. Chloe's roommate.

"I get the feeling she must've been spying on Taylor, too. That's the only way she could've caught me. Because there was no one else around. Or so I thought."

I shook my head.

"She didn't tell you, then, I guess?" Star said, looking sheepish.

"No," I breathed.

"And I saw her talking to Anna the day I left Dearborn— I was getting all paranoid that she was finally telling about my theft. Why now, I wasn't sure."

"Curious," I said.

But it was more than curious. Rhea spying on Taylor shortly before she died. Rhea talking to Anna just days ago.

"It'll be the 10th after midnight," Star murmured. "I'll probably get kicked out of here tomorrow because my fever's gone."

"It'll be good to have you back."

"Maybe you should fake sick and stay here tonight," Star whispered.

It was a tempting idea. But I was eager to get back to Dearborn, in a way. To chase down Rhea, at least. I had a lot of questions, and none of the answers were here in this quiet room with Star.

57

I ate by myself at dinner.

There was no Rhea in sight.

Maylin was gone—probably with Wes at Farnswood. Alex was eating with Chloe. They were at their own table. Chloe was staring at Alex kind of goony-eyed, giggling at whatever Alex was saying, sucking a string of spaghetti into her face. They seemed to be having a good time together—I didn't want to interrupt what might still possibly be a romantic thing.

I thought about the video of me that Taylor had put in her trash folder. I wondered if she'd intended for it to stay there.

Rolling some buttered pasta onto my fork, I noticed Anna noticing I was alone. I took out my *Friendship Is Magic* and flipped through a few pages to look busy. I stared at the big-eyed ponies and felt slightly comforted that something that I'd enjoyed at age ten was still around, and was still somehow the same. Life had gone on, and the world had kept turning, while I'd sunken into myself, then retreated to this weird ivy-covered place.

I thought of Lucia Jackson's Evie Fleming, snow-angeling until she couldn't feel her limbs. And I still didn't know why that passage felt so painfully personal. When I closed the comic, Anna was watching me again. I bused my tray and went upstairs.

✦✦✦

After the dinner hour was over, I pounded on Chloe and Rhea's door.

Chloe opened the door—and I saw immediately that Alex was camped out on the rug, her laptop in front of her.

"Where's Rhea?" I asked.

"She's not here," said Alex. "Are you okay?"

"Where is she?" I demanded, turning to Chloe.

Chloe bit her lip and shrugged. She was wide-eyed—maybe frightened of me.

"We really don't know," Alex said, getting up and stepping between us, sounding apologetic. "Do you want to sit down a second?"

I sat across from her on the rug. "I need to talk to her."

"Because it's urgent?" Alex asked.

Chloe turned from me to Alex and back as we spoke, following our conversation like a tennis match.

"I don't know," I admitted. I wanted to add that I thought Rhea might be trying to get me in trouble, but I didn't want to say so in front of her roommate.

"And what's up with your roommate?" Alex asked. "I hear she's gone?"

"The flu," I offered. "Infirmary."

"That sucks. You're lucky you didn't get it."

Chloe seemed to have lost interest in our conversation. She was sitting on her bed now, playing with her phone.

"Have you heard of anyone spreading rumors, saying I . . . *did* something? Like, um, vandalism?"

Alex put her hand through her hair—which was looking a little limp and dirty at the moment.

"No," she said. "Why? Does this have something to do with Rhea?"

"I'll come back later," I snapped. "You can warn Rhea or not. I'm going to find her eventually."

I resisted the urge to slam the door behind me. On my way through the dining hall back to Dearborn, I took out my phone.

There was already a text from Alex:

Masterpieces of American Wit and Humor

That was the whole message.

What? I typed back. This was obviously a book title. Did Alex think a collection of witty essays was going to cheer me up right now? Put things in perspective?

I glanced at the time of the text. It was sent four minutes ago. Right when we were talking. Of course, maybe there had been a lag—maybe Alex had sent it before I came knocking. And maybe it had just now appeared. But then why would Alex not have mentioned it when we talked? Because I had seemed too angry to discuss book recommendations in that moment?

I thought of Chloe, huddled on the bed, eyes down, typing something on her phone.

Her phone? Or someone else's phone?

Alex's phone.

Had Chloe been typing on Alex's phone?

I tried to remember the exact expression on Chloe's face as she'd listened to Alex and me talking about Rhea.

I Googled the title.

Masterpieces of American Wit and Humor. It was published in 1903.

Back in my room, I searched the school's online library catalog.

Available, it said, and gave the call number. Maybe this book was shelved in a section of the stacks that the studious Rhea liked to hang out in.

I checked the time. The library was open for eleven more minutes.

I threw my jacket on and ran out into the cold.

***

The third floor of the stacks was empty when I arrived.

When I pulled *Masterpieces of American Wit and Humor* from its high shelf, it was obvious there was something shoved into its front cover. A few papers, folded in half.

The gentle ping of the "Get the hell out of the library" closing bell sounded.

I shoved the papers into my backpack, rushed down the stairs, and then carried the book to the front circulation desk. After I'd checked it out, I raced back to Dearborn in the cold, holding my breath most of the way.

In my room, I knelt on my rug, spreading the papers in front of me. There were five pages in all—the first three quite yellowed, the other two less so. It looked like a list, but with something scrawled across the top of the first page:

God sees the heart. I Samuel 16:7.

My heart was pounding as if it could break my rib cage.

I traced a finger down a list of dates and names, some marked with asterisks.

1923 Amelia Hardaker

1924 Ethel Albert*

1925 Helen Wheeler

1926 Emily Quantock

1927 Margaret Campbell*

1928 Sarah Bidwell

1929 Eveline Stoddard

1930 Dorothy Avery

1931 Vera Rainville*

1932 Louise Tackett

1934 Shirley Bishop

1935 Gladys Walker

1936 Erika Clyburn

1937 Phyllis Akerstrom*

1938 Carrie Lovelace*

1939 Muriel Beacham

1940 Rose Cromwell

1941 Anna Lind

1943 Katherine Greenwalt*

1944 Ruth Dierks

1945 Joan Lomis*

1946 Rhoda Scholl

1947 Frances Bleeker

1948 Barbara Strickland*

1949 Patricia Cuttling

1950 Kathleen Fagan*

1951 Mary Vaughan

1952 Elsa Ritter*

1953 Sarah Tabert

1954 Judith Scholl

1955 Sharon Dreyer

1956 Geraldine Tripp*

1957 Norma Wozniak*

1958 Joan Lizotte

1959 Marjorie Dempsey

1960 Katrina Brunswick*

1961 Bonnie Finnell*

1962 Susan Borgeson

1963 Linda Fuller

1964 Janet McCloud

1965 Alice Fusco*

1966 Penny Lebrun

1967 Simone Boucher*

1968 Jane Wetherly

1970 Sabrina Orlando

1971 Paula Bernstein

1972 Gloria Hatfield

1973 Elizabeth Butler*

1974 Grace Lowell

1975 Rosa Hill

1976 Lynn Wentworth

1977 Pauline Harwick*

1978 Erin Copeland

1979 Courtney Greczyn*

1980 Kelly Fabiano*

1981 Kimberley Baum*

1982 Wendy Vargas

1983 Lucia Jackson*

1984 Michelle Moore

1985 Karen Thorn*

1986 Kori Schumacher

1987 Jennifer Garrett*

1988 Megan Holland*

1989 Felicia Hines

1990 Sue Wang*

1991 Maria Zarcone

1992 Jaime Offinowksi*

1993 Nicole Dabbraccio

1994 Jessica Fisher*

1995 Emily Bisset

1996 Rachel Cohen

1997 Shani Green*

1998 Jun Min

1999 Katie McLaughlin

2000 Francesca Morales

2001 Laurel Bouchard*

2003 Summer Wilkos

2004 Cyndi Romero*

2005 Ilma Nehal

2006 Crystal Hemphill

2007 Malinda Jones

2008 Amie Honda*

2009 Helena Martins

2010 Ashley Kuipers*

2011 Angel Anderson

2012 Aretta Lawal*

2013 Skylar Briggs*

2014 Kiara Parker

2015 Lily Bruno

2016 Alexandra Stegall*

2017 Rhea Eggerton

2018 Chloe Schuster

It was apparently the continuation of the list Star had shown me from her files—the one she thought had ended in the early 1920s. It looked exactly the same, with the varying handwriting and the little stars.

Chloe, Rhea, Alex, Lily. The last four names. All part of the same thing. The "Fleming scholarship"? But how could it be the Fleming scholarship if this thing started before Norma Fleming was even born? I scanned over the list again—this time backward, and slowly.

1988 caught my eye.

Megan Holland.

Ms. Holland-Stone. I opened my laptop and checked the faculty directory for her first name. *Megan.* I seethed, thinking of Ms. Holland-Stone opening her folder, producing my damning Western Civ paper. Ms. Holland-Stone, who'd told Star that the early list in the archives was probably a list of on-campus suffragettes. *It wasn't.*

My eyes kept moving upward on the list.

1983 was Lucia Jackson.

Was this a list of women who had been haunted? I opened

my laptop, clicked on the group, and scanned over the names of the women: Suzie Price, Karen Norcross, Darla Heaney, Jane Villette . . . I checked the paper list. None of the "Haunteds" women were on it.

But then, Lucia's description of her own haunting had always seemed rather bloodless, rather matter-of-fact compared to those of the women in the Facebook "Haunteds" group. Hadn't it?

And Bronwyn wasn't on this list.

The year Bronwyn was haunted—the year she was a senior—*Alex's* name was on the list. With a star next to her name.

But Alex *was* potentially haunted. *This* year. Not three years ago. At least, that had been my theory a couple of days ago. But now that theory was feeling a little floppy.

If this was a list of haunted girls, Bronwyn's name would definitely be on it for 2016. But Alex's was there for that year, not Bronwyn's. And there wasn't a haunting every year anyway.

Alex's name was there for the year that Bronwyn was haunted.

My mind shifted uneasily to last night—to how I'd felt when I thought I'd heard that knock on my door. And how it made me feel better to picture the Fox sisters bouncing an apple with a string, or cracking their knees or knuckles. So much better, in fact, that I'd been able to get to sleep. And then I thought of "The Snow Angel," the girl growing cold and exhausted trying to perform bogus magic for her parents.

Some girls say that she's looking for her replacement. That she's tired of being a ghost . . .

My heart gave a jump and I heard a gasp escape me.

I took out my laptop and clicked through to my old photos, calling up the picture of Alex and me on our first day moving into our freshman dorm. I emailed it to my phone and then texted it to Bronwyn:

The girl on the left is me. The girl on the right—does she look like your ghost?

Bronwyn's reply came about three minutes later:

WTF???

I wasn't sure if that was a *yes,* a *no,* or a *leave me alone.* I didn't have all that long to think about it because I had an incoming call seconds later.

"Hello?" I said.

"That's her. I . . . I recognize the eyes. I have goose bumps. Who *is* that?"

"She's my friend. The picture is from when we were firsties."

"I didn't pay all that much attention to the firsties once I was in the upper grades. That's probably why I don't recognize you at all, either."

Bronwyn was silent. And then I could hear her breathing.

"Is she a legacy student?" she asked.

At first I didn't understand why this was relevant. But after a moment, I figured she was trying to work out how Alex could look so much like a ghost. Her mind must have jumped to "great-great-great-granddaughter of restless-spirited dead student." Which was a reasonable jump, under the circumstances. But it wasn't the right jump.

"I'll call you again when I know more," I said. "I just figured something out, and I haven't talked to my friend about it yet."

My friend felt weird on my lips. Was Alex my friend, *really?*

As soon as Bronwyn and I hung up, I ran down the hall and thumped on Alex's door. No answer.

Same thing when I crept over to Barton and tried Chloe and Rhea's door.

When I got back to my room, I texted Alex:

I really need to talk to you. I knocked on your door and Chloe/Rhea's. WHERE ARE YOU?

I closed my eyes. Concentrating, I was pretty sure I heard the *click tap tap* of Anna's boots somewhere down the hallway. Anna was nervous. She'd be cruising past my room a few times tonight, for sure. The meeting with the administrators hadn't gone as planned. Now she had to make sure I didn't do anything weird until tomorrow. The 10th.

But I knew her tip-tapping would end around eleven, when everyone went to bed. And I would wait until then.

♦♦♦

The question, though, was what to do in my room for the next few hours.

I paced the floor for about ten minutes. And then I tried Lucia Jackson's number again.

"Who's calling?" was how she answered.

"It's Haley Peppler. I'm the one who called you about the ghost the other night."

"Yes," she replied. "Of course I know who you are. Have you read my story?"

"Uh." I stopped pacing, sat on my bed, and took a breath. "Yeah. It's really good."

Lucia chuckled. "No. It's not. But thank you. Did you understand it?"

"I think so."

"Good," Lucia said softly. "I'm glad. I'd hoped you would."

I raised the window shade next to my bed, daring myself to look into the dark, choosing my next words carefully.

"You never saw the ghost when you were a senior," I said. "That wasn't true. You were telling a story to satisfy those houseparents—to distract them, or kind of diminish what had happened the year before, with the poor girl who had freaked out?"

"Yes. Right, Haley. Things had gone too far the year before. I lied to shut up those two oddballs, to give them something to chew on. They were *way* too interested in the ghost. I was afraid of what might come of it—what they might figure out. So there was no haunting that year."

Outside, the snow and the crisscross of walkways glowed under the lamplight. Everything held still for a moment. Then a single branch swayed in the wind, and one light shut off in the freshman dorm across the campus lawn.

"There's a list of girls," I said. "Going back a hundred years. You're on it. I have it here in front of me."

Lucia made a sound that might have been a gasp if she'd not recovered herself so quickly. "The list? Who gave it to you?"

"It wasn't given to me in person. Someone . . . sent it to me. Someone on the list who's at the school now, I'm pretty sure. I'm just not absolutely certain which girl."

Lucia was silent for a moment.

"You really should figure that out," she said. "I can't imag-

ine they *all* want you to know. Which might put you in a dangerous situation."

I forced myself to keep looking out the window, willing the
darkness to show me something scary: a face, a figure, a real
ghost.

"I'm *trying* to figure that out." My pitch rose, like it did
sometimes when I was talking to my mother. "What does the
list mean?"

"Well . . . I think you already know." Lucia hesitated. "It's
the master list of ghosts. You need to find out who sent it to you
and let her tell you everything."

"Why can't *you*?"

"Because, Haley, I wasn't there the night your friend died.
So I don't have the answers you want. But I had a bad feeling,
the night you called, that it had something to do with a ghost.
It went too far again, sounds like. Like with the girl who broke
down in 1985, when I was a junior. It went terribly wrong. I
don't know for sure, but I have a hunch it was the same with
your friend."

"Me too," I said, closing the blinds.

"This is the right time for this to end, I think," Lucia murmured. "I'm relieved. Caroline Bromley had to know it would
all be undone someday, by a girl as smart as the ghosts. But I'm
not the right one to end it, honey. I'm sorry for my part. But I
haven't been a ghost for thirty years. I think it's for a *ghost* to
tell you."

"A *ghost*?" I repeated. It was unsettling the way she kept
throwing around that word.

"Yes. That place really *is* haunted, you know. It would have

411

to be, for us to do all of the crazy things we did there. I'm sorry, again, about your friend, Haley. I hope I've been helpful. I hope uncovering this brings you and her some peace. Talk soon, okay?"

"Okay?" I said. I half hoped the uncertainty of my reply would keep her on the phone for a little while longer, and maybe delay the things that would have to happen next.

But she hung up. Like the ghost she'd just confessed to being: here and then gone.

♦♦♦

It was past midnight. It was February 10 now.

I slipped out of my room at 12:45.

I'd texted Alex's number a couple of times.

I'm coming to your room.

You need to open the door.

A response to that came: *Don't bother. I'm not there. Come to Chloe's.*

Grateful for the reply, I crept down the stairs, list in hand, through the dining hall into Barton Hall, and then up two flights of stairs to Rhea and Chloe's room. When I knocked softly on their door, I heard movement in the room. A shuffling, and then a creak of floorboards. I knocked again—though still softly—to let the mover know I wasn't going anywhere.

The door opened.

And then a pasty white face was there looking at me. I gasped but didn't scream.

It was Chloe. Her face was smeared unevenly with white makeup, and she was wearing a white nightgown.

"I was waiting for you," she whispered. "I got your texts."

She let me in without turning the light on. I turned on my phone to give us a bit of light.

I stared at her for a moment. Her eyes seemed unfocused, looking through me.

"Are . . . you okay?" I whispered. "What's on your face?"

Chloe's eyes narrowed in on me.

"At least the girls are sleeping," she said.

I turned on my phone and flashed it around the room. Rhea was on one of the beds, slumped over a closed laptop. Alex was curled up under the covers of the other bed. Apparently neither of them had awoken when I'd knocked.

"I need to talk to both of them. Rhea *and* Alex," I said.

"Not until you talk to *me*," Chloe whispered. "I'm the one who sent you the book so you could get the list."

I hesitated. I considered how quickly she had answered the door. She must have been sitting awake in the dark with that makeup and nightgown on. Sitting silently, waiting for me, looking very much like a ghost. My heart began to flutter.

"*I'm* the one who's helping you," she said softly. "I'm the one you've been writing to tonight. Rhea and Lily are trying to get you expelled before it's too late. Not Alex, but the other two."

I nodded.

"Okay," I said. "We talk first."

Chloe pointed her chin toward the list tucked under my elbow.

"You figured out what this is?" she asked.

"The Fleming scholarship?" I whispered.

"Well. Yes. Since the '70s, the girls have called it that, like code. We're *Flemings*. It's more than that, of course. It's been around for longer than Norma Fleming. They used to call each other *Sunnies*. Because it's the opposite of *Windies,* I guess."

"Did it start with Caroline Bromley?" I asked.

Chloe nodded, her eyes widening a little. "You know a lot. More than they thought, even."

"Who's *they*?" I demanded.

"Oh . . . you know. The other ghosts."

I shuddered at the word.

"Everyone on the list is a 'ghost'?" I asked, my heart sinking, my gaze creeping across Alex's sleeping form again.

Chloe stared at me. Her eyes were wild, and still I wanted to reach out and spit-clean that makeup off her face, like my mom used to do when I got chocolate smudges.

"In theory. But really only the starred ones have performed any kind of haunting. And really . . . truly . . . only *me*. Do you like my ghost outfit? Exact same as I used last year."

Her last words sent a chill up my spine.

"Yes. But . . . who picks who gets on the list?" I asked.

"The senior ghost always picks the first-year ghost. With suggestions from the sophomore and junior ghost, if they want."

"So . . . Lily picked you."

"Yes."

I glanced over at Rhea, wondering why our conversation wasn't waking her up, either.

"Why?" I asked.

Chloe shrugged. "Same reason she was into having a February 10th haunting. The day of Sarah Black's death. She's a traditionalist. Obnoxiously so."

"I don't follow."

"Well . . . I *look* the part." Chloe smiled, twirling her hands up to her gluey white face. "*Don't* I?"

"I . . . um . . . how do you mean?"

"I look like Sarah Black. Small and pale. Some ghosts are into that shit. Although Norma Fleming frowns upon it because she doesn't want just white girls to get the scholarship money. Wants everyone to have a chance at it, encourages breaking tradition, and doing more creative hauntings. Cell phones taped under the bed and whatnot. Etching hearts for girls to find. Technology, psychology. Plus visual hauntings are risky. Only a handful of ghosts have ever tried it."

"Real scholarship money?" I said.

"Yeah. After the senior ghost graduates, she mails her name and a written account of that year's haunting—or an explanation of why she chose not to do one—to Norma, and then she gets her scholarship money. Supposedly she's more generous, though, if you actually haunt."

"But . . . I thought you said this thing was started by Caroline Bromley?" I said.

"Yes," Chloe sighed, settling into a desk chair. "The tradition itself. But Norma added the scholarship to the tradition because she was sad to see it dying off in the '70s. Time-honored tradition started by Caroline Bromley and Leonora Black, to avenge Leonora's poor, sweet older sister who couldn't stand up for herself. She went home because she couldn't hack it, and died a couple of months after that. She got sick—pneumonia—it wasn't anyone's fault. But Caroline and Leonora were so sad, so bitter about how some of those snotty rich girls, the daughters of oil barons and whatnot, had treated Sarah, this is what they came up with. To scare the shit out of one of those girls. Whispering 'God sees the heart' down the pipes or banging doors or whatever other kinds of hauntings they came up with. Maybe visual hauntings, too, we don't know for sure. I guess to make them feel some sort of remorse or make them feel like assholes. Caroline and Leonora were very creative, the story goes."

"I get that Leonora and Caroline were grieving . . . they were influenced by Leonora's spiritualist aunt, but . . ."

"Look at you, doing your research," Chloe murmured.

"My roommate, more like," I admitted. "But why did they ask girls to continue the tradition after the girls they hated were gone? After *they* were gone?"

Chloe scoffed. "I wish I knew. There's always some girl or other to hate or resent, right? The freshman ghost haunts whoever the senior ghost says deserves it. The choice is made by the senior ghost—and her alone. She can choose to haunt no one. But if she haunts, she is supposed to haunt the meanest of the girls, whoever deserves a good shake or to be taken down a peg. But it doesn't *always* work out that way."

"Why Taylor?" I asked softly. A stupid question. I knew why. Taylor was never nice.

"The Jocelyn Rose bullying was the main reason. Not that Lily needed to justify it. The senior ghost has absolute power to pick. The sophomore and the junior support the operation. Stealing keys or setting up sound tricks or whatever. The sopho-

416

more keeps the list, and the junior keeps the other documents and Sarah Black's picture, so they're always separate."

I was speechless. Senior ghost. Junior ghost. Sophomore ghost. *Alex, Rhea, Chloe.*

"Who is the first-year ghost this year?"

I shone my phone flashlight on Rhea again. Something about her posture disturbed me. It seemed like an awkward position to fall asleep in.

"Alex didn't even pick one. Alex wants it to end. Because of last year. Because thanks to tradition, I killed your friend by accident."

"I . . ." I couldn't find the words to reply to this. I started to protest—she was "on drugs," she was suicidal—but none of these theories had ever felt authentic to me. Which was what had brought me here.

"One year ago tonight," Chloe said sharply, her face expressionless. "I made her jump."

The words filled up the room like a noxious smell. I couldn't breathe. It felt surreal to hear her say them, when I had been for so many days making them my own.

I did too, I thought.

"How?" I breathed.

Chloe's lip started to wobble.

"I didn't mean to. Lily wanted a traditional haunting . . . on the traditional day. And the riskiest kind. A real ghost visit. They had me all dressed up in the nightgown and everything." Chloe's face contorted, and she started to let out a sob but gasped it back in. "But Taylor . . . the second she saw me, she flung open the window and . . ."

417

Chloe was sobbing for real now. Loudly.

I flashed my light on Alex. She didn't move in response to the noise.

"Taylor just . . . It happened so fast. She wasn't supposed to be dead. She was just supposed to be *haunted*. Alex keeps saying that it was probably the strength of those brownies she was eating that made her react that way, but you can't say she would've jumped if I hadn't scared her to death." Chloe gulped for air and then kept talking fast. "Right after it happened, Lily shoved me in her closet before she ran to see if Taylor was hurt. I stayed in there for hours. In this dress."

Tears were starting to run down Chloe's cheeks. She thrust open a desk drawer, pulled out a small notebook, and handed it to me.

"It's all in there," she whispered. "I wrote it all down."

"Chloe," I said, heart hammering. "Why aren't Rhea and Alex waking up?"

"I just did to them what they've been doing to me," she whispered.

Absently shoving the notebook and the old list into my fleece pocket, I stepped closer to Alex and nudged her elbow.

"Alex!" I said. One of Alex's legs kicked out, but she didn't open her eyes.

"They can't shut me up anymore. They can't keep me away from that window."

"*Who* wants to shut you up?"

"The ghosts. The other ghosts. *They* get to shut up now. They won't wake up for a while."

"What do you mean?" I demanded, horrified.

"I did to them what they've been doing to me. I put sleeping pills in their food. Well, Alex's food. Rhea got hers in her hot chocolate. I think she got a little more. Alex doesn't eat much lately. She's all fucked up with worry. She's been almost as bad as me."

"*What?*"

"They'll be fine. Just a good night's sleep. They both need it. They've been trading off watching me all night for *days*. Weeks, actually. Like I was a bomb that was about to go off. Well, it's the 10th now and I have something I need to do. And they need their rest."

She reached for the door and opened it. Light from the hallway flooded the room. Her face was a mess of tears and runny white makeup. It reminded me of the washed-out portrait in Norma Fleming's guest room.

"They were trying to keep me out of Dearborn," she sobbed. "Away from the doors, away from that window."

Her voice quavered as she spoke through another rush of tears. "But I only exist at that window anymore. I'm a ghost since it happened."

Chloe ran out of the room.

"Wait!" I yelled.

I shook Alex.

"Wake up!" I screamed.

She gave a little murmur and shifted her elbow away from me. But I couldn't wait for Alex.

As I ran after Chloe down the hallway, I saw she was headed for the stairs. She nearly tumbled down them, she was running so fast. I couldn't catch up with her.

"Chloe!" I screamed as she started through the dining hall that linked to Dearborn. "Chloe, it wasn't your fault!"

I tried to catch my breath, but now she was headed up the Dearborn stairs. Almost a whole flight ahead of me. *Clunk clunk clunk.* Up she went, all the way up to the fourth floor. As I came through the fourth-floor doorway, I heard a key in a door. And as I rounded the corner, I saw Chloe swing Taylor's door open and dash into the room.

She was flinging the window open when I got to her. The blast of air hit us both. She reached for the screen with both hands. But I was by her side, grasping her arm.

"Don't!" I shouted, reaching to pull the window back down, but there was no wax now to make it slide easily—and it was stuck.

"They wanted me to shut up until they could 'resolve things quietly,'" she wailed. "They don't know how it feels to *really* be a ghost."

"Tell me," I whispered. "Chloe. I might be able to understand better than you think."

"They don't understand how it is to keep living with this. To be *this*. A murderer. A ghoul."

She started to claw at the screen. I put my arms around her small waist and pulled her away from the window. She was easy to move, she was so frail.

"Let me *go*," she screamed.

"I want to hear everything," I breathed.

She dug her fingernails into my upper arms and didn't seem to hear me.

"I don't think you really want to go out that window," I said. "Otherwise you wouldn't have told me anything. You wouldn't have sent me to that list."

Chloe stopped thrashing for a moment and stared at me.

"I wanted you to know because you were Taylor's friend," she mumbled. "And because Lily and Rhea were going to get you kicked out. Rhea's been on the phone with Lily for the past couple of days, since you texted Lily. *Haley, Haley, Haley.* That's all she talks about, and thinks just because I'm fucked up, I can't *hear.*"

Chloe took a breath. Since I felt like I was constricting her chest, I gripped one of her wrists and pulled my arms from around her waist.

"Yeah?" I whispered. "Thank you for telling me, Chloe. Thank you."

"They even got Ms. Holland-Stone to help, even though you're not ever supposed to contact old ghosts. But they were desperate."

"She wrote on my paper?" In my disbelief, my grip loosened for a second.

Chloe pulled away from me. She flew at the window, both hands out, and nudged the screen up halfway.

I snatched her arm and pulled her from the window again.

"You're *hurting* me," she cried.

"I need you to stay away from the window." I was trying to use a calming tone, but I could hear the tremble in my own voice.

Chloe reached out and scratched my face. Hard.

I screamed, and in my shock, let go of her again. She leapt for the window. Her feet were already off the ground. I lunged after her again.

She cried out as I pulled her down to the floor.

"This isn't who you are," I said. *"You're not a ghost."*

"I don't feel anything, really," Chloe sobbed. "I don't see myself in the mirror."

"I know. But you will again someday. You're not a *ghost*. It wasn't your fault. You were just caught up in something, you were like the messenger. But this isn't *you*. Not forever."

I wiped my cheek. It was wet—not just with the one tear that had slid from my eye, but a little blood from where she had scratched me.

"Girls! What is going on? *What* is going on?"

I looked up. Anna was standing in the doorway, her purple robe hanging off one arm, her mouth open. I exhaled.

She was not my mother or my friend or the lawyer lady with the beautiful shoes. She was not the most effectual of grown-ups, but I was so glad to see her.

"She was going to try and jump!" I cried, thrusting Chloe's frail, shuddering body into Anna's arms. "I think she'll tell you. But someone needs to check on Rhea and Alex."

"Wait!" Anna yelled.

As I ran, I heard Anna asking Chloe:

"What happened? Did she do something to you?"

I didn't hear Chloe's answer. I was already through the stairwell doors. Down the stairs. I was about to tear through the dining hall doors when Alex came out of them, staggering toward me.

"Alex!" I yelled.

"Chloe," she gasped. "Have you seen Chloe?"

"She's with Anna. Upstairs. Our floor. She's pretty messed up." I grabbed Alex by the arm. "We need to go see if Rhea's all right. Chloe gave you both sleeping pills."

"I thought so . . . ," Alex panted. "I thought so."

"Is Rhea sleeping?"

"Yeah. I tried to wake her, but she was too sleepy to move."

"So she's not dead?" I whispered.

"What?" Alex looked stunned. "No. What happened to your face?"

"Chloe scratched me. It doesn't matter. She told me everything, Alex," I said. "She gave me the list. She told me about all of you ghosts. About Caroline Bromley and Norma Fleming and—"

Alex put her hand on the wall and slid to the floor.

"Good . . . great . . . good. I'm glad. I wanted to, too, but the others . . ."

She was afraid to look at me. Either the scratch on my face was worse than I thought, or it was sinking in for her how much I knew now.

"Is it true *you* were drugging *Chloe*?" I demanded.

Alex pushed her tangled hair out of her face and rested her head against the wall.

"She just needed some sleep," she said. "She was acting crazy, sneaking off to Taylor's room in the middle of the night, opening the window, carving more hearts, carving those words. . . . We didn't realize how bad it was till about a couple of weeks ago. She really thought she was a ghost. I was trying to get her some help, but it was complicated. We needed someone outside the school. We just needed to buy some time. And we needed to get the list from her, but she wouldn't tell us where it was. I wanted to shut it all down. I wrote to Norma Fleming, and she wasn't writing back. Lily and I were fighting about what to do, and she was worried about losing her money or even worse, getting arrested. We just needed a little more time."

"Time for *what*?" I was trying—but failing—to keep my voice down. "What was going to happen that would have fixed things?"

"I don't know." Alex closed her eyes for a moment. "You don't understand. We tried so hard to help her, to tell her it wasn't her fault. Ghosts don't usually room together, but Rhea and I both thought it would be a good idea to arrange it, last year, so she could keep a close eye on Chloe, make sure she was okay. And she *seemed* okay for a while. But the onset of the winter maybe just made something snap in her, brought the guilt back. She started acting weird, saying she was really a ghost, talking about February 10th, disappearing on Rhea in the middle of the night. We were trying to help her, but she was holding us hostage, not telling us where she'd put the list."

Alex exhaled and gazed at me, exhausted but clearly waiting for a reply.

"Meanwhile, Chloe was losing her mind night by night," I said softly.

Alex blushed bright red, her eyes flashing.

"I was doing the best I could with a really messed-up situation, Haley! Do you think *you* could do better?"

"I'm just trying to figure out—"

"You don't know how *lucky* you are. Why didn't the ghosts pick *you*? They almost did."

I put my hand to my face, feeling the stinging part of my cheek. When I pulled it away, there was a little blood on two of my fingertips.

"What?" I said absently.

Alex was staring at me. "They had their eye on you at first. They watched you for a while. Scholarship student, quiet kid, afraid of the place, afraid of everything. The kind of girl nobody sees. Perfect. But then they saw you were starting to hang out with Taylor Blakey. And that's not ghost material, a friend of a girl like that. They had to keep looking. They looked and they looked and then finally they *saw* her. The roommate of their first choice. Quiet and invisible, she almost slipped under their nose. But good thing she didn't. Because when they *really* looked, she kinda looked like Sarah Black, even. Skylar—my senior ghost—was smitten. It was time for a good old-fashioned *haunting,* a sighting, the real deal. Not just the knocks on the doors or the projection camera tricks or the walkie-talkies or cell phones taped under beds. They told me on the night before Halloween when they initiated me—that's when they do it— they had big plans for Bronwyn."

"Could you have said no?" I whispered.

"In October of first year? With barely any friends? When it came with a practically full college scholarship from Ms. Fleming? Would *you* have?"

I hesitated. "Probably not. Do they always pick a fin aid kid?"

Alex shook her head. "No. Usually they do, but not always. It's usually about power, not money. Above all, above even being an invisible sort of girl, the ghost has to be *smart*. Not just to know how to pull off a haunting, but to know when to pull back. When things are going too far. When circumstances aren't good for a haunting, or it's likely to be exposed. Lily wasn't smart, turns out. She wanted *everything*. The exact date, the recorded cell phone ringtone taped under her bed, the door knocks, the Bible quote, scaring Taylor nearly to death in the days before. She even had this ridiculous plastic pole thing she'd stick out her window and scratch Taylor's window with. She thought it was all pretty awesome. She said it was the most fun she'd had at Windham. I mean, she said that before the accident."

The accident.

What happened to Taylor had been an accident. Sort of.

I stood there silent, stunned. A moment later, someone came crashing through the dining room doors.

It was a bald-headed campus security officer.

"Is one of you Haley?" he demanded.

"I am," I said, turning away from Alex.

"Your residential director called us. You need to come with me."

"She didn't do anything," Alex offered weakly, pulling herself up.

"I won't get in trouble," I said to her. "If you help explain."

Alex nodded.

The officer led me back to Dearborn and parked me on the couch in the sitting room. He stood right over me, calling his boss and then Anna, telling them he'd "intercepted her," like I was a football.

I had a feeling that Chloe was going to be their priority for the next little while. I closed my eyes, going over Thatcher's video in my head. Every scary moment had been produced by the "ghosts." Taylor lived right next door to the senior ghost last year: Lily. That made it easy to make scratches on her window. And they'd gotten ahold of one of her keys somehow— probably from the backpack Rhea had taken from Star. A whispered prerecorded ringtone playing from a phone duct-taped under her bed, perfectly timed on multiple nights. Taylor was already haunted—terrified—by the time she recorded that video; she wanted to prove to herself it was real. But hadn't had anyone to show it to.

And it *was* real. The "ghost" was embodied by real girls, year in and year out, for more than a hundred years.

Exhaling, I unzipped my fleece pocket and pulled out the notebook Chloe had given me just before she'd run. I opened it and looked at the first scrawled page:

Thirteen Nights Left

The window is open now, but I don't feel the winter wind. I don't shiver. I don't chatter. Rather, I feel only a sensation of it blowing through the space that used to be me.

58

STAR NORDQUIST

Senior Thesis
Caroline Bromley: From Ghost to Legend

APPENDIX E

We, Caroline Bromley and Leonora Black, declare on this day of June 8, 1892, that Minnie Gardner, Vera Langstrom, and Hattie Brighton are "sisters in spirit" of our Sarah. Please remember Sarah's favorite biblical quote, that "God sees the heart," and perform this tradition in her gentle memory. The primary endeavor of this secret society is not intended to sow terror, but humility. Minnie will designate a younger ghost next year as we have done. In that way, Sarah, and girls like her, will never be forgotten, never be silenced.

Signed,
Caroline Bromley

Dear Ms. Noceno,

As promised, I've attached my full senior project. I had to do a great deal of rewriting, as more than half of it now deals with Caroline's involvement in the creation of the Sarah ghost tradition.

I am honored that you want to include it in the archives. Please credit Haley Peppler and Alexandra Stegall in the file. Haley for obvious reasons, and Alex for being such a willing interview subject on some of the oral tradition passed down among the "ghosts," and giving context to some of the new documents that were turned over to the archives after February 10.

I don't find it as horrifying as some do that Caroline Bromley started the tradition with her bereaved friend Leonora. Caroline spent her life speaking up for the underdog, the voiceless, the penniless, the powerless. Is it so shocking that in this hoaxing she was performing a more adolescent, rebellious version of the same thing? A darkly awkward practice ground for "Our silence, forever broken"?

As you'll read in my paper, it is my theory that Leonora and Caroline disagreed about how to carry on the tradition, to whom they should pass the torch, and perhaps whether it should be continued at all. I have a gut feeling—but can't prove it, so didn't stress it in the paper—that Leonora perhaps started to have second thoughts, as she matured and neared graduation, about spiritualist hoaxing being her sweet, devout sister's legacy. Maybe that was what caused the rift to which Abigail referred in her letter? Or why Leonora didn't sign the May 1892 document? One wonders why Caroline, in that case, was so determined to keep the tradition alive—without the support of the blood sister of the very person it was supposed to honor?

Maybe being a "ghost" was cathartic, and allowed her to leave her bitterness behind—allowed her to become the more positive, progressive, inclusive leader she became? Could she have possibly known that her bitterness would live on here, in a sense, for well over a century? Would she have wanted that? Writing this question gives me the shivers. I confess I am too much of a Caroline fangirl to consider that possibility too deeply. She could not have known she would become so revered and famous—which would lead to what I consider a misplaced reverence for a tradition that I think would have died long ago had not her illustrious name been attached to it.

I'll shut up now. Here I am going on and on again, as usual. Please don't put this note in the archives with my paper.

Thanks. I will miss you. Hope to see you at graduation!

Fondly,
Star

Hi Thatcher,

I'm sorry it's taken me so long to write back. It took me a while to figure out what that video was you sent me. I'm sure the school will be contacting your parents about it. But I would like to talk to you about it, too. And about Taylor.

Thanks,
Haley

59

Graduation was on the sunniest kind of day.

My mother was wearing her favorite springy dress with the splashy red flowers. She looked almost girlish in it, smiling so broadly, her hair swirling around her face in the early June breeze as she handed me a small bouquet of miniature peach and yellow roses—with a triangle snipped out of the cellophane where she'd removed the price.

My brother hung back, yanking uncomfortably at the striped tie my mother made him wear. I texted my father a selfie of me in my cap and gown, and he wrote back seconds later, saying he was proud. I wrote back that I was excited to see him in Illinois in two weeks. It had been his idea to buy plane tickets there for my brother and me instead of a ticket here for graduation. There were a lot of reasons why this was a better idea, and I was grateful no one seemed to need to say them out loud—at least, in this moment.

Star and Maylin and I posed for a couple of shots blowing bubbles in our gowns. My mother mentioned she wished she could take a bookend picture of Alex and me—for me to have along with the one from our first timid day as roommates.

"She's getting her diploma in absentia," I explained, feeling like a jerk as soon as I said the phrase. So prep school–y to say it that way. "I mean, they're mailing it to her."

I knew this because Maylin had been giving me updates on Alex all spring. Alex had left in February when everything went down, and it had taken Maylin a couple of weeks to get over the shock of it all.

If there's any way she could have told someone, it would have been you, I'd insisted, over and over, until Maylin had given in and called Alex. My words might not have been true, but Maylin and I both allowed ourselves to believe them. And I wished Alex well despite the heaviness between us that would probably keep us from being friends again.

Given how hard Alex had worked, given her desperate emails to the Fleming Foundation—and Chloe's persistent claim that Alex was trying to find a solution and end the ghost tradition—the school had allowed Alex to finish her work from home and receive a Windham-Farnswood diploma. This was only possible because I didn't mention the sleeping pills. And apparently Chloe hadn't, either.

A couple of weeks ago, Chloe had gotten out of the residential treatment she'd been in since February 10. She'd sent me an email saying she was doing okay; that her parents were deciding where she'd go to school next. Probably it wouldn't be a boarding school, she said. Sounded like a good call to me.

"Will they have food at this reception thingy?" my brother wanted to know.

"Yeah," I told him. "Little sandwiches, probably."

The reception was designed to be a final goodbye for students and teachers; absent would be Ms. Holland-Stone, who was fired in February.

"Sweet," he growled.

"I'll meet you two there," I assured my mother. "I just want to do one more thing in the dorm. Something I forgot."

♦♦♦

When my brother and my mother had helped me move the last of my things out of the dorm this morning, it had been crazed and stressful, full of nervous parents and sentimental girls. I hadn't gotten a chance to say goodbye to the place.

And I definitely wanted to. I didn't picture myself ever being the type of alum who came back here to nostalgically walk these halls.

There is something about seeing a place for what you know will be the last time; it feels different. The fourth floor was mostly empty when I arrived; everyone was busy getting free finger sandwiches. One lone dad was trying to wrestle an IKEA chair out of a narrow dorm room doorway, clearly trying to get a jump on the final moving wave that would occur in the afternoon. By three p.m., you had to hand in the keys to your empty room to get your diploma.

I gave Star's and my room one last glance and then closed its door resolutely. Strangely, even with the flood of confessions that had followed Chloe's revelations, no one had admitted to pounding on my door the night before the 10th. Chloe claimed not to have done it.

Down the hall, Taylor's old door was, of course, locked. I wouldn't get to see her room one last time. I wasn't sure I wanted to. It was enough just to stand by her door, and to remember what it was like to be inside of it. Like that time she was inconsolable about her calico.

Why can't they just let me love something?

My chest ached at this memory. And the tears on my face now felt familiar, like they were partly hers from that day.

God sees the heart was Sarah Black's favorite Bible quote. The student "ghosts" thought, in a twisted way, they were reminding their crueler peers of that. I didn't know if I believed in God, and I didn't know if Taylor had, either. We'd never discussed that. But I *had* seen Taylor's heart occasionally, when she'd let me. I hoped somehow, since then, she'd seen mine. I hoped she saw that I'd wanted answers for her, and gotten them.

Others would remember Taylor as the girl who filmed Jocelyn Rose. As her friend, I would try to remember her as the girl weeping at the cat shelter, as the girl who put that ridiculous video of me in her trash folder instead of sending it out into the world. And I would know that there had been some warmth hidden inside her—and trust that it maybe would have found its way out, if she had been given more time. *Maybe.* As Caroline Bromley and Norma Fleming and Lucia Jackson had had a chance to grow past the girls they'd been here, both for better and for worse. And as I had a chance now.

I wondered how long the school would keep this door locked—if they'd ever let another girl sleep here. Pressing my hand to the door once more, fingers outstretched, I held a picture in my head for a moment: Taylor on her bed, scratching behind the ears of the illegal kitten on her chest, both of them closing their eyes for a nap.

I propped my mother's roses against the bottom of the door and then ran down the stairs, racing against the tears that I knew would recede once I stepped outside of Dearborn's long shadow.

Acknowledgments

Thank you:

To my family, Ross and Eliza, for support, humor, and love.

To Lisa Walker, Jen Hale, and Emily Stone, for insightful early readings of the manuscript.

To Nicole Moore, for the long chats about boarding school life.

To Laura Langlie, my extraordinarily patient agent, for sticking with me all these years.

To Monica Jean for sharp but sensitive editing.

To Kelsey Horton for graciously taking this book forward.

To Leo Nickolls for the awesome cover art.

To the folks at the Mount Holyoke College archives for their patient assistance.

About the Author

Emily Arsenault is the author of several mysteries, including *In Search of the Rose Notes*, a *Wall Street Journal* Best Mystery of the Year; *The Broken Teaglass*, a *New York Times* Notable Crime Book; and *The Last Thing I Told You*. She lives in Western Massachusetts with her husband, daughter, and cats. *The Leaf Reader, All the Pretty Things*, and *When All the Girls Are Sleeping* are her novels for young adults.

emilyarsenault.com